Range of Heart

STEAMING STONE BOOK 1

STEVI EVELISE

Mager-Lightfoot Publishing, LLC; www.stevimager.com

Book Cover Design by Stevi Evelise

Map Design by Stevi Evelise

Back Endpaper Art by Fay Bec

Developmental Editing by SML Editorial

Copyediting by SML Editorial

Proofreading by SML Editorial

Paperback ISBN: 979-8-9888254-4-9

Hardback ISBN: 979-8-3482586-1-0

Collector's Edition ISBN: 979-8-9888254-3-2

1st Edition, 2025

To anyone who wishes a wolf would eat the ghosts of their past,
and to A, for being that wolf when I need it most.

Content Warnings

Please examine this list carefully before reading further. As much as I appreciate you for wanting to read and experience the world that lies within the pages of *Range of Heart*, your mental health and wellbeing mean more to me.

Beyond this point, please be advised of the following trigger warnings: stalking; discussion of stalking statistics, along with treatment of stalking victims by law enforcement; harassment; PTSD, mental health (panic attacks; anxiety), and trauma representation; violence; blood; explicit language; explicit sexual content; abuse of power by law enforcement officer; non-fatal strangulation; attempted kidnapping.

If you're looking for a closed-door romance, then this book is not for you. No dogs are harmed in this book.

Range of Heart

STEAMING STONE BOOK 1

STEVI EVELISE

Chapter 1

EDARA

The gentle *click-clacking* sounds of my keyboard cease when my fingers still, hovering over the idle keys. Instead of focusing on my laptop screen, my eyes are fixated on my dining room window overlooking my front yard and the street.

Sheer, cream-colored curtains are pulled taut across the glass. They always are. They're translucent enough to let in light, but not so transparent that I lose privacy.

Slowly, I rise from my kitchen table near the backdoor, which has a direct view of the front window thanks to the open floor plan. I tiptoe toward the dining room as if someone is watching me—because that's a strong possibility at this point—with my German shepherd, Elessar, on my heels.

His tail wags once, but the moment he picks up on my body language, his ears perk up. With a low growl, he comes closer to me, his long fur tickling the side of my left knee as we move.

Rounding the wood dining table, I inch toward the curtains and peek out onto the street through the inch gap between the wall and the fabric. Since it overlooks the street, the window gives me the perfect vantage point to investigate what I already know to be true, while still staying safe inside.

That's the third time the red Subaru BRZ has passed by my house in the last hour. The sound is obnoxiously loud for how slow it's moving.

Knowing who is in that car spikes my anxiety.

Moving the curtains out of the way, I push down on the faux wood blinds as much as they'll budge to watch the taillights disappear around the corner. However, I know it's temporary. His absence is only ever temporary.

The infuriatingly easy-to-spot, shiny red exterior passing by for the fourth time is the final straw.

It's official: Raleigh is no longer a safe space. Not for me, at least.

Stress never has been kind to my mental and physical health. It manifests itself in my shoulders, neck, head, and even my chest. Thinking about how often I have seen Brad's car in the last week alone—not to mention in the past few months—makes my anxiety escalate so much that it's now laying high in my chest, rising up and up.

Suddenly struck by lightheadedness, I stumble away from the window and right into the edge of the dining room table. Something hits the floor with a soft thud as my hands take its place against the table in an attempt to hold myself upright. My eyesight has gone bright white with panic, making it impossible to see anything.

Frustration rising, I curl my fingers around the thick, wooden edge and try to breathe through this.

A cold nose brushes against my wrist, his whiskers tickling me, before I feel Elessar's large form lean into my legs. With my vision still white, I place out my right hand and run my fingers through his soft fur. He might not understand the extent of what's going on—of our new reality—but he does sense my panic.

Is this how life is going to be from now on? Hiding from Brad—a man I went out with twice, and who now feels entitled to my time, energy, and body? Never knowing when he'll show or call? Feeling unsafe in my own home?

Damn it, I hope not. The past nine months have already been hell, and I can't imagine this continuing for the rest of my life.

No, this will *not* be my life. Not anymore.

As my anger rises, replacing a little of the stress, I blink away the blinding light distorting my vision. When my eyes focus, I realize it was today's mail that fell. I was too distracted by the car following my every movement earlier that I forgot to sift through the pile after bringing it inside.

With a sigh, I scratch behind Elessar's ear one more time, then slowly lean down to pick up the mess. The small envelope on top of the pile makes me pause. I don't have to open it to know it's the quarterly "thinking of you" card from Aunt Bellamy in Steaming Stone, North Carolina.

A smile tugs at the corners of my lips as I think of the cards I began receiving back in elementary school, and have continued to receive into adulthood. Sometimes they are punny, other times they are sweet, but all of them are thoughtful.

As I open it, I wonder which kind my aunt sent this time. My whole body jumps at the start of a singing gram of barking sounds pieced together to the tune of "Happy Birthday."

I laugh before reading the short note inside:

Eda–

Ignore the happy birthday part of this card, but I just thought it was too cute to not send! Your Uncle Ben and I hope you and sweet Elessar are doing well. We love and miss you, little one, and we hope you'll visit soon.

XOXO, Aunt Bellamy and Uncle Benjamin.

I read the note again, and the last line goes on repeat in my head.

We love and miss you, little one, and we hope you'll visit soon.

We hope you'll visit soon...

In Steaming Stone... Can I?

Before I can talk myself out of it, I drop the card on the counter and make a mad dash to my laptop on the kitchen table.

I don't think twice as I exit out of the blank manuscript document that's been staring at me for weeks. Instead, I pull up a new tab with a mission to book the first cozy, long-stay rental property in the mountains of Steaming Stone, North Carolina.

Clicking the desired dates—with check-in being tomorrow afternoon and checkout being two months from now—my fingers hover over the keypad for only half a second before I nod in determination.

Maybe I'm being a tad impulsive, and maybe I'm desperate, but it feels right. Mostly because it will get me far away from Raleigh. Far away from *him*.

With the click of a button, I lock myself into my mountain retreat. And with it being roughly 24 hours before check-in, there's no backing out. It's happening.

A slow smile splits my face as relief and excitement course through me while I stare at the automated "Thank you for booking Redwood Lane!" message on the page.

I could stay with Aunt Bellamy and Uncle Ben, but I don't want to risk Brad searching for me at their house, or give up my personal space by staying with them for a long period of time. A weekend or two is fine, but not the entire two-month trip I just booked. No, I'd much rather have some privacy and my own space for that long.

Yes, two months to escape to a fairytale-esque home in a picture-perfect mountain town, while I stick my nose in my laptop and let my fingers work their magic to meet my deadline for my next book. At least, that's the hope.

Once I receive the confirmation email with the host's information—Alaric Wülf of Redwood Lane—I close my laptop, tuck it under my arm, and bring it upstairs to my bedroom. Resisting the urge to look out the bedroom window, I grab the remote to turn on the most recent episodes of my favorite reality shows I've been putting off watching.

With the exception of a few quick trips downstairs to feed both Elessar and myself, let him out, and to refill my water bottle, I spend the rest of the night in my bedroom to pack and prepare.

The moment I manage to zip up my two suitcases packed to the brim with things I may or may not need for the next two months, I send off a few quick texts to my two sisters, my best friend, and a separate group chat with both of my parents to fill everyone in on my trip.

I give my sisters a bit more information about the reason why I'm leaving to save my parents from worrying. Although, I know it probably won't stop them; they always say it's their job to worry about us girls.

That's confirmed when my mom texts me back to stay safe and give Aunt Bellamy—her older sister—a big hug. My dad, on the other hand, tells me I'm brave for being willing to drive on the narrow mountain roads, which is the reason why he's been refusing to travel back to the mountains for years now. That does little to help my anxiety about the drive. Thanks, Dad.

My phone continues to chime and vibrate in my hand as more texts come in.

My best friend, Rhiannon, warns me that I better "stay safe, or else," and my little sister, Aurelia, says she's happy for me, but also jealous.

It's the response from my older sister, Cressida, that has me feeling like this trip really is a good idea.

Cressida Lauklan

No way! I'll be in Steaming Stone the second weekend of November to photograph Aunt Bellamy and Uncle Ben's fam before the holidays. Maybe we'll see each other?

Hell yeah, we better see each other.

Cressida's always so polite—reserved, in a way—even with us. It started after she found out her ex-fiancé and high school sweetheart was cheating on her for years, with her learning of the betrayal only nine days before their wedding.

Afterward, she sort of became a shell of the sister I knew, successfully pushing away everyone in her life except for our mom.

Six years later, and it feels like we've become strangers. We still try to do things with each other, and we always include her in group chats and plans we all make. Sometimes she doesn't come, but it just makes it extra special when she does.

Despite feeling as though I've lost her in adulthood, I still hold onto our childhood memories of: the older sister who walked with me to the school bus stop, hand-in-hand, until she went off to high school; the sister who used to wake me, Aurelia, and Rhiannon—who was often sleeping over at our house—on Saturday mornings to build a blanket fort in the middle of the living room and watch cartoons; the sister who teased me relentlessly once she made it to high school, but never let anyone else talk about me.

She's still in there somewhere. *We* are still in there somewhere.

Before I can even think of a response to Cressida's text, green text bubbles pop up, one after another, from Aurelia and Rhiannon chiming in.

Aurelia Lauklan

OK, that's not fair.

Rhiannon Magdalen

Well well well

Lauklan sisters it looks like we're having a family reunion in the great outdoors

But not really the outdoors

Cause nature

You know what I mean

Aurelia Lauklan

Hey Rhia, I think it's about time you get an iPhone. For someone who doesn't like being out in nature, you sure do seem to like seeing green on your screen. Can't say I relate.

Rhiannon Magdalen

Over my cold dead witch blessed body will you ever force an Apple product into my hands

Grinning, I squeeze my phone extra hard with the glee filling me over the thought of getting to see my sisters there. The rental is just big enough for us all to share for a weekend. It'll feel like we're kids again, hanging out way past our bedtimes.

Once my last message is sent to my sisters to confirm our girls' weekend, I manage a record-breaking ten-minute call with my aunt to let her know I'll be in town soon and for how long. After nearly two decades of begging me to visit, she is thrilled to hear her most recent card did the trick. I can already say it's worth the money and the jitters of going alone just to hear the excitement in her voice.

Hanging up, I can't stop grinning as my aunt's happiness bleeds into me, making me feel a little less nervous about traveling.

I lay my head on my pillow and find that joy still lingering on my heart, filling my dreams with adventure after adventure in the mountains.

Before I even get out of bed, thoughts of the rental property are what fill my mind the moment my eyes open. It's all I can think about as I hear the birds chirping their morning song outside my bedroom window and know that, soon, it'll be birds in the mountains singing me awake.

The rental is a cozy, dog-friendly, detached guesthouse. It has a kitchen stocked with everything I'll need and a mountain view I can enjoy from bed. Check-in is set for this afternoon, and I can't wait. Literally. I need to get away from here. *Now.*

Just as I go to roll out of bed, the movement wakes Elessar, who had moved off the bed to sleep on the hardwood floor at some point in the night. Jumping back onto the bed, he dive bombs my chest for pets, which I can't possibly refuse. I laugh into his soft fur as he flops onto me for a good morning cuddle. Being a silver sable German shepherd, his long fur is black and silver, and it's all I can see as I wrap my arms around his back and neck.

The moment my fluffy dog has had his fill and hops off the bed to go outside and eat, I can feel myself itching to leave. Throwing the covers off me, I slip my feet into my fuzzy slippers shaped like wolf heads—the closest I could find to slippers that resemble Elessar—and sprint to the closet to change.

Again, I resist the urge to look out the bedroom window, just in case Brad's car is there. Or, rather, *still* there, if he never even left. The thought alone has me skipping breakfast in my eagerness to rush to a house where I can look out a window and hopefully not have to worry about this anymore.

I silently thank past me for making the decision to permanently park my Jeep Grand Cherokee in the garage. It became a habit after the stalking started, but it also gives me the perfect opportunity to discreetly pack the car with my suitcases and the bags with Elessar's food and vitamins. If Brad is still out there, he'll have no idea what's happening on the other side of the garage door. And if he follows my car as I leave, I'll shake him. Somehow, I will. He isn't going to take my peace anymore.

The sound of the trunk closing is almost like music to my ears. A smile of disbelief mixed with a dash of hope crosses my face as I realize it is officially time for my escape.

In all honesty, I've been looking for an excuse to go to the mountains and write for years now. In the past, not really having free time and the nerves of driving there alone stopped me from making the trip.

But now? Now, I am so freaking desperate to escape Brad, and to also meet my deadline, that my dream of writing a book with a picturesque mountain view is all the motivation I need to push past my fears and make the drive.

With one foot in front of the other, I load Elessar in the car, then hop into the driver's seat. While the garage door slowly ascends to reveal my quiet street and no sign of the red sports car, my vice-like grip on the steering wheel grows tighter as the stress of the past nine months comes to a head.

I *will* make it away from him. And in doing so, I'm going to take my life back. One mile at a time, I will regain control over my life.

Chapter 2

We made it. Somehow, I got past my anxiety and successfully drove us to Steaming Stone, having parked downtown roughly half an hour ago now.

The nerves over the drive lessened a fraction after I saw that Brad's car wasn't waiting for me beyond the garage door, and they continued to lessen with each hour that went by without seeing that shiny red, two-door menace. There was one time when I thought I did, but to my utter relief, it ended up being a false alarm of just a normal person taking the same route somewhere else, eventually veering off onto another exit.

The drive actually went pretty smoothly. It helped that I wasn't alone. I never am with Elessar around. With his harness buckled into the passenger seat of my car, he slept nearly the whole ride with his fluffy head on my right elbow that was resting on the middle console. My arm quickly grew numb from the weight of his snout, but it was worth it.

He always makes for good company. The best, really.

Not being alone had been especially helpful when a particularly narrow, winding road shielded the large semitruck coming toward my car. Even though the truck stayed on its side of the road, panic still ensued within me. My arms shrank in close to my chest, my shoulders shot up to my ears, and my hands clutched the steering wheel for dear life. It was so terrifying that I was practically shrieking instead of singing the chorus to "Don't Stop Believin'" as we miraculously passed unscathed.

Elessar had popped up his head at the sign of distress and the horrible singing—if it could even be called that. With a quick sniff of his cold, wet nose and a little lick for comfort, he laid his head back down in the crook of my arm and fell into another peaceful sleep. How I had wished in that moment that I could someday be reincarnated as a well-loved dog without a care in the world. What a luxurious life that sounds like.

I silently laugh at the thought and memory as I step out of the way of a couple on the sidewalk in downtown Steaming Stone. Elessar follows my lead, prancing as he tucks in between me and the side of the brick building while we walk by them.

"What a pretty dog! It looks like a wolf," the woman half-whispers to the man walking next to her. I smile when she makes eye contact with me, and she grins back as they walk past. "Oh, I can't wait until we get a dog..." her voice trails off, but the smile remains on my face.

When we made it to Steaming Stone thirty minutes ago, I decided to walk Elessar around downtown to discover the local coffee spots, places to grab a bite to eat, and where to pick up groceries if I choose to just stay in and cook for the next two months. Exploring was the right move because I forgot how cute this place is, and there are more shops than I remember. In all fairness, it has been almost two decades since I was last here.

A light breeze hits my cheeks, blowing my hair out of my face, and I can't resist closing my eyes for a brief moment. Oh, the air! It's fresh and crisp, with the slightest breeze that makes me want to light a fire and crawl under a soft blanket with a cup of tea cradled in my hands. Actually, I just might do that tonight. The listing photos showed a fireplace in the living area and a firepit outside at the rental.

When my stomach growls, I make a split-second decision to cross Main Street and have lunch on the outdoor patio of a place called Ruby's Bistro. The chalkboard sign propped on the sidewalk is adorned with chalk-drawn, long-stemmed pumpkins. Their carefully drawn vines frame the words: "Welcome to Ruby's! Seat yourself."

A lone, giant Jack-o'-lantern smiles under the words. I have to do a double-take, but its "carved" mouth is shaped in the silhouette of the mountain peaks that Steaming Stone is known for. The same silhouette that can be found on metal keychains and engrained wood signs I've seen in the windows of quite a few shops now.

I pick a table right up against the bistro's windows because it's the closest to the outdoor dog bowl. Thankfully, it's in the high 60s this morning, which makes it the perfect weather to eat outside.

As quietly as I can muster on the stone-ground patio, I pick up and then position one of the metal chairs up against the restaurant's front window so that I can see both sides of the sidewalk...just in case. I didn't factor in that Elessar—my little shadow—would follow my every step, and he somehow got his leash wrapped around my legs and one leg of the chair.

Satisfied with the spot I chose, I sit down with my back against the window and look from side to side to check the view. Closing my eyes for a second, I feel like I can finally take a deep breath and relax. When I open my eyes again, I barely have time to untangle Elessar's leash from my legs before a server named Neal comes outside and greets me with a menu.

After I take a quick look at the specials, Neal takes my order. Then, he checks that the stainless steel dog bowl is full of water for Elessar, who warily watches him but doesn't move. Checking the water is such a simple act, but the fact that no one here knows us, yet everyone has still been friendly so far has me taking another deep breath and feeling lighter for the first time in...I don't know how long.

Without moving an inch, Elessar watches as Neal walks back inside. It's not Elessar's fault. I was told that a man—his old owner—was not kind to him in his previous life before our paths crossed. I've learned to trust his instincts, because he's a good judge of character.

Once satisfied that Neal doesn't seem like he's going to come back and hurt either of us, he lays down facing the street with his back toward me. He's always on guard; always watching over me like the good boy he is. It's something I've loved about him ever since I first brought him home, but it has been especially comforting this past year.

A few seconds later, he stays laying down, but his nose is twitching high in the air, ears laying flat against his head. I'm not sure whether it's because of the delicious smells wafting from the bistro as the door opens again or the fresh air, but I find myself doing the same. Following his lead, I close my eyes, breathe in the crisp mountain air, and then slowly breathe out some of the stress and fear that have plagued me for months.

The sound of a car horn has me recentering myself to Main Street and the present moment. Both Elessar and I glance in the direction of an intersection, where a car ran a red light. Thankfully, no accident occurs, but it looks like it might have been a close call.

I start to look away to take in more of the shops on the street, but the sight of something red turning right onto this street has me whipping my head back toward the intersection. The breath whooshes out of me when I realize it's not Brad's Subaru.

Laying my hand on my chest, I force myself to inhale through my nose and exhale through my mouth, until my breathing is under control again. It's a technique I learned from my yoga class, which Rhiannon teaches.

As the tightness in my chest loosens and my breathing begins to regulate, I push away the lies the fear wants me to believe and ground myself with a fact: I didn't see him follow me here.

Still, I don't risk closing my eyes again. Instead, I find myself watching the passing cars closely as I sit and wait.

When my food comes out and I take the first bite, I have to swallow a moan. The butternut squash soup and grilled cheese sandwich taste like heaven, and I'm not just saying that because I stupidly skipped breakfast in my desperation.

With every bite and each minute that goes by, I fall in love with not only the food but the staff, who are kind to both me and Elessar. Neal even asked me if we wanted a small cup of whipped topping, which Elessar happily enjoyed.

Twenty minutes later, my bowl and plate are empty, with nothing left but crumbs of bread crust that flaked off and onto the plate. I can already tell I'm starting to feel better after eating and hydrating. I lean back in the metal chair and hand Elessar the largest piece of crust on my plate, sans soup. His tail does a little swish-swish against the stone walkway and brushes against my ankles as he shifts to gently take it.

From my spot at the table, I place an online pickup order at a grocery store to make sure I have enough food for the week. The trip was too spontaneous for me to plan much last night, but after spotting the first grocery store while driving into town, I decided in that moment that I would attempt to save some money by not eating out every day.

However, this little spot will be one I come back to for sure. Especially if I need to step away from my computer at some point. A little fresh air and nice people will do me some good. It already is.

Plus, exploring is the perfect way to kill time until check-in at 3 p.m. Everyone we've encountered on our outing has been friendly and welcoming, which has helped me feel more at ease being in a new place. And, if I'm honest, it also kind of makes me want to move here.

It's an unexpected thought, since I love the city, but there is something about this quaint mountain town that feels...homey. This might all seem new to me—having not been here since I was a kid—but as I look around, it feels familiar. It feels *right*. As if I was meant to come here, and now it's beckoning me to stay.

But I couldn't possibly do that. It's probably just the mountain air and desperation over my situation getting to me. I'll see clearly again when I'm back home in Raleigh—the city I was born and raised in. Choosing to take this trip on a whim was out of character enough for me, let alone picking up my life and moving to somewhere I've only spent a couple hours in.

Although, maybe it wouldn't be such a terrible idea to get a place here and lie low until everything with Brad settles...

A mountain escape of my own? One I could share with my family.

I chuckle to myself as I think about how ecstatic that would make my aunt.

The sudden vibration of my phone makes me jump and a bit of my water spills from my foot bumping the table. Briefly closing my eyes, I exhale through my mouth and tentatively look at my phone. I hope I haven't conjured the man by thinking about him.

When I see it's only my aunt calling, I instantly relax and answer with a smile on my face. "Hi, Aunt Bellamy! I was just thinking about you," I say into the phone, and Elessar's head perks up. He loves her.

"Hi, little one!" Her classic greeting referring to my height of 5'2" always makes me smile, even though I swear she's only a few inches taller than me. "How are you doing? Are you in town yet?" The excitement in her voice is contagious, and my cheeks start to hurt from smiling so hard.

Once more taking in the shops surrounding this area of downtown, I say, "Yes, we got in about an hour ago now. I just grabbed some lunch, and we'll be heading to the rental here soon."

There's a small squeal of joy on the other end of the phone. "Oh, this is just wonderful! How soon until I can see you and my sweet grand-nephew?" she asks, followed by a noise in the background that sounds a lot like a pan hitting a countertop.

I look back down at Elessar—her *grand-nephew*—who has already laid his head back down on the stone patio. By the subtle movement of his silver eyebrows, I can tell he's still assessing our surroundings instead of sleeping, but at least he feels comfortable enough to put his head down. That's a good sign.

Briefly pulling the phone away from my ear to check the time, I think about whether I'm up for company before or after settling in. Except, with that long drive and the stress of life still sitting in my bones, I decide today's probably not the best option. Honestly, maybe not even this week. It's only Monday, and I do still have a lot of work to do, which I explained to her on the phone last night. Thankfully, my family's always been understanding of the fact that, even though I work from home, I'm still very much *working* and don't exactly have a free schedule throughout the work week.

"I might need a few days to settle in first, but I found this cute spot downtown called Ruby's Bistro we could get lunch at." My gaze looks up toward the bistro's sign on top of the stone-faced building.

"Oh, yes! We love it there! Please tell me you tried their delicious butternut squash soup. If not, we're getting it this weekend. It's seasonal, but I wish they served it all year." There's another clink of something through the phone, and I'm tempted to ask her to bring some of whatever she's making. I love my aunt's baking.

Grinning, I look down at my empty bowl of soup. "I did get it today, and I absolutely plan on getting it again." She laughs on the other end. "How does 11:30 on Saturday sound?"

"Aw, Saturday feels so far away!" she says. I know she doesn't mean any harm by it; it's coming from a place of love and having not seen me in a year. Still, I wince a little from the guilt.

"I'm sorry. I just want to be able to really enjoy our time together, and I'm torn between wanting to rest after that drive and wanting to dive straight into work, since we're already halfway through Monday. I'm hoping that waiting a few days so that I can get some work done will allow me to be able to get out of work mode again by this weekend. I just want to truly be present in the moment," I explain, attempting to push down the guilt.

"Don't worry, sweetie." Her voice softens. " I understand. I may not like it, but I understand. As much as I wish I could see you today, tomorrow, and every day after that, I'll happily take whatever time with you I can get. I can't wait to squeeze you! And you'd better bring my little Eless with you."

"I mean, he's hardly little." I laugh. At 80 lb, he's considered petite for a male German shepherd, but still most definitely categorized as a large dog. However, my family and I can't ever unsee him as that little, five-month-old fur-ball resembling a wolf cub who captured our hearts three years ago. Yes, he will forever be my little man.

I bend down and scratch his head. He doesn't lift himself from the stone path, but he does lean into my touch ever so slightly.

"No, but he's the perfect size for a good cuddle and to protect his mama," she says in a way that somehow sounds both loving and stern. It's that classic mom voice she uses. Even though I'm not her child, she's always treated me and my sisters like her own, just as my mom has done for her kids—my cousins.

I'm also grateful that even though I know why she says 'protect his mama,' she doesn't outright mention Brad's name.

"You'll hear no argument from me there," I agree, attempting to keep my tone light, despite the unspoken message between us. Everyone important in my life knows to physically avoid Brad, but that doesn't mean we want to talk about him.

"Of course not. He's the perfect dog," she says, and I can hear a smile in her voice. "All right, sweetie. The oven's beeping at me to grab the pumpkin bread, so I have to let you go. Enjoy the rest of your day! I can't wait to hug you in a few days! Don't hesitate to reach out to us if you need anything before then. Love you lots, my little one!"

"I love you, too, Aunt Bellamy! See you soon!"

When the beep of the call ending sounds, I set my phone down on the metal table and lean back in my chair. I take in the cozy street again, as well as the friendly faces as they pass by, and I can feel it in my bones that I've made the right decision.

Steaming Stone will be good *to* me and *for* me, and I'm looking forward to the adventures I can capture on the page while being here.

Chapter 3

Edara

Nearly three hours later, I'm finally pulling up to 1697 Redwood Lane to check in. After this morning's three-hour drive and a day of exploring, I'm thankful that the host only offers contactless check-in to the guesthouse on his property.

And what a property! The windy, gravel driveway is long, opening up to a secluded home resembling a log cabin and a cute, two-story guesthouse. They're both surrounded by trees, except for the area near the creek on the property, which overlooks the mountains. The trees around the creek perfectly frame the view, and I'm having a hard time pulling my eyes away from it, despite still sitting behind the wheel in the guesthouse parking spot.

It's Elessar's excitement that finally forces me out of the car. He snaps me out of it, and I realize I need to make sure the front door code works, and also get the grocery bags inside.

As I walk the leaf-lined path to the French doors, I pull up my phone with the house rules and information, including the keypad code to unlock the guesthouse: 0127 + lock button. The keypad beeps with each number, and when I press the lock button, the buttons all light up blue and I hear the door unlock.

I briefly glance down at Elessar, whose eyes are bouncing from me to the door, while his tail wags. Smiling, I turn the knob and we enter our new, temporary home.

From the listing description, I already know the rental is a newly renovated loft. Intricate, wood French doors greet me as I enter and I'm immediately blown away by what I see. The listing photos don't do this place justice. It's charming on the outside, but the moment I walk in, I'm transported to a cozy escape. It's misleading in the best way.

The main entrance is on the bottom floor, which leads into an open floor plan with the kitchen, breakfast nook, and living room, along with a small bedroom off to the side. Large windows provide the perfect lighting and a view of the mountain ranges as I take it all in. There are no visible neighbors, which explains the lack of blinds, but there are curtains if I want to close them for privacy.

The backdoor is a Dutch door that I can open the top of to watch Elessar playing outside while I work at the kitchen table. I didn't know that was something I needed in my life, but now that I've seen it, I want it in my own home. Maybe after all is said and done, I'll switch out my current back door for one of these to open on those perfect fall and spring days.

I saw the pictures online, but seeing it all in person as I take a tour of the space has me speechless. It's all so cute and cozy. Everything and more than I could have hoped for during this stay.

It does make me a little nervous to stay somewhere with a stranger on-site—the landlord—but that is one of the many reasons why I chose to bring Elessar and my collection of cooking knives. My dog would never let anything happen to me, and if I need to take extra action, the knives are sharp. A little stabby stab, and all will be fine.

Plus, it is entirely possible the host is married or has a partner. I kind of hope that's the case. Although, Rhiannon is obsessed with true crime documentaries and podcasts, which means that I have heard plenty about how even happily married men can be unsuspecting serial killers.

After putting the groceries away, I prepare to make a cup of Earl Grey tea before taking Elessar out to explore. The listing photos also showed the cutest tea set resting on the kitchen island, and I haven't been able to get it out of my head since. The light blue floral print greeted me and Elessar when we first walked in the front door. It's somehow even prettier in person, just like the rest of the place.

Once the tea has steeped and is sweetened with some milk and lavender creamer, I drag my suitcases up the spiral, metal staircase that leads to the upstairs loft bedroom. It's bigger than I expected, complete with a reading nook in the corner and bath suite with a clawfoot tub and separate shower. Across from the bed are sliding glass doors that perfectly highlight the mountains beyond. It's that view that brought me here, and it's that view that I plan to wake up to each morning for the next two months.

I open the glass doors and step out onto the bedroom balcony. The moment my foot crosses the threshold, I breathe in the mountain air with closed eyes. They pop open again when I feel Elessar shoot past me and down the balcony stairs to the creek below.

Now that we are here and have explored the town, I'm questioning why I ever stayed away to begin with. Well, besides the terrifying drive up the mountain passes, with its windy, narrow roads that are somehow supposed to be two lanes, but barely even feel like one.

Tomorrow morning will begin with me waking up in a loft bed looking over the mountains. This very view right here. A beautiful blue sky and trees with their colorful leaves of every autumn shade, perfectly framing the mountain peaks beyond.

Despite the threat of Brad's presence and the impending deadline my agent nags me about daily, I make the conscious decision to set it all aside and find peace in the birds chirping above.

Honestly, it's about time. This is exactly what I need.

As I sit on the balcony and sip my tea, I close my eyes and create a mental image of this exact moment to store away forever. The calming rush of the stream below. What sounds like a squirrel jumping from branch to branch. Shuffling in the leaves, which could be any sort of creature.

My eyes pop open at that thought, just to make sure it isn't a bear or mountain lion. Eyes following the sound, I sigh when I see it's only Elessar traipsing along the property.

The rental is dog friendly, but only under the condition that the visiting dog gets along with other dogs because the host, Alaric, has his own, as mentioned in the online description. We still have yet to meet him or his dog, but I did see a truck at the main house when we first pulled up. I guess he takes that "contactless check-in" seriously, which I don't mind one bit.

Thankfully, Elessar loves most dogs he comes across. So, the meet-and-greet should be fine. People are another matter, as he is quite selective about who he does and doesn't like. Heck, I also prefer dogs to people, so I can't blame him for being picky when it comes to humans. Not to mention that he has a good reason for it, since his previous owner was less than kind to him.

He tends to warm up faster to women and children than men. However, if he has a strong reaction to our host, then that's my sign that we should leave and not stay here. There are other rental options, and if need be, we can stay with my aunt until I find another long-term place.

Sighing into the tea cup, I close my eyes again and decide it's time to face the real reasons for coming here. Yes, the mountain air is refreshing, and I am looking forward to seeing my aunt for lunch at the same spot I went to today. But the truth is, I am escaping my ex, Brad. If he can be called that, since we only went on two dates. Nine months have passed since I broke things off with him, but he still hasn't taken the hint. No, he's only taken my time and peace of mind.

From keeping an eye on my house to sending his cop buddies out to spy anytime I dare to go out with friends or on a date with someone, he won't leave me alone. He even tried reaching out to my mom and sisters once to see how I was doing and to find out if I was dating anyone new. Since they'd never actually met him, they all either turned the questions on him—mostly my best friend, Rhiannon, matching his energy—or they ignored him entirely, which only seemed to irk him more.

Two months after breaking things off, I blocked his number after he kept calling in the middle of the night. It was scary to realize how conditioned I had become to answering his calls in the beginning. The fear that came with what might happen if I didn't, especially since he's a cop. Even though he wasn't physically in the house with me, I was still somehow so scared of what he'd do if I let the call go to voicemail. It took months to get over, and I still find myself getting nervous when my phone rings.

Despite blocking him, he found a way to call me from other numbers. I'm not sure if they were his friends' phones, or burner phones, but it eventually drove me to getting a new number.

I blocked him again on the new number, and the calls stopped, but the stalking didn't.

Three months in, my family and friends all had to block his number.

Four months in, I finally caved and bought a security system after seeing his car camped out on my street multiple times.

By the sixth-month mark, I was broken. Lost. Stuck. Controlled. Damaged.

On and on it went. This relentless cycle of watching me, scaring me, and not letting me move on. When I worked up the courage to go to the police after month six of being stalked, they told me that they couldn't do anything for me until something happened, and that I needed evidence to prove what he was doing. Of course, it doesn't help that he's a cop himself; they were skeptical of me accusing one of their own.

My fingers rub my temples at the memory. I'm sure they didn't mean it, but it certainly sounded like, until he physically harms or even kills me, I'm on my own. Upon doing research on stalking, it sounds like that was a normal interaction for individuals targeted by stalking. A most terrifying thought.

An involuntary shudder racks my body at the thoughts of *him* and what he could possibly want from me. Instinctively, I take in my surroundings again, making sure he is nowhere to be found. I'd watched the rearview mirror the whole way here, but the bastard has already proved he is sneaky.

Satisfied he isn't lurking behind a tree, I take a sip of my tea and try to relax. Keyword: *try*, as my stress rises once more when I think of the second reason why I'm here.

A number floats in my mind every time I close my eyes, further diminishing the peace my surroundings were beginning to build for me. The reality is, I need to write 80,000 words of the sixth book in my series by Thanksgiving week...which is in two months.

It's going to be a small-town, second-chance romance. A story I feel as though I've already done, but since my amazing and sweet readers somehow still seem to want to hear what my brain creates, I am going to do my absolute best to give them what they want. It'd just be a lot easier if my brain would, well, actually create.

But it can wait another hour...or two.

Now that I am settling in, I decide it's time to send a group text to my sisters and best friend with a picture from where I sit. Branches full with leaves of every shade and shape hover over the creek, framing the mountain ranges in the distance. Clouds floating by have covered the peaks slightly, but it somehow makes it seem even more magical.

Before I can even sit back and bask in the view again, responses immediately roll in with a heart-eyed emoji from my little sister, Aurelia, and a threat to not get killed or else Rhiannon will bring me back from the dead and kill me again herself. My sisters both second that.

I shake my head and chuckle at the responses.

When I texted them last night, I let them know I'd had enough of Brad. The text included where I was going and to not give it away to anyone, in case you-know-who catches wind. To be fair, my sisters would never—and that includes Rhiannon, who has been like a sister to me since we were in elementary school.

Rhiannon swore months ago on her pet hamster's grave that she would never, ever speak to Brad again after going off on him via text. That's a serious oath, considering she plans to name her first-born child—girl or boy—after said hamster, Harrison, whom she loved greatly in elementary school. Harrison was her first love and was named after her other first love, Harrison Ford. So, I know she meant it.

I sigh as I realize what I need to do next.

Taking a deep breath in, I email my agent, Carol, with a brief explanation of where I'll be for the next two months and why—to get words out in order to meet the deadline I promised her months ago. After hesitating for a moment, I also give her the guesthouse address in case she needs to send me anything for work. The message ends with a warning not to tell anyone where I am, with the excuse that the more private the escape is, the more productive I'll be. *Hopefully.*

My agent is somewhat aware of the situation with Brad, who contacted her in the beginning of all of this and pretended to be my boyfriend. Actually, she's still convinced we dated. That's just how good he is at manipulating others. But I don't want to bring it up and risk having a conversation about it right now. In fact, I don't want to encourage any conversation with her at the moment.

When I press send on the email, I stare at my phone and hold my breath for as long as I can before my cheeks puff and I'm forced to suck in air.

A big exhale turns into a groan of annoyance when Carol immediately starts calling my phone. This is why I didn't go into detail.

The phone rings and rings in my hand, until it finally goes to voicemail. That phone call would have only increased my stress level, which was finally starting to go down a bit.

Putting it on Do Not Disturb to drown out the inevitable ten missed calls that will come in from her, I set the phone down on the balcony's patio table.

Twenty more minutes. That's what I silently tell myself and Elessar. Twenty more minutes of enjoying the fresh, chilled air and the picturesque leaves turning. Then, I'll write. I am determined to meet my deadline. Now that I don't have the stress of having my house watched every hour, it is going to happen. I just know it.

The peaceful moment is suddenly interrupted by a faint pounding sound, followed by Elessar's barking. My eyes fly open and my head whips toward the sound coming from the driveway.

Still seated, I stretch my neck to peek over the balcony railing.

There's a man running up the long drive.

Coming toward me.

I can't tell who it is from this distance, but their hair looks like it could be dark blonde...just like Brad's.

The sense of peace is instantly extinguished as pure panic engulfs me.

How did he find me?

Chapter 4

EDARA

Not even the birds chirping can calm my racing heart. That's how I know I'm in trouble.

One shaky hand grips my teacup, while the other grabs my phone. I'm ready to recall Elessar inside and hide. Just in case.

It's the sight of the dog next to the man that causes me to take a deep breath. It can't be Brad, because Brad hates dogs. The loser. Who hates *dogs*? That should have been my first sign that he was crazy. Lived and learned from that mistake.

Dust kicks up in little clouds around the man's ankles as his feet pound into the gravel drive. As he runs farther up the long drive, I get a better look at him. Given his attire and the happy dog next to him—with its tongue hanging out the side of its mouth in a sweet smile—the man looks as if they might be running for fun. That's a foreign concept to me. I'd rather fold laundry for twenty-four hours straight than go on a run, and I loathe laundry.

Yeah, no. The only form of cardio I'm willing to participate in is mind-blowing sex.

He is shirtless, which allows me to admire how his chest and ab muscles flex with each step. And those shorts leave very little to the imagination...

To be fair, it must be difficult to find shorts that would fit those muscular thighs. Suddenly, I'm regretting making hot tea instead of iced, because, *wow*. At least there is a nice breeze to help with the wild heat of attraction building within.

Next to him is an equally gorgeous dog that looks like a Bernese mountain dog, but on the smaller side. Its tail is wagging, and it looks excited to see me and Elessar.

There's a moment when the man notices his dog's attention is on us. His gaze looks up to me on the balcony, and with a small wave, he pivots from running toward the main house to head straight for the guesthouse instead.

Standing quickly, I try to keep the tea cup steady as I adjust my skinny jeans and flannel. It's obvious he is coming toward us, so I set the cup on the table and put my phone in my pocket for easy access. Better to be safe than sorry.

With slow steps, I walk down the guesthouse steps leading off the balcony and I recall Elessar, who comes running from the creek. With a simple command, I put him in a "sit and stay" next to me at the base of the steps to the guesthouse, around the corner from the side Dutch door.

When the man slows from a run to a jog and makes it within ten feet of me, I notice that he barely even looks winded. Ugh, how I envy those who find working out as natural to them as breathing.

Breathing, right. That's exactly what I should do. This handsome man has damn near knocked the wind right out of me. The effect he has on me is strange, but I'm also not complaining. It's been a while since I've been with someone, because Brad drives everyone away. Clearly, I'm missing dating. Well, maybe not the act of dating, but seeing an attractive man and having the option to act on that attraction.

While his eyes look me up and down, I resist the urge to fret and fluff my hair. It's been in a braid since this morning, and I hope it looks okay after the day's travels.

My focus goes on him instead of thinking about what I may or may not look like. He is stunning. Dark brown hair that reflects a lighter shade in the sunlight and a trimmed beard to match. Tanned skin sans farmer's tan—which is probably from running without a shirt. Questionable behavior, but it makes for a nice sight. He's clad with muscles for days *everywhere*.

There's no ring on his finger, which has me feeling more excited than I should be. It isn't clear what color his eyes are from how far away he stands. Brown, maybe? I kind of want to find out. Well, so long as he isn't a serial killer.

"You must be Edara Lauklan. I'm Alaric," he says, not sounding out of breath at all as he accidentally mispronounces my first name as Edd-dare-uh. His voice is smooth, deep, and not at all winded. If I hadn't seen him running just now, I wouldn't believe he'd just exercised. How annoying and attractive all at the same time.

"Yes. I'm *Eee*-dar-uh, but you can call me Eda," I politely correct him on the pronunciation. It's something I've grown used to at this point in life. The price my sisters and I have paid for parents who wanted their kids to have names that weren't popular. "And this is Elessar." At the sound of his name, he thumps his tail once against the fallen leaves, but stays put.

He smiles. And what a great smile it is. "Hi Elessar," he says, waving to my dog before looking back up at me. The sight of this man being sweet to my dog makes my stomach flutter. "This is Blanche." His head dips down in the direction of the Bernese mountain dog next to him. "Elessar is good with other dogs, right?"

I nod. "Yes, but I can go grab his leash if you'd prefer before they officially meet." Elessar's tail is now going crazy in the leaves from excitement, but he won't move until told to. He'll do anything I ask of him. Truly the best boy around.

Alaric's gaze leaves me to assess Elessar, and there's a small smile on his face. "Based on his body language, he looks friendly. But if needed, I have her leash." He raises his hand carrying the unclipped leash and nods his head toward Blanche standing next to him. "You can release him if you're comfortable with it."

Looking down at Elessar's smiling form, his tongue hanging out sideways, I give him the release command: "Vas."

Something flashes on Alaric's face at the term. He looks like he is going to say something, but his attention is immediately drawn to the dogs.

With tails wagging, they both appear to pass the initial sniff test, and play time is initiated almost immediately. Elessar goes down on his front two legs, tail wagging in the air. The second Blanche moves toward him, he takes off.

He has the zoomies from being so excited, and poor Blanche can't keep up despite her long limbs. My mother has a running joke that it was a missed opportunity I didn't name him Flash instead.

I laugh at the sight, and Alaric glances in my direction. With his attention now on me, my fingers nervously pick at a button on my flannel. Why am I feeling nervous? Yes, he is attractive, but that is no reason to suddenly feel like I'm standing in front of a middle school crush.

Turning fully toward me, he asks, "Your release word... What was it?"

Fingers still absentmindedly toying with a shirt button, I explain, "Oh, vas?" He nods. "It's a French command for 'go ahead.' When I had him in training as a puppy, it got confusing for him to have every other owner in the class say 'release' or 'okay.' So, I chose something no one else there did." I shrug, feeling a little self-conscious about my choice in dog training. "And now, I have a bilingual dog."

The look on his face is strange. He almost looks...impressed? "Parlez-vous français, mademoiselle?" *Do you speak French, miss?*

Lips parting in a smile, I stare at him for a moment. He sounds like a native with that almost perfect accent. "Oui, monsieur. Et toi?" *Yes, sir. Do you?*

"Je parle en peu." *I speak a little.* A smile reaches his eyes, and butterflies form in my stomach at the sight. "What made you choose French commands?"

The butterflies sink when I realize he is lying to me about only speaking a little French. No one who speaks that well only knows a little. That doesn't mean he is a serial killer, of course, but it also doesn't mean he isn't. At the very least, a seemingly insignificant lie like that is a yellow flag. Although, maybe he's just being modest.

"My mother studied abroad in France when she was younger. In order to not lose the skill, she taught my sisters and me to speak both French and English growing up." My younger sister and I actually both double majored in French and English Linguistics in undergrad because of it.

Warmth spreads around me at the thought of my family and the love I have for them.

"So, if I had to pick any language other than English, it only felt natural to also teach Eless French." I smile at the dogs still playing. "What about you?"

Alaric nods his head once, but his smile falls, no longer reaching his eyes. "I picked it up for work."

Curiosity piqued, I ask, "For work? What do you do?"

"I now own a gym here in town." His tone is casual, but I don't miss the 'now' part of the statement. That's...interesting. What's he not saying?

Instead of prying, I choose to focus on the gym part for now. "It makes sense why you look like that, then." One of his eyebrows raises and my cheeks grow hot. "Um, yeah, that's cool though. I'm not one for working out. It's not my thing."

He looks like he is about to say something, but the dogs come bounding back. Not used to a dog of Blanche's size, I freeze in place as they come barreling toward me. The next thing I know, Alaric's arms are around my torso as he picks me up, my feet dangling in the air, until I'm standing to the right of him and out of harm's way.

Catching my breath, I look up at him and realize my hands are gripping his bare shoulders for dear life. Prying my fingers off him, I clear my throat and step back at the same time his arm leaves my waist.

"Thanks," I whisper, embarrassed and still a bit in shock. "I'm normally more vigilant around playful dogs, but she's just so...big." While Elessar is considered a large dog at 80 lb., Blanche must be at least 100 lb., if not more. She has to be taller than me when she stands on all fours. Granted, I'm not exactly considered tall, but still.

Thankfully, Alaric shrugs it off. "Don't apologize. It takes most people a little bit to get used to her. She's a good girl, but she's still a puppy getting used to her limbs and size. She doesn't mean any harm, but she's not the best at stopping when excited or running."

My jaw drops. "She's still a puppy?"

Alaric laughs. "Yeah, she's only ten months old."

Mouth still agape, I turn to watch the running dogs. *That* is a puppy? Her back is at least a whole hand taller than Elessar's.

A laugh bubbles up in my chest. "That's amazing."

"She'll keep you on your toes, that's for sure. Fortunately, she's not a quiet one. Just listen for the loud thud of her paws or the sound of her collar jingling, and you'll know she's nearby. You can't miss her." He chuckles as the dogs run by us again.

"If she's ever too much, just holler for me, and I'll come get her," he says, taking a step back, and I instantly wish he hadn't. There was a warmth that radiated off him, and I was beginning to like it

I follow his gaze to the dogs playing before looking back at him. "For being only ten months, she was well-trained to stay at your side when you first came up."

Alaric's mouth twitches as he watches them running. "She's a smart dog, and we train daily."

I nod and smile. "Still, it's impressive that she stayed by your side for a run."

He chuckles. "That wasn't a real run. I just took her out to explore a bit, and then ran up the drive for a little exercise. She won't be able to go on a true run with me until she's at least eighteen-months old. Her joints have to grow properly first."

A man who cares enough about his dog to know what is best for her health? That is a man after my heart.

Fucking hell, did I really just think that? *No one* is getting my heart right now.

"You know a lot about dogs." It surprises me, considering the last guy I was with couldn't even bear seeing Elessar on the couch of *my* house.

"I know a bit. My sister's a vet. She's the real expert," he says, smiling.

While Alaric watches the dogs, I watch him. It's proving to be impossible to not admire the fine specimen before me. That smile. The beard. Those eyes, which I now know are hazel. The way the sunlight shines on the muscles of his shoulders, while also highlighting his abs, his thighs...

When his eyes meet mine again, something flutters far below my stomach. Not butterflies. What was it that British reality show about love called this feeling?

Oh! Fanny flutters.

Fucking hell.

With his eyes now on me, my cheeks flush as I look away. How can I make eye contact while I have *fanny flutters*?

"I, uh, have to go work now," I manage to say.

Yes, work. Because I'm finally feeling inspired to write again, thanks to the handsome man standing in front of me. Actually, I am itching to get the words on the page as they play out in my head. My next romance novel, featuring an Alaric of my own. With a different name, of course. Someone who likes to put those leg muscles to use, and those hands—

"No problem. You should have my number from the booking, but let me know if you need anything during your stay," he says before he calls Blanche back to his side, and I do the same with Elessar.

He smiles before walking toward the main house. A new view I am especially thankful for, considering his back muscles make the flutters more intense. How is that even possible? Back muscles? Never in my life have I been attracted to someone's *back* before, but, wow, there are muscles on top of muscles. Are they painted on? How else could someone have so many?

"Thanks, Alaric. You might be the best host I've ever booked with," I say before he's gone too far.

Looking over his shoulder with one eyebrow arched, his smile deepens a bit more before he continues up the steep drive to the main house.

It is true. In more ways than one. The fact that he is getting me out of my writer's block is enough to give him a five-star review, and day one of my stay isn't even over yet.

Chapter 5

ALARIC

The smell of coffee wafting from the mug in my hand hits me harder than my alarm clock did. It's breathing a little life into me, but only a little. Usually, chopping wood in the crisp mountain first thing in the morning is what helps wake me, but that wasn't the case today. Or yesterday. I'm already done and showered, yet I'm still finding it harder than normal to embrace the day at this hour.

I've slept like shit this week, while a certain little red-haired beauty has been running circles in my mind. When my head hits my pillow at night and my eyes close, it's her face I see and can't seem to push out of my head. Last night was the third night in a row of it, and in defiance, I somehow thought not sleeping at all was a better option. Now I'm suffering the consequences of resisting my dreams being filled with her.

When I first started renting out my guesthouse a couple months ago, I had every intention of remaining the hands-off host. It seemed like the most logical option, since dealing with people really isn't my strong suit—with the exception of those at my gym. Even then, I have staff at the gym who can socialize for me when I'm not in the mood, and a property manager I could technically call on to handle guests at home if needed.

However, after I saw that someone had requested to book long-term, I thought it might be necessary to get a feel for who would be in my space for so long. Not once did it cross my mind as a possibility that I might be so attracted to my long-term tenant that I wouldn't *want* to stay away.

Edara Lauklan has thrown me off my game.

Never in my life have I seen such a gorgeous woman before laying eyes on Eda standing at the steps of my guesthouse four days ago. Going out isn't really something I like to do, but part of me wonders if it's time to get back out there.

Only, the other part that screams, "*no*, never again," wins every time. And I'm kind of okay with that. It would take a serious change of heart for me to open myself up to someone else. Yeah, I don't see that happening any time soon.

Except for when it comes to her it seems, and that is a mystery in itself.

Her striking blue eyes and red hair that shimmers in the sunlight are mesmerizing. The name of her dog—which I recognized as a reference from *The Lord of the Rings* because it's one of my favorite series—and the fact that she knows French have piqued my curiosity in a way that I don't think I've ever experienced when it comes to another person.

When I was in the army, I learned French for my job. Without having anyone to practice with now, I've since struggled to maintain the skill. I wonder if she'd be willing to practice with me and help me sharpen my speaking skills.

No. No, spending more time together than necessary is absolutely not a good idea.

I'll have to continue to remind myself of that, since Eda is renting the guesthouse for the next two months and she is all I can seem to think about. In that time, we could easily avoid one another and remain strangers, or we could risk ending up knowing more about each other than an actual couple might after not even two months of dating. There's a difference between casually dating a person for two months and living in close quarters with another person for two months. For better or worse, people learn way more about someone when they live with them.

I set my coffee mug down on the kitchen island and run a hand down my face and beard. I need to get it together. There's nothing wrong with getting to know a long-term tenant and assessing if it's safe to have them on my property, but there *is* something wrong with wanting to get to know them because I can't get them out of my fucking head.

That almost sounds like a gateway to dating. In my experience, dating never turns out well for me. Which is why, even when it was difficult to pry myself away from her that first day—especially since Blanche was having such a good time—I knew it was necessary. I was extra thankful when she mentioned she had to get to work because it made me feel better about walking away.

The emotions I felt then—and even still now—are alarming. At 36, I've accepted that it's okay to be single and happily living alone in the woods with your dog. In fact, it's more than okay. That's how it has been ever since I got out of the military three years ago, and that's how I like it. Getting involved with someone isn't on my radar. My scars run too deep, and I don't want them to bleed into anyone else. Especially not someone who is as bright of a light as Eda seems to be.

My younger sister, Sawyer, is always telling me that I need to do more things and meet more people. Yeah, no thanks. It's also slightly hypocritical since she's an introvert herself. Plus, there are enough people at the gym I own to drain my social battery daily.

Even if I wanted to date, work and Blanche leave no extra energy for entertaining a woman in my life. That was exactly what I reminded myself of when I walked away from Eda that first day of her stay, and what I've attempted to tell myself since.

I've tried to stay away, but have failed miserably. Every time I see Elessar's silver and black fur out my cabin's windows, I don't fight it when Blanche goes to the front door, asking to go play with him, because it means I get to talk to

Eda. It's lucky for me that Blanche and Elessar get along so well. She gets all of her energy out with him, while I get to enjoy the view of Elessar's owner.

Ugh, that sounds creepy.

There's just something about Eda that pulls me in. Something that I find myself not wanting to fight, even if I don't quite understand it just yet. Maybe that's the allure of it—of her.

How is it that she was able to catch my attention so easily, when I really haven't been interested in anyone in years? It must be those bright blue eyes. I swear they stare straight into my soul. They tell a story of their own each time I look into them.

While she always has a friendly smile on her beautiful face, her eyes sometimes look sad. Scared, even.

I also haven't missed the way she jumps every time either Blanche or Elessar snap a fallen tree branch. A haunting, scared look crosses her face each time at the noise, no matter how far it is from her. She attempts to hide the reaction with a small smile once she realizes there's no threat, which is the only reason why I never mention it. It makes me want to ask her what caused her to react this way, and also gives me this strange desire to want to protect her. I try my best to blame that on why I can't seem to stay away.

Lies.

This morning marks day four of her stay, and when Blanche suddenly runs from the living room window to the front door with a single, loud bark, I know it means that Eda and Elessar must be outside. With a quick glance to the clock on the stove, I make a split-second decision that I'm willing to be late for work today if it means I can get a glimpse of Eda. And who cares if I'm not on time? After all, I am the boss. No one's going to fire me if I show up a bit late to do paperwork.

Shaking my head at how ridiculous I'm being over this woman, I chug the rest of my coffee, rinse out the mug, and stick it in the dishwasher.

Walking to the entryway, I grab my keys and Blanche's leash hanging by the door. She doesn't need it, but I know it makes some of the people at the gym feel better whenever she's leashed while there.

With the keys and leash in hand, I smile down at my happy girl before opening the door and stepping out on the porch. Blanche immediately takes off for the guesthouse, and I eagerly follow, my footsteps quickly picking up pace as I make my way toward the redhead who has been occupying not only my guesthouse but also my mind.

Chapter 6

EDARA

Who knew nature could be distracting? If asked before this trip if I would like to read outside, I probably would have responded with an enthusiastic "yes!" However, now that I've been here for a few days, I've found the outside world to be far more distracting than I anticipated, but in a good way.

I only get about half a chapter into my book before the feel of the breeze against my cheeks has me closing my eyes and relaxing into it. Or maybe three pages in before the sounds of the birds chirping in the trees above make me look up and smile at them.

After the third attempt to read the same page, I accept my fate and set the book down on the outdoor table to look up at the trees and the mountains beyond. My ankles are propped up on the wooden balcony railing, and the stretch to my calves feels nice.

Wrapping my cardigan a little tighter around me, I settle back in the chair and close my eyes to take in the sounds of the birds singing and the leaves rustling.

This place is good for me. It has been good to me, and I've found it's helping me with each day I'm here.

We're only four days in, and I'm already dreading having to leave. In fact, a part of me *never* wants to leave. Maybe it's a little bit of avoidance, but there's no denying Steaming Stone is quickly capturing my heart. Not to mention that I've written more in the past few days than I have in months. Maybe even in the last year, thanks to everything I've been dealing with.

The sense of peace I get here is unmatched. It only confirms that I made the right decision to book a long-term trip. Even though it had been an impulse decision at the time, my gut told me it was what I needed to do, and I'm glad I listened. This feeling I'm experiencing now makes it worth every penny I spent on the extended stay.

Not to mention some of the perks, like the owner of the place, who is not only nice but also nice to look at.

Those back muscles alone inspired me to write for three days in a row. Alaric and his place might be exactly what I need to finish this manuscript once and for all. He is the perfect vision of the new male main character in my book—the one I previously kept blanking on because the only man I could picture before was my gross, cheating ex I dated in college. Well, and Brad, who was *not* about to be the inspiration for the love interest. But Alaric? Ugh, yes, please.

The first night here, I wrote a record-breaking seven-thousand words in four hours. The word count hit almost the same amount the next day before I decided to finally stop for the night. I can't remember the last time that many words came to me in a month, let alone in a matter of days.

As a reward to myself this morning, I decided to pick up one of the many books I packed with me, because one's never enough. Heck, five books aren't enough. However, as good as the book is, I am struggling to focus on it more than this beautiful view before me.

To be fair, it is the reason why I rented this place. I am beginning to wonder if there will come a morning here when I won't be in awe of it. At this point, the answer is a resounding no.

Leaves crunch down below, catching my attention, but the sound is quickly replaced by the rapid thumping of paws running up the balcony steps. With eyes now open, I grin when I see Blanche's smiling snout—tongue hanging out the side—barreling toward me from the top step. I barely have time to pull my legs off the railing before she's in front of me, leaning into my legs.

"Hey there, sweet girl." Laughing, I start rubbing her back. White fur attaches itself to my black leggings, but I don't care. Fur is the most important accessory to every outfit when you're around dogs. "You're just such a happy puppy, aren't you?"

The only response is a wagging tail as she pants with her tongue still hanging out the side. There isn't a care in the world behind those big brown eyes. Just a joy for being alive; a joy for being here in this moment with me. The feeling is mutual.

"Is she up there with you?" Alaric asks, his voice traveling from down below.

Shifting, I lean in my chair toward the railing. Barely able to see over Blanche's back from still being slightly reclined in the chair *and* pinned by her ribs leaning into my legs, I shout, "She is! We're up here."

A few seconds later, Elessar emerges, and by the sounds of the footsteps on the wooden stairs, Alaric is close behind him. My fluffy boy walks over to me, gives me one gentle lick on my hand, and then sits down with his back to me as he waits for Alaric to fully emerge.

With one hand still on Blanche, I scratch behind Elessar's ears. He responds by leaning farther into my left leg, with Blanche now leaning against my right leg to face Elessar.

So far, he's been really good with Alaric, who has been wonderfully patient with him. The first two days were a bit iffy, with Elessar keeping his distance, but still mildly curious about this new man now in our lives here. However, yesterday, he went up to Alaric all on his own. No prompting, no pressure. Just comfortably trotted to him, smelled him, and didn't move until Alaric did.

We're working on him staying around long enough for pets, but it's already great progress in a short amount of time. It also makes me feel better because Elessar clearly doesn't see a threat in our new neighbor.

Before long, Blanche's weight is no longer against my legs and she's giving Elessar her full attention. With another dog companion on the balcony, I'm quickly forgotten by both fur balls. It's just as well, because with the way Alaric looks this morning, my own attention has shifted.

His brown hair looks slightly disheveled and his reddish-brown beard catches in the sunlight beaming through the treetops, making the red strands really stand out. He looks tired, but he still looks handsome.

When he gives me a small smile, I happily return it.

With each step he takes, more of him is revealed. A red and green flannel lays unbuttoned and perfectly sculpts his arms as it sits over a plain, white shirt. Those dark blue jeans hug his muscular thighs, and I can only imagine what it's doing for the rest of his lower body. I try not to stare too hard.

"Sorry about that," he says as his brown boots hit the last step. "Blanche saw Elessar, and then took it upon herself to also come see you, I guess." Before Alaric can even finish the sentence, he is forced to sidestep out of the way as the two dogs barrel down the stairs, practically side by side. Somehow, they squeeze in and make it down together.

The pounding of their paws on the wood steps quickly turns into the crunching of leaves and snapping of twigs as they begin playing somewhere down below.

I chuckle. "It's okay. Blanche is a good girl, and I'm just as happy as she is to be here."

"She likes you," Alaric says with a small smile.

"Well, that's good, because I like her, too." I resist the urge to say that I also like Blanche's owner.

There's a moment of silence between us, as the unspoken words hang in the air. It's not quite awkward, but I still find I want to fill it. Not because I need to, but because I'm intrigued and want to know more about this man.

Noticing the leash in his hand, I point to it. "Were you taking her for a walk?" I ask, attempting to change the subject before I put my foot in my mouth about liking his company or thinking he's attractive.

He shakes his head. "No, just taking her out to get some fresh air before we head to the gym."

I nod and point toward where the rowdy dogs are playing somewhere down below. "Same here. Well, not the gym part," I chuckle. "I'm letting Eless run off some energy, while I attempt to read," I gesture toward the book on the table, "before getting to work here soon."

Alaric's eyes go to my book. Thankfully, the cover's discreet and doesn't give away that it's a spicy fantasy book. Even if it did, that'd be fine. I just don't feel like having that conversation with my landlord at seven in the morning. I especially don't want to risk it leading to a conversation about how I write my own spicy books, and he's currently the star of the most recent one...

His arms cross against his chest, and it's a wonder how the stitches of that flannel are still intact. "You like to read, huh?" he asks. I huff out a laugh, and his eyebrows raise. "Is that a...no?"

"No, I do," I say, smiling. "A lot, actually. It's only funny because you'll probably find me with a book more often than not. The goal was to read this one this morning, but I'm finding *this* to be more distracting than I expected." I gesture in front of me, but there's really no need to. The sky is streaked in the colors of dawn, making its presence known to the day. A light dusting of clouds quickly disperse from covering the peaks of the mountain range, as if they were waiting to unveil the stars of the show for this very moment.

His gaze follows and he nods once in understanding. "Yeah, it's the reason I bought this place. It's hard to beat that." His voice is soft, wistful even, as he takes in the scenery. His features relax a little, and I get the sense that the view puts him at peace just as much as it does me. How could it not?

Prying my eyes from him, I pick up my tea and take a sip. Right as I pull it away from my lips, the hot drink almost spills on me when I jump at a sound below us. The loud *crack* sets off a frenzy of leaves crunching and a bird flapping its wings to get away from the disruption.

My reaction and movement catches Alaric's attention, his eyes now on me as his body language suddenly shifts. But I don't have time to process what he might be thinking right now. I need to work through my nerves before I allow my fear to consume me.

Closing my eyes, I slowly breathe in the scent of the steaming English Breakfast tea still in my hands, then breathe out through my mouth. Doing it again a second time, I remind myself that it was likely just a huge branch snapping below us from the dogs playing. It was them the first fifty times it happened, and it absolutely is them this time, too. They're just playing, and it's only natural for leaves and branches to crunch and snap when we're in nature.

It's not Brad lurking. It's normal. It's safe. It's fine.

I'm safe. I'm fine.

When I open my eyes again, I see that Alaric is still watching me. Embarrassed, I can feel my cheeks heating up. Hoping to play it off as a result of the steam from the mug, I take another sip of the tea. Somehow, I maintain eye contact with him over my mug before setting it back down on the table.

He clears his throat and uncrosses his arms, pointing his right thumb in the direction of the stairs behind him. "I should check on Blanche and head out. Let me know if you need anything, okay?"

"Will do. Drive safe, Alaric." I smile and give him a small wave as he heads for the stairs.

He turns around then, and some sort of staring contest occurs between us. Except, it feels more intimate than a contest. It's more like a mutual desire to not look away rather than a challenge to not break the stare.

I blink away the disappointment that rushes through me when he does finally look away.

"You be safe, too, Eda," he says, and I swear my heart skips a beat at the sound of my name on his lips. I don't think I've ever loved my nickname more than I do at this moment.

With one final nod, he turns back toward the stairs and starts walking down them, while I struggle to process everything this man makes me feel.

Chapter 7

Edara

The bell above the door jingles as it swings open, pulling my attention from my laptop screen to the entrance of the coffee shop. My eyes dart from my dark-mode manuscript to the person in the rather comfortable looking, chunky knit sweater heading toward the counter to place their order.

A harmless person placing an order for a medium caramel apple latte and a chocolate-filled croissant.

Not Brad.

Not a threat.

With a deep, slow breath, I briefly scan the rest of my surroundings before attempting to put my focus back on my laptop.

It has been easy for me to get lost in the zone this week. That's normally something I would celebrate after so long of being blocked, but it's altogether scary when I'm not in the safety net of a familiar place. And while this coffee shop I'm working in is cozy, it's not yet familiar to me, which is making it a bit harder to *stay* in the zone.

When I woke up this morning, I sat up in bed, with Elessar resting against my leg, and looked out the glass doors of the loft patio to the beautiful sunrise over the mountains. I felt so at peace, so hopeful watching it. I can't really explain why. Then, a bird took flight from the tree to the left of the porch, chirping as it soared and landed on a slim branch of the tree to the right side of the porch.

It was a simple, quick trip from tree to tree. Something I've probably watched a hundred times this week, between all the birds inhabiting the trees on Alaric's property. And yet, it made me want to do the same—to go somewhere. Spread my wings and find a new, temporary spot to perch.

With the comfort of knowing that my every move isn't being watched here, I'm starting to realize that I finally can now go about my day and...live. A concept that shouldn't feel as strange or as foreign as it does—it practically feels illegal at this point—but I'm grateful that Steaming Stone has allowed me to feel this way.

With each day that passes, I'm becoming more comfortable with being in my own skin and existing in the world without the constant threat of Brad watching. Right now, I don't feel like I'm just waiting for the other shoe to drop. And wow, does that feel nice.

That's how I've found myself within the walls of The Steaming Cup coffee shop on this beautiful Friday morning. It's cozy, inviting, and most importantly, warm, because I've quickly learned that it gets chilly here first thing in the morning and a few hours after the sun goes down. Granted, that's not much different in theory to Raleigh, but mountain "chilly" and Raleigh "chilly" are proving to be vastly different.

When I left Raleigh five days ago, it was a high of 81°F and still humid. While packing the night before, I looked at the weather in Steaming Stone for the week, and it didn't sound too cold to me at the time. In fact, having weather in the 60s sounded perfect after a particularly scorching summer. However, what I hadn't factored in was the low humidity in the mountains and the crisper air, which weirdly *smells* colder than in Raleigh.

I haven't worked up the courage to head over to one of the many outdoor clothing stores yet to snag a coat. Going shopping and trying on new clothes sounds like such a fun and normal act to many. Once upon a time, I used to enjoy a little retail therapy.

However, I've learned that people—myself included—don't really think about how difficult it is feeling comfortable in the vulnerable state of undress while in a fitting room, when they're terrified that their stalker will greet them on the other side of the door once they reemerge. To be fair, it wasn't until that became my reality that I even considered it a possibility.

Yeah, I'm not quite there yet.

So, for now, I'll stay cozied up next to the indoor fireplace here in the thickest turtleneck I thought to pack. It's a beautiful, double-sided stone fireplace: one side stands as the hearth indoors, with four wingback chairs surrounding it; and the other side is on the outside, with outdoor seating for those who are comfortable enough to sit out in the cold with nothing but the fire and their clothes to keep them warm. That could not be me. At least, not right now. Maybe soon. Hopefully soon.

I'm elbow deep into my manuscript, when Nadine—the woman who took my order—comes up and asks if I need anything else. She has a kind smile, bright brown eyes, and this certain aura about her that instantly puts me at ease. It's helping with the nerves over being alone. I could see myself coming back here, thanks to her warm welcome and genuine kindness.

"Is that chai still okay for you for now?" she asks, pointing to the mug atop a saucer on the wood end table next to the wingback chair I'm in. Her smile is just as bright and genuine as the other few times we've talked this morning.

Nodding, I return the smile. "I think so. It's delicious. Thank you." It just might be the best chai latte I've ever had.

With a nod, she starts to turn back to the register, but then pauses. Her eyes search my face, likely noticing my hesitation. "Are you certain?" Her eyebrow raises.

I huff a laugh at her observation. "Most definitely." Glancing toward the chalkboard menu behind her, I say, "But...I was considering getting a plum cider. Would you recommend it? I've only ever had a regular apple cider before."

There's a beaming smile on her face. "Oh, yes! It's delicious. We mix house-made cider with a local plum tea blend."

Ugh, that does sound delicious, and I'm officially intrigued.

Looking down, I see my mug is still half full. "Well, then. I know what I'll be getting when I'm ready."

"You won't regret it. Just let me know when you'd like it." She nods and turns to ask another customer how they're getting on.

I take that moment to scan the rest of the shop from my spot, taking it all in. I'm the only one occupying the area around the indoor fireplace, thankfully. I don't much feel like entertaining conversation at the moment. Nadine is the exception. The few times we've talked have felt more genuine than the typical small-town, passing pleasantries. She makes me feel more comfortable here.

There are two other people sitting alone. One is reading a textbook and wearing headphones that are almost the same size as their whole head. Based on their choice of reading material, I'm guessing they might be a student at Steaming Stone University. The other person is tapping away at their computer.

That's exactly what I should be doing right now—writing more of the character my new landlord has unintentionally and unknowingly inspired. And I will, after I finish my hourly scan of the place. People watching is too entertaining and important at times.

The chairs at the tables are all cushioned and look comfy, rather than metal chairs most places have that make me want to leave the moment I sit down.

I opted for one of the four armchairs near the fireplace, only because they're upholstered, and one was set up with the perfect view of every spot in the coffee shop. From here, I can see the counter, every table—and everyone sitting at those tables—the entrance, and the sidewalk beyond the glass walls of the building. Just in case.

Whenever I'm engrossed in my laptop, the little bell above the door alerts me when someone's coming in or leaving. Every single encounter I've witnessed or overheard has endeared me even more to this place. Everyone has been so nice—whether to me or to complete strangers going about their days—which matches up with the rest of the town so far.

It's quiet here. Lovely. Cozy. Homey. I don't know, it's nice. No, it's more than nice. I could see myself getting a lot of work done in this spot—when I'm not people watching—but also enjoying coming here even when I don't need to work. Maybe even...on a date? With a certain brown-haired man, who's basically convincing me he's a lumberjack?

Given that dating hasn't been an option since Brad came into my life, I shake off the thought and pull my eyes back to my laptop screen. Instead of daydreaming about going on a date with my landlord, I get back to work writing about it, like a normal person. And this story won't write itself, as much as I wish it would.

Two hours later, I finally ordered that plum cider, along with a pumpkin cinnamon roll. Holy cow, Nadine wasn't wrong: the plum cider *is* delicious. This might be a bit dramatic, but my life will never be the same.

I noticed they sell individual packets of the local plum tea she mentioned, as well as gallons of their house-made cider. All three items—from the tea, to the cider, to another pumpkin cinnamon roll—are on the list of items I will be grabbing to go before I officially head back home today.

Home. Hmm, what an interesting concept. I haven't been in Steaming Stone that long—just five days, to be exact—and the guesthouse has already started to feel like home. Alaric's property has begun to feel like home.

Waking up to the sunrise over the mountains each morning, and then falling asleep to the sounds of the last leaves of fall rustling on the branches while crickets serenade me. Or enjoying a cup of tea and a good book on the balcony, while Elessar and Blanche play on the property below me. Oh, and I can't leave out the part about my lumberjack landlord cutting wood each morning, or when he returns from his runs, jogging shirtless up the colorful, leaf-cluttered driveway toward the main house.

Who knew I'd turn out to be a mountain girl? Heck, Aunt Bellamy probably did. Hence why she's been trying to get me, my sisters, and my parents to come out here for years. While I loved it as a child, it feels different experiencing it as an adult. She probably knew we wouldn't be able to resist the tranquil environment, or this town's irresistible charms.

Although, it helps that it doesn't feel like a small town. Most small towns I've been to have more churches than businesses, but not this one. Personally, I love having options of where to eat or what coffee shops to work in. The ones that are typically so full that they actively drown out the street noise while I pour over my laptop. After all, I'm a city girl through and through.

Or, so I thought.

Warmth works its way down my throat and straight to the center of my chest as I take another sip of the cider I'm holding in both hands. With a content sigh, I close my eyes and lean back into the comfy wingback chair. I've always said tea is a cup full of happiness, but this? This might take the cake.

This whole entire place just might take the cake. The people, the atmosphere, the delicious drinks and food. All of it. And not just this specific spot, but beyond it. Even that bistro Elessar and I went to on our first day in town made an impactful first impression on me.

Could it really be that I'm actually starting to feel comfortable again? Emotion pricks behind my closed eyes, and I scrunch my nose at the feeling, brushing it off.

But I also can't ignore it entirely. I've already started to feel the tension in my shoulders release. I'm looking over my shoulders less and less. I'm not eyeing the door and windows in here as much with each hour that ticks by. I have not even looked at the cars that are passing by in...maybe half an hour?

Yes, this feels right. It feels good for me. All of it.

When I open my eyes again, my sight readjusts to the daylight streaming in. Over the rim of my steaming mug, I catch Nadine and the other barista, Curtis, watching me from behind the counter. With a hopeful, crooked smile, she gives me two thumbs up, as if asking how I feel about the drink.

Taking one hand off the mug, I give her a thumbs up and mouth, *So good.*

She claps her hands together and does a little happy dance behind the counter, her black apron scrunching up around her hips as she does a happy jig. Curtis laughs at her dancing, and I can't help but to laugh as well. Their joy is contagious.

Yeah, I quite like this little spot. And the people within it.

Chapter 8

Edara

There's a slight chill in the air, but the sun is beaming down just enough to make it the perfect temperature out. I smile into the breeze coming my way before crossing the street with Elessar prancing next to me. We had to park two blocks away to accommodate the game-day madness. I knew football was big here, but wow.

Soon, I feel a slight tug on the leash as Elessar spots my aunt standing outside at Ruby Stone's. She's waving excitedly, nearly matching the rhythm of his wagging tail.

"Hi, little ones!" she yells, beckoning us over from the crosswalk.

Aunt Bellamy is wearing skinny jeans, brown knee-high boots, and an emerald sweater that perfectly complements her red hair, making her look like the human embodiment of Christmas in October. The once vibrant red of her hair has faded with age, but this lighter shade suits her well. She's as beautiful as ever. Add in as strong as ever, because the hug she gives me squeezes the breath right out of my lungs.

"Hi, Aunt Bellamy!" I say, squeezing her right back. My body rocks back and forth from the force of the hug.

It lasts a few seconds before she finally releases me and takes a step back to greet Elessar. "My little Eless!" Her arms wrap around his fluffy neck and his tail continues to go wild. "Thank you for taking such good care of your mama," I hear her whisper as she pets his head.

"He loves you so much," I say, my heart full of love for this woman before me, who's like a second mom to me. Her presence actually makes me miss my mom. They're so alike. I'll have to give her and my dad a call later.

"The feeling is mutual," she says as she stands back up and points to the outdoor bistro table. "Is this spot okay? It's the closest to the water bowl." She puts her hand to her mouth, as if she's about to fill me in on a secret. "It was also the only one left."

"Definitely. It's actually the same table that Eless and I got lunch here earlier this week." I smile and get situated into the metal chair as Eless helps himself to the full water bowl.

"How have you been, sweetie? How's the book coming along?" There's a big smile on her face, and I do my best to not make it go away by physically reacting to the question.

It's normal to receive questions about when my next book will be released, especially by those closest to me who love reading them. Being six years into this career now, this isn't new to me—this pressure; the questions; the rehearsed answers to help the conversation go smoothly. However, it's been harder to deal with them recently because I haven't been in a good place with writing. I'm thankful that they care enough to ask and want to read my books, but also, this pressure...

I want to give my readers the next story to read as much as I want this butternut squash soup I know I'm about to devour. However, it's not a simple or quick process. Man, do I wish it was.

My anxiety and harsh internal critic quiet when I think about the progress I've made this week. The progress I've made since meeting Alaric. It's worth celebrating. Small wins, and all.

If I were to step back and really think about it, I might find it a little weird how inspired I've been by someone I only just met. However, I don't have time to get distracted by the reasoning right now. Instead, I'll focus on the positives. First, he's kind and good-looking. Second, he's helping me do something I haven't been able to do in months. Third, I feel safe enough to create and be me.

All things considered, I think it's worth it to not dive too deep into the *why* at the moment. That's future me's problem. She can handle the inevitable future shame over writing sex scenes with him. Well, not *with* him, but about him.

"Actually, the book is coming along. I'd say I'm..." I pause and mentally calculate. "A quarter of the way in."

"A quarter?" Her eyebrows shoot up. "Isn't that..." She pauses and her eyes study my face, which I don't doubt is showing disappointment and shame—everything I'm feeling internally—by her expression. Immediately, her body language and tone shift. "A lot of words? I bet it's going to be your best one yet."

I chuckle at her save and the same words she says to me after each book I finish.

Shaking my head, I say, "I'm not so sure about that, but I'm actually really loving this one. It's a bit different, but it's becoming something I'm quite proud of. I'm also feeling pretty good about the progress I'm making. I've made more of a dent in this project this week than I have all year. And I feel like..." I clear my throat in an attempt to hide that I was about to reveal all my secrets about my hot landlord. "This town has inspired me."

My aunt clasps her hands together in delight. "Ah, I love hearing that! It is a lovely place, isn't it? I'm so happy you're enjoying it and finding inspiration here. It's a shame I can't convince you to stay longer. Who knows how many books you'd write if you lived here?"

It's a joke. I know it's a joke. It has to be. And yet…

My brain is entertaining the thought more than I'd like to admit. More than I ever would have thought it would. I love Raleigh, but it's not the same anymore, thanks to Brad, and there's just something about Steaming Stone…

Fortunately, Neal—the server I met the other day—walks out of the bistro's doors, saving me from having to respond. He welcomes me back—recognizing both Elessar and me—checks the water bowl, and then takes our orders: two bowls of butternut squash soups and two grilled cheeses to dip in them, along with a chai latte for me and a pumpkin spice latte for my aunt.

It's nice being able to catch up with her in person. It's only been a year since we last saw each other, when she, my uncle, and one of my cousins, Meriam, visited my parents' house in Raleigh. Still, that's a year too long.

We talk about my uncle, my two cousins in school, and my other two cousins in their respective careers. Meriam is in a teacher assistantship MFA program at Appalachian State, just like my younger sister, Aurelia, who is graduating from North Carolina State University's program next spring.

My aunt finishes filling me in on my youngest cousin, Lily—named after my mom, Liliya—who's majoring in Political Science at UNC-Chapel Hill just as our food and drinks come out.

Then, as we dig in, I fill her in on all the stuff going on in our family. "Mom and Dad are doing well. Cressida's photography business is kicking off. As you know, she's currently in her busiest time of year, between weddings and family portraits for holiday cards."

"Oh, sweetie, I absolutely know. We already have your sister booked for our holiday cards this year, which means that I'm guaranteed to see both of you this season!" Her joy is eminent as she smiles over her mug before taking a sip.

"She told me! I'm hoping to see her while she's in town," I say, thinking back to the conversation I had with my sisters when I first told them I was coming here. "Rhiannon and Aurelia are also thinking of coming up."

"Oh, how fun!" exclaims my aunt, who nearly spills her coffee with how fast she sets it down to clasp her hands together in excitement. "All of you in one place? How did I get so lucky?"

Smiling, I say, "No concrete plans yet, but we'll definitely all get together with you if they do come."

"You'd better," she says sternly, but then a grin spreads across her face.

"Speaking of Aurelia, she's in her last year of her MFA program and has started looking into jobs teaching higher education. Mostly around Raleigh, but I think she's considering branching out to all over the state," I say as I slip Elessar a small piece of crust. His tail swishes against the brick sidewalk as he gently takes it from my fingers. Sharing a grilled cheese might become our new tradition at Ruby's.

"You know..." My aunt's eyebrows do a little dance and her eyes twinkle. "Meriam plans on applying to teach at Steaming Stone University once her program is finished." She grins as she dips her grilled cheese in her soup bowl. "They have some open positions..." Her shoulders dramatically shrug practically up to her ears. She takes a bite of her sandwich, her eyes still twinkling.

I laugh at her not-so-subtle suggestion that Aurelia should consider applying to teach at the university here in town.

Aurelia and Meriam are only a few months apart, so they were closer growing up than Cressida and I were to Meriam. The idea of them working together at the same college feels full circle when I think back to the two young girls they once were, standing in front of a child-sized chalkboard and pretending to be teachers to me and my other cousins. Sometimes for Cressida, too, but as she got older, she spent less time with us.

I look around downtown and smile, knowing that Aurelia would also love being here, but uncertain if she'd be willing to leave the comforts of our hometown. She probably remembers this place even less than I do, since she's seven years younger than me—with me being 32 and her about to turn 25.

I make a mental note to send her, Cressida, and Rhiannon a text later to confirm they're all coming to visit. A girls' weekend sounds good for the soul. Plus, we could all use a break.

"Rhiannon's told me she's thinking about starting her own yoga business," I tell my aunt, because a family update wouldn't be complete without including my best friend, who's basically a sister to me. "She's sick of the owners at her studio. They pocket too much money and pay their instructors too little for being in Raleigh." I roll my eyes at the greed. "Otherwise, she's good."

Knowing this, my aunt's eyebrows once again raise in a playful manner. It's becoming her signature move at this point. "Hmm... There is a vacant building here in downtown that might make the perfect yoga studio." She clears her throat and sits up a little straighter, cradling her coffee mug. "I'm just saying."

I laugh, but it dies down as I look up and down the street. "Is it nearby?"

She points toward the intersection where I almost witnessed an accident and thought I saw Brad's car a few days ago. It's currently congested with people traveling into town and attempting to find parking for today's football game. "It's just a couple doors down that way. Next to the pretty brick building. You'll see a 'For Lease' sign in the window, but it's currently under construction."

I look in that direction, hoping to see the window sign, but I don't. I'll have to walk that way with Eless after lunch. Just to take a peek. Nothing serious. It's not like I could convince Rhiannon to move here, anyway. And she's been saying she wants to start her own yoga business for years now. I don't see her actually doing it anytime soon.

I turn back to my aunt, whose eyes are on me. "Don't think I didn't notice how you talked about everyone but yourself." She gives me a sad look. "How are *you* doing, Eda?"

Busted.

If I can help it, I don't talk about myself. However, I feel I owe it to her and the rest of my family to give them at least a little bit of information. They worry, and

I can't fault them for that. Admittedly, I'd also worry if the roles were reversed with anyone I know and love.

Pushing my empty bowl away, I grab my chai and cradle the cup in my hands as a safety net. It's also easier to talk about my life when I'm not making eye contact with someone who cares for me. It's not exactly helpful to see the fear—or worse, pity—in their eyes.

Staring at the cup in my hands, I start. "I'm okay. Well, as okay as I can be right now. Being here really has helped a lot already. It's a nice escape, and I…" I never know how much to say. I don't want to worry anyone even more, but I also don't want to lie. And there's really not much to say. There are no new updates. Nothing can be done about what Brad's doing. I'm just…stuck right now.

I adjust in my seat and take a sip to buy myself some time. Looking my aunt in the eyes, I tell her the truth, while still keeping most of it to myself. "I'm okay. I'm happy here. I feel safe, and I'm enjoying myself. That's all I can ask for right now, and I'm going to hold onto it for as long as I can."

Her eyes are watery as she says, "I'm glad to hear that, sweetie. You deserve to be happy."

I nod and look away to prevent myself from also getting emotional. "Thank you for sending all your cards over the years. It was actually your most recent one that made me want to come here."

She laughs. "Oh, you mentioned that on the phone! That was a cute one! I loved the little dogs barking."

I laugh at the memory of the sound of barking to the tune of "Happy Birthday."

"And it's my pleasure. It was a tradition my aunt—your Great-Aunt Betty—had with me and your mom, and I wanted to keep it with you girls." She shrugs, like sharing her love and carrying on a family tradition is no big deal. "While you're here, is there anything you need? Anything we can do for you?"

I shake my head. "No, I'll be okay. I like my landlord, and Eless likes his dog, Blanche. They've been playing nonstop. It's good for Eless to have another dog to get out his energy with."

"Oh? Tell me more. What's your landlord's name? And what kind of dog does he have?" Her body language immediately changes, and I recognize it as her protective mom mode. I know she doesn't love that I'm staying at a 'strange' man's house. Especially since I have another strange man watching my every move. It's a valid concern, but Alaric's...different.

"His name's Alaric. He's nice...and good-looking." Her eyebrow raises and I shift gears. "He owns a gym somewhere here in town. I'm not sure what it's called, but he mentioned that. His dog's name is Blanche, and she's a Bernese mountain dog mix. She's only a puppy, but she's *huge*—even bigger than Eless—and such a sweet girl," I ramble.

My aunt studies my face for a moment before her eyes go big. "Oh my days, Eda! You like this man, don't you?"

I choke on my chai. "No. No, I don't," I say in-between coughs. I cover my mouth with my hand, covering the choked coughs, as tears swell in my eyes. "I don't even know him enough to like him."

"Oh, please. I know you well enough, and I have daughters myself. I can tell when you all fancy someone."

"Fancy?" I set my cup down and laugh. "I hardly *fancy* him."

"Whatever it is you kids are calling it these days." She waves her hand in the air before pointing her well-manicured finger at me. "But don't think I don't see hearts in those eyes."

I shake my head with a smile on my face. "No way. But I will say that he's helped inspire parts of the new book. So, I guess you'll get to know him in that way. Well, not *him*, but the book version of him."

"Well, that settles it. Now I have to meet him." She puts her coffee down on the metal table, as if driving her point home.

My eyes are wide as panic takes over. "No, you don't need to do that." Bad idea. Abort mission. No. No. NO.

"Of course, I do. You're staying at a strange man's home. That alone gives me enough cause to meet him. But now, you're saying he's inspiring your book? I absolutely must meet him." The mom voice is in full force.

I shake my head, panicking. "Aunt Bellamy, there's no need for that. It's a contactless stay, anyway. We don't really interact." Only partially true. He's a hands-off host, but also not. I've enjoyed seeing him around the property, and I hope that doesn't stop.

"Well, we'll make it happen. Just tell him your dear, old aunt is concerned for your safety and wants to meet him."

I give her a small smile because that is absolutely not happening. Yet, knowing her, she'll make it happen.

"You're not old," I say.

"You're sweet for saying that." Her nude-painted nails lightly pat the metal table top and she gives me a gentle smile that quickly drops. "But don't change the topic by trying to flatter me. Tell him I'd like to meet him at his earliest convenience."

I hide my grimace behind my cup as I take another sip. Poor Alaric has absolutely no idea what's coming for him.

Chapter 9

EDARA

By the time my laptop closes tonight, my neck and back are sore and my eyes sting from staring at a screen for hours. Day six of writing is complete, but I'm starting to feel the effects of it.

Elessar trots over and leans into my leg, prompting me to look at the clock on the stove. While I didn't miss his dinnertime—because he would never let me forget—it is time for him to go outside again.

Rubbing behind his massive, pointed ears that he never quite fully grew into, I pull away from the kitchen table and walk toward the back door.

I open the Dutch door, and then immediately close it again. It is freezing out there! When did that happen? As I turn around to scan the small living area and kitchen nook, I realize my thickest cardigan—which I've been using in lieu of a coat—must still be in the car from when I grabbed lunch with my aunt earlier. The car that is currently sitting in the dark of night. In the middle of the woods.

Damn it.

Looking down at Elessar, I say, "This is going to be a quick trip, okay? Your mom wasn't blessed with three coats of warm fur like you."

He just looks up at me with that sweet shepherd smile, oblivious to my woes. His tail thumps on the floor as he sits and waits for the okay to go outside.

With a sigh that dangerously resembles a groan, I resign myself to my fate. Opening the door again, I force myself to walk out of it this time. My hands instinctively wrap around my biceps, hugging my torso as a cold wind hits. Meanwhile, a happy Elessar races into the night.

"Don–n't go t–too far!" I shout between shivers at his retreating form. Within seconds, he's out of my sight and running into the dark of night, his dark fur blending in with the shadows. Resisting the panic rising within, I make a mental note to order a glow-in-the dark collar for him the moment we get back inside. Being able to see him at night was never a concern in my tiny yard back in Raleigh.

Shivering, I listen for the sound of his collar. The clinking of his name tag and rabies shot tag rings into the night. I look around for the source and see that he has found Blanche near Alaric's cabin. That immediately makes me perk up, because it means that Alaric can't be far away. Between his morning runs, off-leash training sessions with Blanche, and routine of chopping wood before leaving for the day, I've only seen him around a little bit this week. Never for more than fifteen minutes or so.

He seems to be taking the hands-off rental host role very seriously. Initially, I was grateful for that, but I haven't been able to get the man out of my head. Literally. A character he inspired now lives in the pages of my book and takes up mental space in my brain.

Still, I have to admit that the man who inspired the character is far more intriguing. *So far.* We'll see how the character continues to develop. Or the human himself. But something tells me there are many layers to unpack with Alaric.

After a quick scan of the dark yard and driveway, I spot him sitting on his porch. He waves, and I take that as a sign that it's okay to approach him. The thought of being an annoying guest makes me hesitate for a brief moment, but I decide to throw caution to the wind and go for it.

"Where's your jacket?" he asks as I make my way closer, the porch lamps lighting my path.

"I–in my car. I didn't t–think I'd be out long, so I d–idn't grab it. But I–I'm not going to deprive Elessar of p–playing with Blanche after he's been co–ooped up with me all day. He d–deserves to play." Despite it being difficult to speak due to my chattering teeth, I manage a smile. Elessar is the best boy, and I constantly ask myself what I did to get so lucky to have him.

As I step closer to the porch, Alaric sets his beer down on a wooden end table on the porch and stands up. "I know what you mean. I try to bring Blanche to work with me most days, but I can tell it's not the same as playing with a dog," he says, smiling. "I've been considering getting another dog for a few months now, so she won't be alone. The way she is with Elessar has solidified that for me. So, thank you."

Before I can respond, he removes his bulky jacket and walks down the steps. His hand extends toward me, offering it to me.

My jaw drops. "Oh, no," I say, waving my hand. "It's t–too cold for you t–to n–not have something."

Instead of putting it back on, he takes the last step down into the yard and stands in front of me. The jacket is around my shoulders within seconds, the hem falling right at my knees. I can't help the audible sigh in relief as its warmth engulfs me.

"That's what I thought." He chuckles at the reaction.

The sudden girlish urge to stick my tongue out at him strikes me, but the feeling quickly goes away when I meet his gaze and realize just how close he is. Only one hazel eye is highlighted in the porch light, and the shadows perfectly frame his strong jawline. He is somehow even more handsome at night.

An image pops into my head of him on top of me, highlighted in the moonlight through the guesthouse's loft windows, while he pounds into me. My cheeks are probably already pink from the cold, but I can feel them growing hotter. I push away the thought, resigning to write the images into my book between my main characters instead.

"I'm sorry, and thank you," I say, choosing to express gratitude rather than attraction. "But now I feel bad. At least you had the sense to grab a jacket before taking your dog out."

A dazzling smile flashes my way. "I've lived here for years. I'm used to it at this point. And it does take some getting used to. It doesn't help that the weather can be kind of unpredictable. We could also get some snow in the next few weeks. Did you bring any snow gear?"

I stare at him. How could I have been so stupid? I booked a mountain rental *in mid-fall*, for crying out loud. "No, I didn't think that far ahead. I mean, I packed a bunch of sweaters. I just didn't realize you all get snow that early in the year."

In my defense, we don't get a lot of snow in Raleigh. Schools shut down at even the whisper of snow, and on the off chance that we do get an inch or two, the roads become a hazard because no one knows how to drive in it. I don't even have a snow coat or snow boots, just a puffer coat and duck boots that I use for snow.

"Yeah, we can get snow as early as the first week of October. It's not common, but it's happened before."

He looks me up and down, as if somehow checking me out under the massive coat resting around my body. Or is that just wishful thinking?

"I can give you the names of some of the best places to get cold-weather gear here. Unless you're planning on skiing or hiking, a good jacket and some boots should be fine."

"Yeah, I can't see myself hiking in the snow. Or skiing." I smile. "Thank you. You might be the best host I've ever booked with." Seriously, though.

He shrugs. "Just making sure you don't freeze to death on my watch."

Is that all?

No, the way he gave me his coat, but still hasn't backed away…it's almost like there is something more here. I can practically feel it zinging in the air. Or is my author brain taking over and imagining things?

"You mentioned you had work to do the other day, and that Elessar has been cooped up all day. What do you do for work?" He shifts on his feet and crosses his arms.

With a single whistle from him, both pups come barreling toward us. Since neither of us give a follow-up command, the dogs continue their playdate, just closer to the porch light.

Smiling at the happy dogs, I respond, "I'm an author. I came here because I need to meet a deadline, and I had to get away from distractions in order to do it." Like a stalker.

"Distractions?" he asks, his tone curious. "Like, a boyfriend?"

My head whips away from the dogs and toward him. He has one eyebrow raised and a glint in his eyes when I meet his gaze. For a second, I think maybe he is asking to see if I am single. Huh, maybe he is…

"*Ex*," I emphasize the word just in case Alaric is interested. "Actually, he wasn't even a boyfriend. We only went out on two dates. But he's been…" What can I say that won't scare Alaric, or make him think I'd bring my troubles to his home?

"Go on," he encourages, taking another step toward me, closing the already small gap between us. His demeanor has changed, and he seems more serious than he was just a moment ago. "He's been what?"

After staring into his eyes for a few seconds, I sigh. Alaric might as well know, just in case Brad soon figures out where I am. A shudder racks my body, and it's not from the cold.

As if to protect myself from an invisible threat, I wrap my hands around each opening of the coat, pulling them close together. I might as well zip it up at this point, but I'm not sure my frozen hands could function with a zipper.

Lost in thought, I gasp when Alaric's fingers gently brush my skin as he tucks a hair behind my ear.

Keeping eye contact with me, he says, "You don't have to tell me anything if you don't want to."

How am I supposed to concentrate while he is so close? And what is that smell? It reminds me of a fall candle. I smell vanilla and...something else. I can't quite put my finger on it.

Blinking to refocus on the conversation, I briefly close my eyes. I might as well get it all out there. "He's been following and harassing me since I broke things off nine months ago. After I saw his car pass my house for the fourth time in an hour, I booked this trip. But I've only told a few people where I am, and none of them would dare tell him. He won't come here," I ramble, but I need him to know I don't intend to bring trouble to his doorstep.

A muscle in his jaw tenses, and his brow furrows as he dips his chin to better look at me. "Considering it was serious enough for you to leave the safety of your home for two months, have you contacted the authorities about him?"

I roll my eyes and huff a laugh in frustration. "Sure did. They said they can't legally do anything until he threatens or harms me."

Alaric's jaw tenses again. "Bastards," he mutters before meeting my gaze again. "One of my best friends is a detective here. With your permission, I can talk to him about it, and we'll see what we can do."

"Oh, you don't have to do that." It's thoughtful of him, but the last thing I want to do is to intrude. Plus, I've heard all I need to know about how much the authorities are willing to help with stalking scenarios, especially when one of their own is involved.

"I want to," he says, and I can tell he means it. Strange, but I like it. It's kind of him, and it feels nice to have someone want to help me who isn't family and feels obligated. "In the meantime, if it makes you feel better, Blanche is a great guard dog—it's in her blood to guard her home and her people—and I was in the army. So, between the two of us, no one's getting close to you."

If my cheeks weren't pink before, they certainly are now. "Oh, Alaric, you don't have to offer that. Seriously, I'm sorry. I didn't come here or tell you all of that to be a burden. I'm sorry for talking about it." Shaking my head, I look away.

"You're not a burden." His voice is deep, stern. "And I'm the one who asked. If anyone should be apologizing, it's me."

I meet his gaze. "You can't say I'm not a burden. You don't even know me."

"Maybe not, but I know enough to not be okay with someone hurting or threatening you." His voice is stern, unwavering.

Something melts in my chest, and it isn't because of the warmth of the jacket. I ignore it the best I can as I say, "But he hasn't technically done either of those things yet." Keyword: *yet*. Which is the reason why the authorities won't do anything.

"Nor will he," Alaric's voice is deep, dark. By the look in his eyes, his words hold a promise. Ex-military, indeed.

Gratitude and relief fill me, and my eyes prick with the sudden onset of emotion. I didn't realize how long I'd been carrying this burden alone, and how good it would feel to not have to do that anymore. Yes, my family knows a bit—just enough to keep them safe and cautious—but I never wanted to worry about their safety, too. The fact that Alaric is capable of protecting himself makes me feel better about him knowing.

"Thank you. You really are the best host ever." I smile, attempting to show-case every ounce of gratitude in that one smile.

His lips twitch. "In the spirit of keeping my reputation of being a good host, would you like some hot chocolate to warm your hands? It looks like they'll be at it for a bit longer." His chin juts out toward the two pups still chasing each other in the yard.

"Sure, that sounds nice," I say, excitement bubbling at the prospect of getting to spend a bit more time with him.

His long legs bound the steps and cross the porch in a matter of seconds. As he opens the door, he turns back toward me. "Are you coming?"

"Oh." My lips part. "I didn't realize you were inviting me in. I'm sorry."

"You apologize a lot, even when you've done nothing wrong." One of his eyebrows raises at me for a moment.

I feel a bit exposed by the observation, but say nothing. Not even the immediate 'I'm sorry' that bubbles up in my throat. I bite my lower lip to keep the words from spilling.

Braking our stare, he briefly glances inside before looking at me again. "Since you'll be here for as long as you are, you might as well get acquainted with the main house—my house. It's where all the firewood will be stored for your fireplace, and if you need anything, but can't get on the roads, you can just come here."

My stomach flutters at the thought of being in the house and snowed in with him. With a silent manifestation, I wish for exactly that. Maybe even before I buy winter clothes so that I'll have the excuse to seek refuge in his warm house.

I internally groan at the thoughts. What is wrong with me?

"I guess they want to come inside, too." He laughs, as the dogs suddenly race past both of us and into the house. Elessar doesn't even hesitate as he walks by Alaric. The trust he's put in Alaric in such a short period of time being here makes me think maybe I can trust him, too. "Do you still want some hot chocolate?"

I look up at him and then back at the door as I realize what just happened. How embarrassing that Elessar let himself in when I'm not even sure *I* should step foot inside!

"Well, seeing as how my dog invited himself into your house, I should probably at least make sure he's behaving. So, sure." My hands wave in the air, trying and failing to hide my embarrassment. First, it was from stealing his jacket, and now it's from stealing his privacy and free time. What else could go wrong?

Stepping into his home, I get another whiff of his cologne and suddenly have the urge to also steal a few kisses from him, too.

I mentally smack myself as I answer my own question: If I give into the urges, *a lot* could go wrong.

Chapter 10

ALARIC

I know I'm supposed to be staying away, but all logic went out the window when she walked outside tonight. After hours—really, days—of thinking about her, finally seeing her again sparked something in me. For some strange reason, the sight of her made me wave in the hopes it would encourage her to come over. It was like I was a kid again, waving at my crush across the yard at recess. But I don't regret it.

When I saw that she was shivering, I instinctively handed her my jacket. I couldn't stand to see her suffering like that. The sound of teeth chattering made me want to help her, to protect her. I told myself it was because my mom raised me right.

The same words ran through my head after rage filled me when she told me about the man stalking her, and the piss-poor police who offered zero help and security. No wonder why she booked somewhere long-term; she needed to get far away from the dickhead harassing her and the assholes not helping her. It also might explain the sadness in her eyes and why she's so jumpy.

It took everything in me to not give into the rage and risk accidentally unleashing that anger on her, because she's completely innocent and doesn't deserve that. So, I kept it reined in as best as I could, and will reserve it for the conversation with Gavin, who's a detective and my best friend. We'll work on a plan to figure out how to protect her.

His specialty is homicide, but I remember when there was a big case in Boone of stalking turned murder-suicide. Being only forty minutes away, we heard all about the tragedy. Surely, Gavin would know how to keep it from getting to that point for Eda. Because, fuck, I can't imagine anyone wanting to hurt her.

It's also easy to blame my sudden desire to be hospitable on my upbringing. Although, this is the first time I've ever invited a guest into the main house. It's strictly off limits to guests. Again, all logic seems to fly out the window whenever I'm around her.

I'm hit with the realization that I don't want to remain strangers with this woman. I want to know more—everything there is to know about her, and everything she's thinking about behind those beautiful blue eyes. Except, that sounds an awful lot like going down the road of dating someone. Which is out of the question.

Yet, seeing her standing in my kitchen now…I'm having the oddest desire to see her here again in the morning. That luscious red hair flowing straight down her back, while she stands there in my shirt that would barely be long enough to cover her ass. Just a peek of cheeks first thing in the morning as she sips her coffee, while I get to cook her pancakes and admire her.

Yeah, that image is probably the most shocking part of all so far. Even more so than inviting a guest into my home. Only my family and closest friends have had the luxury of getting a taste of my cooking, but for some reason, I want to cook for this woman. There is this strong desire to protect her, to satisfy her. It's why I invited her in, and why I'm having the hardest time reminding myself to keep my hands and eyes to myself.

I shake off all inappropriate thoughts of her delicious curves and red hair as I walk toward the cupboard to grab the hot chocolate mix. "Hey, Little Red, can you hand me two mugs in the cabinet to the left of the microwave?"

"Did you just call me Red?" There's amusement in her voice.

I pause mid-rip of a hot chocolate packet before looking at her. "Huh, I guess I did." Except, I said *Little* Red, because she's so tiny. Especially in my coat, which looks massive on her petite frame. But I keep that to myself.

"What an original nickname." She's got me there, and I chuckle. "Wait, did you forget my name?" Her cheeks flush, and guilt churns in my stomach at the sight. How can she think I'd ever forget the name of such a beautiful woman? One living on my property, no less.

"Of course not, Eda. You have a beautiful name." I try to give her the kindest smile I can muster. Since it's not my specialty, I don't know if it's effective. "I just like Little Red more, apparently." No idea what drives me to wink at her, but I can't stop it before it happens.

Unbelievable.

I turn back toward the counter and grimace for only the kitchen cabinets to see.

She laughs behind me.

Our fingers brush when she hands me the mugs, and the touch prompts me to meet her gaze. Her blue eyes sparkle up at me as her lips part, but no words come out. I can tell there is something on her mind. So, I stand there and wait, watching her as it looks like she's trying to find the right words in that pretty little head of hers.

With the clearing of her throat, she finally breaks the silence. "So, since I've told you about my sad love life, I think it's only fair you tell me a bit about yours."

Not expecting that, I stiffen. The reaction causes a flash of emotions on her face before she takes a step back.

What does that mean? Does she think I'm dating someone? Good joke. I don't have enough in me to care for anyone but myself and Blanche. Even then, it took me years to even consider getting a dog. I'm still not sure I deserve the unconditional love and loyalty of a dog, but when my sister introduced me to Blanche at her vet clinic, it was love at first sight. Whether or not I deserve that love, Blanche is mine, and I am Blanche's. Life before that goofy, happy puppy is a blur of going through the motions, and I don't really like thinking about it.

But the love of a dog is different from what Eda's referring to.

Being in a relationship wasn't top of mind for years. Sure, there were some relationships, but never for long. Which is my own fault. Military life is hard enough on service members who chose their careers, let alone their families who didn't really have a choice in the matter. I didn't want to settle down and force anyone into that lifestyle. By the time I got out, I guess I was just used to being alone.

Now, after all the almost romantic partners I turned down in the past, I guess I don't really believe I can love someone else, nor do I deserve to feel that in return. Why should it be on my timeline? And I especially don't believe myself worthy of the love of someone like Eda. Someone who is kind, a bright light, and has won my dog's heart. She has enough troubles on her plate without me adding to it.

The thought sobers me up, making it even easier to keep my hands to myself and my mind mostly out of the gutter.

Instead of saying all of that, I settle for, "I don't date."

Her mouth parts in an *O*, and the image of her on her knees before me, feeling her lips wrapped around my cock is almost too much. So much for being sobered up. Talking about my dating life is helping to keep me from wanting to see if she'd be interested in bringing that vision to life. Just a reminder that I can't cross that boundary.

"Never?" she asks, unaware of my dirty mind wanting to take control.

I turn toward her. "Sure, before, but not now." I shrug, wanting the conversation to be over. "It's not in the cards for me."

Her eyes look down to the front of my jeans, and I can't stop the grin that crosses my face as she looks back up at me. Her cheeks flush red. Is that a sign that her imagination also went straight to the gutter?

I chuckle and grin, the same smile I'd used a time or two in my youth. "That is very much still on the table."

She blushes.

Uh oh. Was that too much?

"Oh, I didn't mean with you," I backtrack, and her face falls. "Wait, no. Not that I don't want to, because I *do*. I just meant that's not the reason why." Why am I rambling? What the fuck is happening to me?

"It's fine, Alaric. I'm the one who assumed I knew what you meant. But it's definitely good to know it still works...and that you're interested in me." She winks.

Our eyes lock, and the amusement that filled hers only seconds ago is now replaced by something that looks a whole hell of a lot like desire. A look I imagine mirrors my own. Based on how her eyelids suddenly look heavy, and the way she bats her lashes, yeah, it's entirely possible she noticed the attraction is mutual.

"Really?" I ask.

"I—" She hesitates, looking like she's having a mental debate of her own on how to proceed. I just hope a line was not crossed by me blurting out how I feel. "Yeah, of course. I'm sure you get a lot of women in your bed. So, it's good that part is fine."

Oh, how very wrong she is. Once upon a time, maybe, but not now.

"What makes you think I get a lot of women in my bed? Or even in my house?" I look around, and her gaze follows.

This is a true bachelor pad, with the bare minimum furniture needed to live and zero decor taking up space. Nothing like the guesthouse she is staying in that my sister decorated. It made sense to decorate that as an investment property, but I don't need a lot of stuff to live here.

"Alaric, you can't look like *that* and not have women interested in you," she teases, her hands gesturing up and down at the word *that*. "Your legs scream 'we're going to have great sex,' and your hands must be in popular demand. I mean," she points to my hands currently swallowing up the normal-sized mugs she handed me, "come on."

With a grin on my face, I set the empty mugs down on the counter and take a step toward her. "My legs scream, 'we're going to have great sex,' huh?"

It's cute how her cheeks grow red whenever she seems nervous or embarrassed, but I find it sexy now because of the topic. They're almost as red as the hair I want to wrap around my hand while inside her.

Her throat bobs. "Well, tell me I'm wrong."

Bold. I like that. She is surprising me right now, and I'm even surprising myself by not ending the conversation and sending her away. I can't decide if that's a bad thing or not. It has been a long time since I desired a woman I just met, and I can't remember ever feeling this strong of an attraction toward anyone.

It's what has me bending down to get closer, and closer, until my lips are brushing the tip of her right ear. "You're wrong," I whisper, and she lets out a faint gasp. "It wouldn't be great. It would be incredible." My voice sounds deep with desire even to my own ears, but I don't care when I see how it sends goosebumps down her skin as she leans closer toward me. I'll have to remember that she likes when I talk dirty in her ear.

When I pull away, her eyelashes shudder as she seems to be collecting herself. My coat suddenly slides farther down her shoulders, and there's a slight sheen of sweat on her skin. Is that from having the coat on inside, or from our conversation?

I want to kiss the soft skin exposed at the nape of her neck, trailing down—

Enough. I turn back toward the hot chocolate packets and discreetly adjust my pants so that she can't see the bulge in them.

"Um, you realize you can't talk to a woman like that and not make good on your promise, right?"

Without hesitation, I drop the open hot chocolate packet and turn toward her again. I study her face and body language, before looking into her eyes. Seeing she means it, I bridge the gap between us in one stride, until we are inches apart.

"Are you saying you'd like to find out if we'd be incredible in bed together?" My voice is low again.

Her lips part without forming any sound, but the moment she catches her breath, she says, "Yes, I am."

Fuck, is this real?

Yes, it is. I can see it all over her face that she means it. My gesture for hospitality just might turn into the best night.

But if we are going to do this, there will have to be rules. Rules set in place for myself to be okay with giving into these desires she ignites, and rules so that she won't get hurt by me emotionally. Honestly, I can't even bear the thought.

"On one condition." My fingers gently graze her chin, tracing up her jawline, then down to her neck. All the delicate places where I want my lips to be at this moment.

Her breath hitches as my feather-light touch goes lower, tracing the curve of her cleavage. "What?"

My fingers deliberately stop moving in between her breasts, right at the deep V of her sweater. Her eyes never leave mine. "Don't fall in love with me."

It's her turn to smile. "That goes both ways."

My lips twitch. If only my heart could love a woman like her, maybe this life would be worth it. But there is no chance of that. I'm meant to be alone. It's a curse I've come to accept. So, I simply respond, "Deal."

The dam of tension breaks when she smiles up at me. My other hand wraps around the nape of her neck as our lips crash onto one another. Soon, my tongue is against her lips, and she lets me in, meeting me with her own.

Passion, heat like I've never experienced before.

My fingers in between her breasts start their movement again, and she moans into my mouth when I pull down the front of her sweater and cup one of her breasts through her bra, kneading it. She leans further into the touch, further into the kiss, while wrapping her fingers around strands of my hair. I devour another moan of hers, and the vibration runs straight to my cock. Her responsiveness turns me on even more.

The moan turns into a groan when I pull away, breaking the kiss, and I huff a laugh at her reaction. There is nothing for her to worry about; there's no way I'm stopping now. Not unless she wants me to.

Holding either side of her face, I look down at her. "Are you sure about this?"

Biting her lip, she nods. "Yes," she says, breathily.

Finding the hem of my flannel shirt, she trails her hands under it, feeling my abs as she starts to undo each button. I can feel her fingers fumbling with the buttons, her nails lightly scraping my abs every few seconds. I reluctantly pull away from her kiss and yank the shirt off, chucking it haphazardly.

Instead of the skin-tight jeans she wore that first day, she is in gray sweats. They're cuffed at her ankles and fitted around her small frame. They should be easy to slide off at any moment...

"Here or the bedroom?" I ask in-between kisses.

"Why not both?" she says on a breath.

It's my turn to moan into her mouth. The sudden need to claim her on every surface of my house sparks something in my chest and makes my cock throb. Yes, we'll start with the kitchen first, and then I'll take her into the bedroom—followed by every remaining room, on every flat surface I can find—and make her mine.

But everything stops when the dogs start barking maniacally. I go still, listening intently. I know all of Blanche's barks, and this is a warning, alert bark. The thought of that guy having found her—which I know she's worried about—sparks my rage all over again. He will never have her.

I peer over her head to the front windows. Keeping my eyes on the yard, my hand wraps around her waist as I gently nudge her to get behind me, so that my body shields her from the open windows. Being this secluded in the mountains, I never considered getting blinds or curtains. Now I kind of wish I had.

"What is it?" she asks, and there's rustling behind me while she fixes her sweater. I can't tell if her breath is shaky from our kissing or from fear. My fists clench at my sides even thinking it could be the latter.

Her small frame goes to peer around my arm, but I sidestep her and gently push her back. If it is this guy—whoever he is—I'm not risking him getting to her. I promised her that.

When she tries again, my jaw tightens and my fingers flex at my sides, itching to act. It takes everything in me to keep from shielding her completely—to protect her—but I don't stop her. If it is him, she has every right to know.

She swears under her breath behind me—no doubt thinking the worst like I am about who it could be. An inner battle ensues of wanting to turn around and comfort her, but also not wanting to take my eyes off what is going on outside.

All thoughts of turning toward her cease when I see car lights coming up the drive, right to the house. Shadows dance along tree trunks as the bright lights round the corner, illuminating the gravel drive and making it difficult to tell what type of vehicle it is.

The lights only make the dogs bark louder. Blanche jumps up on the couch to get a better look out the window, and Elessar only hesitates for a second before he follows behind her, their snouts fogging up little spots on the large window.

My hand instinctually reaches for the throwing knife attached to my waistband.

"Alaric?" she asks. Her voice is so quiet against my arm, where she's still watching.

"Someone's here."

Chapter 11

While watching the car out the window, I take the time to try to process what just happened between us. It was the look she gave me in the kitchen that made me want to kiss her.

Despite the unexpected turn of events tonight, I know my own boundaries. It's why I made sure to warn Eda to not fall in love with me. Whatever happens between us will have to remain casual. Guys like me aren't suited for love. Flings, sure, but not love. The type of love and devotion that a woman like Eda deserves. I've simply never been capable of it, nor am I deserving of receiving it.

Except, after that first kiss, something sparked in me. Not love. Not even lust. No, it's more...primal than that. Something that's making me want to never let her go. Not from my kitchen, nor from my life. And fuck, if that isn't a scary feeling.

Not taking my eyes from the approaching headlights, I reach behind my back, feel for her hand, and give it a slight squeeze. The fear emanating off Eda only fuels my urge to protect her. The way she grips my hand in return has me pulling hers to my lips to kiss it.

My other hand falls back from the knife at my waistband. "It's okay," I say. The tension in my own body immediately releases the moment I recognize the pickup truck pulling up to the house. "It's just my sister."

Eda's hand grips tightly around mine, and I have a feeling it's more from anxiety than fear this time. That's a much better response. One that doesn't make me feel like pulling her into my chest and holding her close to me until she's feeling okay. Well, maybe the feeling is still there...

"Your *sister*?" Her voice squeaks. "You were just going to ravage me when your sister was on the way?" I think it's meant to be a joke, but I can hear the uneasiness laced in her words.

Smirking, I say, "Neither ravaging you—as you say—nor having a visit from my sister were part of my plans tonight." But here we are. Two houseguests in one night, and only one of them was invited.

Turning toward her, I smooth down her soft red hair and kiss the top of her head. From the way her lips part, I can tell the gesture shocks her. It shocks me, too, but I just feel the need to comfort her in that moment. Knowing who we both thought that car could be... I want to wrap her in my arms and keep her locked in my bedroom so that she will be safe forever.

But that's not an option, *crazy idiot.*

Clearing my throat, along with all those thoughts in my head, I say, "She's likely just wanting some firewood. She comes by every once in a while for more, and rarely checks to see if I'm available when she does." Granted, she doesn't need to, because there's nowhere else I'd be, except for my gym.

Eda starts smoothing down her hair and clothes. "Your sister. Firewood. Yeah, okay." She offers me a smile, but I can see the nerves written on her face.

I kiss the crease of worry between her brows before giving her hand another squeeze. "It'll be fine. She'll get some firewood, and then leave."

"What if she's not here because of the firewood?" Her teeth suck in her lower lip, and I have to resist the urge to lean down and replace her teeth with my own—resist wanting to continue where we left off.

"Then we'll figure it out." I smile.

The dogs get louder as Sawyer pops her head in the door.

"Oh! Another puppy!" she says with so much delight in her voice. "And who might you be, you sweet fluffball?" Elessar's tail flicks from side to side as he tentatively smells Sawyer's hand, and Blanche starts to get jealous. She's not used to sharing her people. "Calm down, you giant ball of energy. I have two hands and enough love for both of you."

My younger sister loves animals so much that she chose to go to veterinary school. Now, she runs a successful vet practice not far from here. She's the one who found Blanche when she was just two months old, and the one who will likely find me more dogs in the future. Not that I'm complaining.

Blanche is exactly what I need, and I have a feeling that a second dog will only double the joy in my life. It's something I once thought wasn't for me, but now that I've experienced it, I find I want more of the kind of happiness and unconditional love only a dog can bring.

"Hey, Soy," I say, as Eda shifts next to me. "What's up?"

"Well, I realized I'm running low on wood. So, I—" She stops mid-sentence when she lifts her head away from the dogs and sees Eda and me standing in the kitchen. Her eyes bounce back and forth a few times from me to Eda. "Oh, hello." Sawyer smiles, looking a little too amused for my liking.

"Hi," Eda responds.

I clear my throat, breaking the stare. "Eda, meet Sawyer, my sister. Sawyer, meet Eda, my guest."

I'm hoping she won't ask questions; however, by the way her gaze springs to mine at the word 'guest,' I know I'm in for an earful later. But I don't care. So long as Eda doesn't regret what we started, then neither do I. Although, I'm kind of pissed we didn't get to finish it. We were just getting to the best part when we were interrupted.

"It's nice to meet you," Eda says, meeting Sawyer halfway toward the door.

"You, too." My sister reaches for Eda's hand. "I'm assuming this pretty shepherd is yours?" She gestures toward Elessar.

Eda grins. "Yes, that's Elessar. We're lucky that he and Blanche get along well."

"That's an understatement." I smile and glance at Eda, who gives me a nervous smile. "Those two want to play every chance they get."

"That's good." My sister nods. "Blanche and Elessar…what a cute pair you two make." She dips down to pet them once more, but I don't miss the brief glance my way. "I've been telling Ric that it would be good for Blanche to have a companion. I'm glad to hear I was right. *Again*." Her gaze pointedly meets mine at the last word.

She tried telling me for years that having a pet would help me with my mental health, but neither one of us could have predicted just how right she was. Blanche gives me a reason to keep going, and to actually look forward to the future.

And yes, Sawyer was right about it.

I roll my eyes, but smile. "Let's get you that wood, Soy." I start to walk toward the door, but stop when I see how nervous Eda looks. Her flitting eyes roam my chest, and it hits me then that I never put my shirt back on.

"Right, I'm just going to take Eless and head to bed. It was nice meeting you, Sawyer," Eda says, smiling at my sister before turning toward me. "Rain check on that…cocoa," she says, her cheeks dotting pink at the word *cocoa*.

Understanding exactly what she is trying to say, I feel my lips twitch with amusement and…excitement. "Deal."

"Good night, Eda. It was nice meeting you, too," Sawyer says.

Eda walks out the door, calling Elessar to follow her. With a final look back at Blanche, he quickly matches Eda's stride, prancing with his tongue out as he looks up at her.

The moment the door clicks shut behind them, Sawyer turns on me. I don't even bother sighing outwardly because I knew it was coming.

"Isn't this, like, the first week she's here, Ric?" Sawyer practically screeches, yet somehow manages to keep the words at a whisper level. "I didn't realize you were *that* kind of host."

I need a second, so I turn my back to my sister to pick up my flannel off the floor. Sliding it back on, I fix the buttons Eda managed to unfasten. I see my coat lying on the kitchen floor and clench my jaw when I realize that Eda is walking back to the guesthouse without it.

Since it's unlikely she'll risk returning for it, I pick it up and slip my arms in, preparing to go outside in a minute for the firewood.

Not wanting to deal with my sister's chastising just yet, I grab a rag to clean up the counter where the hot chocolate mix spilled after Eda challenged me to make good on my promise. Brushing the powder into my hand, I toss it in the trash. All the while, I can practically feel Sawyer's searing stare burning a hole into my back.

"Your tone could do with a little less judgment," I finally say. Not that I really care what she thinks. I'm a grown-ass man.

"You'd like me to judge you a little less for jumping into bed with your paid *houseguest* on the first week of her stay?" Sawyer scoffs.

Technically, Eda didn't have the chance to jump into my bed yet, but I don't say that out loud.

"Yeah, that's exactly what I said." I meet her challenging stare.

"Don't look at me like that. I can practically feel the sexual tension in the air." Her nose scrunches as she dramatically waves her hands for effect. "And need I remind you that your shirt was *off*?"

I narrow my eyes at her, but she does kind of have a point about my shirt, which I forgot about until Eda silently reminded me. Still, it doesn't give her the right to talk about Eda this way. We are both adults and can do whatever we want.

Sawyer has always been my favorite sister. Then again, she is my only sister. But at this moment, part of me wishes for a second sibling—one who isn't so nosy or bossy.

Her jaw hangs open for a few seconds. "Alright-y, then. We'll just go on pretending this is perfectly fine and normal behavior for you. No worries. I'll show up with a box of condoms next time, no? How was it? Oh, God, don't actually answer that. No, no. I don't want to know." Her hands wave frantically in the air and her nose scrunches in disgust.

"Dude, you're acting like a prude. I didn't know you had that side to you," I chide, growing irritated. "And the more you chastise me, you realize you're also judging a woman you don't even know?" My hand holding the rag gestures toward the door, where Eda hightailed it out of here only minutes ago. By now, she's probably already in the guesthouse. Alone, instead of with me.

That makes my sister stop. Her arms and face fall. "I'm not judging her, but I am judging *you*." She points at me. "You break up with my friend without warning, and then fall into bed with the next girl you meet?" she hisses.

She can't be serious.

I drop the rag on the counter and turn fully toward her. "How many times do I have to say that Lexi was not your friend? Anyone who talks about you like that, doesn't actually care about you, Soy."

My sister had trouble making friends growing up. Or, rather, finding the right type of friends. So, whenever she thought she'd made one, she'd cling to them for dear life. It's a pattern she's carried into adulthood. Unfortunately, this newest person had manipulated both Sawyer and me, making us believe she was a true friend to her. It didn't take long for me to see through the act.

The last time I spoke with Lexi, she was sitting on the couch of her apartment while I was coming out of the bathroom. I'd overheard her on the phone talking shit about Sawyer, saying she's awkward and clingy, "but at least she has a hot brother." And, well, that was the end of it for me and her.

Granted, there wasn't really anything to "end." We weren't even dating. I took her out twice, and went to her place once, but that was it. It has been over a month since I kicked Lexi out of my life, but I've been unable to kick her out of Sawyer's.

"No, she didn't mean what she said, Ric." Her cheeks flush, whether from embarrassment or anger, I don't know. "And don't turn this on me. I don't care what you do, it's just...odd to break up with one girl, and then immediately get into bed with a *paying* guest."

Patience wearing thin, my knuckles clench and unclench at my sides. Miraculously, my voice remains even as I say, "It's been over a month. I'd hardly call that 'immediately jumping into bed' with someone. And I'm thirty-fucking-six, Sawyer. You don't get to tell me what to do with my life. It's none of your business."

My sister pauses at the mention of her full name. I've called her "Soy"—a shortened version of her name—ever since we were kids.

"Fine, *Alaric*. Don't listen to me." Shoulders falling an inch, she sighs in defeat. "So then, tell me about her. What's she like? She seems nice. Oh, and her dog is adorable!" A genuine smile appears on her face at the mention of Elessar, and I'm glad she's shaking off the Lexi thing to be more like herself.

"Yes, Eda and Eless are nice. Blanche is enjoying having them both here, and so am I." Eager to end the conversation so that I can check on Eda, I walk around the island and head for the front door. "Now, let's get you some wood so that you don't have to stay out too late."

The roads leading up to my house are particularly narrow. There's also no rail or anything against the side of the road, despite driving along the mountainside. Sawyer has complained about them since the day I moved in, and she especially doesn't like driving on them at night. I'm surprised she made the trek tonight.

"That's it?" Sawyer asks. "That's all you know about her, and you still crawled into bed with her?"

My whole body stills. Slowly, I turn toward my sister. My voice is low as I say, "Sawyer, this is the last time I'm going to say this. It's none of your business who I do and don't sleep with. Second, I know plenty about her." Not entirely true, but I know enough. "But just because you asked, after judging us no less, doesn't mean I have to tell you."

"Ric..." Her lips part in shock. "You've never talked to me like this before."

"And you've never treated me like this before. Like I can't make my own decisions." I stand firm, waiting for the argument to end.

"You're acting...weird. But in a grown-up way." She narrows her eyes at me. "I've never known you to stick up for someone in your life like this. Not to me, at least."

"I stick up for you all the time," I gently tease. "Including when you're mean to yourself." The way she was treated growing up is still a sore subject, but we have come to a point where we can make the occasional joke about it now.

She rolls her eyes. "That's not what I meant, and you know it." When her gaze focuses again, her eyes study my face before growing wide. "Holy fucking shit, Ric. You *like* her."

I scoff and back off. "I never said that." I really don't like this conversation. "Let's go."

"You didn't have to say it," she counters.

"Whatever, Soy. Let's just do this," I say, opening the front door for her. "I have some wood I chopped earlier that you can take."

"Nice change of topic," she jokes. "Look, Ric, taking Lexi out of the equation—" Her hands raise in resignation when I glare at her over my shoulder. "I don't care. I was just shocked. Especially considering I walked in on you without a shirt on with a complete stranger." She catches up to me without a problem, since her legs are almost as long as mine. "Tell me you wouldn't react the same way if you found me with my legs around a stranger's body."

My steps falter. "Okay, don't go putting disgusting images in my head like that." In an attempt to banish it from my mind, my palms start digging into my eye sockets. "For fuck's sake."

"Ah-ha!" A punch to the arm drives her point home. "That's exactly what just happened to me. I'm going to have to bleach my eyeballs after this."

I pull my hands from my eyes and meet her gaze for a moment. "Point made, except for the fact that her legs weren't around me," I say, making it to the firewood supply.

"Maybe not, but your shirt was off, and I could tell something happened. Still gross," she says, scrunching her face.

"I guess that means you'll knock next time." Hauling a bundle, I start walking toward her pickup truck.

"Obviously." Her face scrunches up as she emphasizes the word, but then her eyebrows wiggle. "Does that mean there will be a next time?"

"Not your business," I grunt.

"Thank goodness it's not." She laughs. "And I won't tell Lexi."

The bundle lands with a *clunk* in the back of her pickup as I turn to grab another.

"I don't care if you do," I say, shrugging. "We were barely a thing, and we've been over for a while. If she has an issue with it, I don't think that's my problem." Tossing the second bundle into the truck, I turn to look at her. "We hung out for, like, a couple weeks."

"Well, she thought it was something." Her hands go to her hips.

Eyes rolling, I reach for a third bundle. What is it about my sister that pulls her toward the worst type of people? She had always just wanted to fit in. No, she wanted to be liked; accepted by her peers—as everyone deserves to feel, but especially her. Kids here might have been cruel to her, but she never stopped being nice to them.

I got into my fair share of fights with kids who were bullying her, but she always ended up defending them, using her empathy and understanding as her greatest weapons. Meanwhile, mine were my fists to the boy who pulled her hair at the playground, and Jonny, who threw mud on her favorite dress when we were walking home from school one day. He never did that again.

As an adult, she continued that habit of falling into the crowd of people who wanted to use and abuse her. Kids will be kids and have to learn kindness in their own time, but it's a miracle I haven't yet murdered any of these "adults" for the way they've treated her.

Tossing the last bundle, I turn toward her and pull her in for a hug. "I don't care what anyone else thinks. Especially someone who's not particularly nice to my sister." She tries to protest, but her words are muffled into my jacket as I hold her closer. "Believe what you want, but just know that I won't put up with that shit." I kiss the top of her head as she resigns and wraps her arms around my back.

"Ric... Forgive me. It was a shock—"

"All is forgiven," I interrupt as I squeeze my little sister one last time and let go.

She smiles sheepishly. "Thanks. It's really none of my business who you do and don't sleep with, even if it's not Lexi," she tosses in again.

If she brings her name up one more time, my head might actually explode.

As if sensing that, she says, "Ah, before you say anything, I don't care that it's not her." She throws her hands up in the air again in defeat. "Not after seeing you like this."

"Like what?" I ask with a sigh, giving into her prodding.

With one last pat on Blanche's head, Sawyer hops up into her old red and white pickup truck. When she turns to look at me again, her eyes sparkle with amusement as they scan my face. "Curious...and excited."

Whatever that means.

Shaking my head, I close the car door for her. "Right, on you go," I say, giving her a wave.

"Eeeedaaaa and Riiiiic, sittin' in a tree..." she sings in a loud whisper for only me to hear as she slowly pulls away.

"Oh, fuck off," I grunt as I flip her off, but a chuckle makes its way up my chest at her childish antics.

"Good night, Ric!" Her laugh rings out the open window as she pulls off, with Blanche barking after her truck.

What was her deal, anyway? She said I'm curious? Excited? And she said I like Eda. I'm not sure what my sister was on about.

Raking a hand through my hair, I sigh and start toward the guesthouse. Time to clean up this mess.

Chapter 12

Alaric

As I approach the front of the guesthouse, muffled voices from inside grow louder with each step. Confused, I pause and listen, trying to decipher them.

No, it's only one voice: hers. Maybe she's on the phone.

Peeking through a window, I see Eda pacing in the kitchen, talking to herself.. Elessar's right on her heels, his tail wagging as he happily follows her every step.

Is she upset about my sister, or us? Did I do something? Does she regret what we did? Or is it something else?

Like...the guy who won't leave her alone.

My body stiffens and I make a quick scan of the yard. I still plan to check with Gavin tomorrow to see what we can do about the asshole. It won't take much to find out who he is, and what we can do to keep him from Eda without me having to dig a grave for him myself. I can do it without getting caught, but it'd make Gavin's life hell, since he's a homicide detective. He's damn good at his job, but not as good as I am at covering my tracks.

The thought jolts me, since my actions would also impact Eda. Sighing, I run my fingers through my hair. Just another reminder of why I can't taint anyone with my scars or my life. Especially not her.

Straining my neck to hear better, I do my best to listen to what she's saying, making sure it's not something about *him*—that I haven't missed something during Sawyer's visit. Bits and pieces only make it through the glass barrier.

"How could... So stupid!"

Something else about being into it, as she briefly stops and begins fanning herself with her hand.

Yeah, that's my cue to stop being a creep and end this.

Taking a step forward, I turn toward the French doors and knock. There's a gasp on the other side of the doors. Clearly, she wasn't expecting to see me again tonight, but I'm not about to leave her high and dry after what happened. Especially not dry, if I have anything to say—

A door opens, revealing this beautiful woman with a blush along her cheeks and neck. Her long hair is still down, cascading off her shoulders. A few strands flow in the front, near the deep V of her sweater, where my fingers were not too long ago.

"Hi, Alaric." She peers around the corner of the doorframe. "Is your sister still here?"

I fight the urge to smile at her not-so-subtle act of looking to see if I'm alone. "No, she left a few minutes ago."

"Oh, I'm sorry. I hope that didn't have to do with me." Despite the genuine tone, I can see the relief written all over her face.

I smile at that. "I told you, she only needed firewood. She comes every week or so once the weather starts to turn. It's all good."

Hugging herself, she nods. "Right, sure. Is there something I can do for you?"

So, we're being formal again? Interesting.

"That depends." I cross my arms.

"On what?" she asks, her brows furrowing.

"On whether or not you're going down a negative mental spiral or feeling great after we kissed." Her cheeks grow a deeper shade of pink, but I continue before she can respond. "Because it would really do a number on my ego if you felt awful after walking away from kissing me," I say in hopes that giving her a reason to tease me will make her feel less embarrassed about what happened.

It seems to work because she cracks a smile. "We can't have you taking a hit to your ego, now can we?"

I take one step closer to lean against the doorframe, hovering just outside of the threshold. "It would wound me," I tease, uncrossing my arms to place a hand on my chest in mock pain. It's almost scary how easy it is to talk and joke with her. The same thought occurred to me that first day when we talked about French, but I brushed it off. Clearly, it wasn't a one-time thing; it's just natural for us.

With sparkling eyes, her face lights up with a mischievous grin. "What can we do to rectify that, then?" She takes a small step toward me, with mere inches separating us now. I can smell her sweet-scented perfume and it makes me want to kiss it right off her neck.

Fuck. I didn't expect her—or even myself—to respond like this to what I said. "You tell me. You're the one who was left unsatisfied."

Her lashes flutter. "I won't hold that against you, but I also wouldn't complain about being kissed again."

I don't hesitate as I cross the threshold. Never breaking eye contact, I raise my hand, caressing her cheek with my thumb. Trailing my fingers down to her neck, I gently brush the hair off her left shoulder, and then—without looking away from her beautiful blue eyes—I wrap my palm around the vibrant red hair at the nape of her neck. With a gentle tug, I pull her head back so that she is looking up at me. A moan from her pretty lips as she bites them tells me just how much she enjoys that.

My gaze trails from her lips to her bright eyes, watching as her teeth dig deeper into her bottom lip, and oh, how I want to suck it between my own teeth.

Instead, my other hand traces a feather-light touch along the sensitive spot of her neck.

"Don't make me beg for it, Alaric," she says, breathily.

Bending down, I replace my fingers with my lips as I slowly lick that sensitive spot all the way up to her ear. Stopping, I whisper in her ear, "But you'd look so pretty begging for me, Little Red."

She whimpers as I nip at her neck before releasing her. Fuck, I love the mental image of her begging on her knees in front of me.

She sighs, a small, wanting smile on her face, as if she also loves the image my words plant in her mind.

It takes everything in me to not devour that sound, to not bring that fantasy to life, with her hair still wrapped around my hand, and her lips wrapped around my cock. Or to pick up where we left off and just set her on the island of the guesthouse, ready to feast on her.

But my sister's visit reminded me that maybe I did lose control earlier. While I don't regret it—no, how could I ever regret stealing the kisses of such a gorgeous woman?—I can't risk giving Eda the wrong impression. I am emotionally unavailable.

However, if she wants to be with me physically, then I will take anything and everything she gives me. But not yet. Not until I can get a better handle on what exactly I'm feeling, and what it is I want to feel around her.

With every ounce of my self control, I manage to restrain myself. Instead of giving in to my desires, I let go of her hair. Cupping either side of her face, I kiss her forehead.

"Until then. Good night, Eda," I say, pulling myself away from her and walking out the door.

Chapter 13

EDARA

Two days have passed since we kissed. What the hell happened that night? I kissed him, then I left. He kissed me, then he left. Neither scenario was one I wanted to end.

If he's half as good in bed as he is at kissing, then I'm done for.

Don't fall in love with me, he'd said. I might not be in love with *him*, but I sure as hell am in love with those kisses.

I went to bed that night with the biggest smile on my face and an itch I couldn't scratch no matter how hard I tried. And I did, indeed, try. If he has the guts to kiss me like that in the first week, then he'd damn well better finish what he started within the first month. At least, that's what I hope for.

There are three weeks left until we hit a month, and no luck so far.

On a positive note, and to my surprise, words have flown out of me and onto the screen every day since. The steamy levels in this book are off the charts. There is more spice in this first draft than plot at the moment, and I'm surprised to find I am okay with that. Not to mention that it will certainly balance itself out as I write more.

Typically, my books only have a couple of open-door scenes, but when the main male character is inspired by a man like Alaric, how can the draft not hold an abundance of spice in it?

With the exception of Elessar letting me know he needs to stretch his legs, I haven't left my laptop much today.

It's now dinnertime, and as I stretch in the chair, I realize I am officially almost 25,000 words into my word count of 80,000. That must be a record for me. Just over a week in, and I'm already a quarter of the way into my first draft. Booking this rental was one of the smartest things I could have done for myself and my book.

It was a risk going somewhere new, especially when I think about how Brad could have followed me after watching my house the day before I left. I watched the rearview mirror like a hawk—when I wasn't focused on the narrow, windy roads in the mountains—but didn't once see his car behind me.

This getaway is going to be good for me. It already has been for my mind and soul. To get away from the stress of life, between my agent nagging me and a guy not even worthy of being called an 'ex' stalking me. To be somewhere I feel surprisingly safe, with two dogs on the property and an ex-soldier with a detective best friend. To write and read to my heart's content, with a view of the mountains and the sounds of nature. I don't know if I've ever felt so at peace in a place.

There's something to be said about not feeling comfortable in your own home. About not knowing when you are being watched, or what will be safe to do alone outside of the house. Is it okay to go out at night to check on your dog in your own backyard? To put something in the trash or recycling outside? To check the mail? To park in your driveway instead of in the safety of your garage? To fucking live?

It hasn't always been this bad.

We met on a dating app, and despite my gut feeling telling me to cancel, Brad seemed nice enough to meet in person. How very, very wrong I was.

Admittedly, I shouldn't have met with him. And I absolutely should not have agreed to a second date, but I felt bad. Looking back, *he* made me feel bad. I tried to tell him I just wasn't feeling it, but he convinced me to give him another shot and that I wouldn't regret it. I told myself, what the heck, what's one more date going to cost me?

The answer: my freedom; my safety; my peace of mind; and now, my home. Oh, and a whole lot of regret.

After getting home from the second date, I remember feeling like I couldn't slam the lock fast enough once I walked in the front door. I reluctantly put the red roses he gave me in a vase, and felt uneasy the rest of the night. The next morning, I politely cut things off, and he did not like that one bit.

He continued to try to persuade me with notes and flowers—specifically red roses—sending them to my house. After the first bouquet arrived, I texted him and asked how he got my address, to which he responded that he has his ways, with a winky face, as if he thought he was being charming.

I attempted to get him out of my life by not entertaining his advances and going on a few dates with guys I'd met through various dating apps. It took almost a month before I noticed Brad would randomly show up on my dates, whether alone or with "a date" he ignored the whole time. The first time, I thought it was a coincidence. By the third time, I knew something was off. I still have no idea how he knew where I was going each time.

I didn't realize the way I'd been forced to live for so long until I no longer had to live like that. The main drive up to Alaric's guesthouse and main house is far enough away from the street that I noticed cars don't come here unless they mean to, with Sawyer being the only visitor thus far. It's nice, quiet, and safe. Things I took for granted before Brad wrecked my sense of security and peace of mind.

It's hard to know what will happen when I return to Raleigh in a month and a half, but this time away is helping me more than I could have expected or hoped for. So far, I'm surpassing my daily word count goals and getting more comfortable in my surroundings and in my own skin. Something's changing in me, and…I like it.

With each day, I get better and more comfortable.

With each day, I feel his hold on me lessens.

To be fair, I still look over my shoulder when I go out, or when I grab something from the car. Tucked in the woods or not, we are basically just off a main road. Well, the *only* road leading to properties up the rest of the mountain, and the only road going back down the mountain.

My body still freezes when I spot red cars while out in town, but I'm getting better. Knowing that Brad is not in this town makes it easier to recover and breathe after being startled in those moments.

It's crazy what time—and distance—can do for someone. Yes, I still get scared, but at least I'm not having to worry about it being him I thought I saw. I can actually walk alone downtown and know that if I see a tall, blonde-haired man, it is not him following me.

But it could be Alaric. A man whose dark brown hair has secret strands of red that rival my own when in the sunlight, but he is far more handsome than Brad. Kinder, too. Gentler. Tender. Just like his kisses.

Butterflies form in my stomach and I blush as I attempt to shake the thoughts away.

Sitting at the little kitchenette table, where I've been writing for the past three hours, I reach for my now room-temperature pumpkin chai and take a sip. When I put the mug back down, I close my eyes to give them a break from looking at the screen, but all I can see are images of Alaric's smile, his hands cupping my breasts, and then his hand wrapping around my hair.

The last time we spent more than ten minutes together, he kissed me. Not to mention that his shirt was off at one point, as well as my pants. Oh, and the way he'd tugged my hair—so gentle, yet so hot—while never breaking eye contact with me. All in the same night.

"But you'd look so pretty begging for me, Little Red," he'd said.

Begging for someone's affection was not something I ever wanted to do, but the way Alaric said it…it made me want to get down on my knees right then and there and beg until he was inside me.

The blush on my cheeks deepens at the memory of his words and the effect they had on me. Scratch that, are *still* having. Those butterflies are officially fanny flutters now, and I'm having to fan myself with my notebook just to cool off.

It's not working.

When he kissed me, a part of me felt less broken. When he'd grabbed my hair, I expected to flinch, but deep down, I think part of me knew I was safe with him—knew that he wasn't going to hurt me. And when I realized what he wanted—when he looked in my eyes and I saw the desire in his—I suddenly wanted him to take me right then and there.

The way Alaric looks at me makes me feel beautiful, confident. Something I haven't felt about myself in a long time. At the same time, I feel seen by him. He genuinely seems to care and makes me feel less alone…less afraid. I didn't know how badly I needed that—craved it.

With him, I don't have to wonder what he thinks of me. I can see in his eyes just how attracted to me he is. The way he checks me out when he doesn't think I'm looking. The way his eyes practically undress me when I wear my leggings and skin-tight tops. Not to work out, of course, just to lounge in. He also seems to like it when I play with my hair. So, I've started keeping it down and braiding it whenever I'm on the balcony outside and he's nearby.

I unashamedly swing my hips a little more when I walk away from him. I swear I heard him groan yesterday when I walked by him and bent into my car to grab an invisible object that "fell" under the driver's seat. That was a particularly good moment. As much as I wish he'd close the gap already, I've also been enjoying the tease.

I don't know the reason for his change of heart and why he has decided to stay away since our kiss. The day after, I tried waving at him and walking over the few times I saw him, but he just waved back and either went inside or got in his car. The rejection hurt at first, and it still kind of does, but knowing I can still tease him is proof enough that it's not because he doesn't want me. Hell, our kiss that night is proof enough that he wants me. And damn, if that doesn't feel good.

Part of me is telling me it's a problem with me—that I am not attractive enough, not good enough for a man like Alaric. Or maybe I carry too much baggage for him. No matter the message, it's always a cruel voice that likes to take over at times, silencing the kind things I sometimes try to say to myself. It usually wins, but my gut says there has to be something else keeping Alaric away.

The distance started after his sister left that night, which makes me wonder if she said something to him that made him regret kissing me. Or, rather, regret kissing a tenant. That'd be a valid argument to make—and easier to swallow than her—or him—thinking I am not good enough for him. However, that doesn't mean I have to like it. Nor does it mean he has to ignore me.

These are all thoughts going through my head as I decide to take a break from writing to stretch my legs before prepping dinner. I'm officially a quarter of the way into this latest book—the final installment in my first series—but I've been staring at a blank page for almost an hour now. Since my muse is avoiding me, so is my creativity, apparently. Or maybe it's anxiety over the finality of finishing the series.

Either way, this is not great. I'd had a consistent adrenaline rush from crushing my daily word count goals recently, but it's slowing down now.

Yeah, not great...

Some fresh air and a cup of tea will do me some good. Elessar seems to agree, as his tail wags when I grab my thickest cardigan to walk outside before I start dinner. At this point in the season, I'm tempted to wrap myself in the complementary robe hanging up in the bedroom closet. It would do more good than this sweater. However, this will have to do for now.

I'll go shopping soon. Eventually, I'll muster the courage…

Just as predicted, the fresh air feels good against my skin when I open the back door. That is, until I breathe in a little too much of the cold, and my lungs start to feel like they are burning.

Yeah, this will be a short trip outside. I let Eless out and pause before leaving the door propped open for him. It's better for us both if he has some freedom and does this trip outside solo.

Wrapping a throw blanket from the living room around my shoulders to fight off the cold air coming in, I begin tidying up the kitchen.

When I booked this trip, I had a one-track mind. Okay, a two-track mind: 1) get away from Brad, and 2) hole up somewhere to finish this dang book. It didn't really occur to me just where exactly I was going, or that the weather here is different than in Raleigh. Foolish. All I really focused on at the time was somewhere inspiring and cozy, and how much my aunt has made me want to escape here and write for years now.

It still blows my mind a little that I actually did it. It's probably the most daring thing I've ever done. Apart from not properly preparing for the cold, I don't regret it for a moment. I feel free here.

So free that I invited my Aunt Bellamy over tonight to see the guesthouse. Well, it's really because she wants to see *and* meet Alaric after I spoke about the nice, good-looking host of mine. Whether that's because she wants to get a feel for who her niece is staying with or who her niece is interested in is hard to know. Yeah, knowing her, it's likely both.

With the island now clean, I begin prepping dinner. I invited both my aunt and uncle tonight, but he politely declined since he'd have to join my aunt's book club for a night. Apparently, they take turns hosting at each other's houses, and because tonight's meeting is not at their house, he didn't want to chauffeur my aunt and get stuck hearing about a book he didn't read. Or, rather, "crazy gossip about people I don't even know," as he phrased it. I guess book club isn't always about books with their group.

Each time we've talked, my aunt has offered to let me stay with her and my Uncle Ben. While I appreciate it, I like having my own space. I've been on my own long enough that having to share a home with them would feel weird. Not that I don't want to eventually share my life and home with another, but that doesn't mean I want to share it with my aunt and uncle.

So, each time, I remind her that I am enjoying writing at the already-paid-for guesthouse. Not to mention that the views are fantastic. *All* of the views.

The leaves changing color is a pure, picturesque fall scene in the mountains. The kind of sight that can be found on a postcard. In fact, I hear this week is peak leaf-peeping season this year, and I've been warned by my aunt that there will likely be an abundance of tourists in town. It doesn't surprise me one bit, because it's worth the trip. There are so many talented people in this world, but I'm beginning to think no painting or photograph could do the sight justice.

There's also the view of the peaceful creek where Elessar wanders on the property, with its rushing water that soothes my scattered brain. Not to mention the view of the man who lives here, and the way he somehow looks hot as hell whether he's simply walking to his car or chopping wood. The way his back muscles and the veins in his arms flex and pop with each strike of the ax...

But my aunt doesn't need to know all the details. She can simply see it for herself. Heck, she'll probably not want to leave after she does.

I planned dinner and dessert tonight, complete with her favorite red wine and the ingredients for a pineapple Moscow mule for me. Per her request, dinner will consist of chicken stir fry with my homemade sauce over rice and a side salad with ginger dressing. I made my mom's pumpkin roll recipe this morning in preparation. It's my personal favorite fall dessert, and a little piece of home here in Steaming Stone.

I ate a light lunch to prepare for it all, but I'm regretting that now. The house smells heavenly, and my stomach is officially caving in on itself from hunger.

A text from my aunt lets me know her book club is running late and that I should eat dinner, but that I'll be in trouble if I don't save her some leftovers.

Apparently, there is a heated debate on who should be the main love interest of a love triangle in this month's book.

In response, I text back:

> Make the argument that the dark-haired, morally gray guy always wins.

A few minutes later, she responds that she tried telling her friend Cora that, but the woman disagreed and thought it was the blonde guy. I laugh at that, because it's rarely the blonde. I'm not sure why that is. My sisters, Cressida and Aurelia, both hate that, since they are both blonde. It's nothing against them; the people like what they like.

It's possible my aunt might not be as late as she's thinking, and I can wait a little longer. So, I call Elessar inside and grab my e-reader off the back of the couch to start the latest romantic fantasy book on my list. It's a highly anticipated read of mine, with a world full of elves, witches, and all sorts of magical creatures, including some sort of shadowed beast hunting down the main character.

Page one describes her running from the mysterious creature chasing her in the woods, and I can't peel my eyes away from the screen. It hits close to home with my own escape into the woods here, and the familiarity has me on the edge of my seat as I immediately start rooting for her. I'm hooked from the first paragraph alone, and within minutes, I no longer care about the wait as I read about her trying to escape.

Chapter 14

EDARA

After an hour of getting lost in the book's world, I reluctantly set it down and text my aunt again to ask if she thinks she'll be much longer, or if we should just reschedule. Once it's sent, I glance out the window to see if her car showed up without me noticing, but no luck there, either. There are just trees, my Jeep, the drive leading up to the main house, and shadows under the pale moonlight.

Sighing, I decide to get started on the drinks and make myself a pineapple Moscow mule. If she shows up, I'll just make another while I pour her some wine. No harm in that.

Elessar suddenly barks excitedly at the door, startling me so much that I jump and spill a little pineapple juice. Perking up that he might be barking at company pulling up, I set the juice down and quickly wipe up the mess.

I look at my sweet boy with a smile on my face. "Thanks for that, but it was wildly unnecessary."

Elessar only responds with more barking. I laugh as I soak up the last of the juice on the counter. Turning, I set dinner to the side and pull out dessert. It's never too late for pumpkin roll.

With the island now displaying dinner and dessert, I start walking toward the door and smile at how crazy Elessar is acting. He loves my aunt.

"Are you ready to see Aunty Bellamy?" I ask him, and his tail goes nuts. Laughing, I open the door, but instead of the average-height, red-haired beauty of a woman I call my aunt, I'm met face-to-face with a certain tall, muscular man. "Oh!"

"Sorry. I didn't mean to scare you. I was about to knock," Alaric says, just as our dogs start barreling out into the night, acting like they haven't seen each other in days, when it's only been a few hours. If I'm honest with myself, I can understand the feeling as I stand there, staring at his handsome face and feeling weirdly happy about it.

"It's okay," I say, wrapping my arms around my body as the cold starts to bite through my sweater. His eyes follow the movement. "Did you need something?" It's nice to see him again—to talk to him again—but the chill in the air mixed with knowing he's stayed away for a couple of days suddenly sours my mood a little.

He looks down at my crossed arms hugging my torso. "Do you mind if I come in?"

"Of course not." I nod and step aside. "It's your home, after all."

Once he's inside, I peek around and whistle for the dogs to come back. The second they run past the threshold, I quickly close the door to shut out the cold.

Elessar slows when he spots our host now in the foyer. He cautiously walks to Alaric with his snout twitching in the air, then gives a quick sniff against Alaric's dark-wash jeans. Alaric immediately stops moving, allowing Elessar to smell him, which results in a quick lick on his hand. A smile graces his bearded face at the sign of affection, and it melts my heart.

Just as quickly as it came, the moment ends when Elessar jumps away to his spot on the couch, tongue hanging out. Blanche follows his lead, curling up on the other end of the couch. I shake my head and chuckle because I'm sure they'll be back at being wild again in five minutes.

My phone vibrates twice on the kitchen counter, notifying me of a new text.

The sound has Alaric's eyes sweeping from my phone on the island to the food spread out next to it. "Am I interrupting something?" He casually looks around the guesthouse, as if searching for someone.

My gaze follows, spotting the two plates and two glasses I set out on the island countertop. Looking back at him, I smile. Is that jealousy I see on his face? Why does that make me feel good? Maybe it's a sign that he doesn't regret what happened the other night.

As I walk over to the island, I say, "Not really. My aunt is planning to come over for dinner and dessert, but she's running a bit late." I pick up my phone and see the texts from my aunt. "Oh, scratch that. *Was* planning on coming over. She's tired from her book club and wants to reschedule." My eyes scan the food once more before I look up at Alaric.

Smiling, he says, "Well, it smells good."

"Thanks. It's just stir fry and pumpkin roll." I shrug, suddenly growing self-conscious over what now feels like a mediocre meal.

"Still smells great." His lips tip up on one side. "Do you like to cook?"

"I mean, yeah. I dabble in the art of cooking, but that's about it. It's nothing fancy. I just enjoy it." I leave out that I have an entire collection of cooking knives. Or should I make that clear in case he's not the nice guy I thought he was?

I study his face again, get a feel for his energy, and my nerves settle. While my judgment in men might not always be the best, Elessar wouldn't be relaxed around Alaric if he was bad news. I can find comfort in that fact. Plus, there has to be a reason why Alaric feels different, and why I feel so comfortable and safe in his presence.

"It doesn't have to be fancy for it to be good." He smiles at me and I return it. "I also enjoy cooking. I find it calms me," he says, surprising me.

Not sure what to say, we just stand there, looking at each other.

"So," I start, "what can I do for you?"

"Right," he says. "I was just coming to check on you. See if you need anything. Firewood. Food. Blankets. Or…" His voice trails off. "Anything."

My eyes narrow on him. Was this just an excuse to come see me? Maybe he's finally decided to stop avoiding me.

"That was nice of you, but I'm okay." I clear my throat.

"Oh. Good. Good. That's good," he says, but he doesn't move. And why does he sound nervous?

"Is there something else I can help you with?" While I enjoy his company, I feel like there's more to this than just him being a nice host.

"Oh, no. Well, maybe. I—" He runs a hand through his hair and mumbles something under his breath.

I lift my hand to my mouth and stifle a laugh. A flustered Alaric is a new development. The food still on the island countertop suddenly becomes far more interesting as I try to hide my amusement. My eyes sweep over the spread and a thought strikes me.

"Would you… Have you eaten dinner?" I ask.

His eyes meet mine. "Not yet. I was going to whip up something at home."

"Would you like to join me?" My eyes briefly scan the food once more. "There's plenty of it. There's also a salad with ginger dressing in the fridge, if you don't want the stir fry."

"That's nice of you, but I don't want to impose," he says, rubbing his trimmed beard and somehow looking both excited and unsure at the same time. He's looking at me longingly, his eyes crinkling in the corners, but his body is half turned toward the front doors, as if he's not certain he should even be here.

"You wouldn't be." I wave my phone in the air. "My aunt canceled, remember?"

There's a shadow of a smile on his face as his body shifts to fully face me now. "If you're sure, then I'd love to join you."

Butterflies form in my stomach, and I don't hesitate as I say, "I'm sure." I gesture for him to take a seat at the island and turn to start warming up dinner.

Hovering over the barstool on the other side of the island, he asks, "Can I help with anything?"

I shrug as I place the pan back on the burner and turn it on low. With a brief wave of my hand that's not holding the wooden spoon, I point to the fridge. "If you want to dish up the salad, that would be great." His footsteps fill the small kitchen as he makes his way to the fridge before I even finish speaking.

Resisting the urge to watch his every move, I choose to occupy myself by stirring dinner on the stove, making sure the heat is dispersing evenly for the sauce to warm up. But I can't seem to keep my eyes off this man. It's not long before I'm setting the wooden spoon down to lean against the counter and watch him prepare food.

He's wearing a flannel jacket that looks cozy as hell and jeans that perfectly hug everything he has to offer. They're not leaving a single thing to the imagination. Well, there are some things I can imagine...

The sound of the sauce boiling and bubbling on the stove breaks my concentration as I jump up and resume stirring. Once it's ready, I turn off the burner and pivot back toward the island to place the hot pan onto the metal trivet shaped like a mountain range.

"Wine or Moscow mule?" I ask, pointing toward the two glasses.

He eyes the wine for a moment before looking back at the salad bowl. "Wine, please."

I nod and pour him a glass, then grab my Moscow mule to set both of our drinks near our plates.

"Perfect timing," I say as I look over at the big bowl of salad he's prepared for us.

"When you said 'prep the salad,' I thought you meant from a bag." There's amusement in his voice.

I look up at him. "It was from a bag," I say with a straight face as I point to the discarded bags of lettuce and shredded carrots. He gives me a pointed look, and I don't even try to hide my smile. "Although, you're missing a few things."

He pauses and looks up at me as I walk to the fridge to grab the container of chopped cabbage, onions, celery, and red bell peppers I cut and prepped earlier today. He steps aside as I empty them into the bowl.

Mixing it up, I jut my head toward the fridge. "Will you grab the salad dressing, please? It's in the small container with the red lid on the top shelf."

Pushing away from the counter, he opens the fridge. When he walks back over, I stop stirring long enough for him to pour out all the dressing. Our eyes meet, and those butterflies come back in full force. My eyes glance at his lips before I force my attention back toward the bowl.

I finish with the salad and make two bowls as he dishes up both of our plates with the stir fry. It feels easy doing this with him, like it's the most natural and normal task in the world to be prepping dinner together.

Sitting down next to him, I watch intently as he takes the first bite of stir fry. His jaw pauses mid-chew, which has my nerves on edge. Does he like it? Is it bad? Did the sauce not heat enough?

When he swallows, he looks over at me. "What's in this?"

I grip my fork a little tighter to prevent myself from wringing my fingers. "Water chestnuts, bamboo sprouts, carrots, celery, and chicken. Oh, and the sauce is made from apple juice, soy sauce, and a mix of seasonings." It sounds like an odd combination, but it's the best stir fry I've ever had. There's a reason it gets requested by family and friends.

My blood runs cold as a thought strikes me. "You're not allergic to anything, are you?"

"No." He chuckles as he digs his fork back in. "It's delicious."

My shoulders relax at his reaction, and I turn back toward my own plate. I practically moan with the first bite of dinner. It never gets old. He looks over at me, mid-bite, and all I can do is smile with a mouthful of food and give a thumbs up.

He chuckles, and all the tension in my body dies down.

An hour later, we're sitting on opposite ends of the couch with slices of pumpkin roll and a glass of wine each. It was already clear that I enjoy being around him, but he makes for far better company than I anticipated.

I feel at ease with him, which is not always easy for me. There are some people who I feel drained around after spending time with them—to no fault of theirs—but I don't feel like that at all with Alaric. Instead, I almost feel...better than before?

It helps that he's easy on the eyes and heart.

This past hour has been filled with both comfortable silence and good conversations. We've talked about how Blanche entered his life, how Elessar found me, and our families.

We also discussed our previous careers, including my brief career as a fiction editor in Chapel Hill before I published my first novel six years ago and was fortunate enough to switch to writing full-time. He also told me a little bit more about what he did in the army and why he knows some French. Well, he told me as much as he could, and as much as my non-military brain could comprehend.

We also finally exchanged numbers, so that we're not relying on the rental app for communication. Technically, I already had his number from the rental app messages, but him actually wanting me to have his contact information in my phone felt like an intimate step. It shouldn't have excited me as much as it did.

He also told me he bought the first book in my contemporary romance series after I told him I'm an author. Once I got over being mortified at the thought of him reading it, I was relieved to find out he enjoyed it and shocked when he mentioned he finished it in the two days since we last talked.

After years of writing, you can tell when someone's saying they like your book in order to be nice vs. when they actually mean it. Thankfully, he seemed to mean it.

This has been nice. Good conversation after good conversation. What's even better is that I can tell he's truly interested in everything I say, and that he cares about what I have to say.

I stretch my legs out on the couch, and accidentally bump into his thigh. Our eyes meet, and I duck my head in apology. "Sorry," I say.

"For what? Sitting on the couch? You don't need to apologize to me." He smiles and his free hand not holding the empty pumpkin roll plate reaches out to grab my ankle, gently squeezing. "Sit however's most comfortable for you."

Blushing, I daringly stretch out my legs a bit more, and his hand lifts from me as I do so. Before I know it, my feet end up propped on his thigh, partially in his lap.

He looks down at my feet and then up at me, smiling. I raise an eyebrow, silently asking if it's okay. His only response is to put his hand back on my ankle.

Staring into his beautiful hazel eyes, my mind drifts again as his thumb softly rubs against the bare skin between my fuzzy sock and the hemline of my leggings.

Where have guys like Alaric been? I mean, I've put myself out there, and there hasn't been a single guy like him. I've tried the apps, which resulted in freaking Brad. Never again.

I've also tried hitting on a guy at a bar when going out with Rhiannon, which resulted in instant regret. On the other hand, the bar guys who hit on me were usually too drunk to get to know properly, or a little too eager. Sometimes both.

There were also the dreaded blind dates, which I've officially promised myself I'd never do again. I'd much rather take home a blind date with a book from a local bookstore than agree to a blind date that someone in my family has set me up on.

Dating hasn't exactly gone smoothly since things went sideways with Brad. Guys either ghosted me or got too attached, which made me nervous that I'd find myself with yet another Brad on my hands. The one is more than enough.

"What's on your mind?" His voice breaks through my thoughts, and I realize I was staring off into space just then.

Embarrassed, I shake my head. "It's nothing."

My feet shift on his lap as he places his empty plate on the coffee table. Settling on the couch to further face me, he shifts my feet so that they're across both his thighs. His left hand rests on my right foot and his right thumb continues the slow circles against the bare skin at my ankle.

After a few seconds of feeling his eyes on me, I meet his gaze again.

"That didn't look like nothing. Talk to me." He holds my gaze.

My eyes scan his face and see the sincerity there that chips away at my walls.

Sighing, I place my own empty plate next to his on the coffee table, careful not to dislodge my feet from him because I like feeling his touch. Leaning back again, I grab a throw pillow and hold it close to my chest. It seems silly, but it makes me feel a little safer, like donning a shield or a plate of armor.

"My mind drifted to..." The words die in my throat, and I swallow hard to dislodge them. The look in his eyes is soft, encouraging. "I was thinking about Brad—the guy I told you about."

His jaw flexes for a brief second before he regains his composure. "That explains the haunted look on your face a second ago... You want to talk about it?" he asks.

Instinctually, I go to shake my head, but then remember how good it felt to finally not feel like I was carrying this burden alone. Maybe it would be good for me to talk it out. "Would that be okay?"

A small smile tugs at his lips. "I wouldn't have offered otherwise."

I huff an anxious laugh and pull the pillow tighter to me, squeezing opposite corners of the brocade fabric as my arms are crossed against it. "Are you sure?"

"Only if you are." His energy is calm, warm. The way he's looking at me, as if what I have to say is important, is what encourages me to lay it all out for him and allow myself to not feel so alone in this anymore.

Chapter 15

EDARA

The familiar jingle of the bell above the door to The Steaming Cup chimes, welcoming a new guest. My eyes dart to the sound, where a laughing Alaric walks in with who I can only assume is Gavin.

I stand up from the wingback chair that's become my favorite spot and hesitantly wave. When Alaric looks over and sees me, the smile on his face immediately calms my nerves, replacing them with butterflies, and my smile deepens into a more genuine one.

The fluttering feeling plummets in my gut when the man next to Alaric pivots his attention to someone else walking toward them.

"Hello, my Dini dear," Gavin says, planting a kiss on Nadine's cheek.

I would have smiled at the cute moment if I didn't suddenly feel scared. Nadine knows Gavin? Gavin knows Nadine?

"Hi, handsome," she croons and gives him a quick kiss. When her hand cups his cheek, her gold diamond ring twinkles in the sunlight that's coming through the large glass windows. My eyes immediately fall to Gavin's left hand, where there's a matching gold band. Her hand falls away and she goes to hug Alaric. "And Ric! It's been too long!"

"I thought I'd tag along, make sure your husband doesn't get into too much trouble," he says, giving her a quick squeeze by way of a side hug.

"Good thinking," she teases and pats his stomach, returning the squeeze. Then, she follows his gaze...to me.

Her eyes dart like ping-pong balls being hit by overly competitive teenagers as they look from Alaric, then to me, and finally settling on Gavin.

"Eda?" Even though her hand is gesturing in my direction, her eyes are on Gavin, who doesn't confirm anything.

He gives her a pointed look, but stays silent.

She looks back at me. "I didn't know you knew my husband," Nadine says, smiling and looking from Gavin to me. When her eyes land on me again, staying there a beat, her expression falls. My stomach sinks further, as she seems to realize that this is not a casual outing with friends, and that I don't know him on a personal level.

"This is the meeting I mentioned earlier, my love," Gavin says, kissing Nadine's temple and saving me from having to answer.

Something flashes across Nadine's face, and I suddenly have to blink away the tears of embarrassment. How much does he know? How much does she know? How much did he tell her? How could I not have known *this* was her husband? Why didn't Alaric say anything about Gavin's wife working here when I first suggested it as a meeting spot?

Last night, Alaric contacted Gavin after I told him everything about Brad, and Gavin agreed to meet with me today on his lunch break. Way sooner than I expected.

When they asked me where I'd like to meet, I chose the coffee shop in the hopes that I'd feel a bit more comfortable actually talking about this—about Brad and the stalking. It also helps that Nadine is someone I feel comfortable around, and she's been here every time I've come in the past two weeks. She and the coffee shop have started to help me come out of my shell and be less on edge in public. So much so that I've found myself coming here daily this week, even if just for a few hours at a time.

But now, I'm second-guessing the decision to bring the topic of Brad to somewhere that's become a safe space for me. I don't want his name or memory or presence tainting this place. It also doesn't help that the person here who helps make me feel safe will now likely hear about why I've run off to a cabin in the woods like a scared, little girl.

No, that's not fair of me to say about myself. I am scared, and I have good reason to be. Alaric and Gavin seem to think so, too, or else the latter wouldn't have offered to meet with me.

My eyes fall on Alaric, and he steps in like a knight in shining flannel. "Hey, Nadine. Can we get the usual?" His voice is calm, soothing, and it successfully snaps Nadine back into work mode.

"You got it." She claps her hands together, but before she turns back toward the counter, she gives me a soft look. "Let me know if you need anything." Something tells me she's not just talking about another cup of tea.

I smile and nod, feeling just about ready to crawl up the chimney of this fireplace. My cheeks are already burning hot enough as is, might as well burn the rest of me along with it.

"I'd like to introduce you to my best friend, Detective Gavin Jeffers," Alaric says, clasping a hand on the detective's shoulder.

He's a few inches shorter than Alaric, but still tall. He has kind eyes, dark hair with a bald fade haircut, a dashing smile, and zero stereotypical police belly. In fact, he looks like he works out daily. Although, it kind of makes sense, since his best friend owns a gym.

"You must be Eda. Hi. You can just call me Gavin." His hand extends toward me as he closes the gap between us.

"Must be," I say, but then internally cringe. I don't need to make this any more awkward or uncomfortable than it already is. So much for picking a place that I thought would help. I guess this is why so many people can't stand small towns, because everyone knows everyone. "It's nice to meet you." I nod. "I'm Edara. *Eda*. Lauklan."

He already knows that. Breathe, Eda. Breathe.

"It's nice to finally meet you. Although, I wish it was under better circumstances." He gives me a kind smile, a contrast to his firm handshake.

"Hey, Eda," Alaric says, rubbing my arm.

I peel my eyes away from Gavin and look into those hazel eyes that offered such compassion and comfort last night. When he left, he kissed my cheek, and I had half a mind to ask him to stay the night. But there's a reason why he stayed away, and I need to respect it. If he's interested in taking things further with us physically, then I'll be here. Until then, he can talk to me about what's going on with him.

His hand on my arm stills. It gives a gentle squeeze, while his thumb swipes back and forth against my bicep. As I get lost in his eyes, the movement grounds me.

Gavin shifts in front of us, and I suddenly remember we're not alone. I don't look at the detective fully, but I can spy a bright white, toothy grin in my peripheral vision. My cheeks heat up again, but I straighten and face this moment head on. I can do this.

"Hey, Alaric," I say, my voice sounding smaller than I'd like for it to. "Is this spot okay, or would you guys prefer a table?" I ask, gesturing to the wingback chairs surrounding the fireplace.

"This is fine. Whatever works for you," Gavin says. Clearly, this is not his first time talking with someone in an uncomfortable situation. That realization makes me feel slightly better, but also makes me feel sad for anyone else who may be in a similar predicament, or worse off than me.

Alaric sits in the chair next to mine, while Gavin sits in the empty chair across from us. I follow suit, sinking into the deep cushion, which is nice and warm from the fire. I instinctively cross my legs as tight as they will go, while squeezing my hands in my lap. When I feel my shoulders almost at my ears, I look down at the pattern on the rug below us, tracing lines of faded colors with my eyes while exhaling the tension out of me.

This is okay. I am safe. I volunteered to do this. It's going to help. I can do this.

I. Can. Do. This.

When my breathing is mostly under control and my shoulders are back where they're meant to be, I look up at Gavin sitting across from me. "So, how does this work?"

He grabs a notepad and pen from his coat pocket and sets them on the arm of his chair, never breaking eye contact with me. "Why don't we start with you telling me what's going on, and then I'll see if I can help," he says, and I nod once. "If you're okay with it, let's start at the beginning."

Briefly squeezing my eyes together, I sigh and straighten in my seat. "Okay," I say, and then tell the second person in Steaming Stone what's happened to me. No, *happening* to me. The nightmare my life has become and the reality I live in.

When I've finished, I look up at Alaric sitting next to me and fight back tears. This feels like too big of a step. Talking to the police? *Again?* Because it went so well the first time around. What was I thinking?

It doesn't help that I've felt Nadine's concerned gaze on us the entire time we've been sitting here. Opening up was a bad idea. There was nothing the police could do before, and it's not like anything's changed. He's still too smart to let himself get caught. So, what's the point?

Alaric reaches over and grabs my hand. "You did great," he whispers. It's as if he was reading my mind.

I give him a watery smile in return.

The warmth of the fireplace and my increasing nerves were making me sweat, but Alaric being in the chair next to me helped ease some of those nerves. Every once in a while, the tip of his boots would graze my leg ever so slightly. The pressure was barely noticeable, but after the third time, I realized it was intentional. It's like it was his way of telling me I'm not alone in this anymore.

The sounds of Gavin's pen clicking and his notepad shutting have me sobering up, but Alaric doesn't react. If he's embarrassed by his friend seeing any bit of affection toward me—for the second time today—he doesn't show it. Instead, his thumb brushes the top of my hand before he gently lets go, returning it to the arm of his chair.

I reluctantly drag my eyes away from his to look at Gavin.

"Unfortunately, it doesn't surprise me you were told by the Raleigh PD that there's nothing they can do for you. It also definitely doesn't help that the people you talked to were likely coworkers of his," Gavin grunts his disapproval. "As I'm sure you know by now, not all police officers can be trusted to care. It's a sad reality we live in."

I wring my fingers in my lap. Is he trying to tell me he can't help either?

"It's also not surprising you've come here to escape. I might be remembering the numbers wrong, but I believe it's something like one out of every seven stalking victims relocate for their own safety."

I flinch at the term 'stalking victims,' but if Gavin notices, he doesn't react. Alaric, on the other hand, does. The toe of his brown leather boot rubs against the top of my black suede boots, but my attention is on Gavin, waiting to hear what he says next. What I'm feeling is dangerously akin to hope, and I need it to stop. I already know how this is going to go: with zero help from the police and nothing changing.

"Is there anything you can do, Gav?" Alaric's deep voice prompts me to briefly look his way, but his eyes are on his best friend.

The detective grimaces and my stomach drops. This was pointless, just like the first time around. Why did I think this would help?

Gavin sighs. "I'll be honest, there's not a whole lot we can do right now, or in general. Especially since it's not my jurisdiction." His gaze connects with mine. "But that doesn't mean I'm not going to try. You deserve better than how you've been treated, and I will do whatever I can to help."

I exhale and nod slowly as the words sink in. Okay, that's more than I expected. Even if there isn't a whole lot he can do, I still appreciate the sentiment. For a man with a hard job, he's softer than I imagined. And definitely softer than the officers I talked to before.

He takes a sip of his black coffee that Nadine dropped off shortly after I started talking. It feels like a long few minutes of holding my breath before he sets his mug down on the small table next to him and looks at me.

"First, I'll tell my guys to keep an eye out for him and his car. We'll also check to see if he's recently purchased a rental car to keep from being seen if he comes up this way. Not saying he knows where you are," he holds his hands up, "but just as a precaution."

I stop breathing for a second at the thought, but then slowly exhale and nod once. It hadn't occurred to me that he might ditch his red car for another. Now I'll be checking *every* car that goes by...

"I also have a few buddies over at the Raleigh Police Department. Good guys. Not sure if they're in his station, but I'll see if they can give me the lowdown on this *Brad McCray*," his tone is full of disdain as he says his name, "while also keeping an eye on him over there."

His eyebrow raises as he meets Alaric's stare, but lowers again when he shifts in his seat and meets my gaze once more. I look over, but there's nothing in Alaric's demeanor that gives away why Gavin gave him that expression.

"In the meantime, we'll see about getting a restraining order—specifically, a Civil No-Contact Order—in place. You'll have to go down to the courthouse for that, but I must warn you, the initial report is only temporary. It lasts ten days, in which time you'll want to request a hearing in order to determine if a permanent order should go into place. Which, from what I'm hearing, I think it could be a helpful next step. So long as you're okay with it, we'll get that process started. How's that sound to start with?" Gavin asks.

I stare at him for a few seconds. How does that sound? That sounds...like he's not dismissing me; that he believes me. He's right that it's not a lot in the grand scheme of things, but it's better than sending me off and saying there's nothing they can do until I'm physically harmed.

"It's a start and better than nothing. Thank you, Detective."

"Please, call me Gavin," he says with a kind smile as he puts his notepad and pen back in his coat pocket. "I'll send you the information for the courthouse for you to come down and file that report, and I'll have my guys looking into him both here and in Raleigh by this afternoon. If there's anything else you need, let me know. Or let Ric know," he says, jutting his chin toward Alaric.

I nod and stand when he does. He reaches out his hand again, and I accept it. "It was nice meeting you, Eda. I'm sorry for what you're going through, but I'll try my best to help however I can."

"It was nice meeting you, too, Gavin," I say. "Thank you for trying. It means a lot."

He smiles and lets go before clasping his hand on Alaric's shoulder. "Now, if you don't mind, I'm going to go see my wife before I head off."

"Thanks, man," Alaric says. As Gavin starts walking toward Nadine, Alaric turns to me. "Are you okay?" His voice is low for only me to hear and he gently grabs my hand again. Just the tips of my fingers. "For what it's worth, you did great. You are so brave."

I take a second to think before responding. Am I okay? I don't know. That was a lot, and my nerves are still shot. Yet, it feels good. I feel...hopeful for the first time. Like I'm not crazy, and like I might actually be able to make this all stop and take back my life.

Returning his hold by gripping his hand, I meet his gaze and turn to face him. "I'm okay. A bit shaken up, but it wasn't as bad as I was anticipating. He's easy to talk to. And...he seems to care? That's already better than the last officer I talked to."

Alaric squeezes my hand and his jaw clenches at the mention of how I was treated before. "I promise, he does care. We'll do whatever we can to help." His other hand comes up, but then pauses. For a moment, I think he's going to touch my face. And maybe he was going to, but I'll never know because, instead, his hand veers and lands on my arm.

I'm not sure what to make of this affectionate Alaric, but I like it. I'm liking this version of him, and that he's been consistent with his actions since last night. Plus, I'd be lying if I said that he didn't bring me some strength and comfort during this encounter.

The hand on my arm falls away, but he keeps his fingers wrapped around mine. "I know we drove separately, but do you want to get some lunch and then head back to the house together?" he asks.

My mouth falls open on a silent glee of delight, but then I remember that I have to write. "I wish I could, but I need to get some work done here," I gesture toward my laptop bag leaning against the chair I was sitting in, "and then let Eless out." His eyes follow the movement. "But rain check on that lunch date?" I ask, feeling hopeful.

Meeting my gaze again, he squeezes my fingers. "Just tell me when, and I'll be there."

There's a fluttering in my stomach at his words.

His eyebrows pinch together. "Do you need me to let Eless out for you? I'm not sure how long you're going to be, and it's not a problem. I have to get Blanche to take her with me to the gym, anyway."

I go to say no, but pause. Elessar has been so good with Alaric, even falling asleep with his head on Alaric's lap last night on the couch at one point. It could be a good test. The worst that could happen is that Eless doesn't leave the guesthouse when Alaric checks on him.

Trusting in my boy's instincts, I nod and say, "That would actually be very helpful, thank you. Do you remember enough French to handle his commands, or do you need me to text them to you?"

A grin graces his face for a split second before he regains his composure. "I'd like to say I think I'd manage, but why don't you send me them just in case?"

He looks like he's going to say something else, but the bell above the door dings, and a draft of cold air rushes in. My whole body shivers from the chill. Not even my thickest cardigans are cutting it anymore with this almost winter-like weather coming in fast.

He looks down at my sweater. "You still need a winter jacket." Not a question.

I nod and grimace. "Yes, I know. I need to stock up on winter clothes. It's just..." I don't mean for it to happen, but my eyes follow in the direction of Gavin, who's still talking to Nadine. "If I'm honest," I say, whispering as I look back at Alaric, "I've been scared to go into a store and be in a public fitting room. It's too... I feel too exposed. I don't like not being able to..." I sigh in frustration over how stupid I sound, but it doesn't make it any less real of a fear.

Alaric's hand gives mine a little a squeeze in encouragement, and I brush my thumb along the knuckles of his fingers.

Finding my voice again, I whisper, "I feel more comfortable when I can keep an eye on everything and everyone in a store, and I can't do that from behind a fitting room door. I mean, I could just buy a jacket, which wouldn't require me to go into a fitting room," I grimace, "but this is my thickest sweater, and I need more. So..." I shrug.

He goes from being linked with the tips of my fingers to holding my hand in his, and then gently pulls down, prompting me to turn toward him fully. "That's not something I'd considered. I'm sorry." His voice is low and sincere, and it takes everything in me to not shy away from the genuine concern in his eyes. "If you'd feel safer trying on clothes with someone standing outside the fitting room, then I'm more than happy to be that someone for you."

Suddenly, he becomes blurry, because of the tears in my eyes. I blink them away and nod vigorously. "I'll think about it. Thank you," I mumble and look toward the fireplace. A lock of hair falls in front of my eyes, shielding the tears from him. My lips part when he releases my hand to brush the hair from my eyes.

His fingers trace my cheek and come down to lift my chin up, forcing me to look at him. "I mean it, Eda. You won't be a burden to me, so don't let yourself think that. You don't even have to ask. Just tell me when and where, and I'll be there," he says before his hand falls away again.

A shiver runs down my spine, but it has nothing to do with the cold and everything to do with the look in his eyes. Speechless, I nod, not looking away from his gaze.

Ugh, this man. Where did he come from? And wow, what a difference one night can make.

"Hey, Ric, you coming?" Gavin's voice brings me back to reality—back to the coffee shop, and to the fact that we're in public.

Clearing my throat, I step away, but Alaric doesn't move. He doesn't react at all to Gavin's words. Except, he does smirk at my reaction.

Without breaking eye contact with me, he says, "Yeah, Gav. Give me a minute."

I look at Gavin, who's standing in front of the open door, the bell chiming above him. He gives me an amused but curious look before walking out. When it closes shut behind him, I urge my body to not react to the cold as I look back up at Alaric.

His hazel eyes are still on me, studying my face. "I'll see you back at home, Eda," he says, before lifting my hand and kissing the top of it.

As he walks away, his eyes stay on mine before he opens the door and steps out. The sound of the bell has my heart falling a bit. Before I can process that, I spy in my peripheral vision someone walking toward me.

"Listen, if you don't want to tell me what you talked about with my husband, I understand. Frankly, it's none of my business. *But* you must tell me what that was all about with Ric!" Nadine whisper-shouts as she grips both my hands, forcing me to look away from Alaric walking on the other side of the large windows in order to make eye contact with her. "I mean, *Ric*?!"

I shush her, but laugh. Embarrassment washes over me when I notice a couple people in the shop watching us. I can't blame them. If I wasn't the one living it, I'd be people watching out of curiosity, too. She doesn't even bother looking around at the neighborly curiosity she's caused.

"Nadine," I try to say sternly, but it comes out more as a laugh. "Keep your voice down," I urge in a whisper.

"Girl, I own this place. They can deal...respectfully." She looks around at the people watching and nods before looking at me again. "What was that all about? I don't think I've ever seen him so smitten," she says in a gleeful tone.

Smitten? I try not to blush, but really, I can't help it.

"It was nothing." I play it off, because I really don't even know how to explain it myself.

"That was *not* nothing. It was the exact opposite of *nothing*. I've never seen Ric like that. Neither has Gavin, and they've known each other since kindergarten." She guides me back over to the wingback chairs. "I'm taking my lunch break early for this. So, spill. I want to hear everything."

Laughing, I allow her to lead me to the chairs and sit back down as she sits in the one Alaric was occupying. Her excitement has butterflies forming in my stomach again, and it makes me wonder if this is more real than I thought. If maybe it goes beyond more than just one steamy kiss in the kitchen and a nice dinner together.

"There really isn't much to tell, Nadine," I say, honestly. "There's nothing going on between us."

The stern look she gives me has me wondering if maybe I really am wrong. "You think that now," she says, looking down at me over the bridge of her nose.

With a pat on my hand, she says, "Start at the beginning, with how you two know each other, and then *I* will decide if it's 'nothing.'"

Grinning, I do as I'm told, and the more I talk about Alaric, the more excited I feel about the woodsman who's captured my mind and become my muse.

Chapter 16

EDARA

I guide the soft fabric of a beige sweater over my head. Instead of going on smoothly, the turtleneck portion unfurls and stretches out over my face, partially suffocating me while also royally screwing up my hair.

Locking eyes with my reflection in the mirror, I huff in amusement at the sight of myself. I can see the outline of my lips as my breath weaves through the knitted fabric that's still trapping my nose and the lower half of my face. Curling my fingers around the soft knit, I pull at the extra fabric of the turtleneck. The second my nose and mouth are free, I sigh in relief.

With pursed lips, I blow out a forced breath toward the upper part of my face. The flattened hair that was pinned to my forehead and cheek now do a little dance in the air before falling in front of my eyes again.

As I take a deep breath and stare at my reflection in the mirror, I start to wonder why I ever thought this would be a good idea. Although, it wasn't really my idea, but it *is* on me for agreeing to it.

Somehow, Alaric convinced me to go shopping with him to get a coat and warmer clothes. While I was brushing my teeth this morning, my phone vibrated with a text from him, asking if I had some free time today to shop and make good on that rain check lunch date.

I didn't hesitate to answer 'yes,' because I don't think my body can take another day of shaking like a leaf hanging onto a nearly bare branch, fighting the claws of winter as hard as I am. There are many of those around Alaric's property, and I've watched a few lose their fight while drinking my morning tea.

I remind myself of that as I pull the sweater all the way down my torso and admire the way the cream color makes my hair stand out. While perusing the racks for coats, I decided it would also be a good idea to get some more everyday, cold-weather clothes. I didn't find much at the first store, but at this one, I walked up to the fitting rooms with my arms full of options.

Turning toward the selection of sweaters, fleece-lined pants, and jackets hanging up in front of me, I rub my temples at how many items there are. I was just naked in a store...and I have to do it again. And again.

The changing room stalls are situated in the middle of the store and aren't gender specific, which means that Alaric is able to stand on the other side of the door. Having him right here is helping a bit with the nerves over changing without knowing what's happening outside and being this vulnerable in a store. At the same time, his presence is also bringing on a whole other set of nerves, because I'm semi-naked...while so close to Alaric.

Even though it's not technically winter yet, it certainly feels like it to me. Steaming Stone may be calling out to my heart, but my body is struggling to get on board with this mountain weather.

If I'm honest with myself, I think part of why I said yes to this is because yesterday was my court hearing for the Civil No-Contact Order against Brad, and getting out of the house—and out of my own head—felt like a good idea.

Yesterday was...intense. There's no other way to describe it. Except for maybe also 'terrifying.' It was technically a formality to get a more permanent order in place—which was granted—but it was still terrifying. It made this all feel even more real.

Talking to Alaric, Gavin, and Nadine about Brad; hiring a lawyer; filing legal papers; being in court before a judge—I can't ignore what's happening anymore. But perhaps that's a good thing...

I'm realizing that I shouldn't have to hide. My life shouldn't be like this, and now that I finally feel heard and validated in my concerns, I'm willing to do what I can to make it stop.

As per the law, Brad had to be notified of the hearing date. However, to my relief, he didn't show, and the judge's authority to grant the order was not reliant on his attendance. My lawyer, Eliza, explained it as more of a courtesy for him to plead his case than a necessity for the order to be filed and put into effect.

I think it's smart and fair that defendants don't have to be there. I don't think I would have been able to face him. If I needed to, sure, but...that would have required more strength than I think I could muster right now. Plus, then he'd know exactly where I am—especially at that moment, being only feet away from him in the court room—and that defeats the entire purpose of getting away.

Not wanting him to know where I am is the reason why I decided to file in Boone instead of Steaming Stone. They share the same county, but the two towns are about half an hour away from each other. If Brad is aware of where I am now, then hopefully holding court in another city will help throw him off my trail.

A shudder racks my spine at the thought as I slide a turmeric-colored sweater down my torso, the hem resting over black fleece-lined leggings. Closing my eyes, I place my palm on my stomach and clutch the knit fabric. I take a deep breath and release my grip, mentally preparing before I continue trying on the rest of the clothes.

As hard as yesterday was, it helped that I wasn't alone. Alaric, Gavin, and Nadine all came to the hearing, which was kind of them. Their support meant everything to me. Nadine gave me a massive hug after the judge's ruling, and promised me a huge, steaming mug of plum cider at The Steaming Cup the next time I come in.

Alaric has been so kind to me since. He took me out to lunch, and then we took a walk around the park downtown. He successfully helped me get my mind off the day, even if for a brief moment. I've fallen in love with the small town of Steaming Stone, but I love it even more after seeing it through Alaric's eyes. There was something about this place that pulled him back after getting out of the army, and I think I can understand it.

He even offered to make dinner last night. He's mentioned before that he enjoyed cooking, but I hadn't anticipated actually enjoying his food. Lots of people love to cook, but can't cook well, and that's totally okay. However, he does not fit into that category. He made chicken in a creamy sauce consisting of coconut milk, roasted garlic, and lemon juice, with garlic butter mashed potatoes on the side. *Delicious.*

After having such a good time with him recently, it only made sense for me to say yes when he texted this morning. Thirty minutes after getting that message from Alaric, we were in his truck and headed toward Asheville, which is about an hour and a half from Steaming Stone. He suggested it because there are bigger stores with wider selections there.

As I squeeze my way out of this sweater to try on another, I might be somewhat regretting my choices now. I was excited for the trip because I've never been to Asheville, and while it's cute, it's not as charming to me as Steaming Stone is. But I do love a good local spot, no matter where it is. The diner here in Asheville we went to for breakfast was great, and the company even more so...

The drive here wasn't awkward at all. There were moments of comfortable silence, and then moments where conversation flowed naturally. Talking with him is easy. Maybe easier than with any other man I've met. Plus, being in a new city together—where no one knows us or that we're not a couple—made breakfast feel kind of like a date.

It probably doesn't help that I've been on a total high where Alaric is concerned, thanks to my conversation with Nadine last week. Apparently, Alaric's never been this seemingly interested in a woman. Nadine told me that, outside of his serious relationships—the most recent of which ended two years ago—he's never held hands with a woman in public. He's also never made his friend wait for a woman he wasn't dating—let alone for someone he just met—the way he made Gavin wait to leave The Steaming Cup that day.

All of that has been a lot to process, but it's made me look at this with a whole new perspective. Whatever *this* is. Initially, I think I simply wanted a fling—something to enjoy myself and hopefully forget about what's going on. To actually date without Brad's eyes on my every move. But could it be more than that?

After talking with Nadine, I'm not sure if I'm misleading Alaric. Or maybe I'm not. Maybe I'm misleading myself, and this is what I want—to chase whatever makes me happy, even if it's only temporary. My happiness is worth fighting for... Right?

These thoughts circle in my head as I stand half naked in the fitting room. I shake my head, shoving the thoughts from my mind, and slip an emerald green sweater over my head. It's snug in the chest, but it slides down smoothly otherwise.

"How's it going?" Alaric asks, his voice traveling from the other side of the door.

"Not bad." Looking at my reflection in the floor-length mirror, I frown. It's much too tight against my chest. "The green sweater's a bit small, but that's okay," I say, raising my voice a little so he can hear me through the thick door.

"Do you want me to grab you another size?" he asks, his voice getting clearer and louder as he steps closer.

Concerns of being alone and burdening him make me hesitate, but as I run my hands over the soft material, I realize that I really like it. It could very well end up coming home with me, along with the puffer coat hanging on the mounted metal bar next to me, the turmeric-colored sweater next to it, and the fleece-lined leggings held snug to my hips right now.

"It's not a problem if you want me to, and it's not far. It's just right there," he says, and I can picture him pointing right now, which makes me laugh under my breath because I can't see through the door. "But if you're not comfortable with it, that's okay."

I smile even though he can't see it. "Promise you won't take long?"

"Promise. I'll be back in a minute," he says, and I can hear the smile in his voice.

The moment I no longer see his boots under the door, I am instantly filled with regret and wish he hadn't left. There's this sudden sinking fear that causes the hair on the back of my neck to raise. I can't tell if it's simply anxiety, but it almost feels like a sixth sense that something isn't quite right.

Looking up at the ceiling, I close my eyes and try to calm my breathing.

Ugh, it's no use.

The sweater tightens around my chest as my breaths quicken.

My gut churns, my heart beats faster, and as I glance below the stall door to impatiently watch for his return, I see brown boots that aren't Alaric's approaching. There's no proof who it is, but I have a sick feeling I already know.

Panic sets in, and I can't get away from the door quickly enough. As quietly as I can, I slowly back up into the corner of the stall and wait.

The boots don't move. They just stay there, as if the person they belong to is waiting for something.

Then, they turn, the worn leather facing the stall. I hold my breath, but the sound of my heart beating in my ears is deafening.

Suddenly, the door shakes, as if someone's trying to open it from the other side. With each forceful tug, the latch clicks as the lock does its job, keeping me in and the world out.

My mouth opens on a silent gasp and I grab hold of the wall-bolted metal handle, which causes the puffer coat hanging there to fall to the floor. Not taking my eyes off the door, my other hand grips the now empty hanger. A weapon of opportunity is better than nothing.

Then, as if I'd imagined it all, the rattling stops, the door stills, and the boots quickly turn before disappearing.

A few, long seconds pass before a familiar set of boots return under the door and I hear Alaric's voice. "Found it," he says, attempting to pass the green sweater to me through the open space above the door.

It just dangles there.

I see it. I *know* it's there, and I know he's talking to me, but I can't break this spiral of panic within.

Stunned, I remain crouched in the corner.

"Eda?" His boots take a step closer, and the sweater bounces once in the air from him shifting. The lock clicks in its place—adjusting to his closeness to the door—and the sound snaps me out of it.

"Oh shit," he mutters. The sweater raises two inches as he steps away. "Please tell me that's still you in there, Eda, and I'm not talking to a random person."

Blinking rapidly, I stand up. The hanger falls from my hand, landing on the wooden bench, and I jump at the sound it makes.

"Yes, sorry." I close the gap to the door, stand on my tiptoes, and grab the sweater. "Thank you."

"You okay?" he asks.

I rub my hands along the soft sweater and wiggle my fuzzy-sock-clad toes against the cold, wood flooring of the dressing room, attempting to ground myself in the here and now. With a big sigh, I shake off the fear and tension. "Yes, but if you don't mind, I think this is the last one."

"Sure. We can grab some food after this for the drive home."

"Alaric?" I whisper through the door. I just have to be sure. "Is anyone else out there?"

His boots shuffle closer to the door and it shifts as he leans into it. "Just me," he whispers back. "There are a bunch of other people in the store, but I'm the only one right here. Why?"

I sigh in relief. It must have been nothing. Maybe someone was just testing if the stall was vacant.

Except, the breath gets caught in my chest, not fully releasing past my throat. My gut tells me something is off—that someone was here. That *he* was here.

If that's true, wouldn't Alaric have seen him?

"No one in brown boots?" I ask.

The door jerks a smidge as Alaric's boots step half an inch away. When he leans back into the door, I press my hand against it, desperate to hear his next words.

"Most people have boots on, and there are a few brown ones."

"I–is... Do you see..." I almost ask him if he sees Brad, but surely he would have noticed. "Never mind." I sigh.

"No, tell me. What are you thinking?"

"Did you see a man standing here while you were gone?" I ask, my voice low.

"No." His voice is deep, and there's almost a protective note to it.

My shoulders sink in relief, but it is short-lived.

"But I might have had my back turned to the stall for a minute or two, while searching for the right size. I'm sorry," he whispers, and I can hear the disappointment in his voice. "Why? Did something happen?"

My throat suddenly feels tight, but I manage to say, "Someone was here. In brown boots. They tried to open the door."

The weight of the wood shifts again as he steps away, likely looking over the store once again. I wait on bated breath until he's done. When he leans back into the door, my free hand goes to my throat protectively.

"If you're asking about who I think you are, the answer's no."

My eyes shut tight, because he'd know. I showed him a photo of Brad the night he joined me for dinner after my aunt rescheduled. "Are you sure? I... It's going to sound crazy, but I swear I felt him. I swear it was him," I ramble, no longer able to hold it in.

"I believe you," he says, and my eyes prick with tears. He didn't even hesitate to say it. Didn't question it. Didn't question *me*. "But he's not here anymore. I promise. I don't see him anywhere in the store with us." His voice is calm, deep as the words register with me. They sink in one by one.

I rest my forehead against the rough wood door with a sigh. "Alaric?" I whisper his name so quietly, I don't know if he'll hear me at first.

"Yes, Eda?" His deep voice travels through the wood as he leans into it from the other side.

"Please don't leave again." Emotion seeps into the words, but I'm too shaken to care. An apology will likely come later, but not now. I can't think straight right now.

"I'm sorry, Eda. I shouldn't have left," he whispers, and my heart tugs ever so slightly in my chest. "I won't move an inch." And he doesn't. Not even the door shifts, telling me he hasn't stepped away from it.

Satisfied that he's not moving, I step farther into the cramped fitting room and tell myself it's just one last piece of clothing. I'm safe and I can do this. Alaric's on the other side. There's no way Brad followed us to Asheville.

Right? A bone-deep chill holds my body hostage until I shiver, but I manage to collect myself.

I'm okay. This is just one sweater. One more sweater, and I'm out.

As I get undressed, I watch the opening under the door to make sure those other boots don't come back. They don't, and Alaric's never budge. Not until I'm done, fully dressed, and opening the door. I'm not prepared for the look on his face when I do.

His dark eyebrows are pinched together and his eyes are wide with worry while they scan every inch of me. For a moment, he just stands there, as if not sure what to do.

Still shaken up, I look around to make sure Brad's not in the store, and see that Alaric was right.

"I shouldn't have left," he says, his voice low.

I clear the emotion from my throat and take the moment to adjust the piles of clothes I want in my arms. Per the instructions hanging on the wall of the stall, I left the ones that didn't work for me in the stall.

Rapidly blinking away tears from my eyes, I look up at him again. "Alaric, it's not your fault. You couldn't have known. We couldn't have known. And we're still not...sure," I say, as my eyes dart around once again. The fear hasn't left me, it's still sinking into every nerve.

Satisfied that Brad really isn't here, I sigh, but my hands grip a little tighter onto the coat flung over my arm and sweater. When I meet Alaric's gaze again, my heart crumbles.

"I'm sure. If you're sure, then I'm sure. That's all I need to know." His voice is stern.

Shifting the clothes so that they're draped over my left arm, I reach for him with my right hand. "Alaric, it's not your fault. Okay? I'm the one who asked you to grab another sweater. It was me. Not you. You couldn't have known."

Before I know it, he's pulling me in for a bone-melting hug. One of his hands wraps around my shoulder blades, while the other wraps around the back of my head. Shock wearing off, I lean into him, with my cheek resting against his hard chest, and wrap my free arm around his waist.

Planting a kiss on the top of my head, he whispers in my ear, "None of this is your fault. None of this is on you. Do you hear me? You've done nothing wrong."

And suddenly, it takes everything in me to hold back the tears. I didn't realize how badly I needed to hear the words.

I suck in a breath and hold it for a few seconds before releasing it. I look up at him through a sheen of tears. His thumb comes to my cheek, caressing it, and I bite my lip to keep from giving in and kissing him. Almost every part of me wants to, but the fight-or-flight mode—the part of me that's ready to bolt out of this store and hightail it back to the guesthouse—keeps me from giving in.

His eyes fall to my lip between my teeth before he kisses my forehead and lets go. As his arms leave me, I suddenly feel cold and find myself longing for his touch.

"Do you want me to carry those?" he asks, gesturing to the clothes hanging off my arm, which I forgot about thanks to that hug.

Looking down, I shake my head and shift them back to my dominant arm to offset the weight. They're kind of heavy, but it's helping to ground me. Keeping them balanced in my arms gives me something to focus on in the present, not the *what ifs*.

"Okay. Let's get them and head home." His hand falls to my low back, and I step a little closer to him as he guides us to the registers.

My feet move in step with his, but my gaze is unable to stop scanning the store for a familiar, unwanted face. My trust in Alaric gets me to the checkout line because I don't even watch my step, not once worrying I'll run into a display stand or person.

As we wait in line, the only thing grounding me to the here and now is Alaric's right hand holding my waist, and his left hand rubbing up and down on my free arm, before he once again offers to hold the clothes for me. This time around, I take him up on his offer.

Standing in line feels like it's taking hours. Not because the line is slow, but because the wait and uncertainty makes me feel vulnerable; exposed. I'm just waiting for something to happen.

When I've finally paid for my things and we start walking toward the large store door, the women who rang up my clothes says, "Thanks for coming in! Come back and see us soon!"

My steps falter and I'm struck with a desire to never want to come back. Hell, I may never step foot in Asheville again after this. But she doesn't deserve that energy. So, I smile and give her a small wave. "Thanks. Have a good one."

Alaric opens the door for me, gesturing for me to step out before him. I pause in the doorway for a second when the fresh air hits me. It's freezing, but it feels better than the stifling pit of anxiety caving in on me in that store. Breathing in the cool, crisp fall air, I put one foot in front of the other. Alaric's hand is back on my waist, and I lean into his body heat as we walk toward his truck.

I see the hood of the silver truck peeking from behind another large black truck parked next to it and feel a wave of relief wash over me. But it's quickly replaced with crippling nausea and paralyzing fear. I stop dead in my tracks in the middle of the road.

Alaric stops next to me, looking around before facing me. His body is blocking the truck now, but it's too late. I already saw it.

"What is it?" he asks. I know he's standing in front of me, but I feel like I'm seeing right through him. Right to the evidence staring me in the face, screaming at me that I'm not crazy or imagining things.

"Eda?" he asks. When his fingers come to my chin, lifting my gaze to his, I don't fight the movement. It doesn't matter because I couldn't even focus on his face right now if I tried. My vision has turned white with panic. "Eda, talk to me."

"The truck..." I manage to say, and my voice sounds robotic. Void of emotion.

"The truck?" Alaric asks, and I feel rather than see him turn to look back at it. "What about—"

"The truck," I whisper again.

"What the fuck?" Alaric says, as he grabs me closer to him. The feel of his arms wrapping around me is a welcome comfort, but it takes time before I'm aware of what's happening.

Somehow, I don't notice him moving us back inside the store. I don't notice the outside cold being replaced by the heat inside because my blood has run cold. It's not until he's grabbing his phone from his pocket to make a call that I mentally escape my thoughts and return to the present moment. By the sounds of it, it's Gavin on the other end of the call.

"I don't fucking know, man, but it's him," he seethes. The angry tone is a stark contrast to the gentle caress on my back.

The bag of clothes falls down to my wrist when I wrap my arms around his waist. I feel him shift as he looks down at me, but I can't bring myself to look up at him. Instead, I bury my face in his chest. My eyes squeeze shut, but all I can picture is the truck in my mind.

How the fuck did this happen? How did Brad know where to find me? How did he even know where we'd be?

"He got to her in the store when I walked away, and then the fucker left flowers on the windshield of my truck, Gav. It's him. It's fucking him."

My fingers dig into Alaric's coat with each word he speaks as the severity of them sink into my bones.

Brad found me.

And he knows I'm not alone.

Chapter 17

Edara

It's been hours now since we arrived back at Alaric's. I'm curled up on his leather couch, where we've been since Gavin left a while ago. I don't know exactly how long it's been. Time feels as though it has both halted and flown by without me. He met us here to discuss what happened before he and Alaric talked outside. I don't know what they said; I just heard raised, but muffled voices.

Since the protective order went into place yesterday, Brad has technically violated that order. Gavin said that means the stalking crime has been bumped up from a misdemeanor to a felony.

Brad's not going to like that.

I shudder at the thought and how he might retaliate. Both the Asheville PD and Gavin told me they'll be searching for Brad now, and I hope they find him. Soon.

I don't even remember all of what I said to Gavin as he was asking me questions, or what all he said to me, but I do remember that much because the thought of them searching for him *finally* brings me hope. This entire afternoon has felt like an out-of-body experience. Going through the motions. I've felt numb since Gavin left. Hell, I've felt numb ever since I first spotted the roses on the windshield.

No, it was before that. Since the fitting room, when I felt him outside of it, and when he tried everything short of kicking down the door to get to me.

Roses. Red fucking roses because Brad once said they reminded him of my hair. Which is ridiculous because they're not even close to the same shade as my copper-colored hair—a fact that doesn't seem to register with him. When he handed them to me on our second date, he told me he wondered if my hair was as soft as the petals of the roses.

Bile rises in the back of my throat at the thought of him touching me. My hand goes to my throat, cradling it as if that will somehow keep me safe from a hidden threat.

When the stalking started, the roses began popping up out of nowhere. Sometimes a single rose when I opened my mailbox. Sometimes a dozen roses on my doorstep. Sometimes rose petals on the hood of my Jeep when I'd go out to work at a coffee shop in Raleigh. The place and timing changed, but it was only ever red roses.

There's zero doubt in my mind that he was sending a message today. He's been watching me—watching *us.* He even knew which car was Alaric's in the parking lot. Knew what store we were in. Knew that I was in the fitting room, and to leave me there before Alaric returned.

My hands go to my face, covering my tears when I start to sob for the first time today as everything comes crashing down. I don't flinch when Alaric's arm pulls me in closer to him, nor do I fight it when he lifts me into his lap, with my legs draped over his thighs as he holds me close to him. Instead, I wrap my arms around his shoulder blades and cry into the crook of his neck.

If he cares that I'm drenching his shirt collar right now, he doesn't react. With his arms around my back, he just holds me there, offering a sense of security and safety on a level I'm not sure I've ever experienced before. Especially not in the past year.

When the tears lessen and my breathing starts to return to normal, I lay my head on his shoulder. How did my life come to this? How did this happen?

And then, it hits me that I'm crying on the shoulder of my landlord. I can feel the damp fabric of his tear-soaked shirt under my cheek and embarrassment hits me. Without moving to look at him, I squeeze my eyes shut and say, "I'm so sorry." My voice is hoarse, my throat dry. When was the last time I spoke? When Gavin was here?

"Don't be," he says, his hand rubbing soothing circles on my back, and I welcome the touch. "I don't mind."

Shifting a little on his shoulder, I take in our surroundings while working on my breathing some more, and because I'm not ready to look at him just yet. Both dogs are lying on the floor in front of us, and I have to blink back tears when I see Elessar looking up at me with so much love and concern in his big, brown eyes.

"Hi, baby," I say, barely above a whisper. His tail thumps once as he sets his head on the edge of the couch, still looking up at me.

Continuing to scan our surroundings, my eyes fall on the wall of windows in the living room, leading to the front yard and driveway. I notice it's dark out now, and my eyes start to frantically search the yard outside. As if Brad might be out there, hiding behind a tree, or lurking within the shadows of night.

A cold nose on my hand has me looking down and into the amber eyes of my sweet boy. There's concern laced within those brown depths, and I feel my eyes tearing up again as he lays his head on my thigh. I wrap my fingers in the soft fur on the top of his head and breathe through the wave of new emotions hitting me.

Alaric's hand is still on my back, offering comfort and warmth as I continue to collect myself. "What time do you normally feed him?" The tags on Blanche's collar clink together when her head lifts at the sound of his voice.

"Five o'clock," I say, not looking away from Elessar. My voice sounds numb to my ears. Then, I begin to wonder why he asked. I look up at the open windows, seeing the dusk sky beyond the glass. "Why? What time is it now?"

His arm briefly lifts away from me as he checks the watch on his wrist. "It's almost 6:30," he says, returning his hand to my back.

I grimace. Our poor dogs. They deserve better than that.

"We should feed them," I say, my hand on Elessar's head.

"I can do it." Alaric's hand stills on my back. "Tell me where his food is, and I'll go grab it."

For the first time since Gavin left, I look him in the eyes. He looks tired, worried, and that somehow makes me feel worse and better all at the same time.

"Don't leave," I say, and I can't even bring myself to care about the desperation evident in my voice.

His hand wraps around mine. "Do you want to come with me? Or can I just feed him some of Blanche's food?"

Tears prick my eyes again because, no, he can't. "No," I shake my head. "His stomach is sensitive. He...he needs his food. You're right." I nod my head, even though I wish it wasn't the case.

"Do you want to come with me?" he asks again.

My eyes move to the windows again—to the unknown in the dark of night that lays just beyond the glass—and I slowly shake my head. "No. I don't think I can." My voice is so tiny, I almost don't recognize it. But the words did come from my mouth, forced out with what little strength I have left in me.

He kisses the top of my hand, and I look down at our now joined hands. I squeeze his once in gratitude, then shift. Elessar moves his head as I slide off Alaric's lap so that he can get up. Blanche stands up from her spot on the floor, her whole body shaking with excitement, likely from knowing what time it is for her.

"Do you want me to leave them in here with you?" he asks, standing in front of me.

I nod, not able to move. Yes, it'd be better for them to stay here. Well, better for me to know that if someone was coming, the dogs would alert me. I nod again as the thoughts run through my head.

He squeezes my hand gently before slowly walking to the coat closet near the door to grab his jacket. "Will you do me a favor and lock it behind me?"

That makes me look at him again. The thought of the door being un-locked—of being vulnerable—sobers me up a smidge. "Yes."

He nods before reaching for the doorknob, but he meets my gaze as I slowly walk toward him. "Are you sure you're going to be okay alone in here?"

My heart is beating a mile a minute, and I want to say no...but I don't. Elessar needs to eat, and I'm not comfortable going out into the dark just yet. Not when I know Brad's been watching. I wrap my cardigan tighter around my body at the thought, as if that might help shield me from his prying eyes, wherever the hell he is right now.

Elessar comes up to me, leaning into my right thigh, and I smile as he looks up at me. I run my fingers over the top of his head, behind his right ear, and down his back, before looking back up at Alaric. "I won't be alone."

"No, you won't be." He gives me a small smile before looking at both Blanche and Eless. "You be good to her, okay?" His voice is soft and directed completely at our two dogs, who both wag their tails in response.

"His food's in the clear container on the pantry floor," I say.

He turns to me in the cracked doorway and pauses for a brief moment, but then shifts his body toward the porch outside. "I'll only be a few minutes, okay?"

I nod and reach for the doorknob as he walks past the threshold. When his boots hit the top step, I call out, "Alaric?" He turns around, his hazel eyes soft as they land on my face. "Be safe, okay?" I say.

He smiles and nods before turning and walking toward the guesthouse.

My eyes trail away from his broad back to scan the dark of night, which only makes me more anxious. I can't take the thought that Brad could be out there, staring back at me.

I slam the door shut in a hurry and lock both the deadbolt and doorknob. My back crashes into the closed door, and I sink down to the floor. Two cold, wet noses are in my face within seconds, but I steer them away with pets so that I can breathe.

I need to breathe.

My eyes are glued to the digital clock above the stove, watching the minutes tick by.

Exactly eleven minutes after I slid to the ground, I hear Alaric's voice through the door: "Eda? It's me."

Not expecting it, I jump just as the dogs both get up from their spots next to me on the floor, their tails wagging. I pull myself up and unlock the door before opening it for him. Instead of standing in the open threshold like before, I stand out of sight—pinned between the door and the wall—as it opens. I don't really want to look outside again tonight if I can help it, or think about the fact that Brad might be out there right now and could see me in the doorway.

It's silly, really, because he could just as likely see me through the open windows in the living room. However, it feels different when standing behind the barrier of the windows versus in the exposed threshold separating the safety of the house from what lies beyond outside...

The breath is ripped from my lungs when the cold air seeps through from under the door, sinking past the barrier of my fuzzy socks. I suddenly wish I had thought to ask Alaric to grab my wolf slippers.

Eless starts whining excitedly when he realizes what Alaric's carrying.

He sets the container of food down and our hands brush when he takes the handle from me to close the door, shutting out the cold once more.

"How much food does he get?" he asks. His cheeks are slightly pink from the cold.

I shake my head. "It's okay, I can do it."

"Are you sure?" He grabs the container once more to bring to the kitchen, and all three of us follow: me, Elessar, and Blanche.

Once he sets it down, he steps aside and I open the lid. "Yes. You've done more than enough, and I need some sense of normalcy." I grab Elessar's bowl and scoop that are stored inside.

He goes to the kitchen pantry to grab what I'm assuming is Blanche's food.

A few minutes later, we both quietly lean against the counter in different corners of the kitchen, watching them eat at their spots on opposite sides of the kitchen. While they get along well, this is the first time they're eating together. So, we decided we'd rather be safe than sorry by separating them a bit.

Blanche practically hoovers her food. When she's done, she lifts her snout from her empty bowl and looks over at Elessar, who's eating a little slower than her. Alaric calls her over, preventing her from even thinking about getting close to Elessar while he eats. Without hesitating, she walks up to Alaric, who starts petting her as she leans her whole body weight against his legs. Fortunately, he's stronger than me and can handle her without getting knocked off balance.

Once the dogs are both fed and happy, Alaric clears his throat. "I should let them out," His voice is quiet as he pats her side one last time before cleaning up her bowl. "How do you want to handle that?"

They have to go out, I know that, and I'm dreading it. I don't want them outside alone, especially since Brad doesn't like dogs and we don't know if he's out there right now, watching, waiting. I also don't want to be in here alone, either.

But it doesn't matter what *I* want.

My eyes squeeze tight and I feel his warmth close around me. "It's okay if you're not ready to go outside. Just lock the door again, and I'll make sure they don't take long," he says as he wraps his arms around me again.

With my head against his chest, I sigh. "Thank you for being so kind to me and Eless."

Alaric pulls away and I look up at him. "Eda, you don't have to thank me for that. I want to be here for you."

I blush. "I know. I can tell, and I appreciate it. I'm just sorry this is happening. I feel so bad." My voice wobbles.

His hands come to my cheeks and my eyes find his. "You have nothing to be sorry for, do you hear me? Nothing." His eyes search mine.

I nod once, but I don't believe it. There's actually so much.

One hand drops away, but the other stays on my cheek. "I'll be here for as long and as much as you'll let me."

"Thank you," I say.

When a tear falls past my lashes, his thumb is there to catch it. "You don't have to thank me."

"But I do," I say, leaning into his palm against my cheek.

"You don't, but I understand." He offers me a small smile, but it falls as a thought seems to cross his mind. "Have you thought about what you want to do tonight?"

My eyebrows crease, but then relax as I realize what he means. No, I hadn't. I hadn't really thought about anything, or what this might mean. I've only just started to process and *feel* since it all happened.

I shake my head. "I didn't. I'm sorry."

"Stop apologizing," he says with a bigger smile this time. "You're welcome to stay here if you want."

"What? No, I couldn't—" I go to protest, but he interrupts me.

"And before you say you don't want to intrude, or be a bother, or whatever it is you're about to say, don't. If you would feel safer here than at the guesthouse, then I want you here. Okay? You won't be bothering me." His face is stern, but his voice is somehow soft.

"No, Alaric. I can't—"

"If that's what you want, I'm okay with it, Eda," he says, but I'm not convinced. I think he realizes that because he adds, "Fine. If it'll help, then just know that you staying here will actually make me feel better." His fingers fall from my cheek to grip my hand.

I blush and it's my turn to smile now. "Yeah, that does help, actually." I laugh.

He grins in return. "Good. Then I guess I'll tell you exactly how I feel. You staying here would make me feel better about all of this. Knowing you're safe under my roof... Yeah, that would help a lot."

I meet his gaze, and he continues, as if encouraged by my lack of protest.

"Me being able to keep an eye on you tonight would help me sleep better?" he says, and it almost sounds like a question, like he's prodding for what I'm wanting to hear. In his defense, I also don't know exactly what that might be, but I'm enjoying this moment of hearing how he feels. So, I don't say anything.

"You staying here tonight, under my roof, is exactly what I think I need after today," he tries again.

All right, that's enough torturing him. My face softens as I feel myself melt a bit. Having not really had the chance to process it all enough yet, I haven't yet taken the time to consider how he must feel after today. Or how he must have felt after seeing those roses on his car and realizing that Brad's also been watching him. Because of me.

His voice pulls me from the guilt that was beginning to eat me alive. "I'll try again: If you're comfortable with it, then I would be happy if you and Eless stayed here tonight."

Nodding, I squeeze his hand. "Okay. You've convinced me."

"Thank you. I was running out of things to say and was beginning to feel like a broken record," he says with a toothy smile. "I'm gonna let them out now. Are you locking the door behind us again?"

"Yes," I say quickly.

"Listen for my knock, then." He nods and ushers the dogs to the door. "We'll be right outside. I won't keep my eyes off them or the front door."

I stop myself from making a joke that he can't possibly watch both rowdy dogs running and the door at the same time, but the joke dies in my throat when I realize that it's true, he probably can't. Instead, I grip the doorknob as the dogs rush out and he stares back at me from the top of the step. Hazel eyes are the last thing I see before the sound of the deadbolt locking fills the unwanted silence in the cabin.

With my back to the door, I sink down to the floor in the same position as before. One hand goes to my neck and my other wraps around my body protectively. Whether I want it or not, my senses are locked on to my surroundings. I hear every sound outside. Every leaf crunching. Every branch snapping. The playful whines and barks as the dogs undoubtedly chase each other, like they do every night.

When I hear Alaric whistle for them to stay close, I breathe a little easier. The protective grip on my neck loosens just a smidge at the creaking from his boots on the wooden porch steps, coming closer.

Minutes later, when he calls for them to come back inside, I scramble to my feet, unlock the door, and wrench it open before he even has to knock. The dogs come barreling through within seconds, followed by a rosy-cheeked Alaric.

The moment the toe of his boot passes the threshold, I grab a hold of his coat collar and pull him inside before slamming the door shut and locking it. When I turn around, I'm met with wide, hazel eyes, full of confusion and concern.

Without saying a word, I wrap my arms around his waist and squeeze. Not even a second later, the chill still clinging to his coat seeps through the fabric on my back as his arms wrap around me.

"Thank you for doing this. For taking me in; for helping me; for taking care of Eless; for being so nice. Thank you for what you did. Thank you for not letting me have to go through this alone. Just...thank you, Alaric," I ramble into his broad chest.

A hand smoothes the back of my head. "You really don't need to thank me, Eda. I want to be here." His deep voice is soothing on my nerves.

I pull away just enough to look up at him. "Yes, I do. And I know that, which is why I'm even more thankful."

His hand stops moving on the back of my head, cupping the nape of my neck instead. A small smile graces his face, and I'm suddenly thankful for the chill of his coat to stop me from overheating, as well as to keep that stare from melting me completely.

Oh, those lips. Those kissable lips that work magic.

"Since it's clearly no use to say it's not a problem," his smile deepens, "I'll change the topic by asking how you want to handle the sleeping arrangements tonight."

I pause. When he first asked if I'd like to stay here tonight, I really hadn't thought that far ahead. Does he have a guest room here? The couch would be fine, except that there are no blinds to close or curtains to cover the windows. I doubt I'll be able to get much sleep with the naked branches ominously hanging in the sky above while I'm lying down on the couch. Not to mention the sounds of nature keeping me up, making me wonder if it's an unwanted guest or just an animal.

My mouth opens and closes a few times with each unspoken thought that crosses my mind.

Thankfully, he breaks the silence first. "You can sleep in my room, and I'll dig out my old sleeping bag," he says.

"Oh no! I can't ask you to do that." I take a step back, suddenly feeling like I'm already invading his space more than I should.

Grinning, he takes a step forward, closing the gap I just created. His hands grip my forearms firmly but affectionately, brushing his thumbs along my arms.

"You're not asking; I'm offering. And it's not so bad." He shrugs nonchalantly. "That sleeping bag is more comfortable than you might think it is." He laughs when I shake my head in disbelief. "No, really. It's perfect for camping trips, or sleeping on the floor beside a beautiful lady."

My head stops mid-shake, and I start blushing. Avoiding his gaze, I look beyond him to the dogs now resting on the couch and loveseat in the living room. "And what about the dogs?"

He turns just enough to spot them. "Something tells me they'll be just fine together. You could leave the bedroom door open in case they want to come in and out, but I'm sure they'll want to sleep on the bed with you." He looks back at me, and I meet his gaze this time. "And I have a feeling you'll want that as much as they will."

I smile and nod. "That obvious, huh?" He gives me a pointed look and I laugh. "Okay. If you're certain?"

"I am." He drops my arms and his hands are about to come to my face, but it looks like he thinks better of that because they both fall to his sides instead. "Do you need anything tonight?"

"No, I—" But wait, yes. I look down at myself—at the thick cardigan, jeans, and knee-high boots I'm still wearing. "Oh, um, yes. Do you have some clothes I can wear to bed? And maybe an extra toothbrush? And is it okay if I shower?" I have the new clothes I bought earlier today that I can wear in the morning, but I'd rather not sleep in jeans tonight.

"Yes, yes, and yes." He smiles. "I'll grab some clothes for you while you shower."

"Thanks." I smile and nod.

"Do you want to eat dinner before or after?"

I glance toward the kitchen, but don't say anything. I'm not actually hungry. In fact, I haven't had an appetite since breakfast.

He must sense my hesitation because he says, "No way. You skipped lunch. Even if you just eat some soup or a ham sandwich, you're eating while you're staying under my roof."

I look away and smile. "A ham sandwich actually sounds kind of good, if that's okay?"

"Of course it's okay. I'll make you one while you shower."

Meeting his gaze, I smile and nod once. "Thank you, Alaric."

"Anytime, Eda." This time, his hand does come up to brush my cheek, and I close my eyes, leaning into his touch.

Chapter 18

Edara

A loud scraping scares me awake. A little gasp comes out instead of the scream of panic rising within as I sit up in bed, attempting to make out the shapes I'm seeing in the dark. Not recognizing anything—including the noise—doesn't help my fear or anxiety.

Slowly, my eyes adjust to the night, thanks to the moonlight coming in.

Alaric sits up from his spot on the side of the bed and looks around the room. "What is it?" he asks.

His eyes chase the shadows in the room, and I feel his hand cover mine in comfort. I flinch at first, but then the touch grounds me, reminding me of where I am and that I'm not alone in this.

Recognizing the sound that woke me, I look to my left and realize it's just a branch hitting the window from the windy night. Once my breathing is back under control, and I remember what happened and where I am, I start crying. So much for thinking I'd finished processing it all.

Instead of making me feel bad, Alaric hops into the bed and holds me in his arms. I lay my head on his chest as his arms wrap around me.

When the tears stop flowing from my eyes and silent sobs no longer rack my body, he silently returns to his sleeping bag on the floor to the right of the bed.

No words said. No explanation necessary. He just understood, and held me until I was ready.

Lying separately again, I struggle to fully relax as the wind brews on.

When I first laid down in his bed, it felt impossible to sleep after the day's events. I'm not sure how long I tossed and turned in the plaid flannel sheets before exhaustion finally took over. I can already tell the inevitable fatigue and burnout I'll feel tomorrow will make it harder to do anything throughout the day. Not that I want to, anyway.

The idea of leaving the house alone to work is enough to make my anxiety hit in full force. Granted, it's always simmering, just waiting to explode at the smallest thought or sound.

Those thoughts once again bounce around in my head as I lie in Alaric's bed, with tired eyes that are stinging until it becomes too painful to keep them open. I consider just calling it and getting up for the day, but based on the clock on the nightstand, there are at least three hours until dawn. It's still too dark outside for me to be comfortable even attempting to walk to the guesthouse alone, let alone stay there until sunrise.

Part of me wishes he hadn't left the bed. There's no reason for him to be on the floor while I lie in *his* bed.

Screw it, I'm not sleeping, anyway.

Scooting to the edge of the bed, I peer over the side of the mattress at him. He's staring up at the ceiling with his hands interlocked over his chest. The sleeping bag is dark green, and it looks like one he might have got while he was in the army. It's worn, but I have to admit it kind of looks cozy.

Our eyes meet. "Everything all right?" he asks, with one eyebrow raised in question.

I want to say yes, but that isn't honest. The truth is, I'm not sure if I'll be able to sleep again until Brad stops this madness. I'm not sure I'll ever feel safe again at night even long after he's locked up, grows bored of me, or whatever finally makes him stop. I'm not sure if I can let Elessar out again without needing him right by my side, or look at Alaric's truck the same way after seeing it smothered in rose petals. Or if I'll find these woods peaceful again after knowing he's been watching us here.

How can I answer that question honestly without rambling?

Sighing, I lay my head on the edge of the bed and settle for, "No, but I will be." My cheek presses against the soft sheet, and my wrist hangs limply off the side.

"Yes, you will be." Something in his voice makes me meet his gaze. It's stern yet compassionate. It makes me feel hopeful and strong at the same time.

Feeling a small sense of hope, I nod once, and he smiles.

"Can't sleep?" I ask.

Our eyes stay locked for a few seconds before he glances up at the ceiling. "No."

"I'm sorry," I whisper.

His neck sharply turns so that he can look at me better. "For what?"

Gaping, I lift my head off the edge of the bed to better look at him. "For *what*?" My voice cracks, and I clear my throat. "For bringing a psycho to your doorstep. For you now being involved in this shit. For taking over your house and bed—"

The rambling stops when he sits up suddenly. His cold hands cup either side of my face, simultaneously cooling me and encouraging me to hold his gaze. The moonlight illuminates the specks of green in his hazel eyes, and focusing on them twinkling soothes my breathing a bit.

"I can tell I'll have to say this more than once, because you have a tendency to apologize," I feel my cheeks pink as he smiles, "but you have nothing to be sorry for, Eda. *You* did nothing wrong."

Tears brim in my eyes for the...I don't even know how many times in the past fourteen hours. Tears of guilt; sadness; frustration. Defeat. It's a wonder I'm not all cried out at this point.

"I need you to say it," his voice is calm, low, as his thumbs lightly brush along my cheekbones.

A tear drops from my left eye, and his thumb brushes it away.

"I—" Nope. I tried, but it's not happening. These are words that are failing me for a different reason. How can I say it's not my fault? It *is* my fault. My teeth suck in my lip in embarrassment.

Those moonlit, hazel depths briefly drop from my eyes down to my lips. His thumb goes from my cheekbone to just under my lip, where he applies gentle pressure, forcing my teeth to let go. My lips part and I lick them in anticipation, but then his gaze meets mine again. Are his lids heavy because he's also tired?

"Try again. It doesn't have to be full of conviction yet, but I want to hear the words come from your lips," he says.

Okay, I can do this. I can do this. It just has to be said in a way that's somewhat truthful. That will help. That...

"I–I did not...do this," I manage to say.

He smiles. "I'll take it." One hand drops from my face, and the other lingers a moment before he pulls away. "Even if you don't believe it now, I have hope that you will someday."

I nod my head, but I'm not sure if I believe him. Maybe he's right, or maybe he's not, but it's appreciated either way.

As he lies back down on the sleeping bag, his palms rest on his chest again. Without even thinking about it, I drape my arm over the bed and grab his hand. He doesn't hesitate to interlock his fingers with mine. Warmth spreads deep within my chest and I smile at the feel of his hand in mine.

"Good night, Alaric," I say, lying my head on the cold sheets again. His thumb gently brushes the top of my hand, and to my surprise, I feel my eyes growing heavy with sleep.

"Call me Ric," he says, softly.

Eyes blinking rapidly as I fight the sleep taking hold, I smile at him. Before succumbing to sleep with our fingers still interlaced, I whisper, "Good night, Ric."

Chapter 19

ALARIC

Eda was in my bed last night. She's *still* in my bed, wrapped in my sheets, while I remain on the floor. If it had been any other night—any other reason for her to be there—I would have been right next to her.

But it wasn't any other night.

As daybreak hits and the sunlight beams through the windows, my mind wanders to last night, when I heard her rustling. At the time, I had interlaced my fingers over my chest and resisted the urge to rise from my spot on the floor to join her in case it might help her sleep.

When we first got ready for bed after dinner, she'd tried to insist I sleep with her, but I needed to be on guard, alert. And if I had that beautiful woman in bed with me, there's no way I'd be able to resist touching her. Or even just focus on anything but the fact that she was next to me.

She finally fell asleep at one point, until the wind woke us both. While she was struggling to find sleep again, I didn't expect her pretty face to pop over the side of the bed, peering down at me. I wanted to kiss the worry lines from her forehead, to kiss away all of her troubles. Her dainty wrist hung over the edge, just asking to be held. Again, I refrained. That was, until she'd grabbed *my* hand, and I immediately wrapped my own around hers.

And when she'd apologized? *Again.* Everything in me grew angry again, but also sad, at the thought of this beautiful, kind woman believing any part of what's happened is her fault. That she feels she has to hold any of the blame for someone else's actions, or for what has been done *to* her. It made me hopeful when she did her best to admit and accept that none of this is her fault. She really is brave.

It did me in when she abandoned the pillow, grabbed my hand, and fell asleep like that, wanting to touch *me.*

As if maybe it helped her to be close to me.

Damn, I hope so. She deserves to feel safe, and I'm not going to let anything happen to her.

As I lie here now, having slept very little and not caring, I contemplate whether to make her breakfast or stay until she wakes. The thought of her being afraid when she wakes up alone makes me stay put. That, and the fact that even after her grip on my hand went slack, she slept in the same spot on the edge of the bed.

Her hand has been resting limp on my chest for hours, warming the spot right over my heart. I don't dare move. Not that I want to, anyway.

At least, I *didn't* want to, until she stirs awake and those stunning blue eyes land on me, taking me in. A small, sleepy smile spreads across her face, and I almost pull her hand back to me when she raises it to slowly wipe the sleep from her eyes. As she stretches, long hair in the prettiest shade of red splays out over the edge of the bed, inches from my chest, where her hand was seconds before.

"Mornin'," she whispers.

"Good morning, Little Red." I have no idea what compels me to use the nickname again, but I like the way she smiles at it. I take the opportunity to get up and not think about her in my bed anymore. I turn my face to hide my grimace over my sore body. I guess I forgot what it's like sleeping in the sleeping bag. Or not sleeping.

Straightening my back, I turn toward her and say, "If you'd like to shower, I put more towels in there last night, and you're welcome to any of the clothes in the closet."

With a slight nod, she turns over in bed so that she's on her back, tangled in my sheets. Her long, red hair is splayed out all over the pillow and sheets, and it takes everything in me to not straddle her and gather that hair into my hand. That is, until I remember the reason why she's wearing my shirt and in my bed. Memories of the day before flood in, and the desire is instantly squashed.

With clenched fists, I turn away as my anger rises again.

Thankfully, the dogs choose that exact moment to come barreling into the bedroom from wherever they slept and bombard her on the bed.

Standing in the doorway, I look over my shoulder to spy Elessar laid out in Eda's lap and all across her legs, with his head in her lap and his tail thumping against her ankles. She has one hand on his belly and her other arm wrapped around Blanche's neck, trying to ward off my girl's slobbery kisses on her face while still petting her. The sight of the excited dogs cheering her up makes me smile.

Eda's laughter fills the air, echoing down the hall and straight into my chest as I walk away from the beautiful woman in my bed.

When her soft footsteps come down the hall thirty minutes later, I quickly set down book two of her series. I picked it up after cooking breakfast, but I remember how embarrassed she seemed after I told her I finished book one. I don't want to evoke even more unwanted emotions for her right now by catching the next book in my hands.

I shuffle the pile of books on the end table in the living room, placing it underneath a mystery book I've been meaning to finish. Admittedly, her series isn't a genre I typically read, but she's a talented writer. My brain can't comprehend creating the way she does—imagining whole worlds and characters within them. The stories are intriguing, but her words are captivating.

Turning around, I check over the spread of maple and brown sugar oatmeal, bacon, and cinnamon pumpkin pancakes waiting for her. It's my sister's favorite pancake recipe, and I hope Eda will like them. If not, I'm willing to give her my chocolate chip pancakes, or make something else.

I get up to grab a plate for her to sit at the island, but then stop in my tracks when I see her face as she rounds the corner. It's pale, panicked. She almost looks ill.

"What is it?" I ask. My eyes fly to the windows, immediately thinking the worst. Did Brad call her? Did she see him outside? I need to get more cameras and sensors situated outside.

The hand holding her phone lifts, and her mouth hangs open as if she's stunned.

I round the island and put a hand on each of her shoulders. "Eda, what's going on?"

Meeting my gaze, she looks back down at her phone between us. "My agent..." She clears her throat, trying again. "Carol called while I was in the shower. The voicemail... She'd asked if Brad found me." Her voice was quiet, but I heard her well enough.

My hands drop from her shoulders to form fists at my sides. "What does that mean? Did you tell her you came here to get away from him?"

Her head slowly nods and her stare is blank. She's physically looking at me, but it's as if she's not actually seeing me. "Yeah...I did. I gave her the rental address when I first got here in case she needed to send me anything—like book mail or PR—over the course of these two months being here. I told her to not tell anyone." Her voice croaks, but she pushes on. "And she's aware of some of the troubles I had with Brad. Not everything, but enough to know I don't want him near me."

"Can I hear it?" I ask.

She obliges, and I listen to a woman's voice—Carol's voice—try to explain her logic behind giving a stalker any information about the person he's stalking.

"Hi, Eda! Okay, don't be upset, buuuuut you know how I like Brad? Well, I do. I think he's great, and he's good for you. I'm sure of it. Well, anyway, he called me a few days ago and said he has a surprise for you. He knows you're away from home, and was asking if you'd told me where you'd gone. I told him you don't want to be disturbed—I did—*but* he said he just wanted to send you some flowers and a little something else to see if they'd help cheer you up and maybe inspire you.

"So...did you get his surprise? And did it work? How's that manuscript coming along? I haven't heard from you in a few days, and I just wanted to see if his surprise—well, I guess it's now *our* surprise in a way—helped at all. Okay, I hope to hear from you soon. Bye!"

The voicemail ends, and I just stand there in disbelief. "What does that mean? How does she even know him?" Anger rising again, I cross my arms against my chest.

She shakes her head. "He got to her, in the beginning of all of this. Made it seem like we were dating and more serious than we were. Clearly," she says, bitterly. "Carol and I aren't super close. She's good at her job and came recommended to me, but we've never quite clicked outside of work. It's always been strictly a working relationship. Something she's expressed is vastly different than with her other clients, whom she sounds close to, but it works for us." She scoffs. "Or it did."

She glances at her phone again before crossing her arms. "I'm not sure if she was thrilled to finally be in on my personal life or what—even if it wasn't real—but one day, he convinced her that he was my new boyfriend and was reaching out to get her help to surprise me. He asked for my address. That's how he sent me roses the first time." Anger is laced in her words, and I feel enraged on her behalf.

I grit my teeth as she continues.

"He charmed her somehow, and ever since, she's been obsessed with him. Won't hear it if I talk badly about him, or ask her to not tell him anything. She's convinced— Or, rather, *he* convinced *her* that he's good for me. I don't know." Her eyebrows pinch as she looks up at me, meeting my gaze. "I've been working with her for a little over a year now, after my last agent retired. After everything, I didn't think she'd do *this*."

She laughs, but it sounds cold, mocking. "Then again, I guess I had some fear she might. But I had some hope that I'd gotten through to her, and I stressed to her not to tell *anyone* where I was. Not even Brad."

I clear my throat in an attempt to keep the rage from seeping into my tone. "Forgetting about how unprofessional that is, isn't it illegal to give out client information like that?"

Shrugging, she says, "I don't know. Is it?"

"I'm not an agent or a lawyer, but I'm pretty damn certain the answer should be 'yes.'" I try but fail to keep the bitterness from leaking into my tone. With a tense jaw, my fingers rake through my hair. "You should send the voicemail to Gavin later. And your lawyer. Your agent will get what's coming to her for aiding in him harassing and stalking you."

She stares at her phone, the stress evident across her features. It's as if she's already dreading telling them about the call, and I can't say I blame her.

"For now, let's get some food in you." Holding out my hand, she looks up at me and then at my palm before placing her phone in it. I was more so going for her hand to lead her toward breakfast, but if she needs a break from her phone, I'll gladly help. I lock it and place it on the far side of the island, away from where we'll eat.

She sits down on one of the barstools as I warm up the food for her.

Thankfully, the gamble with the pumpkin pancakes pays off, because she loves them. She eats while wearing one of my flannels—the same one I wore the night we kissed in the kitchen—a pair of my thick cabin socks that are way too big on her and go nearly halfway up her calf, and nothing else. Her legs are bare, dangling from the counter-height chair.

That shirt has never looked so good, and I'm tempted to tell her she can keep it. It was made for her.

When I hand her a mug full of hot coffee and a bottle of French vanilla creamer, she happily takes them both and puts an absurd amount of creamer in the mug.

She must see my face, because she asks, "What? You don't like creamer?"

I look from her mug back to her. "I prefer to drink my coffee with creamer, not creamer with a side of coffee."

"Ha-ha," she fake laughs. "So what? I have a sweet tooth."

"Clearly," I say, grinning, before putting the creamer back in the fridge.

"I'm usually more of a tea person because of the caffeine and the taste of coffee, but today feels like a coffee day." Taking a sip, her eyes close in pleasure. Okay, if that's the look creamer puts on her face, I'll make sure she has a lifetime supply.

There's a *clink* as she sets her mug on the island. "Um, do you have tea bags?" The tops of her cheeks grow pink.

There's no way she finished her creamer that quickly. Taking a step closer to the island, I see that there's still coffee in her mug.

I don't even have to ask before she explains. "The tea's for my face."

My eyes fly up, searching her face. She looks shy, as she takes the top buttons of the flannel and wraps the fabric around her neck without securing the clasps. Just holding it there, protectively. Her eyes are a little red and swollen, the color making the blue of her eyes pop, and I instantly don't like that they're more vibrant because she's been crying. Otherwise, there are no marks on her I can see that she might need to take care of. So, why tea?

"I...might," I say, hesitantly, because I'm unsure. "My sister and mom have left some different teas for when they visit." I walk over to the pantry and open the door. "What kind do you want?"

"Green tea, please. If you have it," she says. "It's nice that you keep things around for your family. You mentioned the other night that they live close to you?"

Spotting the green tea box my mom left here, I grab it and turn toward the counter to fill the electric kettle with water. "Yeah, my parents and Sawyer live within twenty minutes of here."

"It must be nice having them so close," she says, taking another sip of her coffee.

"It is." I smile and speak a little louder over the running water. "Sawyer and I were pretty close growing up. We drifted apart a bit when I was in the army, but that's normal. I'd say we're now closer than ever. So, it's nice getting to hang out and make up for lost time."

I set the kettle down on it's electric base and turn it on.

"My parents, Sawyer, and I get together at least once a month, alternating houses monthly for dinner. We try to plan the dinners around each other's birthdays, and we keep holidays at my parents' house. It's a tradition we started after I moved back. My mom insists on seeing us as often as possible, even though we no longer live under her roof. So, they've made the adjustment to come to us every once in a while in a way of respecting us having our own lives."

Smiling at me over her mug, she says, "That sounds really nice."

"Yeah, it's not so bad." I shrug. "What about you? Are you close with your family?"

Her eyes light up before a shadow falls over her face a split second later. She breaks eye contact, looking down instead. "Yeah, we are."

"Then why do you look so sad?" I ask. It might be prodding, but it's a strange reaction for that answer.

A small smile briefly crosses her face, not reaching her eyes before it falls again. "Because I'm going to have to break their hearts and worry them when I tell them what happened."

I grimace. That hadn't crossed my mind. "Will it be easier to do over the phone than in person?"

Her head shakes from side to side. "Yeah, except for my Aunt Bellamy. She's who was supposed to be visiting the other night. I don't know how, but I have to tell her and my uncle. I'll have to tell everyone. Because, if he's been watching us, then he might have seen me with her, and I can't stand the thought of—" Her voice stops mid-sentence, and her mouth hangs open. No tears brim in her red-rimmed eyes, but there's pain and fear in them.

I lean back against the counter. "Do you want to be alone when you do it?"

She meets my eyes, but the chime of the electric kettle goes off before she can speak.

Turning, I grab a mug from the cabinet. When I go to take a tea bag out of the box, she is at my side, her fingers grazing mine as she grabs the mug from in front of the kettle.

"I can make the tea. You've been kind enough," she says, smiling.

When I step back, it's hard not to notice how my flannel shirt hits at just the right spot on her small frame. It covers everything it needs to, while still showing off her legs.

It's nice seeing her in my kitchen and in my clothes. I have no business liking it as much as I do.

After placing two tea bags in the mug and pouring water over them, she turns around and looks at the clock on the stove before meeting my gaze. "I don't know," she says, quietly.

It takes me a moment to realize she's continuing our conversation. She must have been contemplating her answer while she prepped the tea.

"I..." Her arms cross over her chest, making the shirt rise just a little in the front. I keep my eyes on her face. "I think it might help to have you there.

You...make me..." Delicate fingers start to tightly grip her arms. Her throat clears, her hold loosens, and she stands a little straighter. "You make me feel safe," she says, looking me in the eyes again.

Those words tug at me. I take a step toward her, but keep my distance out of respect. Looking into her eyes, I say, "Then I'll be there, if you want me."

She nods with a small smile, but says nothing else as she watches the clock on the stove.

Leaning against the counter, I stand there and let her sit in silence. I'm curious what she'll do next.

When the clock seems to finally hit the time she wants it to, she turns back toward the mug on the counter and takes the tea bags out.

I have to admit, I question her sanity for a minute at what she does next. Instead of tossing the tea bags, she wrings them out over the sink, walks over to the couch, sits down, and then places one tea bag on each of her eyes.

I join her in the living room, but stay silent. Blanche hops onto the couch with me, and I pet her while we wait.

After sitting with the tea bags resting on her eyes for roughly ten minutes, Eda removes them and tosses them into the kitchen trash. Tucking her phone between her left bicep and ribs, she grabs her mugs of tea and coffee in each hand, then comes back into the living room and settles in on the loveseat. It's shocking when I see how her eyes are no longer red and swollen, but now look normal and bright.

Tea bags... Who knew?

Taking a deep breath, she sips the mug of tea, alternating between it and her sweet-as-hell coffee, while Elessar curls up on the loveseat next to her. With Blanche next to me, I sit quietly across from her as she silently stares into space.

It's not until it looks like her mind is tormenting her that I break the silence. "How's work going?" It's the first thing that comes to mind, which is the only thought that keeps me from internally cringing at the attempt at small talk. Selfishly, I'm also asking because I'm enjoying her books.

My eyes glance at book two hidden on the end table next to her. Despite putting her mugs on the same table, it doesn't look like she's noticed it.

Her eyes find mine, and she is silent for a moment.

Breaking eye contact, she sets the tea mug down and switches it out for the coffee. "It's going really well. After struggling for months, I found my groove again since being here. I'm about halfway through the book, and it's only been a few weeks. That's a good sign."

Happiness floods me at knowing that my guesthouse—my home—is a place she's found the motivation she was looking for to write.

"Another book?" I set my glass of water down on the coffee table and start to pet Blanche's head. "I don't think you mentioned before what you're writing. What's this one about?"

"Oh, yeah." She looks away and shrugs. "It was supposed to be a small-town romance about a firefighter and a math teacher."

My eyebrows raise. "Supposed to be? What is it now?"

Looking me dead in the eye, she quickly says, "It's still a small-town romance, but now it's with a lumberjack and a writer." No sooner are the words out than the mug of coffee meets her lips, giving her a reason not to talk.

It takes a second for my brain to register the speed at which she spoke. One by one, the words hit me.

Small-town...

Romance...

A lumberjack...

And a writer...

Grinning, I lean forward. "Little Red, are you writing about us?"

Chapter 20

ALARIC

The mug slowly lowers from her face, but she isn't making eye contact with me. "Um, I believe my lawyer would advise me to say that it's a work of fiction, and any and all similarities to real people are entirely coincidental." Her head nods vigorously. "Yes, we'll go with that."

"Yes, Counselor Lauklan." I laugh, and she grins, her cheeks lighting up in the prettiest shade of pink. "What do these 'entirely coincidental' characters get up to in your book?"

The way her face grows almost as red as her hair tells me everything I need to know, and I have the urge to finish what we started that night. But I want to know what *she* fantasizes about.

Instead of answering, she bites her lip. I have a feeling the silence has everything to do with what she doesn't want to say rather than what she *can't* say. It only makes me all the more curious.

"What do your lumberjack and writer get up to in your book?" I shift, sitting farther back on the couch, and she meets my gaze again. "Tell me what's floating around in that pretty little head of yours."

This time, she doesn't look away. "They have sex. Are you happy now?" She throws one hand up in the air, and the other remains wrapped around the coffee mug.

Grinning, I say, "Only half satisfied."

"I know the feeling..." she mumbles before taking another sip of her coffee.

My head tilts to the side, with a brow raised and my chin pointing downward. Is that a reference to what happened between us? Or rather, what *didn't* happen.

Of course, it is. I'm the fool who left her that night and didn't make up for it after. No, I'd been an asshole and stayed away, allowing my demons to take over my mind and keep me from her. Admittedly, I also let Sawyer get into my head. But the longer I stayed away, the more intense the need to be near Eda became.

"I'm sorry about what happened... You know, before," I say. Her blue eyes go wide and meet mine again over the rim of her mug. "Well, I'm not sorry for what we did, so long as you're not, but I am sorry we haven't talked about it since. I shouldn't have stayed away. I—" A hand rakes through my hair. I'm fumbling. "I'm not one for dating," is all I can say, when there is so much more I want to say.

"Dating?" she repeats. "Who said anything about dating, Ric?"

It's my turn to feel embarrassed. "Well, no. No one did. Yeah, but I just, I don't know. You strike me as someone who's the marrying type—a long-term partner to a lucky man. Or woman. Whoever. Because you could have anyone you want." I'm rambling. Fuck me.

Clearing my throat, I try again. "And that just... I'm just not someone who's good in relationships. I haven't been before. I... And you deserve better. No, you deserve the best. Someone who can make you happy, and make you feel secure." My lips clamp shut, putting an end to this. I'm fucking this way up.

Her eyes stay on mine for a moment, but her lips tip up in the corner. "I thought I was the rambler. Do I make you nervous, Ric?"

A witty remark leaves my tongue when I realize this is an opportunity to be honest; to give her the truth she deserves. "Yes, and no. Fucking this up—hurting you—is what makes me nervous."

Her fingertips slowly and rhythmically tap the sides of her mug a couple times as she sits with my words.

"So, it was something your sister said?" Her tone is calm, but her eyes are fleeting, as if she's the one who's nervous now.

"My sister?" My brows furrow.

She clears her throat before saying, "I could be wrong, but I noticed a change after you spoke to her."

I nod my head once in understanding, especially because I underestimated how observant she is. "Sort of. She just...reminded me that I'm not..." This is hard to say, but I need to get it out. "Talking with her reminded me why I don't date, why I'm alone—and will continue to be—and why you deserve better."

Well, and Sawyer made me realize I might have feelings, which is dangerous. I keep that development to myself, because I undoubtedly have feelings for Eda and don't know what to do about it. At this point, staying away isn't an option. Been there, done that, and hated it. And there's no way I'm leaving her alone now—especially after what happened yesterday—unless she wants me to.

"Why are you alone?" she asks, quietly.

I stare at the blank wall between the coat closet and the front door for several minutes before responding, "My career before this made me feel like it was easier to be alone, especially because of the life I led—always gone for work, never having time for anyone, not even myself. It was just easier to..." I sigh and run my right hand through my hair. "When I got out of the army, they diagnosed me with PTSD. Great for disability benefits, not great for, well, me. Or anyone else in my life."

Needing to collect my thoughts, I pause, but I find a little strength being in her presence. "I never want to drag anyone down in my mess. And you," I meet her gaze, "don't deserve to be dragged anywhere. You deserve to sit on a throne."

Her lips part. "I'm sorry for what you went through in your past life. Thank you for sharing that with me."

I nod, then look over at Blanche sitting next to me. I need to focus on something other than this conversation and what I just admitted out loud.

Clearing her throat, Eda asks, "Did it ever occur to you that what happened that night—and what might have happened—was a mutual decision? One that you didn't get to be the sole decider on whether you'd hurt me."

Fuck, she has me there.

"Honestly? No," I admit.

"I didn't think so." Her tone is soft, but the words strike with a force all the same. "I was the one who made the move, Ric. I was also the one who practically begged you for a single kiss before you left my doorstep that night. If anyone made a fool of themselves, it was me. And if you stayed away out of embarrassment or fear, don't put that on me. Because I was fully conscious of the decisions we were making, and I was more than happy with them."

Damn, if I didn't think that I fucked up before, I certainly know it now. She's right. About all of it.

"At the same time," she continues, "I could understand why you might not want to get involved with a tenant. I just wish we could have talked about it."

Sighing, I lean forward so that my elbows are on my knees. With my hands clasped together, I look her in the eyes. "You're right, and I'm sorry. We should have had this conversation sooner. I shouldn't have taken the easy way out and pretended like it didn't happen."

Her eyes blink rapidly, and she looks confused.

"What?" I ask, sitting back again.

"Nothing. I'm just not used to guys apologizing. Especially not so quickly." She takes a slow sip of her coffee, as if dazed.

I catch myself just in time before I say something about the company of the men she keeps. Even as a joke, I don't want to risk bringing her attention back to yesterday. This is the most she's talked since it happened.

"People make mistakes. It's what makes us human. If you're a decent human, you shouldn't have a problem admitting when you're wrong. And I was wrong. I should have talked to you like the two adults we are, then we could have decided together." I shrug. "It's on me."

"That's mature of you." She looks at me over her mug, and I shrug. "For the record..." she says, as she sets the coffee down and brings the tea to her lips this time. Her eyes are twinkling just above the mug as she continues. "I wish you had finished what you started that night."

The look in her eyes drives me wild.

I hold her gaze as I stand up and walk over to where she sits on the couch. "For the record," I mimic, as I brush my thumb along her cheekbone, "so do I." My thumb trails down toward her lips, which part for me as I trace the plump shape of them. "And I wish I could have done it every night since."

Her breath hitches, and her eyelids grow heavy. Fuck, the sight makes my cock twitch in my pants. Damn it.

"Me too," she says, breathlessly.

"Really?"

"Really." Her teeth nibble on my thumb.

It takes everything in me to swallow the groan working its way up my throat at the sight. But first, I need her to promise me something.

"Will you do me a favor?" My voice is low, serious, because I can't think with *that* head right now.

"After what you've done for me...anything," she says, a little breathless.

"Will you come to my gym with me?" She blinks slowly, then rapidly several times. It's clear by her face that was the last thing she expected me to say. "We'll do a one-on-one self-defense class. Just you and me, and the chance to know you're able to protect yourself." My eyes scan her face, gauging her reaction and if she'll reject it. "Before you say no—"

"Okay," she interrupts me, with her arms crossed.

I stare at her with my lips parted. "O...kay?" The word comes out slow. I remember before when she said she doesn't like working out. So, this is a surprise.

She nods. "If anyone can help me feel safe, it's someone who literally trains others for a living. Saying no crossed my mind for a second there, but I'd be stupid to turn down this opportunity. So, okay."

"Okay," I repeat in shock. "We'll go first thing in the morning tomorrow." The look on her face almost makes me laugh.

"What does 'first thing in the morning' mean to you?" she asks, her voice sounding panicked.

A smile tugs at the corners of my face. "How's six sound?"

Her arms uncross from her chest and start waving in the air. "Nope, nope. I take it back. Not happening."

A deep chuckle comes from me as I lightly rub a hand up and down her arm. "How about we do it after the gym closes for the night? Just you and me there," I suggest.

Blue eyes look down at my hand before looking up at me once more. "I'd like that." Her voice sounds breathy again, but she clears her throat before continuing. "But I must warn you that it's been a long time since I went to a gym...or worked out."

"Then, I guess it's okay for me to confess that it's been awhile since I instructed a class. We can brush off the cobwebs together." Her cheeks spot rosy again, and I can't resist trailing the blush with my fingers.

Her eyelids flutter before she says, "I know I said it before, but thank you for everything you've done. I'm just so sorry it happened. That I brought him here." Tears brim in her eyes, not yet passing her lash line.

My touch briefly halts on her cheek, prompting her to look up at me. "I'll say this as many times as I need to before it fully sinks in. You have nothing to be sorry for. You told your agent not to tell anyone where you were, and she violated that trust. Both she and Brad are to blame. Not you."

With a sniffle, she nods her head.

I gently lift her chin, and her eyes land on mine again. "I mean it, Eda." My voice is low. "It's not your fault. I'll keep telling you until you believe it, but I don't want to hear another apology from you or else."

Her breath hitches. "Or else what?" she asks.

The look makes me hope for something I have no right to hope for. As I realize I'm not imagining what she's feeling, a smile spreads across my face. "Why does it look like you want to find out?"

"Maybe I do." Her voice is breathy.

"Why? Typically, that statement is a threat." My eyes narrow on her, but I can feel my lips still tipped up on the right side, the shadow of a smile likely giving me away.

She licks her lips. "But I know you won't hurt me."

My eyes widen before narrowing again. "I just got done warning you, you deserve better than me." Still holding her chin, I say, "How do you know you haven't run straight into the arms of the Big Bad Wolf, Little Red?" My fingers trail along her jawline before settling on the collar of the flannel shirt, just brushing the tender skin there.

Those blue eyes eagerly meet my stare. "Can't you tell by my choice in dogs that I prefer wolves to men? And how do you know that wasn't my intention, Mr. Wülf?" She smirks.

She's got me there. Elessar does look like a wolf, with his black and silver coloring and wolf mask pattern on his snout. I also fell right into that trap of my own making with my last name.

"You're going to get hurt if you go down this path, Eda," I say. Flirting with her is fun, but I need her to know that if we do this now, she might get hurt.

Or maybe I will. The thought startles me.

She gives me a pointed look, her eyes downcast. "Didn't we already establish that it's my decision to make?"

I huff a laugh, and I can tell by the look in her eyes that she means it. I'm about to bend down and kiss her, when her phone goes off on the end table next to her.

Startled by the sound, she gasps in surprise and breaks our eye contact. As she picks it up, a shadow falls over her face, and I want to banish it.

"What is it?" I ask, fully prepared that it could be her agent again. Or worse, Brad. Resisting the urge to glance down at her phone, I brush my hand against her arm and wait.

Still staring at her phone, she blinks a few times. It looks like she's trying to decide what to do.

When she finally looks up, her brows crease. "Did you mean it when you offered to be there while I talk to my aunt and uncle?" she asks.

Right, the conversation from breakfast. Shifting on my feet, I look from her to the phone in her hand. "I did."

She sighs. "Okay, because they want to meet you soon, which means I have to tell them what happened. And I don't think I can do that alone right now."

"I'll be there, then." I nod, and then pause. "They want to meet me?"

Our eyes meet as she says, "Don't let it get to your head, but yes. That's why my aunt was coming that night. She wanted to meet the hot *lumberjack* next door."

There's no doubt in my mind that the grin on my face is considered cheesing. I put my hand out in front of her. Her brows raise but she doesn't hesitate otherwise as she places her hand in mine, and I help her up. With one arm scooped under her legs and the other around her waist, I pick her up and hold her close to my chest.

Those pretty blues are staring up at my face. A strand of hair falls in front of her right eye, and part of me wishes my hands weren't already full of her so that I can brush it aside. But the other part of me prefers it this way. Feeling her against me...I don't want to let her go.

"If you're up for it, tell them a time and day that works for you, and we can make them dinner together," I say as I carry her to the kitchen.

"Ric, what are you doing?" She laughs.

Looking down at her, I grin.

"I'm going to show the sexy writer next door just how sorry I am."

Chapter 21

EDARA

It's happening, and it isn't a dream this time. Nor is it a scene created for my book.

When Alaric picks me up and sets me atop the island, I want to laugh. But when I see the look in his eyes—the same look I saw that night in the kitchen—the laugh dies and my undeniable desire is brought to life. Just like that. With one look, this man could undo everything I am.

The way he tried to explain the male logic for why he stayed away made me want to roll my eyes. At the same time, it was endearing. That wasn't the first time I'd seen him not calm or collected, but it was the first time I felt my presence affected him in a way that made him as nervous as he makes me. I kind of liked it. Yes, he rambled, but what I heard was that he cares and he's simply scared. So am I, and everyone makes mistakes.

Up until he apologized, I'd planned to let it go and just continue on like this until I felt like it was safe to go back to the guesthouse. The apology was the game changer for me. It was sincere and clear he was remorseful for the decision he made for the both of us that night.

And the questions he asked about my book... The way he was genuinely curious about it, about what *we* do in the book—

"Mmm," a moan escapes me as his lips meet mine. This is so much better than imagining it for the story.

He pulls away, standing at the edge of the island. Which means that I get to admire him at another angle. He's tall, muscular. His beard perfectly fits his face, and I suddenly wonder what it would feel like between my legs.

"You said you also wished for this everyday, but are you sure?" he asks.

My heart swells at his consideration. "Yes." I nod. "You've already proved that I'm safe with you, and...I don't know, it would be nice to not think about what happened. To just *feel* instead of think."

Nodding, he grabs my hand and lightly kisses my knuckles. "We can make that happen."

"Are you sure?" I ask him as his lips linger on my hand. "What changed your mind?"

Meeting my gaze over the top of my hand still in his, he grins and says, "It seems I had a change of heart."

Smiling, I shake my head at him. Thank goodness he did.

"I have a favor to ask. Well, another one," he says, dropping my hand and gently tracing my ankle through his sock I'm wearing. I keep my eyes on him, waiting for him to continue. "Tell me what you've fantasized about while writing your book."

My cheeks grow hot, but I don't look away. "I can't do that," I say.

"Why not?" he asks, as his fingers come to the top of one sock. An eyebrow raises in question, and I nod, giving him permission.

Goosebumps form on my flesh as he gently slides the sock down my ankle and drops it to the floor. He makes eye contact with me when he grabs my other foot.

And I'm suddenly reminded he asked me a question.

"Because..." I say, squirming with embarrassment.

My senses are heightened as his fingers lightly trace the ankle of my other foot. With one eyebrow arched, he slides down the other sock. "Because...?"

"Not happening." I laugh and nudge my bare foot against his thigh.

His fingers lightly trail up my legs as he steps in between them. His lips are close enough for me to bite. Somehow, I drag my eyes away from them to look into his hazel eyes that are full of amusement. "I guess I'll just have to read it, then."

He consumes my laugh as he closes the distance between us, his lips meeting mine.

Wrapping my arms around his shoulders, I pull him even closer into me, and there's a jolt of excitement when I feel the pressure of his arousal in between my legs. The kiss deepens, a dance of tongues and passionate moans.

Breaking away, I catch my breath as his lips slowly trail down to my chin and neck. The soft caress of his beard against my skin adds yet another sensation. It's stolen from me when those lips trail kisses farther down and find the peak of one of my breasts through his shirt I put on after showering.

My hands shoot into his hair, nails digging into his scalp as he sucks and nips at me. While one hand kneads my breast, the other wraps around my waist, exploring my body.

It's not enough. I need more.

Feeling for him, I slide my hand under his shirt and feel his stomach muscles contract at the touch. Breathing heavily, he pulls away from me, and I make it clear that I want his shirt off by tugging on the hem of it.

Chuckling low, he obliges, pulling it off with one hand.

And what a sight. It's just as good the second time around. There are muscles upon muscles, and ab dents I didn't even know existed. And the pecs. Who knew I was a boob gal? My hands explore his body, taking it all in.

Slowly removing my hands and taking them in his, he leans in and kisses my lips so quickly, I don't even have the chance to kiss him back. With half-dazed lids, I open my eyes and find he's watching me. Sliding a finger under the hem of the shirt I have on, I can see the question in his eyes, and I don't hesitate to nod, giving permission to pull it off. One hip lifts, then the other, and he pulls the shirt out from underneath me and over my head.

I'm naked now. Fully, completely, utterly naked before him.

The look in his eyes... A sudden sense of shyness and vulnerability hits me, because I've never been looked at like that before. The desire, the awe—as if I was a piece of art. Or, more fitting for the space, his next meal.

Then, this man—this wonderful, sexy man—gets on his knees before me. His hands wrap around my ankles, sliding up, and there's another question in his eyes. One I crave for him to act on. Unable to speak, I give a slight nod, and he responds by spreading my legs, putting me on display before him.

A smile tugs at the corners of his lips.

"What?" I ask, suddenly growing self-conscious.

Smile still in place, he meets my gaze. "I was just thinking about how lucky it is that I'm at the perfect height for my face to be right where I want it."

My blush deepens, and so does my desire. Equal parts embarrassed to be laid bare before him and aroused that it's exactly what he wants.

He trails kisses from the inside of my ankle, all the way up to my inner thigh. I gasp when he nears my center, his breath tickling.

"Is this what you wrote?" he asks, his mouth hovering over me.

Not this fucking game again. Except, I kind of like it. So does my body, considering my hips buck from the tease of his breath alone. And damn, if seeing this beautiful, sexy man on his knees before me isn't a fucking sight.

"I'm not telling you," I breathe out, then groan when he skips over the spot he knows I want him to touch most. I feel rather than see him chuckle before he kisses my other thigh, giving it the same attention as the first.

"No?" he asks. Then, one flick. One flick of a tease with his tongue against my clit. A breathy chuckle teases the wetness pooling there, and my hips buck at the feel of it, my body begging for action. Something, anything.

Still, I keep my lips sealed, the moans dying in my throat. He's going to drive me crazy. Hell, I might already be there.

"Tell me what you fantasized about..." He hovers over my entrance, but goes no further. "Tell me and I'll make it happen." He's so close. *So* close.

Another flick, and I give in.

"*You*. Me. Us. Here, on the island. In your bed. On the sofa. In the shower," I blurt out in desperation.

A moan tears through me when he starts sucking on my clit. It only lasts a few seconds before he stops again, and I groan.

"All good things, and I'll make them all happen." He kisses that sensitive spot. "But Eda..." Another flick of his tongue, another buck of my hips. "Tell me...what do you want me to do to you now?"

Oh, for fuck's sake.

I sit up on my elbows and look him in the eyes. "Ric, if you don't fuck me with your fingers right now and then with your cock, I will lose my fucking mind."

Something flashes in his eyes before he grins. "Good girl."

A flush of warmth crawls up from my groin to my chest, and then back again.

Before I can respond, a hand goes to my stomach, pushing me back down to the kitchen island. His tongue licks me from top to bottom before going back up to my clit. My hand grips his hair when I feel a finger enter me.

"Yes," I moan.

He sucks harder, and slips another finger in. On instinct, I start grinding, wanting more friction.

"That's it," he says. "Ride my face, Eda." His breath teases me even more, adding an extra element of intimacy to the moment.

A cry of pleasure as he starts sucking my clit and enters a third finger, hooking each one. Oh fuck. I can feel the pressure building in my core, my body ready to release.

"Yes, Ric," I say, breathlessly, and he moans into my center in response. The vibration of it and knowing he's turned on from pleasuring me sends me over the edge.

Pinching my nipples, I let myself feel, to enjoy this moment.

"That's it," he says. "Come for me, Eda."

And to my complete and utter shock, I do. Hard. But he doesn't stop, not until the last wave of my orgasm pulses through me, and the last buck of my hips hits.

My body slowly relaxes against the counter once more.

"Breathe, love. Breathe," I hear him whisper as he kisses my inner thigh and then stands up again.

I slowly open my eyes and look at him from where I'm lying on the counter, the granite cooling my hot skin. A smile tugs at my lips, and then a small laugh escapes me.

"What?" he asks, his hands rubbing the curve of my hip and exploring my body once more.

"Nothing," I huff a laugh. "This is just so much better than in my book."

He grins. "Good."

I match his toothy smile and lift my hand toward him. He grabs it and pulls me up so that I'm sitting up on the edge of the island.

"What now?" I ask, still getting my bearings and coming down post-orgasm.

His hands come down from my hips to in between my thighs, teasing me again, and my breath hitches.

Kissing my temple, he whispers in my ear, "Now, I live up to my character in the book."

A shudder of delight courses through me.

It takes everything in me to not throw my head back in pleasure when his finger presses on that ultra sensitive spot inside of me no one has ever touched before him. If it wasn't for my personal toys, I wouldn't even know it existed. Well, at least not until this moment.

"First, the bed." Another finger.

"Then, the couch." His fingers hook again, expertly reaching that spot inside of me that has all other thoughts leaving me. When his other hand goes to my clit, I grip onto his shoulders for support, nails digging into his skin.

"Then, the shower."

Unable to take it anymore, I wrap my hand around his neck and kiss him deeply as another wave of pleasure hits me. He swallows each and every moan, and he's earned them all. Who the hell is this man that he can make me come so quickly? Magic fucking fingers over here.

His lips come to my temple again as I breathe through this second release. Fuck me. *Literally.*

Pulling away, I smile up at him. "What are we waiting for?"

Grinning, he wraps one arm under my legs and lifts me off the counter. My arms slide around his neck and he holds me close to him. He doesn't break our kiss as he carries me to the bedroom, making good on his promise.

Chapter 22

EDARA

Alaric's fingers gently run through my hair while I lay on his chest in bed. The morning light peers through the window, casting an almost angelic light on the man who made all my fantasies come true all day yesterday, and again last night. An angel, indeed. Or, a sex god might be more accurate. To each their own.

Because I was wrong: He's even better in bed than he is at kissing.

And he was right: We are *incredible* in bed together.

"How are you feeling?" Alaric asks.

"Amazing." I sigh and stretch my legs a little, which rub against his bare calves in the process. There's just the right amount of soreness between my legs to make me smile and blush each time I feel it, but not enough to make it difficult to walk or move. "You're definitely getting a five-star rating from me."

"You rate your sexual partners out of five stars?" he muses and his fingers briefly stop their movement.

I laugh and playfully smack his chest. "No, for the rental property. It was a bad attempt at a joke."

His laugh causes a sudden vibration against my cheek that's resting on his chest, and my head partially rises along with each chuckle. It only makes me smile harder. This—being with him, laughing with him, talking with him—it feels so natural.

When his body shifts a tad underneath me, I lift my head and see him glance at the clock on the bedside table.

"What should we make for dinner tonight for your aunt and uncle?" he asks as his hand lazily rubs up and down my spine.

The pleasant mood plummets as his question reminds me of what plans we made for tonight. I'm not quite ready for what's to come, but it might help to focus on the details rather than the reason for the dinner—that Brad's in the area and has found me. So, instead, I think about what my aunt and uncle might want to eat.

"If you have water chestnuts and bean sprouts, I can make some more of the stir fry I made the other night. It's what my aunt requested that night," I explain. "Oh, and I can make another pumpkin roll."

"That stir fry was delicious, and some more pumpkin roll sounds good." Another chuckle rumbles in his chest under my cheek. "But who has water chestnuts and bean sprouts already at home?"

Grinning into his chest, I say, "I do, usually, but I also make this meal a lot."

"I'll tell you what..." The pressure in his hand goes from his palm to his fingertips as he continues to lightly trail my back. "We can go out and get some stuff for dinner, and then maybe some coffee or ice cream."

Placing my hand in the middle of his chest, I sit up enough to look at him. With my chin resting on his sternum, I take in the man before me. His hazel eyes are focused on my face, the look in them melting something within me and making me feel things I shouldn't be feeling. The up close and personal Alaric is even better than the version in my head I adapted for my book.

He smirks while I admire him, but I don't care.

"Isn't it a little cold for ice cream?" I ask, ignoring my emotions whirring within.

That smirk turns into a full-fledged grin. "Are you telling me you haven't had ice cream in the cold mountains yet?"

I shake my head like a normal person who is barely hanging on in this weather.

"You're in for a real treat." His eyebrow dips for a second as the words register with him. "Literally," he says with a deep chuckle, and I shake my head at him. Who knew he was such a cute dork?

"I do love ice cream," I finally say.

The smile on his face knocks the breath out of me.

"Then it's a date." Something flashes on his face, but he doesn't say whatever it is he's thinking.

"What?" I ask after a few seconds.

His mouth opens, but again, no words come out. I start tracing his pecs with my fingers, while I patiently wait for him to speak.

"Nothing, really." His hand comes to my face, trailing along my cheekbone, then going to my temple. His fingers weave through my hair to the back of my head, before sliding down to my shoulder blades and back up again. "I was just thinking about how maybe I could take you to one of my favorite spots to sit outside and watch the sunset with ice cream. That way you can really experience ice cream in the cold. If you're up for it."

Butterflies flutter in my stomach at the idea of a real date with Alaric, and the thought of going to a spot he considers one of his favorites. "I'd love that," I say, trying not to get emotional, "but only if we can also have hot cocoa. *Finally*, and to help balance the frozen treat," I tease.

A smile comes through, but then he pinches his lips together for a second, as if contemplating my terms. "Was already going to happen. I still owe you a rain check for that hot chocolate." I blush at the memory of the last time we tried to share a cup, but were interrupted by our own desire, and then Alaric's sister. "I think you might like it there." His voice is soft.

I hold his gaze for a second, and then my eyes rove over his face—from his hazel eyes crinkling at the corners to his soft, bare cheeks above a full, trimmed beard that I know intimately after yesterday. In fact, I've become quite familiar with how it feels against nearly every inch of my skin.

I reach my hand up, running my palm over his beard and my thumb over his left cheekbone. I feel his smile stretch across his cheek under my palm at the same time that I see it.

I pull my hand back to his chest, look into his eyes, and think about how he's probably right. If there's a place he loves, then I'll likely love it for that fact alone. There's something about sharing in another's joy and getting to experience a little bit of what makes their heart happy and feeds their spirit. The more I learn about this man, the more intrigued and excited I get.

With my temple resting on his chest again, his hand goes from my shoulder blade back up to my hair. I let out a sigh from the contact. It's like a head massage. Content, I relax into his touch. "Why are you so nice to me?"

The movements in my hair halt. "What do you mean?"

"I don't deserve it," I say into his chest.

The head massage starts again, soothing my breathing and calming my thoughts little by little. "Why do you say that?" he asks.

My shoulders shrug the best they can while lying on a muscular body. "Besides the fact that I trusted the wrong person, or led trouble to your doorstep?"

"It wasn't at my doorstep, and you aren't the first to put your trust in the wrong person." With one hand still in my hair, his other hand comes to rest on my arm lying across him.

Something in his words strikes a chord, and I look up at him. "You, too?"

The only response is a grunt as he looks up at the ceiling, with his head resting on his forearm. I wait a few more seconds and he dips his chin to look at me. "Who hasn't?"

"Touché." Laying my head back down, I say, "Okay, so...you're being nice to me because of your own personal experience? Whatever the reason, I'll take it." I sigh into him, feeling grateful.

"Eda, I don't know what you mean. I've just done what anyone else would do," he says, and I look back up at him. His eyes darken before he gestures to the bed. "Well, besides this."

I shake my head at the joke. "There's no way you think that anyone else would do what you've done, or treat me this way."

A blank stare meets me in return. There's clear confusion written all over his face, which is baffling to me. It makes me feel like I need to explain further, to get him to understand why this isn't what just anyone would do.

"Besides maybe my dad, I don't know a single man who would invite me inside their home after realizing I led a stalker to them, take care of me and my dog, and then sleep on the floor just so I could feel safe. It's far more than most people would do, and it's definitely more than just being nice. You're incredible." How is he not understanding that?

He brings my fingers to his lips and kisses them. "It sounds like you keep the company of boys, not men."

A full-on belly laugh takes over me. "You might be right about that. I certainly know how to pick them." I grimace as the truth sets in.

"There isn't a single man I know who wouldn't have done the same for you," his voice is low and sincere. "Well, maybe not *everything*. Some things are for just you and me." He winks, and I laugh, my smile spreading across my face.

I lean in and give him a peck on the lips before falling back onto him. "Well then, I guess I need to meet more of the men you keep company with," I tease.

He stiffens underneath me, while his hand in my hair tightens slightly. It doesn't hurt. Actually, I kind of like the tension there.

Confused, I turn my head on his chest to glance up at him. My breath catches at the look in his eyes.

"Or not." This time, his voice is low, stern. He glances back up at the ceiling.

"What?" I huff a laugh. "Why not?"

Those hazel eyes meet mine again as he dips his chin, holding my stare. "Because I know them, *well*, and I wouldn't be able to handle it if any of them so much as looked at you in front of me."

My heartbeat falters. When it steadies again, butterflies flit in my stomach. A jealous Alaric is kind of hot.

Clearing my throat, I joke, "Don't go putting your hands on other men for me."

"No promises," he grumbles. "If they touch you, then all bets are off."

Not wanting this moment to end, I hold a little tighter onto the man who makes me feel safe and special.

"Yeah, this is a first for me. I've never cooked with water chestnuts before," Alaric says as he drains a can of them.

"Really? I've lost count of how many times I've done so." I grin. "Do you enjoy experimenting with new ingredients? I try to cook with at least one new-to-me ingredient each year."

"I like that goal." He smiles at me as he shakes the can one last time over the sink and hands it to me. "I guess this would be my new ingredient this year."

Smiling, I take the can from him, empty the water chestnuts out onto a cutting board, and begin cutting them in half.

He steps away to drain the chopped carrots and celery that were boiling on the stove. I glance over my shoulder when I hear his voice again.

"I wouldn't say I don't enjoy cooking with new ingredients, but rather that I don't necessarily make it a goal to seek out recipes with different ingredients. I tend to stick to tried-and-true recipes," he says, placing the now drained vegetables in a bowl before moving toward the stove to stir the chicken cooking there.

I laugh. "Now that, I totally understand."

We've been home from grabbing groceries for a little over an hour now, and as the time passes, I get more and more nervous about telling my aunt and uncle what happened in Asheville. I think Alaric can sense my nerves—they're probably clear as day on my face—and he's been trying his best to keep my mind off it.

When we first started prepping dinner together, he tried to convince me to wear nothing but one of his shirts again. It was a tempting offer, but I didn't want to risk our appetizer happening right before they arrived. One person interrupting us was one too many for me.

Grocery shopping with Alaric had no business feeling as easy and enjoyable as it did. Typically, I just order groceries to be delivered to my house because, between grabbing more than I need or dealing with people everywhere, I can't stand it. It's either overwhelming or boring. But with him by my side, it didn't feel like such a mundane task.

I have to admit, I was a little scared to go out at the risk of running into Brad again—and potentially closer to home this time instead of an hour away. However, Alaric stood by me through it all, his presence easing my anxiety.

Before we left the house this morning, he walked me to the guesthouse to grab some more clothes, the vitamins for Elessar, and all my work stuff. Now that he knows what I'm writing, I didn't feel as embarrassed as I thought I would about him being around my handwritten notes I left out on the kitchen table. Although, he's absolutely not allowed to read anything. At least not yet.

After showering back at Alaric's, I chose my new turmeric-colored, oversized turtleneck, fleece-lined leggings, and knee-high boots for our trip out. Something that's cute and comfortable for the cold weather, while also not being too hot underneath my new coat. The one I'm trying and failing to tie new memories to instead of remembering what happened in Asheville.

I might be crazy, but I feel good when I look good. It's a mental trick. Plus, I like the way Alaric looks at me in this outfit. I didn't miss the look he gave me when he helped me out of his truck in the grocery store parking lot. It isn't as comfortable as wearing nothing but his shirt, but these leggings do look good on me.

Every time we walked by a man in the store, I felt myself instinctively shrink a little closer to Alaric. And each time I looked over my shoulder—feeling the need to observe everything around me—he'd squeeze my hand, reminding me that I wasn't alone.

It also didn't escape me how aware he was of our surroundings. He pulled me in close to his side when someone almost bumped into me with their cart, which I hadn't even noticed at first. His military background clearly taught him how to be observant and prepared, or maybe it's a result of the close call with Brad. Whatever the reason, I'm grateful for it, and for him.

I'm also grateful for the ice cream parlor in town he introduced me to on our way home, as promised. It was some damn good ice cream.

Lost in though, time moves quickly while we cook. Before I know it, I'm pouring the sauce into the wok so it can simmer and then thicken.

"I can watch this if you'd like to get ready." Alaric offers his hand, palm facing up, to take the wooden spoon from me.

If I thought that going out and getting groceries with Alaric felt natural, it was nothing compared to cooking with him. Just like that first night when he helped me with dinner at the guesthouse, we seem to move like an old married couple. He's the perfect sous-chef.

With a kiss on his cheek to seal the deal, I accept the offer.

As I walk toward the bedroom door, I feel his eyes on me. The sensation has me unashamedly swinging my hips just a smidge more for him.

A low, mumbled, "Fuck me," has me stifling a laugh just as a slight breeze from two wagging tails passes me down the hall. It makes my heart happy that Elessar and Blanche get along so well.

Stepping into Alaric's bedroom, I pause in the doorway and take in the bed we slept in. If it wasn't for the absolute hell we went through two days ago, I would think this was all a dream. Although, it still could be.

I sure hope not.

I walk over to my suitcases in the corner near the closet and grab a fitted turtleneck sweater that tailors more to my body shape, a pair of skinny jeans, and the fuzziest socks I own. Grabbing my makeup bag, I head to the bedroom's connected bathroom to finish getting ready.

Alaric suggested I unpack my clothes and put them away in the empty spaces of his closet to feel more at home here, but that feels like it would be intruding a little too much. He could kick me out at any moment, and I wouldn't blame him. He's given me no reason to think he would, but it could happen. Given my track record, it wouldn't be that surprising if he did. So, on the off chance that he does, I'd rather have everything packed and ready to go.

Once dressed—complete with a full face of makeup and freshly curled hair—I follow the dogs out of the bedroom. The smell of dinner cooking makes my stomach growl, but I bypass the kitchen to the living room couch and sit to slide on my boots before they arrive. Looking down at my watch, I realize it should be any minute now.

I wipe my sweaty palms against my jeans as the nerves building in my stomach start to make me feel nauseous. I love my aunt and uncle, but I'm suddenly not sure if this was a good idea. I don't think I'm ready to do this.

Yes, I need to tell them. They deserve to know—all of my family does—but I also don't want to talk about it. Once they know, I'll have to tell everyone: my parents, my sisters, and Rhiannon. Then, everyone else would soon know after that: my other aunts, cousins, and grandparents, who I'm not even close to. My personal business would be out there, and I'd be getting call after call about it. There would be no more ignoring what happened.

Still, my immediate family deserves to know. Especially since they've been targeted by him in the past.

"You okay?" Alaric asks from in the kitchen.

Shaking my hands out, I clear my throat. "Yeah, fine. I guess. It'll be fine."

He walks over to me and pulls me into a hug before kissing the top of my head. I love it when he does that. It's almost as good as his forehead kisses.

"It will be. From what you've said, they love you, and they're just going to want to make sure you're safe and okay," he says, with his cheek resting on the top of my head.

I nod into his chest and take in his calming scent, relaxing a smidge at the smell and feel of him. He's right, but that doesn't make it any easier.

My whole body freezes when the dogs start barking.

Alaric's hands rub my back before he says, "They're here."

Chapter 23

ALARIC

Eda's aunt is almost the spitting image of her, except for the fact that Bellamy is a little older, taller, and has shorter hair. Still, it's obvious they're related. The same shade of red hair; the same blue eyes; freckles in almost the same patterns along both of their cheeks and noses. Even her hugs are as welcoming as Eda's, and her smile just as warm.

The only things that are different are their build, noses, and smiles. Whereas Eda is short, Bellamy is taller—almost as tall as Sawyer. Her aunt also loves Blanche, and Elessar definitely adores Bellamy. He actually got a little jealous earlier when she was petting Blanche instead of him, knocking her hand off Blanche's head to place himself in the way of her affection. At the time, Bellamy laughed and proved to him that she has two hands to give love.

Eda's uncle, Ben, is friendly and doesn't seem to be short of dad jokes. His salt and pepper hair is cropped short, and he has brown eyes that seem to be mostly focused on his wife. Still, I can tell he adores his niece, too.

Just from this one night, I can tell that Eda's close to her family, and I feel lucky to get a glimpse into their relationship. It also explains why she seemed sad when I asked her before if she was close to them. She was nervous all day about telling them what happened, but I'm glad to see her more relaxed and actually enjoying herself now that they're here.

Dinner went well. We ate at the small, wood dining table that really only gets used when my family comes over. The stir fry was just as good the second time around. There were seconds—and maybe even thirds on my plate—but we made sure to leave some to package up for her aunt and uncle to take home.

Once we all had our fill, we moved to the living room. Her aunt opted for a mug of hot apple cider, while her uncle requested a cup of black coffee. Eda and I are both sipping on hot chocolate—a drink that officially makes me think of her every time I make it.

Conversation has been easy so far, but there's definitely an elephant in the room. One I wouldn't dare to bring up unless Eda's ready to broach the subject.

"So, Alaric, is it typical for you to be so close to your rental tenants?" Ben asks. One eyebrow is raised, as if he's alluding to something. Whether that is to how close his niece and I are sitting on the couch, or how close we seem in general, I don't know. He's observant, though.

The question was bound to come up. It was only a matter of *when*.

I glance at Eda for direction. If she's ready, we could take this moment to talk about what happened. But if she isn't, I'll simply spin the tale, while still being somewhat truthful with how I feel about Eda.

Clearing her throat, Eda's grip on her mug tightens. "Well, something happened that brought us closer together." Her voice is shaky.

"Oh?" Ben looks from me to her, not picking up on his niece's change in body language. "Would your dad approve?" He attempts to tease. When Eda tenses, her uncle puts up his hand and shakes his head with vigor. "I'm kidding, Edara. Please, for the love of God, don't answer that," he says, with a nervous laugh.

I scoot a little closer to Eda and meet her gaze, hoping she feels my support in this moment.

With a sigh, she looks back at her uncle and says, "Actually, Uncle Ben, I *should* answer." With both hands on the mug, she rests it on her lap and looks down at it. "Yes, Dad would approve, because Ric helped me two days ago after Brad found us." Bellamy's lips part in shock and Ben's eyes narrow. "He...left a message for us."

The tension in the air grows.

Her aunt breaks the silence. "What do you mean, sweetie?" She has a gentle voice, but fear and concern are evident in her tone.

Eda's hands tremble, making the hot chocolate shake in her mug, nearly spilling it. I reach for her mug, offering to move it. When she hands it over, I set it on the end table next to me. Shifting back to look at her, I place my hand over hers on her lap. Without looking at me, she takes a deep breath and nods.

"Your niece came here to escape Brad, but he found her," I say, before going into more detail of what happened at the store in Asheville. My teeth grind at the memory, but I keep myself from tensing too much so as not to accidentally squeeze Eda's hand.

Bellamy gasps as her hand flies to her mouth. She sits silent for a moment before rushing to her niece's side on the couch, pulling Eda into a crushing hug. "Oh, honey! Are you okay?"

Eda quietly reassures her aunt, who is still holding her.

When I look up, I see her uncle's jaw is tense and his knuckles are white around his mug. "Is he still breathing?" Ben asks, and I instantly like him even more.

"Unfortunately, yes." I grimace. "But my best friend's a detective here in town, and he's on it. If anyone can find him, it's Gavin. Eda's also issued a protective order against him."

Ben dips his chin, his eyes looking down on me. "Thanks for helping her."

I nod and scoot an inch away from Eda and her aunt, giving them some space. Bellamy's chin rests on Eda's shoulder before they pull away from each other. Relaxing next to me, Eda opens her watery blue eyes, which land on me. The sight of her breaking down rips into my chest, but I don't react because she needs the comfort of her family in this moment. She deserves to feel their support and love.

"Have you told your mom yet?" Bellamy asks, her voice cracking a little.

Eda shakes her head. "Not yet. I can't." Tears pass through her lash lines this time. "I don't want to worry them."

There's an overwhelming need to be close to her, to comfort her. I settle for placing my hand on her thigh. She reaches out, grabs my hand, and squeezes it, not letting go.

"It's okay, sweetie. You've been through so much. If you want, I can tell them," Bellamy offers. "I can't promise they won't still call you, or won't want to come visit, but Liliya and Will would want to know. They should know," she says, glancing over at her husband before facing Eda again. "If you can't do it, I can try for you."

Eda nods and wipes her eyes. "Thank you," her voice is quiet, "but I don't know. I'll try to answer if they call, but I just don't want to talk about it. I don't even want to think about it anymore. I know that's not realistic, especially since he's still out there, but I just...can't."

"I understand." Her aunt smoothes down her hair. "If you'll let me, I'll help."

"Thank you, Aunt Bella," Eda says with a small smile.

"Don't mention it, sweetie," her aunt says, while rubbing her back. "I'm just so sorry this is happening to you."

With a blank stare, Eda whispers, "Me too. "

"Eda," Ben's voice grips my attention. It's the tone of a dad; even though he's her uncle, he's clearly a dad first. His tone forces Eda to snap her gaze to him. "They're going to find him, and when they do, you'll find some peace. You won't ever have to deal with him again."

Eda nods absentmindedly in response, seemingly unconvinced. I know how little faith she holds in cops right now, being that they didn't help her with one of their own when she needed it most before.

There will come a day when she never has to see Brad or worry about him again. I'll do whatever I can to make sure that day comes soon.

Chapter 24

EDARA

Dinner last night went so much better than I ever could have expected it would. Alaric's presence helped make me feel brave while I talked to my aunt and uncle, and I was thankful when my aunt offered to tell my parents everything for me.

After waking up this morning, I decided that I needed to just rip the Band-Aid off and do it myself. It does mean that I spent all of this morning on the phone—between calls with my parents, sisters, and Rhiannon. I had to talk about it over and over again in detail, and then reassure them all that I was safe and sound.

I'm finally taking a break and decompressing from all the talking and emotions. Admittedly, I put it off because I knew it was going to be tough, but it took more out of me than I even expected.

My sisters and Rhiannon are planning to come up this weekend to see for themselves that I'm okay. I told them it wasn't necessary, but they're still insisting. Alaric says they'll be safe in the guesthouse, where he plans to install more security cameras this afternoon. Butterflies fluttered in my stomach the moment

I realized that him offering them the guesthouse means he wants me to stay here in the main house with him.

I find myself smiling again at the thought as I sit in his living room.

Things with him have been nice. Much better than nice, actually. Since staying with him, I've felt comfortable. Safe. Important. He makes me feel things I haven't felt in a long time, if ever.

While I enjoyed lounging in his clothes that first day, I'm happy to have my clothes again. I'm curled up on the sofa in my new sage green, faux fur-lined leggings; white, fuzzy socks that are actually mine this time; and a cream-colored turtleneck sweater.

A mug filled to the brim with a London fog is cradled in my hands, close to my chest, as I absorb its warmth. Steam rises, caressing my cheeks. It's like a facial, but without the high price tag or relaxing spa—both a pro and a con.

A major pro to being here is the company a spa can't provide: the comfort of a dog.

The warmth from our two dogs—with one at each of my sides—also helps against the cold. With one hand leaving the heat of the mug, I weave it through Elessar's soft fur, rubbing along his back. His tail begins to lazily thump on the couch, causing Blanche's to join in out of excitement.

After a few seconds, I switch my mug into my other hand and do the same to Blanche on my left side. Her equally soft fur wraps around my fingers. Before meeting Blanche, I was convinced that no dog's fur could ever be as soft as Elessar's, but she proved me wrong. They're both the softest, most perfect personal heated blankets a girl could ask for.

Needing to get out of my own head for a bit after the seemingly endless phone calls, I offered to take over Blanche's daily training session this morning. I watched Alaric train her before we went grocery shopping yesterday, and I felt confident in helping out. It's also good to brush up on Elessar's training every once in a while.

It was an interesting task having one dog speak English and the other French, but after walking in on us doing a "sit and stay," Alaric told me I should give French a go with Blanche.

We started with the basics: *assis* (sit down); *coucher* (lay down); and *reste* (stay). She's a smart girl and picked them up quickly. I might tackle some more tomorrow after reinforcing what she learned today.

The rhythmic sound of an axe splitting wood has me looking up from the dogs and out the window. Alaric didn't leave today. Actually, he refused to for the third day in a row. No, he's outside chopping wood. Well, sort of. Sometimes he uses his ax, and other times he pries pieces open with his bare hands. Which is *hot as hell*. How can one man be so sexy, strong, and single at the same time?

Single. That word makes me pause. Is he still single if he wants me to stay with him? Or does it mean nothing and is just because my sisters will be here this weekend, occupying the guesthouse?

Yes, of course, he's still single. So am I.

The thought makes my mind briefly go to that day in the outdoor store... Maybe I deserve to be single forever for the trouble I've caused by bringing Brad into my life and the lives of those I care about. Maybe I deserve to be alone. Maybe I should be. It would keep everyone else safer.

No. That is exactly what he wants—to isolate me. I've read about it when researching stalking tactics, and Gavin confirmed as much when we talked after the incident. I won't give Brad the satisfaction of winning.

Forcing away the thoughts of Brad, I lift my chin and look out the window again. It's perfect timing because there's no ax in sight, as he uses his bare hands to pry open a log. A loud *crack* echoes through the window and into the otherwise silent living room from the white oak splitting into two pieces.

How is that even physically possible for a human to do?

Since he's been staying home with me and hasn't been going to the gym, he said he needed to blow off some steam, but didn't want to be too far away. I don't mind, especially because it means I have a great view out the window while I cuddle with the dogs on the couch.

In addition to chopping firewood for himself and his family, he told me that some of the wood goes to local carpenters, since white oak makes for beautiful, solid furniture. There are plenty of bundles already stored away in his shed, but I understand why he needs this. Physical exercise is his way of coping with his frustration and anger over what happened.

Mine is reading and writing. I tried to write earlier after the phone calls, but my happy, carefree manuscript is suddenly turning not so light and airy with the week's events. I had to stop before I started writing a thriller rather than a romance with a happily ever after.

It won't always be like this. There's at least some comfort in that knowledge. However, knowing that he's been watching me here means it will take awhile for me not to feel on edge again, which is nowhere near as comforting.

Not yet being able to shake this will undoubtedly eat into the little time I have left to meet my deadline, but at least I'm deep enough into the manuscript after only a few weeks of writing here. That's promising, and it gives me a bit of a cushion of time to heal. When the time is right, I'll get back into it. Forcing creativity isn't the answer.

As for forcing myself to do things... I grab the mug with both hands again as thoughts come to mind of working out with Ric tonight. We are still planning to go to the gym so that he can teach me some self-defense moves.

Working out is probably my least favorite thing to do. However, if it means I can protect myself if need be, then the sweat and hyperventilation will be worth it. Right?

Right.

I rub my temple with my right hand, which is warm from the mug. I still can't believe what happened.

While talking to Rhiannon this morning, she offered to break up with my agent for me after she violated my trust and privacy. While it's tempting, this is something I need to do on my own. Carol's number is already blocked, so she can never contact me again, but I want to get my lawyer's advice before officially sending the written termination letter.

If I don't find a way to release this stress, I'll give myself a headache here soon.

Sighing, I reach for my e-reader and pull up the romantic fantasy book I started the other night. With one hand on my London fog and the other on my e-reader, I sit nestled in between two sweet dogs. The loud cracking sounds of wood being chopped fill the air, but they're soon drowned out as I get lost in my book.

He's shirtless. That's my first thought. Actually, the *only* thought that consumes my brain, until I start to get worn out and the sounds of our breaths fill the space. Granted, my breathing is louder, since I'm more winded than he is at this point.

Still, I find some satisfaction in knowing Alaric's not so superhuman that he doesn't need to breathe while working out. Specifically, a sense of satisfaction in knowing that I'm the reason for his heavy breathing.

My skin tingles and heats up whenever he touches me, despite it literally being a faux attack so I can practice defending myself. That doesn't matter though; it's still him.

Glee overcomes me and a smile appears on my face each time I successfully copy his demonstrations—even if it's with poor execution. The butterflies in my stomach go wild whenever he tells me I'm doing well, praising me for picking up what he's teaching. Although, I think it's more a testament to his teaching than my physical capability.

The arms of my long sleeve workout top are rolled up my forearms halfway through the lesson. I have half a mind to take it off and practice with him in just my sports bra, but I don't want to risk anyone else seeing me like that.

It's just us here, but there's no telling if someone will show up. Alaric released everyone home for the night and locked up so that it would just be the two of us for the lesson, but my paranoia isn't going to allow me to take the chance. Especially not after Sawyer walked in on us before. Yeah, I don't think I'll ever let that one go…

All thoughts about the long sleeves and getting caught go out the window when it happens. The sexy man with muscles upon muscles is somehow pinned to the mat under me, exactly where I want him. Pride fills me as I look down at my thighs on either side of his hips, locking him in place.

I did it. I really did it!

An unbelieving breath slips through my lips and I stare into his hazel eyes twinkling with amusement. A girl could get lost in them.

The smile he flashes kills me, and my cheeks grow hot at the effect he has on me. "That's my girl," he says, with speech slightly difficult now that my knees are digging into the sides of his ribs.

Oh, hell. More praise. And he said, *my girl*. It's not the first time he has called me *his* girl, but it is the first time he's said it when his head isn't between my legs. At the time, his hazels eyes had been hooded and looking up at me as he—

Nope. Focus, Eda.

Too late. The images are forever ingrained in my mind. My eyes flutter, my head suddenly feels light, and the fanny flutters are back in full force.

Maybe I *should* take my shirt off. Do I really care if someone sees? If he is under me and between my legs like this, I doubt I'll be thinking about anyone else, anyway. No, I'd be focused on him and only him.

He takes advantage of my reaction to his words by twisting and pinning me, my back now against the mat.

"Oh!" Surprise and excitement are laced in that one word. Thinking I finally won, I wasn't expecting him to get me back, nor was I expecting how much I like having him on top of me in public. Granted, we are alone, but it is technically a public place, and it never gets old having him above me like this.

Who am I kidding? Of course, I like it. What isn't to like about this sexy man touching me?

"You did really well." He smiles. "For someone who can't stand working out, you're a quick learner."

The tops of my cheeks heat up from the compliment, and I look away. My eyes catch on a fluffy tail, and I smile.

Since no one else is here, we brought the dogs. I'm also thankful for that; I can't imagine leaving Elessar right now after finding out that the mountains aren't exactly Brad-free. They are currently curled up next to each other a few feet away from us.

Alaric gets up and reaches his hand out to me, helping me to my feet. I successfully stand on wobbly legs, taking a deep breath in.

"I think that's good for tonight." Walking over to where our water bottles and towels are, he hands me one before asking, "How do you feel?"

"Thank you," I say, taking the bottle. "And yeah, I'd say my legs are quitting on me." I laugh as my thighs visibly shake. "But I do feel good about the progress." I smile at him before taking a sip of water.

"You should be proud," he says, and I return his smile.

Putting the cold bottle to my lips again, I take the opportunity to marvel at the man before me. Those back muscles inspired a whole character in my book, and seeing him shirtless never gets old. Who knew that back muscles would do it for me? Hell, anything and everything about Alaric does it for me.

That beard... I've always liked a little facial hair on a man, but I had no idea how much I'd like one on a lover. Now, I know exactly how it feels against my palm, or in between my legs. And I know exactly how that bare skin feels under the caress of my hands when he's on top of me, under me, next to me...

As if he can read my thoughts, he turns and catches my gaze over the rim of his own water bottle. A smirk tugs at the corners of his lips as he lowers it. Instead of shying away from his gaze, I smile back. That smirk turns into a full-fledged grin.

He looks down at me and a finger grazes my cheek. My eyelashes flutter as I look up at him. Given the unmistakable look of desire in his eyes, I'm not expecting the question he asks. "How about some ice cream to celebrate on the drive home?"

"From Stone-cold Sweets?" I ask, my smile widening. I quickly grab my jacket and Elessar's leash from the wooden bench. Hearing the sound of the leash hardware clinking, the dogs immediately jump up from their spots on the floor.

Alaric gathers his own bag and Blanche's leash in one hand. "The one and only."

I reach out for his free hand, lacing my fingers with his, and eagerly pull him toward the door. "Let's do it."

Chapter 25

EDARA

My sisters are here. All three of them: Cressida, who is the oldest; Aurelia, who is the youngest, and Rhiannon, who is only five months older than me. Technically, she isn't my biological sister, but we still grew up together like sisters. Even Cressida and Aurelia think of Rhiannon as the sister they never wanted, but now can't picture themselves living without.

Poor Alaric. His house hasn't been quiet for hours now, not since they arrived this morning. That sweet, sexy man doesn't seem to care though. He's been giving us space, which I appreciate. It's good to have it be just us girls and feel somewhat normal. Then again, with Brad still out there, it helps knowing that Alaric isn't ever too far away.

Rhiannon keeps commenting on how cold it is here. Her shoulder-length, purple hair is curled and bounces slightly with each shiver that takes over her body. I tried to remind her we are in the mountains—where it is cold—to which she responded by flipping me off. How I've missed her.

In terms of weather difference, Steaming Stone's late-October weather feels like Raleigh's mid-winter weather in January. So, to us, it's way past freezing here.

Really, Aurelia's the only one who allowed to complain more than once because she has Raynaud's Disease, which means that the cold weather affects her circulation. But even I have to admit that it's a little chilly. Although, not as much as I once found it. To my surprise, it appears I'm growing used to the weather. Or maybe it's just because I'm finally dressing properly for it.

Like me, my sisters didn't pack properly for their impromptu trip. So, after they got here, I offered them each some thick sweaters, and Alaric offered extra coats of his. Cressida politely turned them down—opting for a cozy, faux fur blanket instead—while Rhiannon and Aurelia accepted. They're also bundling up with mugs of hot apple cider and some of the faux fur throws around the living room.

In their defense, the leather sofas don't help matters. Why have leather in the mountains, when the fabric will just absorb the cold? I don't understand that. Based on photos of the other rental listings I saw when I was first searching for a place to stay, the material is quite common for mountain cabins.

Looking around, I imagine how cozy a cream-colored sectional would feel in the space. Along with velvet recliners to replace the current leather ones. Yes, it would warm up the space, in more ways than one.

Knowing we're cold, Alaric comes in every once in a while to stoke the fire for us. His presence always grabs our attention while we lounge in his living room. My sisters' reactions are amusing, but I also find myself admiring the hunk of a man working to keep us warm. Despite being fully clothed, I can practically see the muscles in his back rippling with the movements as he tends to the fire.

Each time he finishes, he always smiles and casually winks at me before walking away. But just me. Only ever me. While it doesn't come off as rude—because he isn't exactly ignoring my sisters—it does something to me that he thinks I'm worthy of his attention. It surprises me to find that a little voice in my mind agrees that, yes, I am indeed worthy of his attention and affection. That I am worthy...

And maybe I am?

A tear pricks in my left eye at the thought, but I blink it away and avoid my sisters' gazes. I rub my hand up my sweater and toy with the high neck, unfurling and re-furling the edge of the turtleneck.

The sound of footsteps behind me pulls me from my thoughts.

"I'm going to let the dogs out really quick, and then I have an errand to run," Alaric says.

At the sound of his voice, I turn my head and see he's standing in front of the coat closet, putting his jacket on.

Slipping his arms into the sleeves of his jacket, he asks, "Are you going to be okay here? Do you have everything you need?"

Rhiannon speaks up before anyone else can. "We're fine. She'll be safe with us."

For a moment, Rhiannon and Alaric meet each other's gazes, and a silent conversation passes between them. It looks very much like he's contemplating her ability to protect me, while her stubbornness and conviction shine clear on her face. She's protective of her family—of her people—and I feel lucky to be considered one of them.

After a solid stare down, Alaric finally nods his head, seemingly satisfied that Rhiannon will be able to handle business if needed. As if he isn't helping me learn how to do that for myself. We've had two lessons this week, and I'm improving...I think. At the very least, I can only get better from here.

Fortunately, I found the interaction between my best friend and my...whatever Ric is to me—my *woodsman*, I suppose—sweet.

Walking over to me, he bends over the back of the leather couch and kisses the top of my head. Butterflies flutter in my stomach and my eyes briefly close from the tender act.

"I'll be back, Little Red," he whispers into my ear.

Goosebumps form along my skin from the gentle caress of his voice and the endearing nickname.

Looking up at him, I smile. "Don't be long, okay?" I say for only him to hear.

With a small smile, he whispers, "I couldn't stay away if I wanted to. I mean, I do live here." He winks at me.

Okay, he's got me there.

"If I let them out with me, would you be willing to let them in?"

"Sure. I can do that." I nod. I'm still not super comfortable being out in the open alone. So, I appreciate him for offering a solution that both benefits the dogs and helps me feel comfortable.

"All right, you two lovebirds. You're going to make me sick." Rhiannon groans. Her body shivers again, and she raises her blanket higher, nearly covering her entire neck.

"What do you mean? I think it's sweet!" Aurelia says, clapping her hands together over her heart. If it was possible for someone to embody the heart-eyes emoji, it would be my little sister at this moment.

Alaric's chuckle is cut off as he closes the front door behind him and the dogs. It's hard not to watch him and the dogs in the yard without me. When I'm not watching Elessar's movements to make sure he's safe, my eyes are on the man who has been taking care of both me and my dog.

That fact makes it even harder to watch as he waves at me through the window, gets in his truck, and pulls out of the driveway, inching farther away from the house. Farther away from me.

Looking away from the window, I get up and let the dogs inside. I linger in the doorway for a moment, watching the taillights of his truck disappear through the trees lining the long driveway. My anxiety rises to alarming levels for the first time since staying in the main house with him. If it wasn't obvious to me before how safe he makes me feel, I certainly know it now.

But this is okay. I'll be okay.

It helps that it's still light outside; that the dogs are inside now and will alert us to anything suspicious outside; and that my sisters are here with me. Still, I hope he doesn't stay out too late. It's fall, which means it gets dark before dinnertime. And it's impossible to know what lurks in the dark...

I certainly didn't until Asheville.

"So, tell us everything. Don't leave any single juicy detail out," Cressida says, pulling my gaze away from the spot where Alaric's truck disappeared minutes ago.

When I stare at my sister with wide eyes, Cressida's mouth hangs open for half a second before she backtracks. "I meant about Alaric. Your lumberjack. You two together. Not...the other thing. I'm sorry. You don't have to talk about that."

My older sister's sitting on the floor, opting for the rug instead of the leather sofa. Smart woman. With her blonde hair in her signature chignon, she's bundled up with two blankets and her steaming hot mug she just reheated for the third time.

I'm the odd one out, with my fiery red hair, while Cressida and Aurelia were born with the same light blonde hair as our mother. All three of us have blue eyes, but Aurelia's are more of a navy like our mom's, while mine and Cressida's share the same light blue color as our dad's eyes. Beyond that, I always have looked more like my aunt than I did my parents or sisters. Meanwhile, my cousin Meriam—my aunt Bellamy's daughter—looks like she could be Aurelia's twin. Genetics are strange.

With a chuckle, I close the door and lock it. "He's not actually a lumberjack. He just chops wood." I settle back into the cold sofa and pull a blanket over me.

"Eda, that's a lumberjack," Rhiannon says, flatly, before taking a sip of her cider. Her purple hair looks lighter than normal from the firelight.

Shaking my head, I laugh into my mug of plum cider. I bought out nearly the entire stock of ready-to-purchase plum cider the last time I went to The Steaming Cup.

"Okay, you heard Essie. Spill," Aurelia chimes in, agreeing with our older sister. The big, blue eyes of my hopeless romantic sister are full of excitement.

Blowing on my mug that's hot but not steaming anymore, I sit there for a second before responding, "There's really not much to tell. He helped me that day, and I've been staying in his home ever since."

"Liar, liar, pants on fire," Cressida says, as she leans over from her spot on the floor and pokes my knee. "You had sex. I can tell."

Coughing, I choke on the rather hot cider. What a poor time to misjudge the temperature of it, because it's most definitely burning my throat.

"Oh my! You did! You totally did!" Aurelia shrieks, looking way too excited. When did my little sister become someone I talk to about sex? Yes, she's technically old enough, since she's finishing up her grad school program, but that's not the point. When did the little girl who once followed me around like a lost puppy become an adult?

Rhiannon grins. "All right, Lauklans. It looks like we need something a little stronger to pry the truth out of her." She stands up and wraps the faux fur throw around herself like a cape. "Eda, where's the wine?"

"Rhia, it's not even noon." I laugh.

"So? It's five o'clock somewhere." Rhiannon shrugs as she walks to the kitchen. "With what you've been put through, I'd say a glass of wine—or a whole ass bottle each—is in order."

"I don't know where the wine is," I say over my shoulder.

"No matter," she says back. "I'll find it."

Turning in my spot, I look over at her. "Rhia, are you using this as an excuse to snoop?"

Her upper body is already practically hidden in the pantry, and her purple streaks are barely visible from behind with how far she's in it. "No idea what you mean," comes her muffled reply.

Rolling my eyes, I face Cressida and Aurelia again. Cressida's gaze softens, and I fight the tears in my eyes at the sight of my sisters worrying about me.

"How are you really?" Cressida asks.

A big sigh comes out. "I'm fine. At least, I will be. I feel safe here, with Ric. Not safe alone yet, but I do with him. It's helping. *He's* helping," I ramble, but I don't care. If there's anyone I can be honest with, it's the three of them. "He's even teaching me some self-defense moves at his gym."

"You? In the gym?" Cressida's eyebrows raise.

"Yeah, I never thought I'd say that." I laugh. "But it's fun training with him, and it helps me feel a little better knowing I could...I don't know, hold my own? I don't really know how to explain it, but I do think it's important training, and yeah, he's been helping me a lot." Unsure of how much I want to share about Ric and me, I start furling and unfurling the fabric of my turtleneck again to give me time to think.

"I'm glad you have him. What luck that it was his rental you booked." Cressida's head shakes.

"And don't worry," Rhiamnon says from the kitchen. "We'll stay here with you until he gets back. And even after." There's a grin on her face as she holds up a bottle of wine. "Found it."

Before I know it, a much too full glass of wine is in my face, and I gladly accept it.

Smiling, I look each one of them in the eyes. "Thanks, guys. You have no idea how nice it is to have you all here. I... Thanks for making the drive up here. You didn't need to, but it really means a lot." I missed them all, and having them here makes things feel a bit more normal. As if nothing has happened.

As if I have nothing or no one to fear.

"Always," Aurelia says, smiling. Since alcohol doesn't mix well with her medication, she topped off her mug with some plum cider instead. The rest of us are enjoying some of Alaric's wine, which I fully intend on restocking for him.

With a big sigh, I sit back with my wine and cider in each hand, and allow myself to relax and cherish this moment with my sisters. The sisters Brad harassed after he started stalking me. The sisters who drove three hours to see and comfort me after he found me.

Brad has taken enough of my joy and moments of my life that I'll never get back. He isn't going to take anymore from me. Not now, not ever again.

So, I embrace the warmth from the cider and the way the wine loosens my mind, banishing my anxiety with each sip. I'm going to enjoy this moment with them, while looking forward to the day my life is Brad-free.

Chapter 26

Edara

After waking up this morning, Alaric looked down at me in his arms and said that today is the day we're finally going on that ice cream date. The one where he promised to take me to one of his favorite spots, and he's making good on that promise.

We just picked up our ice cream from Stone-cold Sweets, and I'm trying to keep the nosy dogs from smelling the bag. A difficult task with them both leaning over from their spots in the backseat of the truck.

The employee working the drive-thru saw the dogs in the back through the driver's window and gave us two small cups with a little whipped topping in them for the dogs. It's something the employees at Stone-cold have done the few times we've gone with the dogs, and it's undoubtedly why they are so excited.

To ward them off, I make them both sit as best as they can on the leather backseat, and give them their cups one at a time. When a blob of whipped topping falls out of Blanche's cup and onto the leather interior, I'm feeling more in favor of the leather for its easy clean-up, as opposed to fabric seats. It definitely helps that Alaric's truck has heated seats. Otherwise, I might not be able to survive in here. The icy material even seeps through my fleece-lined leggings.

As we drive, the main roads of downtown turn into some windy, narrow backroads, which have me holding onto the "Oh, shit" handles each time a car pops up around the bend. Thankfully, we pass each one of them unscathed.

Nerves settle in when his truck starts to slow and I see the "PRIVATE PROPERTY" sign attached to a chain linked on two cement posts, creating a barrier separate from the rest of the road.

Before I can ask what we're doing, Alaric hops out of the driver's seat—leaving the door open—and starts walking to the front of the truck. I suddenly feel like I need to reapply deodorant or something because of the way I start sweating when he unhooks the chain and it slams into the dirt road with a loud *thud*.

Whose property is this? Are we even allowed to be here?

When he hops back into the car and puts it in drive, clearly planning to drive over the sign and chain, I look at him with my jaw on the floor. "Are you mad?" I ask.

And this man—this beautiful, kind, infuriating man—has the audacity to silently grin in response.

We keep driving, and my eyes are searching everywhere for any clue of where we are or if we're even allowed to be here. Fortunately, I can see clearly because it's still daylight out, with the sunset likely coming within the next hour or so. But I don't know where we are, and there are no buildings or landmarks around for me to recognize.

"Alaric, where are we?" I practically whisper, as if someone might hear us and catch us on their property. It's terrifying when I think about how people in the south carry weapons and don't take kindly to trespassers.

As the car slowly trudges along, the dirt path opens into a grass field.

His hand slides to my thigh and squeezes before he laces his fingers through mine in my lap. "It's okay. This land is owned by the Wülfs," he says, and I slowly look up at him. Before the question can pass my lips, he nods in confirmation. "It's my parents' property. So, we have permission to be here." He gently squeezes my thigh again before letting go to return his hand to the wheel.

A small comfort to know we're not trespassing. I exhale all the anxiety I was holding in and allow myself to admire the land we're driving through.

As my eyes settle forward once more, the breath gets robbed from me at the view before me. We're driving toward a clearing that overlooks a river below. On the other side of the riverbank are beautiful mountains with leaves in every fall shade imaginable. They're not the biggest mountains I've seen in this area, but they're still beautiful and magnificent in their own right.

Suddenly, the truck turns, and the mountain view in the windshield is replaced by a large clearing with dead, dried grass from the season. It feels like it goes on for miles before meeting the forest's edge.

And then, a thought strikes me: if this land is owned by his parents...am I about to meet them? Looking around, I don't see a house here.

Feeling nervous again, I glance over at Alaric. "What are we doing here?"

He sits back in his seat and his eyes look up to the mountain range now visible in the rearview mirror. "Sometimes, I like to park my truck here and sit in the bed to watch the sunset." His gaze flits to mine. "I've been doing it since I was a teen and had my first truck."

He huffs a laugh before looking back at the mirror. "Well, not exactly. It was technically my dad's truck, and I would sneak it out in the evenings after he got home from work. This quickly became my own little sanctuary. A quiet spot to just...be."

Watching him for a moment, I feel a newfound warmth in my chest, and it has nothing to do with the heated seats in his truck. Before I can process what that might be, or what it could mean that he decided to take me here—a place he considers a sanctuary for himself—he looks over at me again.

Smiling, he asks, "Ready?"

Matching his energy, I nod. "Ready."

When I unbuckle, his hand comes to my left thigh again. That smile hasn't left his face, but it falls just a bit, as if he might be a little nervous. Is it because he's taken me to one of his favorite places and isn't sure how I'll react? Or is it something else?

"What?" I ask, looking from his hand to his face.

His fingers rub my thigh before he lets go. Without breaking eye contact, he asks, "Will you wait in the car with the dogs for a moment? I have a surprise."

"I—" A surprise? Wasn't *this* the surprise? The mix of nerves and excitement on his face makes me all the more curious. "Okay," I say, trusting him.

And I have come to trust him with so much.

"Okay," he says excitedly.

I stay in the passenger seat while he grabs the two travel mugs of hot cocoa that were resting in the cup holders to cradle them in one arm.

I stay in the passenger seat when he sticks out his free hand, asking for the bag with our cups of ice cream.

And I continue to stay in the passenger seat when he gets out of the truck, shuts the door, and then heads around to the truck bed.

That doesn't mean I'm not curious. I try my best to see what he's doing from the rearview mirror, but I have no luck because the dogs in the backseat are just as curious. Their long-haired, fluffy tails wag in a frenzy at watching him walk around the truck without them.

At least five minutes pass before he comes to the passenger door and opens it for me. "All right, it's ready for you." He offers his hand to help me climb out of his tall truck, and I happily take it. Not because I need the help, but because I like touching him. Well, and the help is nice. It's quite the drop for my little legs.

The truck door closes behind me as I adjust my coat and take in the rushing water and mountain ranges before me. It's even prettier when there isn't a glass barrier and I can take in nature as it was meant to be admired.

Quite a few leaves have already fallen, but the majority of the trees are still full enough to give us this beautiful view. And what a view it is.

"It's lovely," I say.

He opens the car door beside me, letting the dogs out of the backseat. With tails that never seem to wag when they're around each other, the dogs rush out into the field. Blanche takes off running, clearly familiar with this space, while Elessar takes his time sniffing every blade of grass.

Alaric comes up beside me. His eyes are on the mountains when I look up at him.

"It is, isn't it?" He glances down at me and places his hand on the dip of my low back, guiding me to the bed of the truck, where the liftgate is down. A small gasp escapes me when we round the corner and I see what he was working on.

He's set up an array of blankets and pillows in the bed of the truck, with a small, wooden tray holding our mugs and bag of ice cream. The truck bed is facing the mountains. Considering the time of day—and what he used to love doing here when he was younger—I'm guessing it's so that we'll have the perfect spot to catch the sunset.

"Oh, Ric," I whisper.

His jacket makes a crinkling sound as he shrugs beside me. "It's not much, but I thought it might be nice."

Turning to him, I get up on my tiptoes and kiss the smooth skin just above his beard. I feel his cheekbone move against my lips as he smiles. "It's more than 'nice.' It's perfect."

He leans down and kisses my forehead. "Thank you for coming with me."

Curling my unzipped jacket around me, I take his hand as he helps me climb into the bed of his truck. The cold metal bites at my palms, making me crawl faster to the blankets and pillows he's laid out for us.

As I move toward them, I hear the crunching of leaves under boots behind me. When I turn to settle back into the pillows, I see Alaric reaching down to grab something from the ground on the driver's side of the truck. With ease, he places a ramp on the open liftgate. A swift whistle passes his lips, and Blanche barrels up the ramp and toward me within seconds. I laugh as she smothers me with her kisses and love.

Looking up, I watch Elessar run toward the truck, then dig his back paws into the dried grass, abruptly stopping in his tracks when he sees the ramp. Panting, his brown eyes are wide as they glance from me and Blanche in the truck bed, and then to the ramp blocking his path to us.

I've never taught him how to use one, but Alaric doesn't hesitate. Reaching into his pockets, he grabs treats and sweetly encourages him up the ramp. He's so gentle and patient with my boy, and I'm proud of Elessar for coming as far as he has with Ric.

I tell Blanche to sit next to me, and then reach closer to the ramp. "Come on, little man," I say, encouraging him. "You can do it."

His tail flits from side to side as he lets out a bark. His front paws find their way onto the ramp—claws out, madly gripping the rough surface—but he pauses there.

"That's a good boy!" I say, clapping to hopefully praise him along. "Come on. Just a little more."

Another nervous tail wag, accompanied by a second bark.

"Good job, Eless," Ric says as he lays a trail of treats up the ramp and into the truck bed. He tosses a few to me, which I assume are for Blanche, so that she's not tempted to take the ones laid out on the ramp. I happily give them to her, but save one for when Elessar finally makes his way up.

Elessar stretches his neck of long, silver and black fur to eat the first treat Ric laid out. Slowly, treat by treat, he inches his way up the ramp. All the while, his nails are digging into it for dear life.

But he does it! He's such a brave boy. Scrambling up into the truck bed, he comes barreling for me, and I give him the last treat I held onto just for him.

"Bon chien!" *Good dog!* "That's a good boy, Eless!" I say as he comes up and sits in my lap, panting from the excursion.

Blanche comes over and licks his snout, and I have to shift on the blankets just to keep from getting trampled by them. With catlike reflexes, my hand snatches up our hot cocoa travel mugs on the tray before they can knock them over.

Since they're all over the place in front of me, I have to sit on my knees to try to figure out what scraping noise I'm hearing. Peering over the backs of the two dogs, I see Alaric collapse the ramp and place it off to the side of the truck lift, in case the dogs want to come and go.

"Hey," I say, grabbing the dogs' attention. They both whip their heads toward me, tongues lolling, and I try to not laugh at the sight. Clicking my tongue, I pat the blankets laid out and say, "Coucher" *lay down.*

Without hesitating, Elessar plops down, tongue still out and eyes on me. Still learning the French commands, Blanche glances from me to him, and then finally lays down, following Elessar's lead. Their soft heads and cute faces are just begging to be pet, and I oblige. Why are they so freaking cute?

Now that they've calmed down, I settle back into the bed of pillows behind me. Alaric climbs in, and I'm thankful for the lids on our mugs, or else the hot cocoa would be spilling all over me from the way the truck rocks as he crawls past the dogs and up to me. A joke about him playing Twister to get over the dogs dies on my tongue, because seeing this man come toward me... I suddenly forget we're out in the open and what we're doing here to begin with.

"You comfortable?" he asks, settling in next to me on my right.

I snap out of it. "Yeah, the pillows were a good idea." He smiles at me. "Want your hot cocoa?" I ask, attempting to get my mind on more appropriate things.

"Yeah, just give me one second," he says as he reaches over for the paper bag with our ice cream. In one hand, he takes his travel mug from me—holding it out in front of him—at the same time he gives me my blackberry ice cream with his other hand. I happily take it.

With the travel mug of hot cocoa now tucked between his thighs and his mint chocolate chip ice cream in hand, he's looking so content, I can hardly bear it.

When he glances over at me, warmth spreads through me, down to my core, suddenly making me feel like I no longer need the hot drink.

"Keep looking at me like that, and I'll have to kick the dogs out of the truck," he whispers before slowly taking a bite of ice cream.

My cheeks heat a smidge and I take the opportunity to cool off with my own frozen treat. It's so cold, though, I have to pull out my gloves in my coat pocket just to hold it. However, as I take the first bite, I have to admit that Alaric was right: ice cream in the cold is a combination that somehow just works.

The dogs look so cozy in front of us. I set my ice cream down on the tray again and pull out my phone to take a photo of them together. Then, I snap a few shots of the mountain range and river before us. Something to hold onto this moment forever. The end of November is approaching faster than I'd like, and I have no idea when or if I'll ever make it back here.

The thought hits me like a train. I only have two-and-a-half weeks left on my rental—which I haven't stayed in for almost three weeks now—and roughly 12,000 words left to write in my manuscript before I send it off to my new agent, Fay, whom I'm really liking. An author friend of mine who's local to Wilmington—Noreen Fisk—recommended her to me, and I'm so glad she did.

But soon, I'll meet my word count, finish my draft, the trip will come to an end, and I'll have to return to Raleigh. Where Brad will likely be waiting for me.

There has been no word of him since he left the roses on Alaric's truck in Asheville nearly three weeks ago. No word, no sighting. Just the frustrating game of waiting to see what he'll do next. If he'll risk doing anything more after the police got involved in Asheville and the protective order went through.

"What's on your mind?" Alaric's voice cuts through my head.

I pry my eyes away from the mountains to look at the handsome man next to me. His brown hair is a little ruffled, but in a cute way, and the orange glow of the slow-setting sun is highlighting the little bit of red in his beard. Maybe I should start calling him Little Red instead.

The joke makes me laugh a little, which has his eyebrow raising. There's a small smile on his face, which makes him look even more handsome. "What?" he asks, and I suddenly remember he'd asked me a question before this.

"Oh, nothing." But I'm a terrible liar, and my face splits into a grin. "Just happy to be here. With you." I shrug, because that part is not a lie. "Thank you for taking me here." As I look over the view again, I realize that not even climbing the highest peak in these mountains would give me the same adrenaline rush that seeing him does.

His left hand slides under the blanket I'd placed over my lap and squeezes my thigh before leaving to hold his ice cream once more. "Thank you for trusting me to surprise you." I look over at him again and smile before resting my temple on his shoulder. He lays his head on top of mine for a few seconds before kissing the top of my head.

We go back to silently eating our ice cream while the sun starts to set. This ice cream parlor hits every time. My sisters would love it there, and I think I should take them when they come back this weekend. It'll be their second visit here, and now that I'm feeling a bit more comfortable leaving the house, I can show them more of Steaming Stone, like Stone-cold Sweets.

The ice cream shop has this nostalgic feel, with red and white striped poles and an old diner vibe, but with both classic and new flavors of ice cream. They've already ditched their Halloween decor and started decorating for Christmas, despite it not quite being Thanksgiving yet. On the other hand, The Steaming Cup—where I also plan on taking my sisters—*is* embracing the fall and Thanksgiving decor. Their seasonal drinks and pastries are *the best*.

I pause mid-bite as a thought comes to me. "Hey, do you think Sawyer would want to join us this weekend while my sisters are here? I was also thinking about inviting Nadine." His hazel eyes land on me, crinkling in the corners. "I think they'd all get along, and it might be fun."

"Yeah, I think she'd like that. I'll talk to her about it, and I can give her your number so you guys can talk if you want."

I nod. "Definitely. That would be great."

His smile falters a smidge. "Just know, Sawyer takes a bit to warm up to people." His gaze briefly falls on our two dogs snoozing on the blankets in front of us. "Kind of like Eless." He looks back at me. "Especially when other women are involved. She didn't have the easiest time fitting in with other girls growing up, and somehow, that bad luck has followed her as an adult."

His face looks grim, and there are hard lines of concern in his forehead. "Maybe it's from living in a small town, where a lot of people never really seem to grow out of the high school mentality. Just...don't take it personally if she's a bit shy or quiet around you all at first. Once she warms up to you, she probably won't stop talking." He chuckles.

I nod in understanding. "I'm sorry to hear that. Some girls can be cruel, and speaking from experience, some women can be, too." I put my spoon down in the paper cup and rub his arm, but it's a sad attempt against the thick fabric of his coat. My gloved hand barely makes it two inches before the fabric stops me. So, I resign to resting my palm on his bicep. "I promise my sisters are nice. We'll take it at her pace."

"They are nice." He smiles at me. "And I trust you with her." The look in his eyes has my heart fluttering. The mix of the expression and the tone of his voice, it feels like a great honor to have his trust where his family is concerned. "Plus, it might help her having Nadine there. They know each other because of Gavin."

I smile. "Good. It's always nice to have a friendly face with you."

"Thanks for thinking of her." He holds my stare, his eyes soft.

"Of course. I think it'll be fun," I say.

He nods and goes back to eating his ice cream.

I take the last bite of mine and place the empty container back in the paper bag. "Oh, and you were right about ice cream in the cold. It's somehow even better?"

"Right?" He grins and takes his last bite of mint chocolate chip before putting his empty container in the same bag and setting it aside.

A post-ice cream shiver racks through me, causing a full body spasm. Pulling my jacket further around me, I finally zip it up. "Or maybe not."

Alaric chuckles deep as he takes the mug of cocoa from between his legs and props it upright against a pillow next to him. Leaning forward, he grabs another plaid blanket—a large one with a deep purple and black pattern—and wraps it around his shoulders.

Spreading his legs, he taps the blanket in front of him. "Come here," he whispers.

I look from in between his legs and then back up at his face before obliging. He certainly doesn't have to ask me twice to be close to him, or to get in between his legs.

Dragging the blanket I was already using, I sit between his thighs and spread it out over both of our legs. I lean back against his chest with my head on his shoulder as he wraps his plaid blanket around us, his hands coming together to rest on my torso.

One shiver, two shivers, and then they stop before his warmth spreads into me.

He nestles his face into my hair at the crook of my neck. I feel his lips on my skin before he begins leading a trail of kisses from my neck to my jaw to my cheek, and finally, my temple.

"Thank you for being here, Eda," he whispers against my hair, his breath sending a different kind of shiver through me. I have a feeling the meaning of the words goes far beyond me just being here with him in his favorite spot.

I pull his hand out from under the blanket and kiss it before curling our fingers under the warmth once more. "Thank you for letting me be." I look up at him and feel there are more words that want to breach the safety of my lips, but I stop them. Not yet.

I lean back against his shoulder and watch as the sun makes its descent, and appreciate this moment. Just me and him and our two dogs.

Chapter 27

Edara

Football is on the TV, and it's not because Alaric's home. In fact, he and Gavin are watching today's games at Bash's house—another friend of theirs. No, the sound of sports being on is the telltale sign that it's football Sunday and my sister, Aurelia, is in the house.

The voice of her childhood best friend—and whom I suspect to also be her childhood crush—Atticus Phillips, rings out in the living room as he chimes in with his co-announcers. He's giving his predictions for the games set to play today, and while Aurelia is locked in on every word, I keep trying to tune it out.

Atticus is the son of our mom's best friend, Ingrid. He's a few years younger than me and four years older than Aurelia. While he and I are almost as far apart in age as they are, the two of them always hit it off more than he and I did. They spent so much time together that they were nearly inseparable, until he went off to college on a football scholarship, later joining the NFL to play for the Minnesota Vikings.

This season, he's been announcing instead of playing after getting injured for the... I've lost count. Or perhaps I've just done a poor job keeping in touch. Football's not really my thing. So, I can't say I've followed his career much.

However, when my mom first told us that Atticus wouldn't be playing this year—news we heard before the rest of the nation because she's still best friends with his mom—my dad said that Atticus lasted longer than most at seven years. Apparently, the average time a player stays in the NFL is around three years. It's alarming thinking about how dangerous of a sport football is, especially when I take into account his injuries.

Aurelia's the only one watching the TV, sitting on the floor about five feet from it, whereas the rest of us are doing our own thing. The faint sounds of sports announcers talking commingle with the clinking of glasses as Nadine and Rhiannon both get to work making drinks in the kitchen.

Nadine put herself in charge of the mimosa bar at the island, complete with juice options such as cranberry, orange, grapefruit, and even some apple cider, which sounds delicious as a mimosa. Leave it to her to introduce me to yet another cider drink this season, and I have no doubt I'll love it.

At the kitchen counter behind her, Rhiannon decided to put her previous bartending skills to work and prepare the other drinks, including a pineapple Moscow mule she's currently making for me and a spicy margarita for herself.

The sound of computer keys tapping has me looking over at Cressida sitting crisscross on the loveseat. She's not drinking yet because she's currently pouring over her laptop to edit photos from the family photoshoot she did yesterday with our aunt and uncle. She has more hours yet to work on it, but she likes to try to get sample photos done within a day or two for all her clients. She's said she'll have a mimosa after to celebrate another shoot done.

Aurelia rarely ever drinks because alcohol doesn't mix well with her medications or high blood pressure. Knowing that, we got sparkling cider at the store earlier for her to have mocktails.

Sawyer's occupying herself with the dogs, opting to sit with them where they've sprawled out on the floor in front of the loveseat. I noticed that she seems to be the most comfortable when one of them is nearby. She's sweet and a bit shy, but when she has her hand on a dog, her smile is a little more genuine and she seems more at ease.

I take a mental note of that to make sure she remains comfortable here. My sisters and I can be a lot for anyone, but especially when meeting us for the first time...or when alcohol is involved. I hadn't quite factored that in when I first thought about inviting her.

Still, it's proving to have been a great idea to invite them both. Just as I'd thought and hoped, they get along well with my sisters so far. Nadine fits right in with our chaotic conversations. It's like she has always been one of us, which might have something to do with her having sisters of her own. Sawyer also fits in, but took a minute to warm up, which is totally fine.

I think most people, myself included, experience those first, awkward moments of social anxiety when meeting someone new. With the exception of maybe Nadine, who is most definitely an extrovert in the best way. It might also help that Nadine and Sawyer know each other since Sawyer also grew up around Gavin. So, the two women both have a familiar face here.

Looking around at each of them—including the back of Aurelia's blonde head as she stares intently at her...whatever Atticus is to her—it feels so good to have them all in the same space.

To have my sisters, including Rhiannon, who have been with me through every stage of my life, good and bad.

To have Nadine, who I had an instant connection with and has become a safe space here in Steaming Stone.

And to have Sawyer, the sister of the man who has brought me so much security and happiness over the past several weeks. It feels like a bonus that I like her. Actually, I liked her from the moment she walked in the door that first week, when she patiently approached Eless and without judgment for his timidness.

He also warmed up to her quickly that day, which told me everything I needed to know.

If she wants to be, I have a feeling we could become fast friends. However, I'm not going to force anything. Especially when I'm not even sure who her brother is to me.

Rhiannon comes up next to me, hands me my drink, and plops down on the couch beside me. The leather makes crinkling sounds as she settles in crisscross applesauce, miraculously not spilling her almost too full glass.

"All right. It's been three weeks of being in his house, and two weekends total of us in the guesthouse instead of you. Which, by the way, thanks for renting that out for us." Rhiannon lifts her glass and winks. "But, for real, tell us what's going on. We want all the juicy details about what you've been up to. *All* of them." Her eyebrows raise up and down a few times above the rim of her glass as she takes a sip, and we all get the picture.

"Oh, gosh, please don't. I don't want to know anything, or imagine my brother doing anything of the sort. Not with anyone," Sawyer says, her tone half panicked, half amused, as she frantically waves her hands in the air in an X motion before returning them both to one dog each.

I mouth a silent, *Thank you* to her.

I don't particularly want to talk about my sex life either. Pre-Brad, I would share every sexual and non-sexual encounter with Rhiannon, as she does with me. But, for some reason, things with Ric feel more intimate, more sacred than with anyone else I've ever been with. So, I'm thankful for her aversion to the sex talk, which I both respect and greatly appreciate. My sisters, on the other hand...not so much.

Aurelia turns away from the TV and says, "Awww," in such a disappointed tone, "but it's so fun hearing how happy they are, isn't it?"

"Rellie," I huff my nickname for my sister out on a laugh and halfway hide my face behind a hand. When she was born, I had a hard time saying 'Aurelia' properly. So, my seven-year-old brain simplified it to just 'Rellie,' and it sort of always stuck. Everyone else calls her Aurie, but she'll always be my little Rellie.

"I suppose." Sawyer scrunches her nose. "But happiness from a romantic situation and happiness from a sexual experience are two entirely different things." Her eyebrows furrow as she looks around and takes in my sisters' demeanors over the topic of me and Ric. "I don't know, maybe it's different with sisters?"

"You have no idea." Cressida laughs over her laptop. "Life with these three is never dull. We're open books about everything—whether we want to be or not." She grins at me before looking at Sawyer again. "It's probably odd from the outside looking in."

Rhiannon grunts. "That doesn't mean you're not being a party pooper by raining on our sexcapade." Her tone is light and teasing, and thankfully, Sawyer doesn't seem to take it to heart.

Instead, she shakes her head and laughs. "Not sorry."

I snort from laughing so hard, but I also can't correct my best friend and say it's hardly a sexcapade. Because it was—*is*. It's been the best sex of my life. Passionate, hot, pleasurable on so many levels, and beyond anything I've ever experienced before. I've had a decent amount of partners over the years—nearly two handfuls—but being intimate with Alaric is more than I ever thought could be possible with someone.

"I can confirm," Nadine chimes in from the kitchen, where she's just opened the last bottle of juice to pour herself a cranberry mimosa. "I have two younger sisters, and we've been gossiping about boys since we were all teens. Of course, we're all married now, but that doesn't mean it's stopped." She grins and takes a sip of her drink before joining us. She steps around the obstacle course that is Sawyer and the dogs to sit next to Cressida on the loveseat.

"Sisters are *wild*," Rhiannon agrees, and I laugh as Cressida and Aurelia both smile at her, knowing everything the four of us have gone through together.

Sawyer looks over at her, then waves to everyone in a general sweep. "Listen, until one of you finds *your* brother with his pants around his ankles, you don't get to be mad at me for not wanting to discuss *my* brother's sex life," Sawyer says, then winces. "Sorry, Eda."

Ugh, I had hoped that topic wouldn't come up. Cringing, I meet Sawyer's gaze and say, "I'm sorry, too."

"Hold up. Hold up," Rhiannon says, with her free hand raised in the air. "You found *what*?" Her honey-colored eyes quickly shift from Sawyer's to mine. "When? Why are we just now hearing about this? You're holding out on us, Lauklan."

Groaning, I say, "Maybe because I didn't want to talk about it?"

Sawyer laughs. "We met the first week she was here." She waves her hand in the air. "His pants weren't actually around his ankles, thank goodness, but he didn't have a shirt on. Ugh." Her face scrunches up in disgust at the memory.

His pants being around his ankles was exactly where that kiss was going if she hadn't stopped by.

I make a point to look away, knowing my cheeks are likely red with how hot they feel. They probably match my hair at this point.

Rhiannon catches onto my not-so-subtle attempt to mask the embarrassment, and I want to wipe the smug grin off my best friend's face. With wide eyes, I silently plead for her not to say a word, to which she winks in response. An unspoken promise that she won't further tease me...too harshly. Knowing her, she's most definitely still going to enjoy every moment of my torment, and privately ask about it all later.

I still haven't decided if I'll give in and tell her. Part of me feels guilty about that, but I kind of just want to hold onto this bubble with Alaric for as long as I can...

"Either way, you still should have told us," Rhiannon pokes fun, to which I just roll my eyes.

"Agreed. You had the chance last time, but you held out on us," Aurelia pipes up, briefly looking over her shoulder at me before focusing her attention on the TV again.

Taking a sip of my drink to buy myself some time, I smile. "Because nothing happened." A little white lie, but also mostly the truth. While it had been a steamy kiss we shared, and *something* was definitely about to happen, nothing actually did happen before Sawyer interrupted us. That's no longer the case, of course. He's more than made up for the interruption since then.

I take another sip of the drink in an attempt to hide the blush crawling up my neck. Not from embarrassment this time, but from desire at the images flashing of me and Ric together since. While I might not want to discuss mine and Ric's sex life with my sisters—or *his* sister—there is certainly a lot to enjoy and discuss. *If* I want to, that is.

Rhiannon has her fair share of stories to tell, as she's not ready to settle down and is very comfortable with her sexual life. Cressida grew private about her love life after her ex-fiancé cheated on her, and Aurelia isn't a casual dater. My younger sister is holding out hope for that special someone in her life. Secretly, I believe that someone to be Atticus Phillips. The way her eyes are still glued to him on the TV as she absentmindedly eats from a bowl of popcorn tells me all I need to know.

I smile into my cup and look from my younger sister to my older sister. Cressida's a mystery to me. Granted, she went through quite a lot with her high school sweetheart and ex-fiancé, Justin, who cheated on her with the same woman the entire five-and-a-half years they were together—from high school and onward.

She found out about a week before the wedding, and thank goodness she did. I'd hate to think what life would have been like for her if she'd never found out. None of us suspected Justin of such a thing, but he proved us all wrong.

She's kept her cards close to her chest ever since, understandably so. Although, I've slowly seen the light igniting in her eyes again over the last couple of years as she's healed behind closed doors. I can't say if she's fully healed or even moved on from him yet, but I do feel like she's getting there. Whomever sweeps her off her feet is going to be one lucky man.

My eyes land on Rhiannon, who's already watching me intently. There's a small smile on her lips, but she stays silent, as if knowing I need this moment to take in my family.

Rhiannon's been there for as long as I can remember. How many people get to say they've known their best friend since preschool? We're some of the lucky few. Day one of Mrs. Davis' preschool class, we were immediate best friends and have been inseparable since.

The years when times were tough at home with her mom and her mom's boyfriends, Rhiannon stayed with our family. My parents and sisters accepted her as one of our own back in elementary school, and if my parents could have adopted her, I think they would have. They definitely view her as a daughter.

Knowing her, she's not looking for anything serious. It would take a special someone to get Rhiannon Magdalen to settle down. She's fiery, spirited, and the one person I don't think I could do life without. Everyone in my family means a lot to me, but she's the one person who I feel completes me. She's my person.

With tears brimming in my eyes, I reach out and squeeze Rhiannon's free hand. A moment of understanding passes between us, as we've learned to communicate without speaking, and she returns the gentle gesture.

"We're ready to have you back home," she whispers for only me to hear. "It's been hard to have you so far away during all of this."

With my eyes downcast to our still joined hands, the lightness I felt from being surrounded by family and friends turns heavy with guilt and dread. I don't want to leave Alaric, Blanche, or Steaming Stone. I've been avoiding the thought, my impending deadline, and the fact that my time here is going to end. Soon, I won't be able to ignore it anymore and I'll have to leave.

Looking back up into her eyes, I blink back tears and nod. "I'm sorry."

Her eyebrows pinch together. "Don't be. Brad's the one who should be sorry, and he will be," she whispers, with a deadly promise in her eyes that makes me hope the police find Brad before she does.

Maybe it is better to just let karma take over here. Then, I won't have to bail my best friend out of jail. If she even gets caught, considering the knowledge she possesses from all of the true crime documentaries she watches and podcasts she listens to. Now that I'm thinking about it, she's kind of terrifying, and I love her for it.

I squeeze her hand in gratitude, but the heaviness weighing on my heart doesn't go away.

"All right, mimosa time," Cressida exclaims with the clap of her laptop shutting as she sets it aside. "And then, maybe we can play a game?"

Aurelia's head whips away from the TV again. "Ooh! Cards Against Humanity?"

Letting go of Rhiannon's hand, I laugh. The most innocent one of us all somehow loves the most diabolical game we own as a family. "Yeah, we can play it. If that's okay with everyone?" I ask, looking around.

Sawyer nods from her spot on the floor, and Nadine gives a thumbs up as she downs the rest of her mimosa and stands up for drink two. "Count me in, but don't go crying to your mamas when you find out that my humor is superior. I crush that game every time."

Aurelia's grin is the most devilish one I've ever seen from her. "You're on."

Chapter 28

EDARA

I wake up ready to tackle the day, but the second I sit up in Alaric's bed and look out the window, I see an ominous mist overpowering the mountain tops. It's impossible to see anything and looks like something straight out of a thriller movie. If I hadn't already enjoyed the view for nearly two months now, I wouldn't have known what lay beyond that fog.

Despite the sight being slightly jarring at first, it's also arguably the perfect writing weather. And it couldn't have come a day too soon because I plan on finishing my manuscript today. It will happen. I know it will.

Hands reaching up toward the wooden headboard, I stretch my achy, tired muscles. Sleep did not want to come for me last night. All I could think about was finishing this manuscript. The worst part is, I'm so close to being done. *So. Close.*

The closer I get, the harder it is to write. It's not because the story isn't coming to me, or that the characters aren't speaking to me. No, it's flowed from me for nearly two months now. As I was lying in bed last night, staring at the ceiling, I realized that it's not the story's fault, but mine; I've been procrastinating.

There is zero doubt in my mind that I don't want to finish it. This story deserves to be told, but I'm not ready for it to end. Because then...I'll have to leave. This will all be over. Whatever this is between Alaric and me will have to end. This fondness I've developed for Steaming Stone will become a mere memory subjected to occasional visits because I'll have to leave it all behind.

I'm scared to finish. Scared of what comes next.

However, I realized that I can't drag it out anymore. I have to finish it. The time has come, and whatever happens, happens.

With a cleansing breath, I rub the tears from my eyes that I refuse to let fall. Sliding the flannel sheets and quilt off me, I tentatively put my bare feet on the cold, hardwood floor. He desperately needs a rug in here.

I smile, thinking about Alaric, who I can hear chopping wood outside. He has plans for a guy's night at his friend Bash's tonight, which means that he'll take over watching the dogs during the day while I go out to write, and I'll watch them this evening before he gets home. It's a good plan, one that feels so normal between us now, but I already miss him, even though I haven't even left yet.

With a big stretch in bed, I quickly stand up and practically run to the bathroom to shower and start the day. This floor is like ice on my feet.

Shivering, I turn on the water in the shower, letting the cold pipes wake up. Wearing only one of Alaric's shirts, which hits me mid-thigh, my legs and arms are bare. A terrible idea in the cold of this cabin. We moved all my things from the guesthouse to here a couple weeks ago, but I still prefer to wear his shirts to bed. Or nothing at all, depending on our moods.

Stepping under the hot, steaming water in the shower feels like stepping into a heated building from the snow. Based on the chill inside, I'll have to bundle up well before heading over to The Steaming Cup. Nadine is expecting me today, but she said she's taking the later shift so that she can stay after hours if needed for me to finish. She's so freaking sweet, and probably right, because with the way I'm taking my time with this one, I might need every minute she can buy me today.

Once I finish my manuscript—and once my rental booking is up—I have to return home. I have to. Not just to my home in Raleigh, but to my life there. Or, what's left of it.

The police still haven't had any luck in finding Brad after what happened. He's been MIA since—even from his work in Raleigh. So, I don't know what that life will look like when I return. It'll be the same day-to-day—with me possibly still hiding and avoiding Brad—but it'll also be different.

Life after Steaming Stone...

I don't know if I'll be able to get this place out of my system. Or if I'll be able to get Alaric out of my system, for that matter. If I even want to. His eyes. His smile. His heart, warmth, kindness.

A life post-Alaric sounds...sad. Colorless. Lifeless.

I'll be alive, but I won't be living the same way I have been these past two months. I simply existed this past year with Brad tainting my life. But here—in Steaming Stone, with Alaric and our dogs—I've never felt more alive.

However, I also know I can't drag Alaric into this life anymore than I already have. He deserves better. Knowing him, he'll allow himself to continue being dragged into it. He'll likely go willingly without me even having to ask, diving headfirst into the disaster I left back in Raleigh. He might even offer to try long-distance, or suggest I come here and risk Brad finding us again.

Can I really upend his life and the lives of his friends and family for the sake of my happiness?

No. I can't do that to him. He deserves better. Hell, I also deserve better, but seeing as how this is to be my fate until further notice... Only one of us can cleanly get away from this.

If we continue as we are, I'm scared that I'm going to bring that trouble to him even more than I already have. Yes, I know he can handle it, but I refuse to put him through that. Staying somewhere—anywhere—long-term means that Brad will follow.

He found me in Asheville on a trip we took on a whim. He knew I was in the fitting room that day. He knew Alaric's truck, which means it's highly likely he already knows where Alaric lives, and it's only a matter of time before he makes his presence known.

Again.

I might have been able to escape him for now, but I can't escape him forever. I refuse to subject Alaric to a life like that. A life of living in the shadows—of living in fear, even if the fear is only my own. Because he's so brave; he doesn't seem to be afraid of anything.

Standing under the steaming water, I rest my head against the cold, tile wall.

What a fucking mess.

And what does this even mean? What am I even saying? That I'm resigning myself to a life of being stalked forever? Fuck, wasn't that always the plan? Steaming Stone was only ever supposed to be temporary. Even the protective order is temporary, with an expiration date of a year. I knew I'd eventually have to return back to my reality. Before I'd have to go back to Raleigh—back to Brad. Well, his haunting presence, anyway.

Some of the officers Gavin works with think that Brad has given up after the protective order was filed and he was almost caught in Asheville, but I don't think so. There's no way he just stopped after all this time. Neither Gavin nor Alaric think so, and my gut says it's only a matter of time before he makes himself known again. Plus, he's likely pissed that the order's been filed. It's only a matter of time before—

No, I can't think like that. I *won't* think like that. My hand comes to my chest, trying to control my breathing, and I have a feeling this sudden full body heat isn't just because of the water temperature.

To help, I turn the hot water down a smidge to cool my body off.

What do I do about this? How do I tell Ric what I'm feeling and thinking? What I'm fearing? How do I tell him this can't go on?

Or does he already know? Is he just waiting for the right time to tell me he feels the same? That he can't agree to this long-term? Can't agree to willingly be a part of my life? Are we just biding our time?

I run my hands over my wet hair and bite back the tears burning in my eyes. I grip my chest when a sudden pain burrows a hole there—an Alaric-sized crater making its way across my heart.

My hand comes to the cold, tile wall, and I slide down until my knees hit the shower floor. Cradling my legs close to my chest, I tuck my head onto my knees and let out the pain as the water beats down on my head and back. Unable to decipher what's water and what are my own tears, I stay that way until the sharp pains of loss and heartbreak are replaced by a bitter numbness built from dread and fear.

Chapter 29

EDARA

When I got to The Steaming Cup this morning, I set up at a table near the fireplace, put on my headphones with a "Lord of the Rings" playlist on repeat, and dove into the last chapters of the final book in my series.

Patrons have come and gone, but I've stayed in this chair for hours. Having had the chance to get to know the staff of the coffee shop in my time being here, I know that they are aware of my situation with Brad, and—with my permission—Nadine showed each employee a picture of Brad to make sure he's not allowed in. As it turns out, Gavin had already done that with a couple of them.

Knowing they're all aware of the situation and his presence makes me feel less on edge here and keeps me from constantly watching the door.

Initially, I was embarrassed that more people were finding out—and especially the people I see on a regular basis, since this has become a regular writing spot for me. However, the more I've talked about it, the less embarrassed I've felt over the whole situation. I think I'm starting to realize that this whole thing isn't my fault and I have nothing to feel guilty about. It's been a slow process, but I'm getting there.

Being here in The Steaming Cup, I can now fully immerse myself in my manuscript without fear of him sneaking up on me. It's paying off. The only time I've moved is to walk down to Ruby Stone's Bistro for lunch and to stretch my legs, but then I was right back at it.

Nadine clocked in around one, and ever since then, I've been catching her gaze on me. I finally had to tell her that staring at me won't make me type any faster, to which she laughed and apologized. The stares have lessened, but only a smidge. It's okay, it just makes me laugh.

It's now after hours, with Nadine having closed up about half an hour ago. When I told her I can leave if she needs me to, she reminded me that she owns The Steaming Cup, and we can stay as long as we want.

Since Gavin's with Alaric and their friend, Bash, tonight, I have the pleasure of her company while she waits for them—and me—to finish. She's been cozied up in one of the wingback chairs by the fireplace, reading book five of my series in anticipation of book six coming out.

She told me she started reading book one after learning that I'm an author. She admitted that she didn't initially tell me she was reading them because she didn't want to risk not liking the books. Instead, I guess she fell in love with my books and the characters within them, and called me her new favorite auto-buy author. One of the best compliments I can receive. Knowing how much she's enjoying the series, I've already promised her she can be an ARC reader—someone who receives a copy of the book to read pre-release.

The next time I catch her staring at me, I grin and flip the laptop screen to look at her. In the biggest font size I could put it at without separating the words on the line, she reads: "THE END."

The way her face lights up and she shoots out of her chair has me feeling so proud and giddy.

I did it. I really did it.

"Eda!" she screeches and hurries over to me, pulling me up and into a hug. She bounces me in a circle.

Laughing, I finally have to pull away when I start to get dizzy.

"You did it!" she says, clasping my hands in hers. "How does it feel?"

I pause, reflecting on the question so that I can answer honestly. It's wild to think that I've finished an entire series. Not just one book, but six—*all* of the books in this series. I finished.

I finished.

I *finished*.

The more the overwhelming thoughts and feelings hit me—and my emotional shower from this morning comes back to me—the more I feel my smile fall.

I give her a small smile with watery eyes. "Bittersweet, I guess."

"Oh, honey." She pulls me over to the wingback chairs. "Talk to me. What's going on?"

I shake my head and cover my mouth, trying to stifle a sob. So much for thinking I'd cried it all out this morning. I guess that numbness was only meant to be temporary to get me through the day.

Looking into her concerned eyes, I sniffle and ask, "You promise not to tell anyone what I'm about to say?"

She nods and trails her finger across her chest. "Cross my heart and hope to die. Your secrets are safe with me."

I squeeze her hand in gratitude, and then let it all out. All my fears about Brad. All my heartache about this needing to end with Alaric. All my pain of subjecting myself to more of this life of stalking and barely living. All joy mixed with sadness over finishing my first series.

She sits there, letting me vent as she silently takes it all in.

When I'm done, she lets out a big sigh and sits back in her chair.

"That was a lot. I'm sorry," I say, instantly regretting unleashing on her.

"Don't be." She leans forward again and takes my hand. "Don't be," she repeats. "It's okay. You were holding a lot in, and it's healthier to get it out." She squeezes my hand before letting go again. "Have you talked to Alaric about any of this?"

I shake my head. "No. How can I? You know how he is; he'll just tell me we'll figure it out and put up with me. But also, I'm sure he must suspect something. I mean, my rental is coming to an end, and he knows I was here to finish my draft today. Maybe he feels the same way?"

She nods solemnly, staring off toward the register. "He's a smart guy. He's probably already thought about what this means. But, knowing him…" she pauses to look at me. "I've never seen him this way, Eda. He's normally a one or two date guy, max. He has no problem cutting people off to protect his own peace and mental health. *None*," she emphasizes that last word.

More tears brim in my eyes as she continues.

"He doesn't normally let himself get attached—doesn't normally want to. And he certainly doesn't let women stay at his house, or go out in public with them and show affection." She keeps going, and with each statement, the feelings I have for Alaric not only root deeper but cause more tears to fall.

I attempt to dry my eyes and cheeks. When my hands fall in my lap again, she squeezes them.

"Trust me, Eda, if he didn't want to be spending his time with you, or have you in his home, he wouldn't. You'd still be in that guesthouse, and you likely wouldn't have had any interaction outside of polite conversation after your first date. Second date, if you're lucky." She huffs a laugh. "I love him dearly, but he's not one for commitment." A smile slowly spreads on her face. "*Wasn't* one for commitment. I have a feeling that's changed."

Is it possible that she's right? That what we have might be different, and something he might actually want?

Her soft voice breaks me from my thoughts. "Tell me, how many dates have you been on? If any?"

I look away, counting in my head. There's the first time we got ice cream, and then grocery shopped together. Does that count as a date? As simple of a task as it was, it felt like one with him. Then, he took me to lunch and dinner a few times. But were those really dates, or him just being nice? For sure, ice cream and hot cocoa while watching the sunset over the mountains was a date. I smile at the memory. That was a beautiful night.

Nadine's laugh pulls my attention back to her. "That many? Wow. Yeah, girl, I think you're going to be just fine. You couldn't get rid of him even if you tried. I saw sparks flying between you two the first time I saw you standing together," she points downward at the rug, "in this very spot."

I look down and remember when his presence and the feel of his fingers intertwining with mine was all I needed to calm down after talking about Brad. It was also the first day I felt in my gut that I could trust him with Elessar when he offered to let him out so that I could work.

She continues. "That man—the broody, hard, noncommittal man I've come to adore like a brother—is smitten by you. And I know him well enough to know that he won't just let you walk away because you're scared. If there was some other reason, like you not wanting to be with him, sure." She shrugs. "He'd take it like the gentleman he is. But not because you're scared of the outside world coming in. And he won't walk away out of fear. He knows that anything worth having is worth fighting for, and you, my dear, are certainly worth it."

My hands come to wrap around my torso as a tear falls down my cheek. I don't deserve him. I don't deserve his kindness, his commitment, his—

"Eda..." Nadine's soft voice breaks through the loud voice in my head. I look at her through watery eyes. "You love him, don't you?"

I shake my head. I can't. I can't possibly. Not because he doesn't deserve it—he does—but because I can't subject him to what a life of loving me would look like. It's not fair, and saying the words would hurt more.

As if she understands, she comes up and wraps her arms around me. "It's okay, honey. It'll be all right. Okay?"

We stay that way for a few minutes until the sobs subside. When she pulls away, her shoulder is soaked.

"I'm so sorry," I say, gesturing toward her shoulder as she stands. "I–I'm so sorry for all of this. You didn't stay here tonight for me to drown you like this in my emotions or tears."

"Oh, stop it," she says, brushing my apology away. "What are friends for?" she asks, smiling.

I smile back—and I mean, really smile. She's got me there. It feels good to know she sees me as a friend the same way I have come to see her.

"How are you feeling now?" she asks me as we stand in front of the fireplace.

I cross my arms. "A little better. I think I'm realizing that I just need to talk to him."

"Yeah, the dreaded communication. I hate how necessary it is." She rolls her eyes and nods. "Okay, now that we have the emotions out of the way, are you ready to celebrate?" Her hands clap together.

My eyebrows raise. "I don't typically celebrate beyond just sending it off and closing my manuscript."

Her jaw drops. "Seriously? That's it?"

"Yeah." I nod my head and shrug. "Why? What did you have in mind?"

Caramel-colored eyes light up as they look at me. "Wait here." She sprints over to behind the counter and disappears in the back.

A minute later, she resurfaces with two plates of baked goods in her hands and a balloon with the word CONGRATS tied to one wrist. As she comes closer, I see pumpkin cinnamon rolls, a slice of pumpkin pie with an ample amount of whipped topping, and pumpkin bread with maple cinnamon glaze on each plate.

I practically start salivating at the sight. "Nadine. This is too much!" I say as she sets the plates down on the end table between the wingback chairs."

Waving her hand at me, she says, "It was nothing. If it makes you feel better, it was leftovers from the day. They needed to get eaten, anyway."

I laugh. "In that case, I take it back. This is amazing. Thank you."

"Please. It's not every day I get to celebrate an author finishing their book, let alone a friend." She grins at me and I feel so grateful that our paths crossed. She's helped make this town feel like home, and helped to give me a safe space here.

She gets up to pull out some sparkling cider and two glasses, and as she sets them down on the table, I realize that I've missed out by not celebrating these wins with anyone. It's kind of nice that someone wants to be with me. Maybe she's right—maybe I should celebrate this accomplishment each time. Actually, maybe she's right about a lot of things.

After I leave here tonight, I'll head straight home, and we'll have a much needed conversation when he gets back. No matter the outcome, at least I'll have been honest. And no matter what he tells me or decides, I'll be okay.

I've fallen in love, in more ways than one, and there's no way that love will allow me to stay away for too long. My heart has fallen for Steaming Stone, and one resident in particular. So long as he feels the same way, not even Brad can keep me from this newfound happiness. I won't let him.

Chapter 30

ALARIC

"**I** heard you've got yourself a pretty, little redhead, Ric," says Sebastian, with humor and curiosity laced in every word.

I roll my eyes and don't even reward him with a look.

Sebastian and I met in middle school, when Sawyer started riding lessons at his family's riding academy. We immediately hit it off, and I introduced him to Gavin.

Having grown up around the academy, Sebastian successfully convinced us to give riding a shot. And since he is the heir to the Swanson Estate, the three of us were able to go riding around the property without an escort. Which means that we might have gotten into trouble a time or two...

"She's pretty, all right. And little. *And* has our guy in the palm of her hands," Gavin chimes in before chugging his beer.

This time, I do look. When I take a swig of my own beer, I lift up my middle finger on the hand wrapped around the bottle.

A low chuckle from Gavin sounds in response, along with Sebastian's low whistle.

"Subtle, but it only confirms what he said, man," Sebastian says, leaning against the bar top.

Cassie, the Swanson's in-house bartender, asks if he wants a refill of his amaretto whiskey, and he nods his head with a smile.

"Whatever," I mumble and head for the Pac-Man game in the corner of the billiard's room.

This is one of many rooms in the Swanson mansion that doesn't seem real, like the heated indoor pool, the movie theater, the massive garage full of cars that's more like the size of a warehouse than a garage, or the two-story gym. Despite having his own gym here, Sebastian still makes a point to support me by coming to my gym, which I appreciate.

Along with unsupervised rides along the estate property, we have spent a lot of hours in this billiard's room. Games have been added since, but the nostalgia is still there each time I step into the room.

The walls are a light green, with the top half adorned in framed artwork of all sizes, and the bottom half decked out in dark wood paneling. It's more extravagant than a game room should be, but it's not unexpected, considering the Swanson's are one of the richest families in town, between their famous winery and prestigious riding academy.

"When do I get to meet her?" Sebastian asks.

"Never," I say without hesitation.

Another low whistle sounds from him. "That serious, huh?" His black eyebrows dance up and down and there's a playful twinkle in his eyes.

"No, dickhead." *Yes, actually.* "I just don't want her falling madly in love with the heir of the Swanson Estate." Not that I actually think that would happen, but Sebastian has a way with women, even if he doesn't mean to. It comes naturally to the man. Whether because of his good looks, status in society, or fortune, who knows.

"If he won't tell you about her, I will," Gavin says.

I shoot him a look, which only makes both men laugh again. Even Cassie cracks a smile from behind the bar as she hands Sebastian his drink.

"He's screwed, isn't he?" I hear Sebastian whisper rather loudly to Cassie, who only grins harder.

"I'm staying out of it, Boss Man." Her hands lift in surrender before she picks up a white rag and starts wiping down the dark wood counter.

I shake my head. "Is there nothing better for us to talk about on guy's night than my private life? Really, gentlemen? What have we come to?"

They slowly glance at each other for a moment before looking my way again. "Isn't talking about women, sports, and life *all* we do?"

"Yeah, normally it's just Bash's list of countless international supermodels who want a piece of him, and whatever gal Sawyer tried to hook you up with most recently," Gavin says.

He's not wrong. Once he married Nadine, we respected his desire to keep the details of his marriage private. As for me and Sebastian? Maybe it's the detective in him, but Gavin's the one who asks the most questions out of the three of us.

Something flashes on Sebastian's face at the words. Gavin and I can both see that he is not really interested in any of the ladies who practically throw themselves at him—or rather, his fortune and the life he could offer any partner. He politely turns down most, and occasionally enjoys the company of some, but none of them have really seemed to get him or strike his interest enough to earn more than a third date.

It's almost like he's holding out for something—someone—else, and my gut has told me since I was a teenager that this someone might be my sister, Sawyer. If I'm honest, I probably suspected it when we were in high school, and he couldn't keep his eyes off Sawyer, who was still attending the riding academy.

But knowing how strict his parents were about Sebastian's future and the person he would marry someday to help him run the estate, I forbid him at the age of sixteen from even considering it. I didn't want to risk him breaking her heart when his parents turned her away for not being up to their pedigree. He agreed.

Now that they've both passed away, I'm not sure what's stopped him from trying. Although, maybe I'm wrong. Maybe she's not the one he wants.

Gavin's voice brings me back to the present moment, and I catch the tail-end of his little speech about Eda. "Cut us some slack for wanting to know more about the lady who has you skipping days at the gym and practically showing PDA in a public coffee shop."

Sebastian's mouth drops. "PDA?! From Alaric? Who *are* you? It's like we don't even know you anymore." His tone feigns mock hurt.

This time, I don't bother disguising my finger from around the beer bottle. Raising my arm, I show him loud and clear exactly how I feel about his poking and prodding. But when I look up, I see a portrait of Sebastian's grandpa staring at me, eyes shrewd, and suddenly feel like that thirteen-year-old boy shrinking from his scolding stare in real life all over again. My bad, Grandpa Swanson.

"Plus, it's only fair for us to ask questions when she's..." Gavin's voice trails off, which isn't like him. He's normally better with his words than that.

I turn away from the portrait, but stop when I notice his grave expression.

"She's what, Gav?" I ask. My eyebrows pinch together, having a feeling what he was going to say. "Say it."

He clears his throat. "Chill, dude. I was just going to say it's only natural for us to be worried."

"You mean, because of her past?" I ask, my voice gruff.

"Well, yeah, and present and future. You heard what I said in that coffee shop about the stats for stalking. This isn't— Fuck, man. It's not going away anytime soon. He's proving to be smart enough to not get caught, and she lives too public of a life as an author to truly hide." Gavin's hand comes up for emphasis.

Sebastian's eyes go wide as he hides his face behind his glass and takes a sip.

"That's not her fault." I set my beer bottle down on the poker table cover and cross my arms.

Gavin's black eyebrows dip. "Of course, it's not her fault. I never said that. I just said that I'm worried about you, man. We both are."

I look at Sebastian, a burning question in my eyes. "Is that so?"

He meets my gaze over the rim of his glass and shrugs. Lowering it, he sighs. "Can you really blame us, Ric? You'd feel the same way if the roles were reversed." He looks sheepish, but I only stare harder.

"Not to mention what happened in Asheville. You've clearly made it on his radar. This fucker knows what your truck looks like, for crying out loud, Ric!"

"You don't think I know that? I'm the one who had to tell the Asheville PD what happened and watch them bag the stupid flowers," I bite back.

"And what about what's happened since? You've practically hid away. I don't see you at the gym anymore. Not even Dean or Lydia have seen you there recently, and they're your *employees.*"

"Of course, they've seen me!" I throw my arms in the air incredulously.

"Not the way they used to. Not like normal," Gavin says, pointing his finger at me before taking another sip of his beer.

Am I hearing this right?

"So, I've taken a few days off work. Is that so bad? For me to have a life outside of work? You guys and Sawyer have been pestering me about that for years now. That I need to start doing more outside of the gym. To live more. And now that I am, it's an issue?" I look at Sebastian. "Seriously?"

Eyes wide, he puts his hands in the air, drink still in his right hand. "Hey, don't come at me, man."

Gavin turns to him. "What? Am I the only one who feels this way? You're really going to put this all on me?"

Turning to him now, with hands still up, Sebastian says in a faux innocent voice, "No, Mr. Detective, sir."

Gavin blows out a laugh, breaking the tension.

Sebastian finally lowers his hands. "You both just need to take a breath. Relax. I think we got a bit off track here." He turns back to me. "Let's be very clear:

we're not telling you how to live your life, how to run your business, or who to spend your time with."

"It sure as hell sounds like it," I say.

He pins me with a stare. "Maybe, but it's not what we mean. We just care about you, man. We've known you for...longer than I'd like to admit." He smirks and I want to hate him for making me chuckle, but I can't. Because he's right; I've known him so long that he's basically family. He *is* family. These two men are my brothers.

I shake my head and pick up my beer again, sighing before taking a sip.

"I'd like to think we've earned the right to express concern, or tell you flat out when we're worried about you," Sebastian says, and Gavin nods as he speaks.

"And that extends to you getting to pass judgment on who I choose to spend my time with, or her life?" I ask. I don't mean it. Well, the question, yes, but not the tone. I know they're coming from a good place.

"There's no judgment, dude. You know us better than that." Gavin sighs. "I know what's happening to her is out of her control, but I'm not going to apologize for being worried about *you*—my friend."

My beer bottle hovers inches from my lips before I shake my head. "I understand." Gavin's brow raises and I smirk. "Get off your high horse, dickhead. I'm not saying it's cool. I just get it. Okay? But you're also not going to tell me what to do." I point my finger at both of them for a few seconds each. "Neither of you bastards get a say in who I spend my time with. Got it?"

"Got it," Gavin says. I give him a look, and he returns it, turning an eyebrow down at me. "I mean it. You're a grown-ass man, Ric."

"Thanks for acknowledging that, Dad," I joke. Switching tones, I say, "Listen, I get it, and I appreciate the concern. I do, and you're right, I'd probably be just as concerned if the roles were reversed. But they're not, and you're just going to have to trust me. Okay?"

After a few seconds, Gavin nods his head. "Okay."

I look at Sebastian, who's glancing back and forth between the two of us. Seemingly satisfied, he claps his hands together. "Good. We're back to normal. Now I can beat your asses at pool."

I laugh. "When have you ever beat me?"

He walks toward the pool table and grabs a stick. "About a million times in my dreams, asshole."

Gavin and I sport matching grins. "You dream about me, Swanson? That's cute," I tease.

He looks at me over his shoulder and winks. "Only on days that end in Y."

I let out a much needed belly laugh—a much needed reprieve from the tension in the room. Leave it to Sebastian to make me laugh in a moment like this.

As they set up the pool table, I hang back a minute, their words ruminating in my head. Are they seeing something I can't? Is it worth taking into consideration how concerned my best friends are? Outside of my family, they've known me longer than anyone.

The train of thought is interrupted when I feel my phone buzz in my pocket. Pulling it out, I see it's a notification of motion detected on one of the security cameras at home.

Wondering if Eda's made it back from writing at the coffee shop with Nadine, I pull up the camera on the side of the house, facing the drive. The recorded clip shows shadows and leafless tree branches blowing in the wind, but there's nothing more to see.

Exiting the recording, I pull up a live view of the camera, but it's the same—nothing. I guess she's not home yet.

Clicking out of the security app, I send off a quick message to Eda.

> Hey beautiful. How's it going?

A response comes back less than a minute later.

Little Red

Hey, you. Really well. In fact, I'm done. It's bittersweet. We're finishing up a bottle of sparkling cider, since we have to drive back home after. Once it's gone, I'll be heading home. :)

Home. I like the sound of that, and I can't help the smile that tugs at my lips.

Look at you go. I'm so proud of you. We'll celebrate with a proper bottle of champagne tonight. Enjoy your time with Nadine. I'll see you soon :)

Little Red

I can't wait to see you tonight. Have fun and be safe, Ric. :)

Me too. I'm already missing you. Is that weird to say? And don't worry, I know my limits. You be safe too Eda :)

Little Red

Not weird at all, unless you think it's weird that I'm most definitely missing you.

I smile. She did it. I never doubted her for a second. Pride fills me, but it's quickly replaced by a sinking fear.

She did it.

She's *done*.

Which means she'll be leaving soon, and I'm not ready for that.

"You just going to be on your phone all night?" Sebastian asks, tearing me from the realization hitting me like a freight train.

"Yeah, give me a sec." I exhale and walk over to the bar. "But this might be my last game tonight." I put my phone on the bar counter so that the vibration will be louder and easier to hear if Eda texts me.

"Wait, really?" Gavin asks, looking at the watch on his wrist. "It's not even eight o'clock, man."

"What can I say, I'm an old man." I shrug and grab my beer.

Eda and I talked about her watching the dogs tonight while I'm here, but I have this gut feeling that I need to be there with her tonight. Or maybe it's just because I want to be—that I'm feeling desperate for every minute I can get with her, knowing it could all come to an end at any moment now that she's finished what she came here to do.

As I walk over to the pool table to grab a stick, I attempt to shake off all thoughts and focus on the rest of tonight with my friends. I can think about all that later.

Except, my brain has other plans in mind, and a certain little redhead dances tirelessly in my mind, knowing I'll get to hold her again soon. The only question is, for how much longer?

Chapter 31

Edara

After helping Nadine clean up, I leave the coffee shop with a stack of food containers from leftover baked goods and a full heart. The cold wind strikes the breath from my lungs when I step out of the coffee shop. Shivers rack my body when the wind sneaks through the unzipped front opening of my jacket.

I tuck the edge of my scarf up, covering my nose to shield against the icy wind so I can breathe. The street is semi-lit, with some businesses still open, and others having lit up storefronts, despite having already closed up. It gives the illusion that it's earlier than nine o'clock at night.

Grounding the balls of my feet into the brick sidewalk, I lift up my heeled boots just enough to spin in place to face the door again, where Nadine is locking up.

I've enjoyed this time with her, and I'm looking forward to the next time we're going to hang out. Preferably outside of her workplace, where she can truly have fun. However, I cannot wait to see Alaric again tonight, and to cuddle with the dogs before he gets home. He never said when he plans to be back, but

I hope it won't be too late. I already miss him, and we have quite a bit to talk about.

Shifting the containers of baked goods I'm bringing home for Alaric, myself, and some pumpkin bread for my aunt, I wrap my now free arm firmly around Nadine's shoulder blades. "Thank you for tonight. I appreciate you so much, and I'm extremely grateful I met you."

"Right back at you, girly," she says, squeezing me in return before pulling away. "And I say we make this a tradition, which means that you have to finish every manuscript of yours in Steaming Stone from here on out." She points at me and winks.

I laugh, reading between the lines. "I'll see what I can do about that."

"See that you do." She nods curtly and breaks out into a grin. "Get home safely, okay?"

"Same to you!" I shout over my shoulder while walking to my Jeep that's parked only a few cars down.

As I get closer, the joy in my heart ceases and the smile on my face drops. The plastic food containers in my hands crinkle against my white-knuckled grip, holding them closer to my chest as fear grips me.

"Nadine!" I yell.

Footsteps come from behind me a few seconds later, and I whirl around to make sure it's her and not someone else. "What is it?" she asks, panic written all over her face. The moment she sees it, she freezes in place. Her mouth opens and closes, not uttering a single sound, and yet, I understand every word.

I turn back toward my car, where there's a bouquet of naked, thorny rose stems on my windshield. Only a single red rose remains intact, though it hangs there limply, as if it fought to survive. The bare bouquet looks like it's been stomped on, mutilated, and maybe even thrown about. Red petals have been spread all over the hood of my car, and while some have blown off onto the street, the intent is impactful.

What's worse than the presence of the roses are the words that those remaining rose petals spell out:

HE'S DEAD

"Ric," Nadine whispers behind me. Coming to the same conclusion, she said what my brain was too afraid to.

I shift my feet to turn to face her, keeping both her and the Jeep in my line of sight. The panic in her eyes somehow dampens the fear inside of me, and I suddenly feel like I need to protect her from this.

"Hey, I need you to do me a favor." Fully facing her now, I block her view of the car, making her look at me. "Go back inside, lock the door behind you, and look at the security cameras. See if you can find any video of who did this and when." The words that come out of my mouth shock me. They're calm, collected—nothing like how I feel on the inside. I guess that it's one thing for me to be the target, but another when people I care about are involved.

She nods her head once and starts walking backward toward the coffee shop door. The whole way, her eyes remain on my car, before finally landing on me in concern.

The headlights of my car blink as I unlock it. Opening the driver's door, I toss my purse, laptop bag, and the food containers over to the passenger seat before hopping in. "And call Gavin. Right now!" I call out the door before shutting it.

I start the car and turn on the windshield wipers, getting off as many of the petals as I can that made their way to the windshield, likely from the wind. The wipers come crashing down on the naked stems of the bouquet, violently squishing them further. It does little else; they stay there, their thorns staring at me.

Turning the wipers off, I scowl at the remaining bouquet and stubborn petals. I'll enjoy watching them fly off the car one by one as I drive.

"Where are you going?" Her voice is muffled through the closed door.

I don't respond, and her footsteps halt in her retreat to The Steaming Cup's entrance. She shakes her head at me through the windshield, because she already knows.

But then, as if she understands why I must do this, she yells, "Be safe, Eda!"

I nod once and wait for her to get safely inside before I back out of my parking spot and head for Alaric's. I try to call him, once, twice, but both times go straight to voicemail.

"Fuck!" Tossing my phone onto the passenger seat, I grip the steering wheel with white knuckles and resist the urge to drive recklessly in order to get there faster. These narrow, windy roads are already dangerous in daylight, let alone at night with deer around.

With each mile that goes by, my heart pounds harder in my chest, and nausea builds at the thought of what I might find.

I just hope I'm not too late. I can't be.

Chapter 32

EDARA

Pulling up the long driveway of Redwood Lane, I sigh in relief when I see Alaric's truck's not here. Lights are on in the house for the dogs, who I can hear barking, but I don't see him inside the windows, either.

I look around the yard, but it's nine o'clock and too dark to see anything. It does bring me a little comfort knowing that Alaric has added more security cameras on the property. If Brad had come here tonight, it would have set off the cameras and Alaric would already know.

He was just toying with me.

My forehead rests on the steering wheel and I let out a sigh, releasing as much of the fear and tension in me that I can. It's not effective. My nerves are shot after seeing the rose petals. The record-breaking seventeen minutes it took me to get here felt like a lifetime.

Sitting up, I grab my phone from the passenger seat to see I have three notifications from two minutes ago. All three text messages are from Nadine.

Checked the cameras and someone in a black hoodie got to your car about 30 minutes before we came out

I called 911 and they're sending patrol cars out to look for him around here and at Ric's

I'm about to call Gavin but wanted to check on you first. Please tell me when you get there

Fear grips me like a boa constrictor. My hands start to shake, dropping the phone. I flex my fingers and put them on the steering wheel, gripping hard. When my knuckles turn white, I let go, trying and failing to relax all the muscles in my body. Frustration builds with each second that passes. Not sure how to react, I rest my head back against the headrest and fight tears.

Tonight was too close of a call. He was so close. *So* close! To both me and Nadine. The nausea grows stronger at the realization, and I feel like I might be sick.

Maybe Nadine was wrong this morning, and maybe I was right. I need to leave so that Alaric will be safe. I've put him, my friends, his friends, his family, my family—*everyone*—in danger by coming here and staying. I can't do this to him anymore.

I need to pack my things and leave. *Tonight*.

My book's done. I sent it off to my new agent before I left the coffee shop. My goal here is complete, and now, I need to go.

Fighting tears of sadness, which I feel like I've been doing a whole hell of a lot today, I spot the dogs barking like crazy in the window and know I need to get to them. With a deep exhale, I steel my spine and decide to set aside my fears for their sake. And because I know I'll feel safer once I'm inside, with the dogs surrounding me while I pack.

Grabbing my purse from the passenger seat, I don't give a second glance to my laptop bag, deciding to leave it, since all of my work stuff is basically packed in it already. One less thing to do. I climb out of the car and take another deep breath as my feet hit the ground. The sound of the door shutting rings into the silent night, accompanied by the gentle rustling of the tree branches above.

I lean against the car door for a moment, breathing in the cold air. This time, the icy chill is welcomed, with how much I was sweating on my way here.

Hearing the dogs barking from inside makes me smile a little, but then I realize that I'm also going to have to leave Blanche tonight. I clear my throat, swallowing a sob.

Pushing off the driver's door, I remove the scarf from around my neck and step around to the front of my car. The words and bouquet itself are gone now, having flown off in my mad dash to get here, but I notice there are still a couple petals stuck under the wipers. Holding firm onto one end of the scarf, I toss the other end like a rope, hoping to dislodge them.

Realizing I'm too short to get them off, I blink back tears of frustration and put the scarf back on. Determined and angry, I start searching for a long, thick branch. Having no short supply of fallen branches with all the trees around, I grab one and use it to carefully remove each red petal from my car.

Dropping the branch, I see a shriveled petal that landed on my boot. I sneer, kick it off, and stomp it, burying it beneath mud and countless dried leaves. Satisfied that I can't see the vibrant red color anymore, I turn toward the house.

As I start walking the path from the driveway to the front porch, my nerves dig deeper into me and my senses heighten in response. I'm sure it's just from being on edge after finding my car in the state I did and knowing Brad knew where I was at The Steaming Cup.

When I feel my skin prickle with goosebumps underneath my thick cardigan and coat, my eyes spring to the trees around the property. It's probably just because of the cold wind. It's... Yeah, that's it. It's really cold tonight. Alaric said we should be expecting snow soon, and I believe it.

Still, I pick up the pace to the porch, cutting through the dried grass and leaves instead of the walkway, just to be on the safe side.

The closer I get, the harder my blood pounds in my ears.

When my foot reaches the bottom step of the porch, the sudden creaking of wood and a fast-approaching shadow make me freeze in place. My stomach sinks as disbelief courses through me.

"Hi, Eda," Brad says. There's no warmth in his tone.

Before I can catch my breath—or even think—my purse is falling off my arm and my back is slammed against a hard surface. The back of my head hits the siding of the house, and my eyesight blurs from the contact. His hand is around my throat before I can catch my breath. The scarf I just used to wipe off the flower petals is now gripped in his hand, as he twists it tighter around my neck.

With vision bright white from the impact and overwhelming panic, I can't see him anymore, but there's no mistaking the voice I heard or the face I saw.

Blonde hair, longer than I remember, just past the tips of his big ears. Big, light blue eyes that are creepier than they are pretty. Rough, unshaven facial hair that wasn't there before, and a crazed, toothy smile that makes him look deranged.

He might look slightly different—more haggard than before—but it's very much still him.

Brad found me. How did I ever think I could be safe?

The blood in my veins freezes over, but my skin feels like it's on fire all at the same time as panic sets in. Tears prick my eyes from fear mixed with the pain of his hold, but I blink them away and my vision starts to clear. Seeing the outline of his tall, thin frame sets a fire in me as I claw at his wrist and hand.

It's no use. He's too strong.

I try to think back to my training with Alaric, but I can't think of anything to get me out of this hold he has me in. Crippling fear takes over. I don't have the strength, and he holds all the power right now.

Brad tilts his head, and I'm able to see him clearer with the living room light shining onto the porch through the window. The yellow light reflects off his dark blonde hair and his eyes pierce straight through me. There are dark circles under his eyes, as if he hasn't been sleeping well. *Good.*

"You've been hiding from me." With a sadistic smile, he says, "And what's with this little protective order I heard about? You've been a naughty girl, Eda." Leaning in close, his nose nudges against my cheek, and my skin crawls at the contact. "You could never be rid of me, babe."

His hands release my neck, and I immediately suck in a breath. Before I can even think or react, he grabs my wrists and starts pulling me toward the steps. I dig my heels into the wood boards of the porch and pull against his hold to try to get to the front door, where I can hear the dogs barking even louder.

"Enough!" Brad shouts and pulls me so far forward, I lose my balance. With my hands still in his hold, I can't stop myself from falling on my face.

I gasp as my chin bangs into the rough wood, jerking my head back with the force. But he doesn't loosen his hold or stop his retreat down the porch. Sharp pain shoots through me as the wooden steps dig into my ribs one by one and my knees and ankles bang against the steps. My shoulder blades start to burn from his tugging, and I can practically feel his fingers digging into my wrist bones.

With the pressure on my chest from being dragged, no scream will breach my lips no matter how hard I try, but I'm not going down without a fight. My toes dig into the ground as I shake my hands and try to get free.

He lets go of my arms and I'm only able to suck in half a breath before he hauls me over his shoulder. The bone of his shoulder digs into my stomach, making it difficult to breathe as he takes me toward the woods.

The sounds of the dogs barking become quieter and the lights of the house dim. I start slamming my fists against his back, while trying to wiggle a smidge to gather enough breath to scream. Only a mangled cry comes out as my whole body bounces up and back down when he trips over something.

Irritated, Brad stops walking and throws me on the cold ground. Ignoring the pain from my body slamming into the hard surface, I wince and reach out into the icy leaves and damp soil. Looking around in desperation, I spot Alaric's ax stuck in a tree trunk just ahead. Without hesitating, I try to crawl away—to crawl toward a weapon—but Brad is too quick.

A large hand wraps around my neck, while his other hand goes to the shoulder, where my disheveled jacket has slid down. The skin there is left bare to the elements from my sleeveless blouse under the cardigan I wore in preparation for getting too hot while writing by the fireplace today.

A whimper escapes me from his bruising grips on both my throat and shoulder.

His gaze lands on my bare skin and he jerks me up so that my face is level with his. Maybe it's the close proximity, but his eyes look bigger than normal in his rage. "Did you wear this for him? You just couldn't wait to jump into bed with the next man who paid you even the slightest bit of attention, you whore," he sneers.

My eyes go wide and I stop scratching at his hands as I realize he's talking about Alaric. Where has Brad been the last month we've been searching for him? How long has he been watching me here? How much did he see us? Was this ever truly an escape, or just a waiting game for him?

"What did you think would happen? Did you really think I wouldn't find you?" I flinch as spit flies from his mouth, hitting me almost as hard as the hand that connects with my left cheek. Pain stings along my cheekbone and mouth as my teeth dig into my top lip from the impact. But there's no time to process it all as his hand around my throat tightens further.

That same hand brings me even closer to his face, distorted with his anger, and we are almost nose to nose. His eyes are big, wild. "No one could ever want you after what we've been through. What did I tell you? You're mine, Edara Lauklan. *Mine*," he seethes through his teeth that look bigger than normal this close up.

I try to protest, but nothing comes out of my mouth. Tears threaten to spill as he moves his hand from my throat down to my scarf, twisting it again.

I try clawing at his hand around the scarf when he steps back and continues to drag me by my arm farther away from the house. The lights of the house almost look like they're getting brighter for a second, but just as quickly as it came, it left. It's too far now. I can't hear the dogs anymore, and I can barely make out the shape of the house through the trees.

Unsure of where we're going, my eyes bounce from left to right, but all I see are trees and more trees. His red Subaru car wasn't nearby when I pulled up to the house. So, where is he taking me? I can't figure out his plan. It's getting harder to breathe, to think.

"Damn it!" When he stumbles over something in the dark and stops, I use that moment to take in a deep breath.

I kick at him, but my movements are slow, and he easily dodges them. In a movement that feels too fast for my eyes to process, his hand is coming toward my face again before it grips my throat.

"Now, now, Eda." Smiling in a way that eerily reminds me of The Joker, he says, "I haven't decided how I'm going to punish you just yet." His grin deepens, stretching further on his face—a most terrifying sight. "But it's going to be good." The wink he gives makes his expression all the more horrifying.

Fuck no.

I know I need to get away—to get to Alaric's ax, to the road, to the house, anywhere but in Brad's clutches—but it's getting harder to breathe. My vision starts to grow white and spotty, and there's a buzzing in my ears. I can't think straight. I can't—

Air.

Air hits me, rushing into my throat and lungs, as his hand releases my neck. I double over, with legs wobbling but standing strong as my eyes begin to focus once more. There's a loud noise, and I don't know if he's still trying to talk to me. I can't hear anything clearly from the ringing in my ears.

Slowly, I gather my bearings again. With my hand set possessively around my throat in an attempt to protect it from him, I start to rise and see—

Alaric.

Alaric and Brad are rolling on the ground, fighting. It's hard to see in the dark of night, but one of them—the one whose back isn't as broad—looks like he has blood on his right shoulder. A lot of blood.

Their grunts and curses match my wheezes and coughs as I fight to catch my breath.

Another person comes up, running toward me. A tall man I don't recognize. I stumble back, but I'm too weak to get more than a couple feet away.

"It's okay," the voice says, with hands put up in surrender. "I'm Bash, Alaric's friend. We came together."

I stare back and forth between him and Alaric. Bash, right. The friend hosting guy's night. I nod once, then twice, as I realize this stranger's probably speaking the truth.

He steps forward, hands reaching toward me. "Are you okay?"

I open my mouth to speak, but I can't. I *can't*. My throat hurts so much. Nothing's coming out but croaks. I point to my neck, and understanding quickly dons on Bash's face.

His arm wraps around my shoulder blades and his other hand comes to my forearm, offering me support to stay upright. Leaning into him, I hold on like a lifeline as I watch Alaric, feeling useless in that moment.

It's like everything is happening in slow motion and fast forward at the same time.

Alaric rolls off, and Brad starts to scurry away. Without hesitating, Alaric sprints and grabs the ax I attempted to reach earlier.

"Ric, no!" Bash bellows into the wind, but the words get lost in the night.

My lips part in an *O* as Alaric holds the ax over his head and launches it at Brad. It whizzes by Brad's ear, lodging into a tree just ahead of him, but not before a yowl comes from him that I didn't know a human could make. Yelping, he clutches his left ear, but doesn't stop running. His footsteps only falter for a moment before he catches his balance and continues running into the trees toward the street.

Just then, sirens blare and flashing lights illuminate the road. His path now blocked by two patrol cars, Brad switches directions, but Alaric's faster, blocking his way to the woods. Still clutching his ear, with blood running down his neck, Brad tries to run to the side, evading Alaric, but a police officer tackles him before he can even make it a foot.

The words coming out of the police officer's mouth are drowned out as Brad stares at me with a mixture of shock and anger.

With Brad now apprehended, Alaric comes running to me, taking over support from Bash.

"What the fuck were you thinking, man?" Bash asks, but Alaric ignores him, and I can feel his eyes on me. Except, my eyes haven't left Brad, who's handcuffed and being read his rights.

"Are you okay?" Alaric asks, his hands cupping my face. "Look at me, not him. Me. *Me*, Eda. Are you okay?"

I can't look away until the blood on the back of Brad's black coat is no longer visible as he's led into the backseat of a patrol car. Meeting Alaric's gaze, I try to answer him, but only a pitiful squeak comes out of my mouth. My throat feels sore, raw. Like shards of glass every time I try to speak even a single word.

"Are you okay?" he asks, his words are soft, but I can hear the fear in his tone.

Still, words fail me. All I can do is whimper and nod my head in answer, while tears of pain and frustration and fear brim to the surface.

"Take your time and breathe, then we can talk," he tries to tell me, not understanding what I'm trying to tell *him*.

He wipes away a tear on my cheek as I point to my throat, attempting to show him it hurts to talk.

"Ric, she can't..." Bash starts, and Alaric whips his head toward his friend before looking at me again.

When his eyes settle on my throat, they turn dark, dangerous. His head whips back toward the direction of Brad, but I grab his arm before he can go running after him again.

"N—" I croak, trying to keep Alaric from leaving and doing something stupid. He's already in custody. There's nothing more Alaric can or should do.

This man could easily overpower me, throw me off him, and run after Brad. Instead, he pauses before he places his hand over mine on his arm.

He turns back toward me, and the longer his hazel eyes look into mine, the more his face relaxes. Just a little. I can still see pure rage, but his features are growing softer.

"I'm so sorry, Eda." Cupping my face again, and with tears in his eyes that never fall, he makes a vow: "For as long as I'm breathing, he will never lay another hand on you again. *No one* will."

Stunned and touched, I can't stop the tears from flowing. It's probably from a mix of everything, including the fact that Brad's in the back of a patrol car right now. Behind it, an ambulance pulls up in the driveway, the lights of which are reflecting onto the trees, dancing with the shadows. I haven't processed anything that's happened, and my mind is still reeling. But his words send me over the edge of emotion.

He pulls me into his chest and rubs my hair as I sob into his coat.

"Sh, shh. You're okay. I've got you now. You're safe," he says. Kissing the top of my head, his lips linger there for a moment. I lean into it, lean into him, as the tears slow and my breathing evens out a little.

His coat sleeve rustles as one arm leaves my back. I hear the name 'Gavin,' which prompts me to look up at him and see he's talking on the phone. He looks down and smoothes my hair again before kissing my temple.

"Yeah, Gav, she's safe now. An ambulance just pulled up. We'll get her checked out, and then I'll let you know." There's a pause before he says, "Thank Nadine for me, and give her our love. I'll call you later."

Hanging up, he looks into my eyes and holds me a little tighter, seeming to know exactly what I need right now. "Nadine called Gavin, who was still with us at Bash's. He put her on speakerphone and I heard everything. He went to her, and Bash came with me to you. But, Eda, I'm so sorry I missed your calls earlier."

There are tears in his eyes as his hands go to either side of my face, his thumbs tracing my cheekbones. "The guys were teasing me for being on my phone too much, mostly from just waiting for a message from you." He gives me a small, sad smile. "And..."

Bash sucks in a breath through his teeth next to us. "I fear I must apologize. It's completely my fault. After Ric put his phone down, I snuck over and clicked the button to turn it to silent. I...I just thought I was helping him unwind. I'm very sorry it led to this."

Alaric's hands are still on my face as I glance from Bash and back to him. There's an awkward silence while Bash seems to catch on and saunters away with his hands in the pockets of his slacks.

"I swear, if I'd known, if... I swear I wouldn't have put it down if I knew you needed me. I'm so sorry." His fingers continue their gentle caress. "I tried to call you back after Nadine called us, but you weren't answering."

He did?

I start to shake my head, but then stop. My eyes look over to where I think my car is in front of the house, as I realize that I left my phone on the passenger seat. It never made its way back into my purse after I tossed it in frustration. I squeeze my eyes shut tight. What a night to make such a stupid mistake.

Reaching up, I cup his cheek with my hand and nod, letting him know it's okay. This wasn't his fault. It was mine.

He sets his forehead against mine, and we stay like that until a paramedic asks to take a look at me. During which, an officer comes to take our statements. Throughout it all, Alaric's eyes remain on me, and I don't take my eyes off him as guilt floods me further, numbing the pain.

Chapter 33

ALARIC

I should have killed him.

I should have grabbed the ax sooner, and just ended it. Consequences be damned.

When Nadine called during guy's night with news about what happened to them at The Steaming Cup and that Eda was on her way to make sure that *I* was okay, I immediately grabbed my car keys and hightailed it out of Sebastian's house, with him close on my heels. I hadn't expected him to come with me, and Sebastian being Sebastian, he joked that it might be the only way he'd ever get to meet her.

And I damn sure hadn't expected to arrive home to see anyone with their fucking hands on her. It took everything in me to not kill the bastard right then and there. I heard Bash's warning, but I didn't give a fuck. I wanted him dead for ever touching her.

As soon as we pulled up and I saw Eda's purse lying on the porch, we started scanning the yard, looking for her. Then, I heard the bastard yelling at her in the woods, and I took off. Hearing an angry, male voice and loud rustling on *my* property had all thoughts leaving my head. Except for one: get to Eda.

When I saw Brad dragging Eda, I grabbed the knife at my hip, balanced it in my fingers—the motion and feeling of pure instinct after doing it hundreds of times before—and threw it directly into the shoulder of the arm holding her. Brad dropped her, and I saw red as I ran and tackled him to the ground. In a controlled rage, I hit everywhere on his body that I could connect my fists with.

When I grabbed the knife and pulled it from Brad's shoulder, I tried to use it on him again. I'm certain I cut him somewhere else, but I couldn't see clearly with the moonlight barely filtering through the branches above.

Just as I was driving the knife down toward Brad's chest, the lucky bastard slid on the slick leaves, giving him a chance to move away just in time. He got lucky a second time when the only damage my ax did was slice the top of his ear. If only I'd aimed for the ax to hit him instead of just scare him. Just a little down, and a little to the left for a bullseye in the back...

With a deep breath in and out, I let go of that desire. *For now.* Her safety and well-being is all that matters right now. If I leave her in order to seek revenge, she'll be alone. And looking into her eyes tonight, seeing the trust in them, I can't do that to her.

The thought of her alone and vulnerable again strikes a chord, igniting a fire inside of me to protect her.

At the time, I thought it worked out for the best so that Gavin didn't have to arrest me for murder. But when I saw that he'd actually hurt Eda—between her neck and the scrape on her chin from falling—every part of me wanted to pull him from that patrol car and finish the job.

She held me back then, and as I stare at her now, curled up in my arms on the couch, that mental debate is still warring within. If I asked, I'm sure Gavin would let me have a minute or two alone with Brad. Or maybe not... But I know what I'd like to do if given the chance.

What if something had happened to her? What if Nadine hadn't called when she did? What if we'd been too late and he'd managed to take Eda wherever he planned to?

Over my dead fucking body.

It's been over an hour since the police left. Bash stayed a little after out of concern, but when Eda mentioned she wanted to hop in the shower and wash the night's events off her, I told him he should go home. I just want to be with Eda tonight, to hold her and make sure she's safe.

With a deep sigh, I do just that. I hold her a little tighter to my chest, not wanting to let her go. Not even when her sobs stop and her breathing evens out a bit more. And even then, I don't let go right away.

Reluctantly, I loosen my hold when she straightens in my arms and sits up in my lap.

"I'm sorry," she mumbles, while wiping her wet lashes and damp cheeks. Her voice is still hoarse, but at least she's able to talk a little now.

My eyes fall to the thick fabric of her turtleneck, where I know bruises lay underneath from his hands. My molars grind, but I set aside my emotions and focus on her.

Looking back up at her face, I gently brush away a tear she missed on her cheek. Her lips part and her lids flutter at the contact, but the movement is slow because her eyes are slightly swollen from crying. The sight reminds me of the morning she asked me for green tea bags to help with her swollen eyes. I briefly glance at the pantry, where the tea is stored for my mom and sister—and now, Eda—before looking back into her blue eyes.

"For what?" I ask. My fingers linger on her cheek, and I wish I could take away every ounce of her pain and fear.

Those pretty blue eyes suddenly go wide, and she scurries out of my lap. I'm already missing the feel of her against me. Standing up, she straightens her sweater and goes to Blanche, petting her.

"What just happened?" I ask, confused over her sudden change in demeanor.

Her head shakes, as if to say, "Nothing," as she pets Blanche, kissing the top of her head. Then, she motions for Eless to come with her down the hallway leading toward our bedroom.

"Are you okay?" I shoot to my feet and follow after them. Maybe she's tired and ready for bed?

When I step into the threshold of the bedroom, I see she's pulled her suitcase onto the bed. Slowly, she packs her things, one by one.

Dumbfounded, I stand there, watching. "What are you doing?" I finally ask.

She says nothing, and I don't know if it's because of her throat hurting, or because she doesn't want to. The latter has my heart constricting.

"Eda?" I ask again. Still, no answer, but she sniffles.

Fine. We'll play it her way, then.

Walking over to the top shelf of my closet, I grab my overnight bag and put it on the opposite side of the bed so that I can face her. Her hands pause in folding a sweater to look at me, an unspoken question in her eyes.

Shrugging, I say, "It looks like we're going somewhere. Should I pack warm or cold?"

Her eyes start to water and the sweater limply falls from her hands. I take that as a sign to close the distance between us. Wrapping my arms around her, I pull her in close. My hand cups the back of her head as her arms go to my waist. It feels good to have her in my arms. It feels right.

But I hate seeing her like this, instead of happy and smiling at me.

When her shoulders stop shaking with silent tears, I pull away to look at her. With a light touch—careful of the small cut there—I lift her chin up so that she's forced to look me in the eyes. "What's going on?" I ask.

She shakes her head, tears still brimming in her eyes.

Letting go, I step away and walk over to her nightstand drawer to pull out the pen and notebook she put in there for when she gets hit with late-night writing inspiration. Opening to a blank page, I walk back over to her and place the pen and pad on top of her things in her suitcase.

"I know you can't talk, or maybe you don't want to risk making your voice worse by talking, but we are still going to talk. You need to tell me what's going on, and how I can help."

Her eyes go wide, looking from the notepad to me, and then back again. With a slow nod, she picks up the notepad and sits against the pillows on the bed.

Her eyes are glassy as she protectively holds her throat in one hand and the notepad in the other. Staring at the blank page, it looks as if she's trying not to let the tears boil over.

I stay standing as the pen scribbles on the notepad. Every few seconds, she's scratching something out and starting again. With each scratch of the ink tip, I get more anxious to read what she's writing.

After a couple of minutes, I realize this isn't going to be a quick task. So, I sit on the edge of the bed, trying to wait patiently. All the while, my mind is running wild. Could she need a break from the cabin after what happened tonight? That would be completely understandable. I'd be happy to go away with her somewhere else. Anywhere.

Or does she need time away by herself? To be alone, or away from me?

I've felt her pull away this past week, but I just wrote it off as her being stressed with work. Of course, it hadn't slipped my mind that her rental booking is also ending soon—which I plan on refunding her for—but I figured we'd have that discussion when she was ready. I didn't want to add any more pressure to her impending deadline, and it's not like I'm itching for her to leave. I don't want her to. So, yeah, maybe I was avoiding the conversation.

Finally, she sets the paper down in her lap. The movement has me looking at her with eager eyes. Slowly, she hands it to me, and I take it, my gaze remaining on her face. Her eyes are glassy as she holds her mouth with her arms close to her chest, as if she's trying not to let the tears boil over and cry.

The sight tugs at my chest and dread fills me. What did she write?

Exhaling, I look down at the page. Multiple lines and words have been scratched out, making two lines stand out more.

I'm so sorry for everything. Eless and I will leave tonight. Just let me pack, and we'll be gone.

Chapter 34

EDARA

Fidgeting with the edge of the quilt next to me, I watch Alaric as he reads and then rereads the note.

"What is this?" he asks, with eyes still on the notepad.

No words come from me. Not because I can't, but because I don't know how to answer. Speaking is becoming a little easier for me with each hour that passes, but my voice sounds weird, and I've been trying to resist using it if I don't have to.

And, yes, maybe I'm being a bit of a coward. I'm scared to tell him what's on my mind, to tell him how I feel about him, and to tell him I need to leave.

His eyes meet mine. "What does this mean?"

I scrunch my nose, fighting back the stinging of tears building. "I–I'm leaving," I croak.

"I see that," he says, lifting the notepad up before setting it down on my open suitcase. "But what I don't get is why." Holding my gaze, he slowly gets up off the end of the bed and comes up toward me. He pushes the suitcase aside and sits down in front of me. Taking my hands in his, he asks, "Eda, it's over now. You don't have to run anymore."

Shocked, my lips part and my eyes squeeze shut. Is that possible? Can it really be over? Brad's a cop. Surely, he has some connections that will help him get off the hook. And he could always escape. It's not like he doesn't work with handcuffs on a daily basis.

"Do you really think it's over?" I whisper. Tentatively, I open my eyes, afraid of what the answer might be.

"Yes, I do," he says, leaning in and kissing my forehead. "He's locked up, and there's no way he's getting away now. Gavin won't let that happen."

Tears well in my eyes and a wave of emotions run rampant through me.

Relief. Anger. Irritation. Sadness.

What now? Home?

Except, Raleigh hasn't really been home for a while now, has it? The memories I hold of my house back in Raleigh taint the place. There's a reason why I left, and I'm not sure if I'll ever view one of my favorite cities the same way after Brad made me feel unsafe there. He took so much from me. *So* much.

It's not my home anymore. The thought saddens me even more.

But...this also isn't my home. As much as it's started to feel that way, it's not. It's Alaric's. And now that Brad is out of the picture—as much as I'm having a hard time believing that's true—there's no reason for me to stay here anymore.

My bottom lip trembles, but I clear the painful lump in my throat, lengthen my spine, and look away from his gaze. "I guess this means you want me to leave now? I can go stay in the guesthouse tonight, and you can keep the rental money—"

"Eda, stop," Alaric says, shifting closer to me. "What are you talking about? I don't want you to leave. Why would I want that?"

"Because there's no threat anymore." I hate how pitiful my words are, let alone how raw my voice sounds. Clearing my throat again, I raise my chin but avoid his gaze. "Which means I can go back to the guesthouse now."

"No, I don't want you to leave. I don't want you to go back to the guesthouse. Not because he's gone. Not at all." I meet his gaze again and see the sincerity in his eyes. "Not unless you want to."

"Are you sure?" My voice cracks.

An eyebrow raised, he looks taken aback. "Fuck yes, I'm sure. Why would I want you to leave? I've never been happier than waking up with you in my arms, or going to sleep at night to the sound of you snoring."

Scoffing, I playfully hit his arm. "Ric! I don't snore."

He smiles. "It's not a bad thing. It's cute."

"Snoring is so not cute," I grumble, but there's a small smile on my face.

"*Your* snoring is cute, and I don't want to stop hearing it next to me at night." Pulling my hands into his lap, he holds my stare.

Tears brim in my eyes again, and for the first time in a long time, they're tears of pure happiness. "What are you saying, Ric?"

"I'm asking you to stay, Eda. If you want to only stay for the rest of however long you booked my guesthouse for, then fine. But...if you want to stay even after that, I'd like nothing more." Something flashes in his eyes. Desperation? Pleading? Whatever it is, it pulls at my heartstrings. To see this man before me ask me to stay does things to me. Makes me feel wanted, needed. Like maybe I'm enough. Enough for him, and enough for myself.

The thought brings the strangest sense of happiness and hope to my heart.

"Are you sure, Ric? Because you can kick Elessar and me out at any time," I say, but secretly hope that he won't change his mind.

"Never." There's a shadow of a smile on his face. "You guys can stay for however long you want to." His hand rests against my cheek now. Closing my eyes, I melt into the touch.

"That could be a long time," I whisper into his palm.

"If you stayed here with me forever, it wouldn't be long enough," he whispers, pulling my hand up and kissing the tops of my knuckles.

A tear falls from my eye, and his fingers brush it away.

"You can't possibly mean that, Ric. You barely know me," I say. But I hope he does mean it. I really do. Because I feel the same way, as crazy as that sounds.

"I don't know you?" He grins and I shake my head, smiling back at him before he continues. "I know enough to know I'm right. And more importantly, I know myself. No one has ever made me feel the way you do. No one. And in the time you've been here, I've come to rely on knowing I will have you and the dogs to come home to, no matter how hard life is getting me down that day."

I squeeze his hands. "I'm honored that you feel safe with me. You deserve to feel that." He does. He absolutely does.

"That means something to me, Eda. *You* mean something to me. A whole hell of a lot, really. You make me feel more than I ever thought I could for a person, and I...I'd like to believe you feel the same."

My heart might as well be a puddle on the floor right now. Knowing that he'd doubted himself when he spoke with his sister—after allowing himself to believe he doesn't deserve to be happy, to be loved—I'm touched by his words.

His hand comes up to my cheek, brushing against the line of my cheekbone. "I told you not to fall in love with me, but it was me who fell in love with you."

My mouth falls open on a silent gasp. His eyes briefly follow the movement before he grips my hands again and continues.

"I love you, Eda. And if I have a choice in the matter, I'm not about to let you just walk out of my life. If that's what you want, then fine. I will help you pack your things for you, and as much as it'll hurt, I'll wish you happiness." There are tears in his eyes as he speaks, as if the mere thought of me leaving pains him.

Seeing this man who has only ever shown strength and courage cry before me almost makes me break down. My left hand goes to my mouth, containing a small sob at the sight of his sadness and pain.

Gently grabbing my hand from my mouth, he squeezes it and says, "But if you're asking me if that's what I want," he places my hand on his chest, "if my heart wants to see you leave...then the answer is hell no."

I can't keep the tears in any longer. Wrapping my arms around him—palms on the nape of his neck and fingers in his hair—I pull him down for a hug. He immediately wraps me in his arms, hugging me tightly to him in a grip that feels like he never wants to let go. Maybe he doesn't, and I definitely don't want him to.

When I catch my breath and find my voice again, I speak into his chest, "Ric?" His body stiffens as I pull away to look up at his face. "I do feel the same way," I say, with a hand on his cheek.

Eyes full of tears that never fall, he leans his face into the touch.

"And for what it's worth, you're not hard to love. You're worthy of love. Of happiness. Of living your life with someone who adds value to it. And I hope to be that someone for you. I hope..." I clear my throat, choking back a sob full of both emotion and pain. "I hope that someday, you see yourself the way that I do, and know that you are worthy. Because you are. Because...I love you too, Ric."

His eyes close, and a tear falls from his lashes and onto my hand. We stay like that for a moment.

He sighs before pulling away to grab my hand and kiss the palm of it. With eyes now on me, he says, "I hope the same for you, Eda." His voice is quiet, soft. "I don't care if I have to say it every day until you believe it, but it'll happen someday. We'll make it happen. Because you deserve to be happy, Eda. No one in this world deserves love and happiness as much as you do."

I huff a laugh at that. Plenty of people do, but it's the thought that counts. Plus, the fact that I agree that, yes, I do deserve happiness and love, is a big step for me. One step at a time. For both of us.

Smiling, I say, "I guess we'll just have to help each other out, won't we? For however long it takes."

"And even after?" he asks, with so much hope singing in his voice.

Placing my hands on either side of his face, I say, "Even after. Especially after."

A grin lights up his handsome face. "Good, because I'm not ever letting you go." He pulls me against his chest as I pull his face down for a searing kiss. One that seals the spoken promises between us—sealing a fate that I feel was etched onto my heart long before this moment.

Epilogue

ONE YEAR LATER...

The cold of the hardwood floors seeps into me from sitting crisscross in front of a floor-length mirror in our bedroom. Elessar is lying on the floor next to me, his fur providing some warmth along my left thigh, as I put on my makeup.

The light tapping sound of Blanche's nails on the hardwood in the hallway gets louder as she comes closer to the bedroom door. Her fluffy, smiling face emerges a few seconds later, with Alaric right behind her.

Elessar's head raises, his tail thumping against the floor at the sight of them.

"Hey, Little Red," Alaric says, leaning in the doorway.

"Hey." I smile at him, feeling the corners of my eyes crinkling.

"How much time do you need?" He never rushes me, but I know it's helpful for him to know when he should start getting ready. We've learned the hard way that we run late to things if he starts getting ready *after* I'm already done.

I glance from my reflection in the mirror—makeup half done and hair ready to go—then over to the floor-length, black velvet dress draping over the closet door, with the hanger hooked on the top of the door.

Looking up at him again, I say, "Hmm, maybe twenty minutes? I need to finish my makeup, and then get dressed."

Tonight's my first book signing for my newest release about an author and her lumberjack hero who swept her off her feet. It's a private, intimate event to kick off the press tour, and also the first one that Alaric's ever gone to with me. I don't know who's more nervous—me or him—but it's really cute, and I appreciate that he wants to support me.

His eyes look up and down at the dress hanging on the door. "Is that what you're wearing tonight?"

I look at it again and then back at him. My cheeks heat. "Yeah, why? Is it too much? Should I wear something else?"

His eyes crinkle. "No. It's perfect. You're going to look like a dream in it, Little Red." He winks, then walks over and kisses the top of my head—careful not to mess up my hair.

My cheeks grow hotter, and I break eye contact. Even after a year, his compliments still make me blush, and the way he looks at me gives me butterflies.

Turning on his heel, he calls Elessar to his side and walks back down the hall with both dogs running ahead of him.

With my personal heated blanket now retreating down the hallway, along with my handsome woodsman, I ask, "Where are you taking him?" I lean over a little so that my voice travels down the hall, but I don't look away from the mirror as I apply mascara.

"Just taking them out one last time before I start getting ready," he calls back down the hallway of our home.

Our home. Calling it that will never get old.

The past year has been full of so much love, happiness, and many adventures between the four of us—our little family we've formed. I kept my house in Raleigh for the first six months of our relationship, but after only returning once in that time, I decided to move all of my stuff out. Some of it was put in storage, and other stuff—like my desk and favorite reading chair—came here. Now, it's being rented out by a lovely family Cressida knows.

My sisters also fell in love with Steaming Stone, just as I knew they would. Upon graduating with her master's degree, Aurelia accepted a teaching position at Steaming Stone University starting this past fall semester. It also just so happens that Atticus accepted the head football coach position at the same university. As if parking downtown wasn't crazy enough on football Saturdays...his presence and success so far this season have brought a lot of publicity and tourism to our small town.

His presence has also made my younger sister smile more, which makes me happy to see.

In August, Rhiannon signed a rental agreement lease for a place downtown—right down the street from The Steaming Cup—that has both a commercial space on the main floor and a residential apartment on the second floor. It's the perfect size for an intimate yoga studio. After helping her get everything situated, she officially opened the place a few weeks ago.

The grand opening was just in time for a Halloween-themed yoga night, which included instrumental Halloween songs on a playlist, as well as a movie night for anyone who wanted to stay after class. Nadine and The Steaming Cup helped cater the event. It was such a hit that it has inspired Rhiannon to do more themed nights.

We're working on convincing Cressida to move here, but we'll see. She has a solid client base in Raleigh, but I think we're finally wearing her down. The more she visits, the more I see her softening to the idea of coming. I doubt my parents would be up for the big move, too, but my aunt's trying her hardest at convincing them. Then, we really would be one big, happy family here.

That includes Alaric's side. I've loved getting to know his family over the past year. His parents, Henry and Daphne, are so sweet. They welcomed Eless and me into their family with open arms, even inviting us to their monthly family dinners.

I've grown closer to Sawyer, who is now Elessar's vet and my friend. She and Nadine always come to the girls' nights I host with my sisters. At this point, it wouldn't feel complete without them there.

A few times now, Bash, Sawyer, Nadine, and Gavin have joined us for dinner. It hasn't gone unnoticed the way Bash and Sawyer look at each other... Alaric told me all about their history, and I wouldn't be surprised if they finally stop lying to themselves and just act on their feelings. Maybe they just need a gentle nudge in the right direction...

As for Brad, he's officially been sentenced to twenty years in prison for first-degree kidnapping; five years for non-fatal strangulation; five years for felony stalking; and ten years for violating a restraining order. Needless to say, we won't be seeing him anytime soon.

I hope he rots and has to live with the consequences of his decisions and sick mind, being tormented day in and day out. I don't know which is worse, wishing death upon him or not.

At the same time, if Brad had never developed this sick obsession with me enough to drive me out of Raleigh, I never would have met Alaric. I'd hate to be grateful for anything he's done, but fate brought Alaric and me together.

I finish applying my mascara, then start to get dressed. Sliding the dress over my head, the smooth velvet cascades down and over my curves like it was made for me.

Elessar and Blanche come barreling back in the room, jumping on the bed, as I slide my foot into one heel. Alaric walks in after them. He glances at the dogs on the bed first, then me, and gives me a quick kiss on the cheek before moving to the bathroom.

I admire him as he walks away. He's wearing tan slacks that are snug in all the right places and an emerald green button down that always makes the green tint of his hazel eyes pop.

"You already changed?" I ask as I hear him moving stuff around on the bathroom counter.

Quickly sliding the second heel on, I stare at my reflection in the mirror, smoothing out the creases on the dress. With the shoes on, the outfit is complete, and I'm feeling ready to conquer this event.

"Yep, in the guest bath. I figured it would give you more time to get ready in here." He pops his head out of the bathroom with a smile, eyeing me and then the dogs on the bed, before going back to whatever he's doing in there.

I walk over to where the dogs are resting and plant a kiss on the tops of each of their soft heads. "You be good babies tonight, okay?" I say, rubbing each of their necks. I pause when something sharp on Elessar's collar digs into my right palm.

Leaning down, I move his long fur that's practically a wolf's mane around for his white collar to make sure the metal hooks of his tags haven't come loose. I don't want it poking into him, or Blanche if she play bites his neck.

The creaking of wood behind me tells me that Alaric has entered the bedroom again. "Sorry, I'm just checking Eless's collar. It feels like something's come loose," I say as I continue my search.

But there's so much fur, I can't see anything, and I don't feel it again. Maybe I imagined it?

Standing up, I sigh. "Never mind." I look at him leaning in the doorway of the bathroom and shrug.

He smiles at me and looks at Eless, walking over to the bed. "I'll take a look just in case."

"Thank you," I say, watching in concern. There's still a slight white mark in the palm of my hand, indicating something did, indeed, scratch me. There's most definitely something sharp there.

"You're looking extra pretty today, little man," I hear Alaric say as I walk to the closet and grab my burgundy wool coat off the hanger. It's sweet that he's adopted my family's nickname for him.

"He always looks pretty. They both do," I say a little loud so that he can hear me from inside the closet.

"Yeah, but he's looking *extra* pretty today," Alaric says, and I laugh.

Sliding the coat on, I step back out into the bedroom and gasp.

In front of the bed, Alaric's on one knee before me with a ring sparkling in-between his fingers.

Dumbstruck, I just stand there, frozen. My heart stops beating for a moment, and I think I've forgotten how to breathe. How does one do that again? What does breathing even mean?

"Eda…" The sound of his voice and the movement of his lips as he speaks have me blinking several times. I forcibly will air into my lungs and try to focus on what he's saying to me.

"My entire adult life, home was never a place. It was never a constant for me. Yes, I had this house," he waves a hand at the four walls of our room, "but I did not have a home. I bought this property after getting out of the army and before getting Blanche, but even then, it wasn't home. It was simply a place to lay my head at night." He briefly glances behind him at our fluffy girl, whose tail thumps at the sound of her name.

"And after adopting her, it started to feel right, like little pieces were falling into place. But, still, something was missing." He holds out his hand toward me. My feet miraculously move as I close the gap between us and place my shaking hand in his. "A piece was missing. And I've come to realize that was you, Eda. You and Eless." His thumb starts brushing along the back of my hand. "You three, you are home. You are my home."

My other hand comes to my mouth, hiding my wobbling lips as my eyes water.

"You are the ones I look forward to seeing every day. You are the ones who can make me smile when no one else can. You are the ones who are making me fall in love with life again. Or, perhaps, falling in love with it for the first time." He gives me a small smile. "While I also get to fall in love with you, more and more every day."

Unable to hold back the tears anymore, I rapidly blink them away so that I can see his handsome face clearly as he continues.

He squeezes my hand gently. "And if you will have me, I want to continue falling in love with you over and over and over again. If you will have me, I want to come home to you each and every day for the rest of my life." His voice cracks a little as tears well in his eyes.

I take my free hand to his cheek, wiping away a tear that fell. Closing his eyes, he leans into the touch and kisses my palm before looking at me once more.

"Edara Michelle Lauklan, will you do me the great honor of continuing to be my home? Will you marry me?" Hopeful, hazel eyes stare up at me, and my heart bursts at the love I see in them.

"Yes—" Before I can say everything going through my head, his lips are on mine. "Yes!" I say again in-between kisses.

Coming up for air and holding my face in his hands, he rests his forehead against mine, with his eyes closed. I take advantage of the added height the heels give me and kiss the tip of his nose, whispering, "Yes," as I do. Now on my tippy toes, I go to kiss the lashes of one eye. "Yes." Then, I kiss the other. "Yes." He gives me a toothy grin, and I kiss each corner of that delicious smile. "Yes...and yes."

His hands are still on my face, and I mirror the action by putting mine on either side of his face. "A thousand times yes, Ric."

He pulls away just long enough to slide the perfect ring onto my finger. It sparkles in the bedroom light as I replace my hands on his face.

Holding my gaze, he says, "I love you, Eda."

"I love you, Ric."

Taking my left hand and kissing just above the ring that signifies our love and commitment to one another, he chuckles. "You're stuck with me forever now."

I grin. "I wouldn't want it any other way."

What's the Recipe?

If at any point while reading you found
yourself wanting to know the recipe for a
food or drink mentioned in this book, then
this page is for you!

Simply scan the QR code below, or visit
www.SteviMager.com/recipes
for a list of recipes found in this book.

Don't see one you're interested?
Contact Stevi at info@SteviMager.com!

Author's Note

I know that most people don't read these notes in novels, but I enjoy them. It's fascinating to me seeing the research that some authors delve into while writing, or seeing how their incredible minds work to take a concept and turn it into a great story. Personally, I also love knowing I'm not the only one who goes down rabbit holes of random knowledge while doing research for my novels. So, if you're like me, this Author's Note is for you.

This note includes information about the originally published fairytale, *Little Red Riding Hood,* as well as adaptations and retellings published since, and how the various versions inspired me and my book.

At the end, I will also discuss the research I conducted on stalking behavior and statistics.

Little Red Riding Hood of France, 1697

Range of Heart by Stevi Evelise was inspired by the classic fairytale *Little Red Riding Hood,* which was first published in 1697 by Charles Perrault. While he was the first to publish it, it's worth noting that the original tale was not his. The original author is a mystery, because it was an oral tale shared for centuries before Perrault published the first copy. However, Perrault's version is said to not be as dark as the European oral tradition, which featured elements such as cannibalism.

The majority of the concepts in *Range of Heart* came from my own imagination; however, my research into the various renditions of the fairytale inspired important elements throughout the story. I'd like to discuss some of those here, while also sharing more about Perrault's tale, as well as some adaptations and retellings that have since been released.

The Dangers of Man in *Little Red Riding Hood*

The biggest inspiration I pulled was a concept noted by Perrault himself in the first publication of *Little Red Riding Hood*. He states that the wolf in the original story was inspired by predatory men in France.

In his own author's note discussing the moral of the tale, he warned young women to not even smile at a strange man, for it may be all the encouragement he needs to act on his dangerous desires. Perrault's version is "a cautionary tale about charming men who would lure innocent young women to bed and ruin them."[1]

While the years have gone by since Perrault's publication, this is sadly something people still have to worry about today. Centuries later, we are *still* dealing with men like this all over the world.

The concept of simply smiling at a man or showing kindness leading to untoward advances inspired the storyline of Brad stalking Eda in *Range of Heart*. She gave him a second chance with another date, and that one, simple act led to him believing he was entitled to her. His character was inspired by the Big Bad Wolf in Perrault's version.

---

1. Source: https://www.nottingham.ac.uk/manuscriptsandspecialcollectio
ns/documents/exhibitions/rags-to-witches/little-red-riding-hood.pd

There have been many versions of the tale released since its first publication in 1697. In Perrault's tale, no one saves Little Red Riding Hood from the wolf, who devours her and her grandmother. In some tales, a woodsman saves Little Red Riding Hood and her grandmother.

Then, there are versions where the grandmother defeats the wolf, saving both herself and Little Red Riding Hood. There are also versions where Little Red Riding Hood saves herself.

Alternatively, some more modern retellings have the wolf as the hero, and the villain as a man. This male character is often inspired by the woodsman from older versions, or sometimes, it's a new male character introduced for that specific retelling.

For *Range of Heart*, I pulled inspiration from: 1) Little Red Riding Hood saving herself; 2) the wolf saving Little Red Riding Hood; and 3) the Big Bad Wolf from Perrault's version.

In *Range of Heart*, Edara Lauklan sees the danger she's in and, in order to keep herself and her dog safe, picks up her belongings and changes her circumstances and surroundings. She later agrees to learn self-defense in order to protect herself. While she never should have had to leave, she took back control of her life in her own way.

We also have Alaric Wülf, whose character was inspired by two versions of the tale. Alaric is both 1) inspired by the woodsman who saves Little Red Riding Hood in one of the later adaptations; and 2) my version of the wolf helping to protect Little Red Riding Hood from a dangerous man, hence the last name "Wülf."

This is one of the reasons why I say the novel is *loosely* inspired by the classic fairytale, with a contemporary, modern twist.

Names and Dates

As stated above, Little Red Riding Hood was first published in 1697 by Charles Perrault. The year of publication inspired the street address for Alaric Wülf's property: 1697 Redwood Lane.

In 1888, Charles Marelle published a reimagined version titled, *The True Story of Little Goldenhood.* In this version, Little Red Riding Hood finally has a name that isn't just 'Little Red Riding Hood.' We meet Blanchette, the young girl with a "gold and fire-colored" hooded cloak. (In Marelle's tale, the cloak and the grandmother are the heroes, and both possess magical powers.)[2]

Marelle's choice to give a name to the character inspired me to use that same name in *Range of Heart.* It's the reason why we have our lovely Blanche. She's young, curious, and friendly, just like Blanchette/Little Red Riding Hood/Little Goldenhood.

Veering away from Little Red Riding Hood, I'd like to mention the inspiration behind the name for Elessar, our sweet silver sable German shepherd in *Range of Heart,* who resembles a wolf. His name comes from *The Lord of The Rings,* with 'Elessar' being Aragorn's elven name. Elessar is also inspired by my real-life black seal German shepherd, Strider, who is named after Aragorn's Ranger alias. Much of Elessar's personality came from Strider (my dog, not the character), to the point where readers who have met him said they felt like Strider was right there with them while they were reading it. He's a precious boy, and I love that this book now feels like his.

Inspired by Fairytales & Myths

I've always enjoyed reading fairytales and myths from different cultures. In fact, when I graduated from undergrad, I earned a minor in History, with a concentration in Ancient Greek and Roman History and Mythology. Since

---

2. Source: https://sites.pitt.edu/~dash/type0333.html#marelles

then, exploring mythologies and fairytales from different cultures has become a passion.

Writing a book loosely inspired by a fairytale felt like a great adventure—one where my imagination took the driver's seat, and research became the backseat driver commentating when needed.

With one fairytale-inspired romance done, I'm looking forward to diving into the next in the series! Stay tuned to find out who's coming to Steaming Stone next, and which classic fairytales and/or myths inspired their story!

<u>Stalking Statistics and Resources</u>

I'd be remiss to close this letter (can I call it that? It feels like a letter to you) without first touching on the research I did on stalking behaviors and statistics. I must preface that I mostly researched information in the state of North Carolina, specifically how to obtain a restraining order in the state when stalking is involved.[3] [4]

While I did try to stick to statistics and laws in North Carolina, I also found a great resource about stalking statistics, behaviors, and tactics, as well as safety strategies from Domestic Violence Services Network, Inc., (DVSN) based in Massachusetts.

I'm not sure how the laws in North Carolina differ from other states. Although, I imagine there are many differences from state to state, considering "Fewer than 1/3 of states classify stalking as a felony in all circumstances,"

---

3. https://www.charlesullman.com/domestic-violence-lawyer/steps-obtain
-north-carolina-restraining-order

4. https://www.smithdebnamlaw.com/article/the-basics-of-restraining-orde
rs-in-north-carolina/

and "More than 1/2 of states classify stalking as a felony upon the second or subsequent offense, or when the crime involves aggravating factors."[5]

One January 2024 article from DVSN stunned me with its statistics across the entire US. The majority of which are referenced from research shared by Stalking Prevention, Awareness, and Resource Center (SPARC) based out of Washington D.C.

Some of these statistics include:

- "Nearly 1 in 3 women and 1 in 6 men have experienced stalking victimization at some point in their lifetime."[6]

- "11% of stalking victims have been stalked for 5 years or more."[7]

- "Among undergraduate students, 1 in 7 transgender and nonbinary/genderqueer and 1 in 10 female reported experiencing stalking, compared to 1 in 17 of all students."[8]

- "Active duty service members identifying as LGBT are two times more likely than non-LGBT service members to experience stalking."[9]

---

5. https://www.stalkingawareness.org/wp-content/uploads/2019/01/SPARC_StalkngFactSheet_2018_FINAL.pdf

6. https://www.stalkingawareness.org/wp-content/uploads/2019/01/SPARC_StalkngFactSheet_2018_FINAL.pdf

7. https://www.stalkingawareness.org/wp-content/uploads/2019/01/SPARC_StalkngFactSheet_2018_FINAL.pdf

8. https://www.stalkingawareness.org/wp-content/uploads/2021/09/SPARC_Stalking-LGBTQ-Fact-Sheet.pdf

9. https://www.stalkingawareness.org/wp-content/uploads/2021/09/SPARC_Stalking-LGBTQ-Fact-Sheet.pdf

- "Transgender and nonbinary/genderqueer student stalking victims (33%) were more likely than cisgender student victims (28% cis-women, 29% cismen) to contact a program or resource for help."[10]

And more.

The footnote link for the last three statistics above also shares support services for the LGBTQIA+ community. Don't ever be afraid to reach out to these support services if you need to. Please. The article also shares a guide for victim advocates to better help LGBTQIA+ stalking victims.[11]

Additionally, DVSN's article referenced above not only talks about statistics, behaviors, and tactics, but the impact stalking has on victims, safety strategies, and seeking help.[12]

When the concept for *Range of Heart* first came to me, I knew I wanted a human character that embodied the Big Bad Wolf, but I must admit that I didn't truly weigh the gravity of the topic until I did research. Even then, I know that I cannot fully grasp the severity of stalking and the realities victims and survivors face on a daily basis.

While it is meant to be fiction, I also understand this is a serious topic and something millions of people in the US (and the world, for that matter) face, oftentimes without help. That is why I did not want to end this letter without talking about it.

If you need it, *please* reach out to 888-399-6111. This is DVSN's helpline.

---

10. https://www.stalkingawareness.org/wp-content/uploads/2021/09/SPA RC_Stalking-LGBTQ-Fact-Sheet.pdf

11. https://www.stalkingawareness.org/wp-content/uploads/2023/01/SPA RC-Supporting-LGBTQ-Stalking-Victims.pdf

12. https://www.dvsn.org/january-2024-stalking-stats-tactics-impacts/

Acknowledgements

I first want to thank you—you brilliant, kind reader—for taking a chance on my book. I hope you enjoyed reading Eda and Ric's story as much as I enjoyed writing it.

To *all* of my readers—thank you for being here. You are the main reason why I haven't let the cruel, ever-present imposter syndrome win. Thank you to every reader who has taken a chance on my books. Thank you to the special readers who have graced me with their vulnerability to tell me they felt seen in my words and in my characters. Thank you to the readers who have reached out to tell me I'm officially an auto-buy author for them. Thank you to the readers who have used quotes from my books in their email signatures. Thank you to the readers who have reached out specifically to tell me I'm their new favorite author. Thank you to all of you—you are the reason why I'm able to do what I do.

To the North Carolina mountains—your beauty is indescribable and your mountains underrated. While Steaming Stone is a fictional town created from my imagination, it is loosely inspired by Blowing Rock, Boone, and Banner Elk, NC, which are of just some of the many mountain towns that were hit hard by Hurricane Helene in 2024. Our mountains in NC are beautiful and vast, and if you have the chance to visit and support the many great mountain towns post-storm, you absolutely should. Many businesses and towns in the mountains are just waiting for your arrival!

To my husband, A—thank you for being you. You help to keep the voices of imposter syndrome and self doubt from taking over. You never let me give up; you never let me give in. You believed in me before I even believed I could craft a novel, let alone multiple series. And as the dedication states, thank you for being the wolf who eats the ghosts of my pasts when they start haunting me.

To my alpha readers, beta readers, and ARC readers—thank you for taking the time to read my words and sending me all your unhinged, in-real-time reactions. You have no idea how much I love having you on my team!

To my C&S babes—thank you for pushing me to write this story. If it wasn't for all of you, I never would have been inspired to write Eda and Ric's story, let alone finish writing it in less than two months. You all are my chosen family. Thank you for being in my corner.

To my cover designer (of the paperback and ebook versions), Kloé—thank you for putting up with my multiple emails and notes for the cover, as well as being flexible with the timelines as life got in the way. Also, thank you for being such a talented artist that your premade cover (now the cover for *Range of Heart*) inspired an entire scene in this book that didn't exist prior. (Note: If you're curious, it's the truck bed scene, which just so happens to be one of my favorites in the whole book.)

To my entire family—thank you for all of your support and love. I feel it with every new story idea, every release day, and every book signing. You mean so much to me, and I'm incredibly lucky to have you all in my life.

To my dear friend, Anaïs—thank you for always being my sounding board and for carving out time to read my words before anyone else. Thank you for hyping me up in my moments of self-doubt, and for putting up with me randomly sending you book art without even first saying hello. Thank you for helping me take brain breaks with our craft nights. Even when we simply sit in silence, your presence and friendship is always exactly what I need in those moments. Thank you for always being there.

To my friend who has always felt like more of a sister than a friend, Jess—thank you for being the best friend I needed in our teens, and for being the one I've needed in adulthood. Every friendship is different, but I find there's beauty in the ones that survive without daily communication. The ones that you can go days, weeks, maybe even months without talking, and yet, when you do talk, it feels as though no time has passed. There's just a whole lot of love and support there. Always. I cherish that, and I appreciate you.

About Stevi Evelise

Stevi's mind lives in fiction, and her heart in fantasy. If she's not writing, she's daydreaming about it. When she's not at her computer, she can be found getting lost in a book, trying a new recipe, or on her tippy toes at a rock concert.

Stevi also writes romantic fantasy under the pen name Stevi Mager. Find more of Stevi's books at www.SteviMager.com